AMOS WALKER
The Complete Story Collection

AMOS WALKER
The Complete Story Collection

Loren D. Estleman

TYRUS
BOOKS

Published by
TYRUS BOOKS
1213 N. Sherman Ave. #306
Madison, WI 53704
www.tyrusbooks.com

Library of Congress Cataloging-In-Publication Data has been applied for.

12 11 10 09 08   1 2 3 4 5 6 7 8 9 10

978-1-935562-24-5

Contents

Amos and Me

I hesitated over that title. The machinery falters whenever I refer to him as Amos. After thirty years we're still not on a first-name basis.

To get close is to intrude. Yes, he tells his stories in first person, probably over a glass of cheap scotch with some new injury keeping pace with the beating of his heart; but he draws the shade just short of the reveal, preferring to test his theory in practice. As he says somewhere, "I hate being wrong in front of witnesses."

I doubt I could describe Walker physically in the amount of detail you'd need to pick him out of a crowd, although I'd know him at a hundred paces. I never took the time to provide more than a few Impressionistic strokes to keep the reader from supplying his own image. Since Walker's the one telling the story, it's unlikely he'll be confused with any other characters. I bring this up to warn other writers away from describing their protagonists in mirrors, which apart from being a clanking cliché just slows down the action.

But others have written at length about Walker, flaying him open like a medical cadaver and weighing his brain, which lists heavily toward the centers of irony. I've held the scalpel a number of times myself, but the more I do that the more I watch myself work later, being careful to make Walker behave as represented instead of letting him go about his business with me stumbling along behind, the way I've done from the beginning. I'd rather write him than write about him. It's his longevity I want to discuss.

When *Motor City Blue* appeared in 1980, there was no Internet. There were no cell phones, no cordless phones of any kind. There was only one telephone company. The broadcast networks ruled television. Pee Wee Herman was a major star. Videocassette recorders were new on the market, priced far outside the budgets of most Americans: If you missed a movie on its first release, you waited ten years for it to appear on TV, edited to pablum to avoid violating FCC regulations and cut up to sell beer and automobiles, and if two programs you wanted to see aired in the same time slot, you had to pick one and wait for the summer rerun season to see the other instead of recording one to watch at your own convenience. (Reality shows would not crowd out repeat broadcasting for another twenty years.) The Berlin Wall was observing its twentieth anniversary. The USSR had just begun the invasion of Afghanistan that would bring the Soviet empire down in ruins by the end of the decade. DNA was a mystery waiting to be unlocked.

It's a different world, to be sure, but in many ways little has changed. There is fighting again in Afghanistan, but the USA is leading it, and finding the place as difficult to bring to heel as the Russians did. Iran is still a threat, and peace in the Middle East remains as elusive as when Lawrence of Arabia was campaigning in Egypt. And Amos Walker is still sitting in his third-floor walk-up office on Grand River Avenue in Detroit, contributing to the nicotine smudge on the ceiling above his desk when he isn't out exposing the back of his head to some handy bludgeon on some troublesome errand.

Private eye fiction—a mainstay of the American mystery since 1920—was all but dead when I wrote *Motor City Blue*. Ross Macdonald was ailing and would write no more Lew Archers. Mickey Spillane was doing commercials for Michelob. Arthur Lyons and Robert B. Parker were just getting started and were flying well below the radar. The entire suspense genre was considered to be in decline, held above water only by the espionage thrillers of Robert Ludlum and Ken Follett. Romance novels were nudging everything else off the racks. It's hard to imagine a more inopportune moment to begin a series about a postmodern knight errant slaying his ogres one at a time armed with nothing but a revolver and a laminated license. But I was stubborn; which as we'll see has always been my most reliable weapon of small destruction. I'd written westerns, I'd leapt aboard the bandwagon of Sherlock Holmes pastiches that proliferated after the success of Nicholas Meyer's *The Seven-Percent Solution*. I needed a break from horses and gaslight.

I was warned against it. What I'd considered my greatest asset, the Detroit setting so rarely used in detective stories, yet so eminently adapted to that seamy world, was the very reason, fellow Detroiters assured me, that the book would never find an audience. Mayor Coleman A. Young was six years into his rape of the city; it would continue for another fourteen, and sixteen years after it ended, Detroit shows no sign of recovering. The national media took sadistic glee in exposing its blasted neighborhoods, its soaring murder rate, its Devil's Night arsons, and the administration and the three local television stations concentrated on polishing the city's image instead of acknowledging the source of all the bad publicity and taking the measures necessary to eliminate it. But to mangle a notorious aphorism uttered by a top General Motors executive, what's bad for a city is good for a crime novel. Where others saw desolation and despair, I saw color. It's the worm in the apple that makes the apple interesting. I wrote:

Dry, grainy snow—the kind that usually falls in the city—heaped the sills of unused doorways and lined the gutters in narrow ribbons, where the wind caught and swept it winding like white snakes across the pavement, picking up crumples of muddy newspaper and old election campaign leaflets and empty condom wrappers and broken Styrofoam cups as it went, rattling them against the pitted sides of abandoned cars shunted up to the curb; weathering the corners off ancient buildings with bright-colored signs advertising various hetero- and homosexual entertainments; banging loose boards nailed over the windows of gutted stores defiled with skulls and crossbones and spray-painted graffiti identifying them as street-gang hangouts, Keep Out; buckling a billboard atop a brownstone two blocks south upon which a gaggle of grinning citizens gathered at the base of the Renaissance Center, near where its first suicide landed, urged me in letters a foot high to Take Another Look at Detroit...

The book was rejected twice, first by my editor at Doubleday, who wanted me to write another novel set in Victorian London, the second time by another publisher who said it wouldn't stand a chance in the marketplace. But my agent, Ray Puechner, was relentless, and placed it with Ruth Hapgood at Houghton Mifflin, who would go on to edit the next nine books in the series. Two of those titles would be named Notable Books of the Year by the *New York Times*, and the fifth, *Sugartown*, would win the first of four Shamus Awards given by the Private Eye Writers of America to the series. The books were picked up in the United Kingdom and Australia and translated into French, Italian, Spanish, German, Danish, and Japanese. As of this writing, twenty Amos Walker novels have been published, with a twenty-first awaiting its time in stores and libraries.

It's not quite a rags-to-riches story; more of a rags-to middle-class respectability. Amos Walker has never cracked a national best-seller list, but he's survived a number of fictional detectives who have. The series has been with four publishers, not counting mass-market and trade-paper reprints, and for seven years I was enjoined from writing about Walker in a book because of a dispute over contracts. However, the fact that readers embraced the character all over again after so long a silence testifies to his durability.

Here again is where my congenital muleheadedness paid off. When asked the reason for Walker's long tenure, my reply is always "applied denial." Publishing wisdom says that there is no percentage in picking up a series after it's been dropped by a competitor, but I've never been one to let someone else's wisdom stand in my way. After Houghton Mifflin bowed out of an auction, and after I canceled a contract with the high bidder over professional differences, I took the series to the Mysterious Press, where an editor I'd known for years was eager to show what he could do with it. When, four books later, that editor was terminated in the ill-fated AOL/Time-Warner merger, I offered the series to Forge, which had been publishing my historical westerns for years, and there the novels have remained to this day. On occasion, these changes of venue have involved smaller cash advances, but never so small as to be unworthy of my best efforts, and in the long run the books have earned as much if not more through royalties. I need money to live, and I enjoy spending it when there's anything left over after my belly is full and my mortgage is paid, but I've never considered it an indicator of my value as a human being or as an artist. I don't keep score with figures involving dollar signs.

So much for the novels—although I hope there is a great deal more to be heard from and about them. The present collection contains more than thirty short stories featuring Walker beginning in 1982. Walker connoisseurs, assuming such creatures exist, may note that the stories place less emphasis on photorealistic style and more on leanness of prose. It's an often-repeated misconception that not a single word can be excised from the Estleman canon; going back over my earlier work, I always find bales of stuff I could do without. I'm one of those critics I hate.

Economy is crucial to the short form, but when you pare a thing too close to the bone you risk nicking the marrow. It's not enough to say the air is cold and leave it at that. If you want the reader to feel the cold, you need to lay a piece of metal alongside his spine; only you can't do that, and I can't either, because I already have. If I repeat the image, the reader will remember it from before and wind up thinking about that instead of how cold it is. In a novel, I can spend a paragraph comparing ice floes to tipped-over tombstones, frosting noses with tiny needles, and bursting the cores of trees; but this isn't a novel, it's piston-driven, I'm being paid by the word; okay, you made your point, it's cold. What happens next?

A novel is a broad canvas. You can hide coarse brushstrokes in the expanse. Short stories are miniatures, where flaws of any sort are immediately obvious. A Botticelli would never have attempted one. There are highly accomplished novelists who blanch at the prospect of writing short fiction. William Faulkner once said that he'd tried poetry, couldn't do it, then tried short stories, couldn't do that, and so he wrote novels. More prosaic writers have compared writing short stories to making love on an elevator and having to finish before it reaches the top floor. They're an intolerant form. When I type the last period on a short story I consider satisfactory, I feel a sense of accomplishment (and exhaustion) that I don't necessarily feel at the end of a novel that took me six months to complete.

The stories in this book satisfied me, when I wrote them. Looking back from the perspective of years or even weeks, I can always see something else to be done, but if in the rereading I wasn't sufficiently happy with the result, I wouldn't be offering it here. This is the humblest way I can think of to say these are good stories. Walker himself owes them a personal debt: They kept him alive when I was prohibited from writing about him at book length.

These stories originally appeared in Ellery Queen's Mystery Magazine, Alfred Hitchcock's Mystery Magazine, and various other magazines and anthologies. They're arranged in rough chronological order for those who care to track Walker's progress through time beginning with "Robbers' Roost" in 1982, two years after his debut in *Motor City Blue*. Amateur anthropologists of this stamp might discover a somewhat sadder and wiser detective in "Rumble Strip" than the one they made the acquaintance of in "Greektown."

Or perhaps not; but I'm a somewhat sadder and wiser man myself than I was when the only place you could look up a telephone number was in the Yellow Pages. I have to believe that some of life's lessons have spilled out into print.

As I said, the outlook for private eye fiction in 1980 was dismal. Within two years, other series had sprung up against the backdrop of every major city in the U.S. A national organization of private detective writers was chartered, with applications for membership streaming in from as far away as Australia. I can't claim credit for this renaissance, because others were developing their characters at the same time. But I can state that most of those writers have moved on to other subjects and that some have left the trade entirely. Meanwhile, Amos Walker and I remain. I have, of course, many readers to thank, as well as editors Ruth Hapgood, Cathleen Jordan, Janet Hutchings, Bill Malloy, Jim Frenkel, and Linda Landrigan, as well as the staff responsible for the present book, and agents Ray Puechner, Barb Puechner, Millie Puechner, Robin Rue, and Dominick Abel. Finally, I can't emphasize too strongly the importance of the City of Detroit to the series, and the courageous people who maintain the place with little help from the people in office.

—LOREN D. ESTLEMAN
January 2010

Greektown

One

The restaurant was damp and dim and showed every indication of having been hollowed out of a massive stump, with floorboards scoured as white as wood grubs and tall booths separated from the stools at the counter by an aisle just wide enough for skinny waitresses like you never see in Greektown. It was Greektown, and the only waitress in sight looked like a garage door in a uniform. She caught me checking out the booths and trundled my way, turning stools with her left hip as she came.

"You are Amos Walker?" She had a husky accent and large dark pretty eyes set in the rye dough of her face. I said I was and she told me Mr. Xanthes was delayed and sat me down in a booth halfway between the door and the narrow hallway leading to the restrooms in back. Somewhere a radio turned low was playing one of those frantic Mediterranean melodies that sound like hornets set loose in the string section.

The waitress was freshening my coffee when my host arrived, extending a small right hand and a smiling observation on downtown Detroit traffic. Constantine Xanthes was a wiry five feet and ninety pounds with deep laugh lines from his narrow eyes to his broad mouth and hair as black at 50 as mine was going gray at 33. His light blue tailormade suit fit him like a sheen of water. He smiled a lot, but so does every other restaurateur, and none of them means it either. When he found out I hadn't eaten he ordered egg lemon soup, bread, feta cheese, roast lamb, and a bottle of ouzo for us both. I passed on the ouzo.

"Greektown used to be more than just fine places to eat." He sighed, poking a fork at his lamb. "When my parents came it was a little Athens, with markets and pretty girls in red and white dresses at festival time and noise like I can't describe to you. It took in Macomb, Randolph, and Monroe Streets, not just one block of Monroe like now. Now those colorful old men you see drinking retsina on the stoops get up and go home to the suburbs at dark."

I washed down the last of the strong cheese with coffee. "I'm a good P.I., Mr. Xanthes, but I'm not good enough to track down and bring back the old days. What else can I do to make your life easier?"

He refilled his glass with ouzo and I watched his Adam's apple bob twice as the syrupy liquid slid down his throat. Afterward he was still smiling, but the vertical line that had appeared between his brows when he was talking about what had happened to his neighborhood had deepened.

"I have a half brother, Alexander," he began. "He's twenty-three years younger than I am; his mother was our father's second wife. She deserted them when Alexander was six. When Father died, my wife and I took over the job of raising Alexander, but by then I was working sixty hours a week at General Motors and he was seventeen and too much for Grace to handle with two children of our own. He ran away. We didn't hear from him until last summer, when he walked into the house unannounced, all smiles and hugs, at least for me. He and Grace never got along. He congratulated me on my success in the restaurant business and said he'd been living in Iowa for the past nine years, where he'd married and divorced twice. His first wife left him without so much as a note and had a lawyer send him papers six weeks later. The second filed suit on grounds of brutality. It seems that during quarrels he took to beating her with the cord from an iron. He was proud of that.

"He's been here fourteen months, and in that time he's held more jobs than I can count. Some he quit, some he was fired from, always for the same reason. He can't work with or for a woman. I kept him on here as a busboy until he threw a stool at one of my waitresses. She'd asked him to get a can of coffee from the storeroom and forgot to say please. I had to let him go."

He paused, and I lit a Winston to keep from having to say anything. It was all beginning to sound familiar. I wondered why.

When he saw I wasn't going to comment, he drew a folded clipping from an inside breast pocket and spread it out on the table with the reluctant care of a father getting ready to punish his child. It was from that morning's *Free Press,* and it was headed PSYCHIATRIST PROFILES FIVE O'CLOCK STRANGLER.

That was the name the press had hung on the nut who had stalked and murdered four women on their way home from work on the city's northwest side on four separate evenings over the past two weeks. The women were found strangled to death in public places around quitting time, or reported missing by their families from that time and discovered later. Their ages ranged from 20 to 46, they had had no connection in life, and they were all WASPs. One was a nurse, two were secretaries; the fourth had been something mysterious in city government. None was raped. The Freep had dug up a shrink who claimed the killer was between 25 and 40, a member of an ethnic or racial minority group, and a hater of professional women who had had experiences with such women unpleasant enough to unhinge him. It was the kind of article you usually find in the Science section after someone's made off with Sports and the comics, only today it had run Page One because there hadn't been any murders in a couple of days to keep the story alive. I'd read it at breakfast. I knew now what had nagged me about Xanthes' story.

"Your brother's the Five O'Clock Strangler?" I tipped half an inch of ash into the tin tray on the table.

"Half brother," he corrected. "If I was sure of that, I wouldn't have called you. Alexander could have killed that waitress, Mr. Walker. As it was he nearly broke her arm with that stool and I had to pay for X rays and give her a bonus to keep her from pressing charges. This article says the strangler hates working women. Alexander hates *all* women, but working women especially. His mother was a licensed practical nurse and she abandoned him. His first wife was a legal secretary and *she* left him. He told me he started beating his second wife when she started talking about getting a job. The police say that because the killer strangles women with just his hands he has to be big and strong. That description fits my half brother; he's built more like you than me, and he works out regularly."

"Does he have anything against white Anglo-Saxon Protestants?"

"I don't know. But his mother was one and so was his first wife. The waitress he hurt was Greek descent."

I burned some more tobacco. "Does he have an alibi for any of the times the women were killed?"

"I asked him, in a way that wouldn't make him think I suspected him. He said he was home alone." He shifted his weight on the bench. "I didn't want to press it, but I called him one of those nights and he didn't answer. But it wasn't until I read this article that I really started to worry. It could have been written about Alexander.

That's when I decided to call you. You once dug up an eyewitness to an auto accident whose testimony saved a friend of mine a bundle. He talks about you often."

"I have a license to stand in front of," I said. "If your half brother *is* the strangler I'll have to send him over."

"I understand that. All I ask is that you call me before you call the police. It's this not knowing, you know? And don't let him find out he's being investigated. There's no telling what he'll do if he learns I suspect him."

We took care of finances—in cash; you'll look in vain for a check-book in Greektown—and he slid over a wallet-size photo of a darkly handsome man in his late twenties with glossy black hair like Xanthes' and big liquid eyes not at all like Xanthes' slits. "He goes by Alex Santine. You'll find him working part-time at Butsukitis' market on Brush." A telephone number and an address on Gratiot were written on the back of the picture. That was a long way from the area where the bodies were found, but then a killer hardly ever lives in the neighborhood where he works. Not that that made any difference to the cops busy tossing every house and apartment on the northwest side.

Two

He looked like his picture. After leaving the restaurant, I'd walked around the corner to a building with a fruit and vegetable stand out front and a faded canvas awning lettered BUTSUKITIS' FINE PRODUCE, and while a beefy bald man with fat quilting his chest dropped some onions into a paper sack for me, a tall young man came out the front door lugging a crate full of cabbages. He hoisted the crate onto a bare spot on the stand, swept large shiny eyes over the milling crowd of tomato-squeezers and melon-huggers, and went back inside swinging his broad shoulders.

As the grocer was ringing up the sale, a blonde wearing a navy blue business suit asked for help loading two bags of apples and cherries into her car. "Santine!" he bellowed.

The young man returned. Told to help the lady, he hesitated, then slouched forward and snatched up the bags. He stashed them on the front seat of a green Olds parked half a block down the street and swung around and walked away while she was still rummaging in her handbag for a tip. His swagger going back into the store was pronounced. I paid for my onions and left.

Back at the office I called Iowa Information and got two numbers. The first belonged to a private detective agency in Des Moines. I called them, fed them the dope I had on Santine, and asked them to scrape up what they could. My next call was to the Des Moines *Register,* where a reporter held me up for fifty dollars for combing the morgue for stories about non-rape female assault and murder during the last two years Santine lived in the state. They both promised to wire the information to Barry Stackpole at the Detroit *News* and I hung up and dialed Barry's number and traded a case of scotch for his cooperation. The expenses on this one were going to eat up my fee. Finally I called Lieutenant John Alderdyce at Police Headquarters.

"Who's working the Five O'Clock Strangler case?" I asked him.

"Why?"

I used the dead air counting how many times he'd asked me that and dividing it by how many times I'd answered.

"DeLong," he said then. "I could just hang up because I'm busy, but you'd probably just call again."

"Probably. Is he in?"

"He's in that lot off Lahser where they found the last body. With Michael Kurof."

"The psychic?"

"No, the plumber. They're stopping there on their way to fix De-Long's toilet." He broke the connection.

Three

The last body had been found lying in a patch of weeds in a wooded lot off Lahser just south of West Grand River by a band student taking a shortcut home from practice. I parked next to the curb behind a blue-and-white and mingled with a group of uniforms and obvious plainclothesmen watching Kurof walk around with Inspector DeLong nipping along at his side like a spaniel trying to keep up with a Great Dane. DeLong was a razor-faced twenty-year cop with horns of pink scalp retreating along a mouse-colored widow's peak and the kind of crossed eyes that kept you wondering where he was looking. Kurof, a Russian-born bear of a man, bushy-haired and blue of chin even when it was still wet from shaving, bobbed his big head in time with De-Long's mile-a-minute patter for a few moments, then raised a palm, cutting him off. After that they wandered the lot in silence.

"What they looking for, rattlesnakes?" muttered a grizzled fatty in a baggy brown suit.

"Vibes," someone answered. "Emanations, the Russky calls 'em."

Lardbottom snorted. "We ran *in* fortune-tellers when I was in uniform."

"That must've been before you needed a crowbar to get into one," said the other.

I was nudged by a young black in starched blue cotton, who

winked gravely and stooped to lay a gold pencil on the ground, then backed away from it. Kurof's back was turned. Eventually he and DeLong made their way to the spot, where the psychic picked up the pencil, stroked it once between the first and second fingers of his right hand, and turned to the black cop with a broad smile, holding out the item. "You are having fun with me, Officer," he announced in a deep burring voice. The uniform smiled stiffly back and accepted the pencil.

"Did you learn anything, Dr. Kurof? DeLong was facing the psychic, but his right eye was looking toward the parked cars.

Kurof shook his great head slowly. "Nothing useful, I fear. Just a tangible hatred. The air is ugly everywhere here, but it is ugliest where we are standing. It crawls."

"We're standing precisely where the body was found." The inspector pushed aside a clump of thistles with his foot to expose a fresh yellow stake driven into the earth. He turned toward one of the watching uniforms. "Give our guest a lift back to Wayne State. Thank you, Doctor. We'll be in touch when something else comes up." They shook hands and the Russian moved off slowly with his escort.

"Hatred," the fat detective growled. "Like we need a gypsy to tell us that."

DeLong told him to shut up and go back to Headquarters. As the knot of investigators loosened, I approached the inspector and introduced myself.

"Walker," he considered. "Sure, I see you jawing with Alderdyce. Who hired you, the family of one of the victims?"

"Just running an errand." Sometimes it's best to let a cop keep his notions. "What about what this psychiatrist said about the strangler in this morning's Freep? You agree with that?"

"Shrinks. Twenty years in school to tell us why some j.d. sapped an old lady and snatched her purse. I'll stick with guys like Kurof; at least he's not smug." He stuck a Tiparillo in his mouth and I lit it and a Winston for me. He sucked smoke. "My theory is the killer's unemployed and he sees all these women running out and getting themselves fulfilled by taking his job and sometimes snaps. It isn't just coincidence that the stats on crime against women have risen with their numbers in the work force."

"Is he a minority?"

"I hope so. " He grinned quickly and without mirth. "No, I know what you mean. Maybe. Minorities outnumber the majority in this town in case you haven't noticed. Could be the victims are all WASPs because there are more women working who are WASPs. I'll ask him when we arrest him."

"Think you will?"

He glared at me in his cockeyed fashion. Then he shrugged. "This is the third mass-murder case I've investigated. The one fear is that it'll just stop. I'm still hoping to wrap it before famous criminologists start coming in from all over to give us a hand. I never liked circuses even when I was a kid."

"What are you holding back from the press on this one?"

"You expect me to answer that? Give up the one thing that'll help us separate the original from all the copycats?"

"Call John Alderdyce. He'll tell you I sit on things till they hatch."

"Oh, hell." He dropped his little cigar half-smoked and crushed it out. "The guy clobbers his victims before he strangles them. One blow to the left cheek, probably with his right fist. Keeps 'em from struggling."

"Could he be a boxer?"

"Maybe. Someone used to using his dukes."

I thanked him for talking to me. He said, "I hope you *are* working for the family of a victim."

I got out of there without answering. Lying to a cop like DeLong can be like trying to smuggle a bicycle through Customs.

Four

It was coming up on two o'clock. If the killer was planning to strike that day I had three hours. At the first telephone booth I came to I excavated my notebook and called Constantine Xanthes' home number in Royal Oak. His wife answered. She had a mellow voice and no accent.

"Yes, Connie told me he was going to hire you. He's not home, though. Try the restaurant."

I explained she was the one I wanted to speak with and asked if I could come over. After a brief pause she agreed and gave me directions. I told her to expect me in half an hour.

It was a white frame house that would have been in the country when it was built, but now it was shouldered by two housing tracts with a third going up in the empty field across the street. The doorbell was answered by a tall woman on the far side of 40 with black hair streaked blond to cover the gray and a handsome oval face, the flesh shiny around the eyes and mouth from recent remodeling. She wore a dark knit dress that accentuated the slim line of her torso and a long colored scarf to make you forget she was big enough to look down at the top of her husband's head without trying. We exchanged greetings and she let me in and hung up my hat and we walked into a dim living room furnished heavily in oak and dark leather. We sat down facing each other in a pair of horsehair-stuffed chairs.

"You're not Greek," I said.

"I hardly ever am." Her voice was just as mellow in person.

"Your husband was mourning the old Greektown at lunch and now I find out he lives in the suburbs with a woman who isn't Greek."

"Connie's ethnic standards are very high for other people."

She was smiling when she said it, but I didn't press the point. "He says you and Alexander have never been friendly. In what ways weren't you friendly when he was living here?"

"I don't suppose it's ever easy bringing up someone else's son. His having been deserted didn't help. Lord save me if I suggested taking out the garbage."

"Was he sullen, abusive, what?"

"Sullen was his best mood. 'Abusive' hardly describes his reaction to the simplest request. The children were beginning to repeat his foul language. I was relieved when he ran away."

"Did you call the police?"

"Connie did. They never found him. By that time he was eighteen and technically an adult. He couldn't have been brought back without his consent anyway."

"Did he ever hit you?"

"He wouldn't dare. He worshiped Connie."

"Did he ever box?"

"You mean fight? I think so. Sometimes he came home from school with his clothes torn or a black eye, but he wouldn't talk about it. That was before he quit. Fighting is normal. We had some of the same problems with our son. He grew out of it."

I was coming to the short end. "Any scrapes with the law? Alexander, I mean."

She shook her head. Her eyes were warm and tawny. "You know, you're quite good-looking. You have noble features."

"So does a German Shepherd."

"I work in clay. I'd like to have you pose for me in my studio sometime." She waved long nails toward a door to the left. "I specialize in nudes."

"So do I. But not with clients' wives." I rose.

She lifted penciled eyebrows. "Was I that obvious?"

"Probably not, but I'm a detective." I thanked her and got my hat and let myself out.

Five

Xanthes had told me his half brother got off at four. At ten to, I swung by the market and bought two quarts of strawberries. The beefy bald man, whom I'd pegged as Butsukitis, the owner, appeared glad to see me. Memories are long in Greektown. I said, "I just had an operation and the doc says I shouldn't lift any more than a pound. Could your boy carry these to the car?"

"I let my boy leave early. Slow day. I will carry them."

He did, and I drove away stuck with two quarts of strawberries. They give me hives. Had Santine been around I'd planned to tail him after he punched out. Pounding the steering wheel at red lights, I bucked and squirmed my way through late afternoon traffic to Gratiot, where my man kept an apartment on the second floor of a charred brick building that had housed a recording studio in the gravy days of Motown. I ditched my hat, jacket, and tie in the car and at Santine's door put on a pair of aviator's glasses in case he remembered me from the market. If he answered my knock I was looking for another apartment. There was no answer. I considered slipping the latch and taking a look around inside, but it was too early in the round to play catch with my license. I went back down and made myself uncomfortable in my heap across the street from the entrance.

It was growing dark when a cab creaked its brakes in front of the building and Santine got out, wearing a blue Windbreaker over the clothes I'd seen him in earlier. He paid the driver and went inside. Since the window of his apartment looked out on Gratiot I let the cab go, noting its number, hit the starter and wound my way to the company's headquarters on Woodward.

A puffy-faced black man in work clothes looked at me from behind a steel desk in an office smelling of oil. The floor tingled with the swallowed bellowing of engines in the garage below. I gave him a hinge at my investigator's Photostat, placing my thumb over the "Private," and told him in an official voice I wanted information on Cab No. 218.

He looked back down at the ruled pink sheet he was scribbling on and said, "I been dispatcher here eleven years. You think I don't know a plastic badge when I see one?"

I licked a ten-dollar bill across the sheet.

"That's Dillard," he said, watching the movement.

"He just dropped off a fare on Gratiot." I gave him the address. "I want to know where he picked him up and when."

He found the cab number on another ruled sheet attached to a clipboard on the wall and followed the line with his finger to some writing in another column. "Evergreen, between Schoolcraft and Kendall. Dillard logged it in at six-twenty."

I handed him the bill without comment. The spot where Santine had entered the cab was an hour's easy walk from where the bodies of two of the murdered women had been found.

Six

I swung past Alex Santine's apartment near Greektown on my way home. There was a light on. That night after supper I caught all the news reports on TV and looked for bulletins and wound up watching a succession of sitcoms full of single mothers shrieking at their kids about sex. There was nothing about any new stranglings. I went to bed. Eating breakfast the next day I turned on the radio and read the *Free Press* and there was still nothing.

The name of the psychiatrist quoted in the last issue was Kornecki. I looked him up and called his office in the National Bank Building. I expected a secretary, but I got him.

"I'd like to talk to you about someone I know," I said.

"Someone you know. I see." He spoke in cathedral tones.

"It's not me. I have an entirely different set of neuroses."

"My consultation fee is one hundred dollars for forty minutes."

"I'll take twenty-five dollars' worth," I said.

"No, that's forty minutes or any fraction thereof. I have a cancellation at eleven. Shall I have my secretary pencil you in when she returns from her break?"

I told him to do so, gave him my name, and rang off before I could say anything about his working out of a bank. The hundred went onto the expense sheet.

Kornecki's reception room was larger than my office and a half. A redhead at a kidney-shaped desk smiled tightly at me, found my name on her calendar, and buzzed me through. The inner sanctum, pastel green with a blue carpet, dark green Naugahyde couch, and a large glass-topped desk bare but for a telephone intercom, looked out on downtown through a window whose double panes swallowed the traffic noise. Behind the desk, a man about my age, wearing a blue pinstripe and steel-rimmed glasses, sat smiling at me with several thousand dollars' worth of dental work. He wore his sandy hair in bangs like Alfalfa.

We shook hands and I took charge of the customer's chair, a pedestal job upholstered in green vinyl to match the couch. I asked if I could smoke. He said whatever made me comfortable and indicated a smoking stand nearby. I lit up and laid out Santine's background without naming him. Kornecki listened.

"Is this guy capable of violence against strange women?" I finished.

He smiled again. "We all are, Mr. Walker. Every one of us men. It's our only advantage. You think your man is the strangler, is that it?"

"I guess I was absent the day they taught subtle."

"Oh, you were subtle. But you can't know how many people I've spoken with since that article appeared, wanting to be assured that their uncle or cousin or best friend isn't the killer. Hostility between the sexes is nothing new, but these last few confusing years have aggravated things. From what you've told me, though, I don't think you need to worry."

Those rich tones rumbling up from his slender chest made you want to look around to see who was talking. I waited, smoking.

"The powder is there," he went on. "But it needs a spark. If your man were to start murdering women, his second wife would have been his first victim. He wouldn't have stopped at beating her. My own theory, which the *Free Press* saw fit not to print, is that the strangler suffered some real or imagined wrong at a woman's hand in his past and that recently the wrong was repeated, either by a similar act committed by another woman, or by his coming into contact with the same woman."

"What sort of wrong?"

"It could be anything. Sexual domination is the worst, because it means loss of self-esteem. Possibly she worked for a living, but it's just as likely that he equates women who work with her dominance. They would be a substitute; he would lack the courage to strike out at the actual source of his frustration."

"Suppose he ran into his mother or something like that."

He shook his head. "Too far back. I don't place as much importance on early childhood as many of my colleagues. Stale charges don't explode that easily."

"You've been a big help." I said and we talked about sports and politics until my hundred dollars were up.

Seven

From there I went to the Detroit *News* and Barry Stackpole's cubicle, where he greeted me with the lopsided grin the steel plate in his head had left him with after some rough trade tried to blow him up in his car, and pointed to a stack of papers on his desk. I sat on one of the antique whiskey crates he used to file things in—there was a similar stack on the only other chair besides his—and went through the stuff. It had come over the wire that morning from the Des Moines agency and the *Register*, and none of it was for me. Santine had held six jobs in his last two years in Iowa, fetch-and-carry work, no brains need apply. His first wife had divorced him on grounds of marriage breakdown and he hadn't contested the action. His second had filed for extreme cruelty.

The transcripts of that one were ugly but not uncommon. There were enough articles from the newspaper on violent crimes against women to make you think twice before moving there, but if there was a pattern it was lost on me. The telephone rang while I was reshuffling the papers. Barry barked his name into the receiver, paused, and held it out to me.

"I gave my service this number," I explained, accepting it.

"You bastard, you promised to call me before you called the police."

The voice belonged to Constantine Xanthes. I straightened. "Start again."

"Alexander just called me from Police Headquarters. They've arrested him for the stranglings."

Eight

I met Xanthes in Homicide. He was wearing the same light blue suit or one just like it and his face was pale beneath the olive pigment. "He's being interrogated now," he said stiffly. "My lawyer's with him."

"I didn't call the cops." I made my voice low. The room was alive with uniforms and detectives in shirtsleeves droning into telephones and comparing criminal anecdotes at the water cooler.

"I know. When I got here, Inspector DeLong told me Alexander walked into some kind of trap."

On cue, DeLong entered the squad room from the hallway leading to Interrogation. His jacket was off and his shirt clung transparent to his narrow chest. When he saw me his cross-eyes flamed. "You said you were representing a *victim's* family."

"I didn't," I said. "You did. What's this trap?"

He grinned to his molars. "It's the kind of thing you do in these things when you did everything else. Sometimes it works. We had another strangling last night."

My stomach took a dive. "It wasn't on the news."

"We didn't release it. The body was found jammed into a culvert on Schoolcraft. When we got the squeal we threw wraps over it, morgued the corpse—she was a teacher at Redford High—and stuck a department-store dummy in its place. These nuts like publicity; when there isn't any they might check to see if the body is still there. Nick the Greek in there climbs down the bank at half-past noon and takes a look inside and three officers step out of the bushes and screw their service revolvers in his ears."

"Pretty thin," I said.

"How thick does it have to be with a full confession?"

Xanthes swayed. I grabbed his arm. I was still looking at DeLong.

"He's talking to a tape recorder now," he said, filling a Dixie cup at the cooler. "He knows the details on all five murders, including the blow to the cheek."

"I'd like to see him." Xanthes was still pale, but he wasn't needing me to hold him up now.

"It'll be a couple of hours."

"I'll wait."

The inspector shrugged, drained the cup, and headed back the way he'd come, sidearming the crumpled container at a steel wastebasket already bubbling over with them. Xanthes said, "He didn't do it."

"I think he probably did." I was somersaulting a Winston back and forth across the back of my hand. "Is your wife home?"

He started slightly. "Grace? She's shopping for art supplies in Southfield. I tried to reach her after the police called, but I couldn't."

"I wonder if I could have a look at her studio."

"Why?"

"I'll tell you in the car." When he hesitated: "It beats hanging around here."

He nodded. In my crate I said, "Your father was proud of his Greek heritage, wasn't he?"

"Fiercely. He was a stonecutter in the old country and built like Hercules. He taught me the importance of being a man and the sanctity of womanhood. That's why I can't understand…" He shook his head, watching the scenery glide past his window.

"I can. When a man who's been told all his life that a man should be strong lets himself be humiliated by a woman it does things to him. If he's smart he'll put distance between himself and the woman. If he's weak he'll come back and it'll start all over again. And if the woman happens to be married to his half brother, who he worships—"

I stopped, feeling the flinty chips of his eyes on me. "Who told you that?"

"Your wife, some of it. You, some more. The rest of it I got from a psychiatrist downtown. The women's movement has changed the lives of almost everyone but the women who have the most to lose by embracing it. You're wife's been cheating on you for years."

"Liar!" He lunged across the seat at me. I spun the wheel hard and we shrieked around a corner and he slammed back against the passenger's door. A big Mercury that had been close on our tail blatted its horn and sped past. Xanthes breathed heavily, glaring.

"She propositioned me like a pro yesterday." I corrected our course. We were entering his neighborhood now. "I think she's been doing that kind of thing a long time. I think that when he was living at your place Alexander found out and threatened to tell you. That would have meant divorce from a proud man like you, and your wife would have had to go to work to support herself and the children. So she bribed Alexander with the only thing she had to bribe him with. She's still attractive, but in those days she must have been a knockout; being weak, he took the bribe, and then she had leverage. She hedged her bet by making up those stories about his incorrigible behavior so that you wouldn't believe him if he did tell you. So he got out from under. But the experience had plundered him of his self-respect and tainted his relationships with women from then on. Even then he might have grown out of it, but he made the mistake of coming back. Seeing her again shook something loose. He walked into your house Alex Santine and came out the Five O'Clock Strangler, victimizing seemingly independent WASP women like Grace. Who taught him how to use his fists?"

"Our father, probably. He taught me. It was part of a man's training, he said, to know how to defend himself." His voice was as dead as last year's leaves.

"We pulled into his driveway and he got out, moving very slowly. Inside the house we paused before the locked door to his wife's studio. I asked him if he had a key.

"No. I've never been inside the room. She's never invited me and I respect her privacy."

I didn't. I slipped the lock with the edge of my investigator's photostat and we entered Grace Xanthes' trophy room.

It had been a bedroom, but she had erected steel utility shelves and moved in a kiln and a long library table on which stood a turning pedestal supporting a lump of red clay that was starting to look like a naked man. The shelves were lined with nude male figure studies twelve to eighteen inches high, posed in various attitudes. They were all of a type, athletically muscled and wide at the shoulders, physically large, all the things the artist's husband wasn't. He walked around the room in a kind of daze, staring at each in turn. It was clear he recognized some of them. I didn't know Alexander at first, but he did. He had filled out since 17.

Nine

I returned two days' worth of Xanthes' three-day retainer, less expenses, despite his insistence that I'd earned it. A few weeks later, court-appointed psychiatrists declared Alex Santine mentally unfit to stand trial and he was remanded for treatment to the State Forensics Center at Ypsilanti. And I haven't had a bowl of egg lemon soup or a slice of feta cheese in months.

Robbers' Roost

I was met at the door by a hatchet-faced woman in a nurse's uniform who took my card and asked me to accompany her to Dr. Tuskin's office. I hadn't come to see anyone by that name, but I said okay. I have another set of manners when my checks don't bounce. On the way we passed some old people in wheelchairs whose drugged eyes followed us the way the eyes of sunning lizards follow visitors to the zoo. The place was a nursing home for the aged.

"I can't let you see Mr. Chubb," announced Dr. Tuskin, after we had shaken hands and the nature of my visit was established. The nurse had withdrawn. "Perhaps I can help you, Mister"—he glanced down at my card—"Walker?"

He was tall and plump with very white hair and wore a three-piece suit the color of creamed anything. His office wore a lot of cedar and the desk he was standing behind was big and glossy and bare but for the card. I didn't think he'd scooped any paperwork into a drawer on my account.

"I doubt it," I said. "I got a telephone call from Mr. Chubb requesting my services. If he hasn't confided in you we've nothing to discuss."

"He is infirm. I can't imagine what reasons he'd have for engaging a private investigator at this time in his life." But his frost-blue eyes were uneasy. I played on that.

"I don't think they have anything to do with the operation of this home or he wouldn't have made the call from one of your telephones." I dropped the reassuring tone. "But I have a friend on the *News* who might be interested in finding out why a private investigator was denied access to one of your patients."

His face tightened. "That sounds like blackmail."

"I was hoping it would."

After a moment he pressed something under his desk. Reappearing, Hatchet Face was instructed to take me to Oscar Chubb's room on the second floor. Dr. Tuskin didn't say good-bye as we left.

Upstairs lay a very old man in bed, his pale, hollow-templed head almost lost amidst the pillow and heavy white quilt. The nurse awakened him gently, told him who I was, and moved to draw the blinds over the room's only window, which looked out over the choppy blue-green surface of Lake St. Clair.

"Leave it," he bleated. "It's taken me eighty years to get to Grosse Pointe. I like to be reminded."

She went out, muttering something about the glare and his cataract.

"As if it mattered." He mined a bony arm in a baggy pajama sleeve out from under the heavy spread, rested it a moment, then used the remote control atop the spread to raise himself to a sitting position. He waved me into the chair next to the bed.

"I hear you're good."

"Good's a pretty general term," I said. "I'm good in some areas. Missing persons, yeah. Divorce, no. I have a low gag threshold."

"Have you ever heard of Specs Kleinstein?"

"Racketeer. Retired, lives in Troy."

He nodded feebly. His eyes were swollen in the shriveled face and his head quaked. "I want him in jail."

"You, the Detroit Police, and the FBI." I stuck a cigarette in my mouth, then remembered where I was, and started to put it away. He told me to go ahead and smoke. I said. "Sure?"

"Don't worry about killing me. I'm hardier than I look."

"You'd almost have to be."

He smiled, or tried to. The corners of his lipless mouth tugged out a tenth of an inch. "You remind me of Eddie."

"Eddie?" I lit up.

"He's the reason I want Specs behind bars. The reason you're here. You know about Robbers' Roost?"

I blew smoke away from the bed. "If I answer this one right, do I get the range or the trip to Hawaii?"

"Indulge my senility. You won't find the Roost on any map, but if you ask any old-time Detroiter about it he'll grin and give you directions a blind man could follow. It covers ten blocks along the river in Ecorse where rumrunners from Canada used to dock during Prohibition. Eddie and I grew up there."

"Eddie was your brother?"

"Yes and no. His last name was Stoner. My folks adopted him in nineteen twelve after his folks were killed in a streetcar accident on Woodward. You ever see an old Warner Brothers picture called *Angels with Dirty Faces?*"

"A time or twelve."

"Well, it was Eddie and me right on the button. We were the same age, but he grew up faster on account of a four alarm temper and a pair of fists like pistons. When college time came and my parents could afford to send only one of us, it was Eddie who stepped aside. After graduation I joined the Ecorse Police Department. Eddie got a job delivering bootleg hooch for Specs Kleinstein.

"I asked him how far he thought I'd get in the force when it got out that I had Mob connections. He said, 'Probably chief,' and I knocked him down for the first and only time in my life. He moved out soon after."

Chubb closed his eyes. Whatever breathing he was doing wasn't enough to stir the quilt over his chest. But his nostrils were quivering and I relaxed.

"One day I pulled over a big gray Cadillac for running a stop sign on Jefferson," he went on. "Eddie was behind the wheel with a girl in the passenger's seat and ten cases of Old Log Cabin stacked in back. The girl was Clara Baxter, Kleinstein's mistress. Eddie laughed when I told him to watch his butt. Well, I took them in, car and all. They were back on the street an hour later with everything returned, including the liquor. That was how things worked back then."

"Back then." I flicked some ash into a pantscuff.

Chubb ignored the comment. "I never saw him again. That winter the river froze over, and the boats went into drydock while old cars were used to ferry the stuff across. I still have the clipping."

A yellow knuckle twitched at the bedstand. In the drawer was a square of brown newsprint fifty years old. BOOTLEGGER DIES AS ICE COLLAPSES, bellowed the headline. I read swiftly.

"It says it was an accident," I said. "The ice gave way under Stoner's car and he went to the bottom."

"Yeah. It was just a coincidence that Specs found out about Eddie stealing his woman the day before the accident and threatened to kill him. I have that on good authority."

"You tried to nail him for it?"

"For thirty-two years, until retirement. No evidence."

"What made you decide to try again now?"

He opened his huge eyes and turned them on me. "In confidence?"

I nodded.

"This morning I had a little stroke. I still can't grip anything with my right hand. Nobody here even knows about it. But I won't survive another."

I smoked and thought. "I wouldn't know where to start after all this time."

"You do if your recommendation is any good. Try Walter Barnes in Ecorse. He was my partner for fourteen years and he knows as much about the case as I do. Then you might see what you can do about recovering Eddie's remains."

"He's still down there?"

"I never could get the city to pay out to raise a gangster's body. The car isn't a hazard to navigation."

I folded away the clipping inside my jacket and stood. "My fee's two-fifty a day plus expenses."

"See my son. His number's on the back of the clipping."

"Be seeing you."

"Don't count on it."

Two

I found Walter Barnes watering the lawn of his brick split-level on Sunnyside, a tall man in his early seventies with pinkish hair thinning in front and a paunch that strained the buttons on his fuzzy green sweater. He wore a hearing aid, so naturally I started the interview at the top of my lungs.

"Stop shouting or I'll spray you," he snapped. "Who'd you say you were?"

I handed him my card. He moved his lips as he read.

"Amos Walker, huh? Never heard of you."

"You're in the majority. What can you tell me about Eddie Stoner?"

"Who'd you say you're working for?" His eyes were narrow openings in thickets of wrinkles.

"Oscar Chubb. You used to be partners."

His face softened. "Oscar. How is he?"

"Dying."

"I been hearing that for ten years. Who was it you asked me about?"

"Eddie Stoner." I made strangling motions with my hands in my pockets.

His lips drew back over his dentures. "Eddie was bad. He was the reason Oscar took so long getting his stripes. The brass didn't like having a hoodlum's brother on the force, blood kin or no."

"Tell me about Eddie's death."

His story was loaded with repetitions and back-telling, but I gathered that it was one of Barnes's snitches who had carried the tale of Kleinstein's death threat. Clara Baxter had blurted out the details of her fling during an argument. A scuffle with Eddie followed; Kleinstein's eyeglasses got broken along with his nose, and he sputtered through the blood that Stoner wouldn't see Thursday.

"Way I see it," the ex-cop wrapped up, "Specs wormed his way back into Eddie's confidence somehow, then let him have it in the car that night on the ice. Then he got out a spud and chopped a circle around the car so it broke through, and headed back on foot. But he never could prove they were together that night."

"What happened to Clara Baxter?"

"She left town right after the fight. Last I heard she was back and living in Detroit. Married some guy named Fix or Wicks, something like that. I heard he died. Hell, her too, probably, by now."

"Thanks, Mr. Barnes. Who do I see about fishing Eddie's remains out of the river?"

He turned off the nozzle and started rolling up the hose with slow, deliberate movements of his spotted hands. "In this town, no one. Money's too tight to waste solving a murder no one cares about anymore."

"I hope you're wrong, Mr. Barnes," I said. "About no one caring, I mean."

He made no reply. For all I knew, his hearing aid needed fresh batteries.

Three

A Clara Wicks and two C. Fixes were listed in the Detroit directory. I tried them from my office. The first was a thirty-year-old divorcee who tried to rape me over the telephone and the others were men. Then I got tricky and dialed the number for C. Hicks. No answer. Next I rang Lieutenant John Alderdyce on Detroit Homicide, who owed me a favor. He collected on a poker debt from a cop on the Ecorse Police, whose wife's brother knew a member of the city council, who had something on the mayor. Half an hour later Alderdyce called back to say that dragging for the submerged car would start first thing in the morning. Democracy is a system of checks and balances.

There was still no answer at the Hicks number. The house was on Livernois. I thought I'd check it out, and had my hand on the door handle of my war-torn Cutlass when two guys crowded in on either side of me. Together they'd have filled Tiger Stadium.

"You got a previous engagement, chum," said the one on my left, a black with scar tissue over both eyes and a sagging lower lip that left his bottom teeth exposed. His partner wasn't as pretty.

I was hustled into the rear of a dark blue Lincoln in the next slot down, where Gorgeous sat next to me while the other drove. After that the conversation lagged.

Kleinstein was leaning on a cane in the living room of his Troy townhouse when we entered. His white hair was fine over shiny scalp and his neck and hands were spotted, but aside from that he was the Specs whose picture I'd seen in books about Prohibition, down to the thick eyeglasses that had earned him his nickname. He had on a pastel blue sport shirt and gray trousers with pleats.

"You're working for Oscar Chubb." His Yiddish accent was faint but there. "Why?"

"I'm supporting a habit. I have to eat every now and then."

His cane slashed upward. A black light burst inside my temple. I reeled, then lurched forward, but the gargoyles who had brought me stepped between us. Unarmed that day, I relaxed.

"Next time don't be flip," warned the old man. "What've you found out?"

"If you hit me with that cane again I'll make you eat it."

Gorgeous lumbered toward me, dropping one shoulder. I pivoted and kicked. The side of my sole met his kneecap with an audible snap. Howling, he grasped it and staggered backward until he fell into an overstuffed chair. He started to blubber. His partner roared and lunged, but Kleinstein smacked the cane across his chest, halting him.

"All right, you're a hardcase. The cemetery's full of them. Some guys are just too dumb to scare. You're here because I want you to know I didn't kill Stoner."

"Who told you I cared?"

He smiled dryly. The spectacles magnified his eyes to three times their normal size. "Let's stick to the subject. Five witnesses swore I was nowhere near the river that night."

"My client says different."

"Your client is senile."

"Maybe. We'll know for sure tomorrow. The City of Ecorse is raising the car Stoner died in."

He didn't turn pale or try to walk on the ceiling. I hadn't really expected him to. "How much evidence do you think they'll find after fifty years?" He flushed. "Look at this house, Walker. I've lived like this a long time. Do you think I'd risk it on a cheap broad?"

"Maybe you wouldn't. The old Specs might have."

He spat on the carpet. The thug in him would always come through in moments like this. Turning to the uninjured flunky: "Take this punk back to his building and get a doctor for Richard on your way back." To me: "Step soft, Walker. Things have a way of blowing up around people I don't like."

I took him literally. When the gorilla dropped me off I checked under the hood before starting my car.

Four

The Hicks home stood in a seedy neighborhood where old jalopies went to die, a once-white frame house with an attached garage and a swaybacked roof, surrounded by weeds. When no one answered my third knock I tried the door. It was unlocked.

The living room was cozy. Magazines and cheap paperbacks flung everywhere, assorted items of clothing slung over the shabby furniture and piled on the colorless rug. In the bedroom I found a single bed, unmade, and a woman's purse containing the usual junk and a driver's license in the name of Clara Hicks, aged 68. I was in the right place. A small, functional kitchen boasted an old refrigerator, a two-burner stove, and a sink and counter where a sack of groceries waited to be put away. The sack was wet. Two packages of hamburger were half-thawed inside.

There was a throbbing noise behind a side door. My stomach dropped through a hole. I tore open the door and dashed into a wall of noxious smoke. She was lying in the back seat of a six-year-old Duster with her hands folded demurely on her stomach. Her mousy gray hair was rumpled, but aside from that she was rigged for the street, in an inexpensive gray suit and floral print blouse. I recognized her sagging features from the picture on her driver's license. Coughing through my handkerchief, I reached over the seat to turn off the ignition and felt her throat for a pulse. After thirty seconds I gave up.

I climbed out and pulled up the garage door, gulped some air, then went back and steeled myself to run my fingers over her scalp. There was a sticky lump the size of a Ping-Pong ball above her left ear.

Five

Two hours after I called him, I was still sitting in a chair in the kitchen talking to John Alderdyce. John's black, my age, and a spiffy dresser for a cop. In the garage they were still popping flashbulbs and picking up stray buttons.

"It could be suicide," I acknowledged. "She bought groceries today and left that hamburger thawing out in case you boys in Homicide got hungry."

The lieutenant made a disgusting noise. "That's what I can always count on from you, sincerity," he snarled. "The M.E. says she probably suffered cardiac arrest when the blow was struck, an hour or so before you found her. Who would you fit for it? Specs?"

"Maybe. I can't help wondering why, if he was going to do it, he didn't have her iced fifty years ago. The fact that I was with him about the time she took the blow means nothing. He could have had it catered. You'd better talk to Barnes."

"Not that I wasn't planning to anyway, but why?"

"Aside from Specs and Chubb, he was the only one who knew I was on the case. Someone had to tell Kleinstein."

"That opens up all sorts of unpleasant possibilities."

"Buying cops was invented in the twenties," I said. "Look up his record. Maybe he knows who dropped the contract on Eddie Stoner."

"That one's yours. I've got enough new murders on my hands. I don't have to tinker with old ones too."

I fumbled out a cigarette and stuck it between my lips without lighting it. My throat was raw from them as it was.

"Someone doesn't agree with you. This particular old murder bothered him enough to make committing a new one seem worthwhile."

"Barnes is the one told you about the Baxter woman in the first place."

"He knew I'd suspect him if he didn't. He very conveniently forgot her married name, remember. Of course, I'm assuming she hasn't made enemies in the interim. That one's yours."

"Thanks. I wouldn't have known if you hadn't told me."

He put away his notepad. "That'll do for now, Walker. Your help is appreciated."

I'd heard sweeter thanks from muggers. "Don't mention it. Finding little old ladies sapped and gassed is a favorite hobby of mine."

That night I dreamed I was out swimming on a warm evening when I came upon a vintage car sunk in the mud, moonlight shining on it through the water. Peering inside, I was snatched by flabby hands and found myself grappling with an old woman whose face was blotched gray with death. We rolled over and over, but her grip was like iron and I couldn't shake her. I awoke as drenched as if I had actually been in the water.

The telephone was ringing. It was John Alderdyce.

"Good news and bad news, shamus. Sheriff's men got Barnes at Metro Airport a few minutes ago, boarding a plane for L.A."

"What's the bad news?"

"We looked up his record. There's nothing to indicate he was anything but square. I wish to hell mine were as good."

That tore it as far as getting a good night's sleep was concerned. I sat up smoking cigarettes until dawn.

Six

The day was well along when Alderdyce and I shared the Ecorse dock with a crowd of local cops and the curious, watching a rusty sedan rise from the river at the end of a cable attached to a derrick on the pier. Streaming water, the glistening hulk swung in a wide, slow arc and descended to a cleared section of dock. The crane's motor died. Water hissed down the archaic vehicle's boiler-shaped cowl and puddled around the rotted tires.

Uniforms held back the crowd while John and I inspected the interior. Decayed wooden crates had tumbled over everything. Something lay on the floor in front, swaddled in rags, and what remained of the upholstery. White, turtle-gnawed bone showed through the tattered and blackened fabric.

"Not much hope of proving he was sapped or shot," said the lieutenant. "The denizens of the deep have seen to that."

"Even so," I said, "having a *corpus delicti* makes for a warm, cozy feeling. Is Barnes still in custody?"

"For the time being. We won't be able to hold him much longer without evidence. What is it?"

A longshoreman who had been pressed into service to unload the cargo had exclaimed as he lifted out the first of the crates. "Awful light for a box full of booze," he said, setting it down on the dock.

A crowbar was produced and the rotted boards gave way easily to reveal nothing inside. Alderdyce directed another crate to be opened, and another. They were equally unrewarding.

"I wonder why Eddie would risk his life for a carload of empty boxes," I mused, breaking the silence.

Seven

In the end, it was the boxes and not the body that broke him. After an hour of questioning, Alderdyce dropped the bombshell about the strange cargo, whereupon Barnes's face lost all color and he got so tongue-tied he couldn't keep his lies straight. When he started confessing, the stenographer had to ask him twice to slow down so she could keep up.

Outside Oscar Chubb's room that evening an orderly with shoulders you couldn't hike across grasped my upper arms as I started to push past and I asked him to let go. He squeezed harder, twisting the muscle and leering. I jabbed four stiffened fingers into the arch of his ribcage. When he doubled over I snatched hold of his collar and opened the door with his head. Inside, a gentle boot in the rump laid him out on his face.

Dr. Tuskin and the hatchet-faced nurse were standing on the other side of the bed. An oxygen tent covered Chubb's head and torso and he was wired to an oscilloscope whose feeble beep disconcertingly resembled a countdown. The noise echoed the beating of my client's heart.

"Call the police," Tuskin told the nurse.

"Uh-uh." I blocked her path. "What happened?"

Tuskin hesitated. "Stroke. It happened shortly after you left yesterday. What right have you to break in and batter my staff?"

I studied the gaunt face behind transparent plastic. "Is he conscious?"

Before the doctor could respond, Chubb's eyelids rolled open and the great eyes slued my way. To Tuskin I said, "This will only take a minute. It'll be on tonight's news, so you can stay if you like."

He liked. I spoke for longer than a minute, but by then no one was watching the clock. The dying man lay with his eyes closed most of the time. I had only the peeping of the electronic whozis to tell me I still had an audience.

"I confirmed it in back issues of the *News* and *Free Press* at the library," I went on. "That wasn't the first load of hooch Specs paid for and never got. His rumrunning boats and cars had a habit of sinking and getting hijacked, more than those of his rivals. Eddie bought the stuff in Canada with the boss's money, stashed part of it to be picked up later, and saw to it that the empty crates he'd replaced it with got lost. He was making a respectable profit off each load. Kleinstein got wind of it and threatened him. Eddie and Clara never were an item. That was just Barnes's story."

Chubb's lips moved. I didn't need to hear him.

"Sure you saw them together," I said. "They were retrieving a load from one of their caches. If Barnes was Eddie's pipeline into the police department, as he's confessed, Clara was his spy in Specs's inner circle, ready to sound the alarm if he ever got suspicious. When he did, Barnes panicked and had Eddie taken out to keep him from talking."

I read his lips again and shook my head.

"No. I thought Barnes had killed him too until we checked out his alibi. The night Eddie went down, your partner was sitting vigil in a Harper Woods funeral parlor with a cousin's remains. Two people who were with him that night are still alive, and they've confirmed it. There was only one other person who had a stake in Eddie's death, who he would have trusted to go with him that last night."

His lips didn't move this time. I hurried on.

"It was the girl, Mr. Chubb. Clara Baxter. She shot him and spent all night chipping a hole under the car to cover the evidence. Barnes hasn't changed much in fifty years. When I started poking around he lost his head again and tipped Kleinstein anonymously to get me out of the way while he offed Clara. He knew she wouldn't confess to Eddie's murder, but if Specs got suspicious and wrung the truth about the swindle out of her, Barnes was cold meat. In court he stood a chance. The underworld doesn't offer one."

I waited, but he didn't respond. After a brief examination Dr. Tuskin announced that his patient had lapsed into coma. I never found out if he was conscious long enough to appreciate the fact that he'd spent half a century hating a man for the wrong reason. He died early the next morning without telling his son about our arrangement, and I didn't have enough capital on hand to sue his estate. But I wasn't the biggest loser by far.

Three days after his arraignment on two counts of murder, while awaiting trial in the Wayne County Jail, Walter Barnes was found strangled to death in his cell with the cord from his hearing aid. The coroner called it suicide.

Fast Burn

The old man wrestled open my inner office door and held it with a shoulder while he worked his way inside, supporting himself on two steel canes, dragging one foot behind him that clanked when he let his weight down on it. He had a corrugated brow and a long loose face of that medium gray that very black skin sometimes turns with age, shot through with concentration and pain. His brown suit bagged at the knees and no two buttons on the jacket matched.

At that moment I was up to my wrists in typewriter ribbon, changing spools on the venerable Underwood portable that came with the office, and unable to get up from behind my desk to assist him— not that he looked like someone who was accustomed to receiving help from anyone. I simply said hello and nodded toward the customer's chair on his side. While I threaded the ribbon through the various forks, hooks, and prongs I heard him lower himself thankfully onto semisoft vinyl and make the little metallic snicking noises that went with undoing the braces securing the canes to his wrists.

I took my time, giving him breathing space. Going to see a private investigator isn't like visiting the dentist. I come at the desperate end of the long line of friends, relatives, friends of relatives, friends of friends, and guys around the corner whose friends owe them favors. By the time the potential client gets around to me he's admitted that his problem has grown beyond him and his circle. So I let this one resign himself to the last stop before the abyss and didn't realize until I looked up again that I was playing host to a dead man.

You know dead once you've seen it a few times, and the old man's cocked head and black open mouth with spittle hanging at one corner and the glittering crescents of his half-open eyes said it even as I got up and moved around the desk to feel his neck for an artery he didn't need any longer. His face was four shades darker than it had been coming in, and bunched like a fist. He'd suffered six kinds of hell in that last quiet moment.

I broke a pair of surgical gloves out of a package I keep in the desk, put them on, and went through his pockets. When someone dies in a room you pay rent on it's only polite to learn who he is. If the driver's license in his dilapidated wallet was valid, his name was Emmett Gooding and he lived—had lived—on Mt. Elliott near the cemetery. What a crippled old man was doing still driving was strictly between him and the Michigan Secretary of State's office. There were twelve dollars in the wallet and a ring of keys in his right pants pocket, nothing else on him except a handful of pocket lint and a once-white handkerchief that crackled when unfolded. He was wearing a steel brace on his left leg. I put everything back where I'd found it and dialed 911.

The prowl car cop who showed up ten minutes later looked about 17, with no hair on his face and no promise of it and a glossy black visor screwed down to the eyes. He put on gloves of his own to feel Gooding's neck and told me after a minute that he was dead.

"That's why I called," I said, knocking ash off a Winston into the souvenir ashtray on my desk. "I wanted a second opinion."

"You kill him?" He laid a hand on his sidearm.

"I'll answer that question when it counts."

Creases marred the freckles under his eyes. "When's that?"

"Now." I nodded at the first of two plainclothesmen coming in the door. He was a slender black with a Fu Manchu moustache and coils of gray hair like steel wool at his temples, wearing the kind of electric blue suit that looks like hell on anybody but him. I knew him as Sergeant Blake, having seen him around Detroit Police Headquarters but not often enough to talk to. His companion was white, short, fifteen pounds too heavy for department regs, and a good ten years too old for active duty. He had a brush cut, jug ears, and so much upper lip it hung down over the hollow in his chin. I didn't know him from Sam's cat. You can live in a city the size of Detroit a long time and never get to know all the cops on the detective force if you're lucky.

Blake's flat eyes slid over the stiff quickly and lit on the uniform as he flashed his badge and ID. "Anything?"

"Just what's here, Sarge," reported the youngster, and handed me a glance meant to be hard. "Suspect's uncooperative."

"Okay, crash." And the uniform was off the case. When he had gone: "They're running too small to keep these days."

The short fat cop grunted.

"Amos Walker, right?" Blake looked at me tor the first time. I nodded. "This is my partner, Officer Fister. Who's the dead guy?"

I said I didn't know and gave him the story, leaving out the part about searching the body. Cops consider that their province, which it is. Fister meanwhile wrapped a handkerchief around his fingers and drew the dead man's wallet out of his inside breast pocket. He had probably run out of surgical gloves years ago. He read off what mattered on the driver's license and inventoried the other contents. Blake watched me carefully while this was going on, and I made my face just as carefully blank. At length be gave a little shrug. That was it until the medical examiner arrived with his black metal case and glanced at Gooding's discolored face and looked at his fingers and took off the dead man's right shoe and sock and examined the bottom of his foot and then put all his instruments back in the case, humming to himself. He was a young Oriental. They are almost always Orientals; I think it has something to do with ancestor worship.

Blake looked at him and the M.E. said, "Massive coronary. We'll root around inside and spend a hunk of taxpayer's money on tests and it'll still come out massive coronary. When their faces turn that shade and there's evidence of an earlier stroke"—he indicated the leg brace, part of which showed under the dead man's pantsleg—"it can't be much else."

The sergeant thanked him and when the expert left had me tell the story again for Fister's notepad and then again just for fun while the white coats came to bag the body and cart it down to the wagon. "Any ideas about why he came here?" Blake asked. I shook my head. He sighed. "Okay. We might need your statement later if Charlie Chan turns out to be wrong about the heart attack."

"He didn't act like someone who's been wrong recently," I said.

Fister grunted again. "Tell me. I never met one of them croakers didn't think his sweat smelled like lilacs."

On that sparkling note they left me.

Two

I spent the rest of the week tailing a state senator's aide around Lansing for his wife in Detroit, who was curious about the weekends he was spending at the office. Turned out he had a wife in the state capital, too. I was grinning my way through my typewritten report at the desk when Sergeant Blake came in. He wore a tired look and the same shocking blue suit. There couldn't be another like it in the city.

"You're off the hook," he announced. "Gooding's heart blew like the M.E. said. We checked him out. He was on the line at the Dearborn plant till he took his mandatory four years ago. Worked part-time flagging cars during road construction for County, had a stroke last year, and quit. No family. Papers in his dump on Mt. Elliott said he was getting set to check into a nursing home on Dequindre. Staff at the home expected him this week. Next to his phone we found Monday's *Free Press* folded to an article about employee theft that mentioned you as an investigator and the Yellow Pages open to the page with your number on it."

"That was a feature piece about a lot of dead cases." I stapled the report. "What did he want with me?"

"*¿Quien sabe?* Maybe he thought this was the elephant graveyard for old Ford workers. I'd care if he died any way but natural."

"Okay if I look into it?"

"Why? There's no one to stand your fee."

"He came looking for help with something. I'd like to know what it was."

"It's your time." He opened the door.

"Thanks for coming down, sergeant. You could have called."

"I'm on my way home. I dropped off a uniform to drive Gooding's car to the impound. We found it in the lot next door."

He went out and I got up to file my carbon of the report to the woman with the generous husband. The window behind the desk started chattering, followed an instant later by a massive hollow *crump* that rang my telephone bell. At first I thought it was the ancient furnace blowing. Then I remembered it was June and got my

.38 out of the desk. I almost bumped into Blake standing in the hall with his Police Special drawn. He glanced at me without saying anything and together we clattered down three flights to the street. Something that wasn't an automobile any longer squatted in a row of vehicles in the parking lot next to my building with its hood and doors sprung and balls of orange flame rolling out of its shattered windows, pouring black smoke into the smog layer overhead. Sirens keened in the distance, years too late to help the officer cooking in the front seat.

Three

Shadows were congealing when I got away from Headquarters, dry-mouthed from talking to a tape recorder and damp under the arms from Sergeant Blake's enthusiastic interrogation. The bomb squad was still looking at the charred husk of Gooding's car, but it was a fair bet that a healthy charge had been rigged to the ignition. Gooding was Homicide's meat now and my permission to investigate his interest in me had died with the uniformed cop. So I called an old acquaintance in Personnel at the City-County Building from a public booth and asked for information on the old man's brief employment with the Road Commission; if I'd had brains to begin with I would have invested in two chinchillas instead of a license and waited for spring. My acquaintance promised to get back to me next day during business hours. I hung up and drove to Dearborn, where no one working the late shift at the Ford plant had ever heard of Emmett Gooding. The turnover in the auto industry is worse than McDonald's. I caught the personnel manager just as he was leaving his office, flashed my ID, and told him I was running a credit check on Gooding for a finance company. Reluctantly he agreed to go back in and pull the old man's file.

The manager was small, with a shaved head and a very black pointed beard that didn't make him look anything like the high priest of the Church of Satan. He scowled at the papers in the Manila folder.

"He was a steady worker, didn't take as many sick days as you might expect from someone nearing mandatory retirement. Turned down the foreman's job twice in eighteen years. No surprise. It's a thankless position, not worth the raise."

"Is there anyone still working here who knew him?" I asked.

"Probably not. A robot's doing his job these days." He winced. "I had a computer expert in here recently bragging about how the machines free workers from inhuman jobs to explore their true potential. In my day we called it unemployment."

There was nothing in that for me, so I thanked him and got up. His eyes followed me. "What's a man Gooding's age want with a loan?"

"He's buying a hot tub," I said, and got out of there.

That was it for one day. I had a bill to make out for the bigamist's wife, and contrary to what you read, private stars don't often work at night, when most sources are closed. The bill complete, I caught a senile pork chop and a handful of wilted fries at the diner down the street from my office and went home. There was just a black spot on the parking lot pavement where Gooding's car had stood.

After breakfast the next morning I drove down to the City-County Building, making a gun out of my index finger and snapping a shot at the statue of the Spirit of Detroit on my way in. The Green Giant, as we call him, was still threatening to crush the family he was holding in one hand with the globe he was gripping in the other. The blunt instrument symbolized Progress.

I owed my contact in Personnel to having sprung his younger brother from a charge of assaulting a police officer upon producing evidence that the cop had a history of trying to pull moving violators out of their cars through the vent windows. It had cost me some good will at Police Headquarters, but the access to confidential records was worth it. My man looked like 14 trying to pass for 40, with freckles, hornrims, and short sandy hair parted with a protractor. Never mind his name.

"What you got?" I slung my frame into the treacherous scoop chair in front of his gray metal desk and lit up. He pushed a spotless white ashtray my way. He was one of those non-smokers who didn't mind a little more pollution in a sky already the color of sardines. "Not a lot," he said. "Gooding was with the Road Commission off and on, mostly off, for only about five months before taking a medical." He told me which months. I took them down in my notebook.

"What sort of worker was he?"

"How good do you have to be to hold up a sign? Nothing remarkable on his work sheet; I guess he was reliable."

"Where'd he work?"

He started to read off street names, quadrant numbers, and dates from the printout sheet on his desk, then swore and slid it across to me. I wrote them down too, along with the foreman's name and home telephone number. "Anything else?"

"Nothing the computer noticed," he said.

"Okay, thanks." I got up, shook his hand, and went through the door, or almost. Blake and Fister were on their way in. The sergeant's fist was raised to rap on the door. When he saw me I pulled my head back out of range. He hesitated, then uncurled his fingers and smoothed down one side of his Fu Manchu. He said: "I should have guessed. The guy in Dearborn said someone was around asking about Gooding last night."

"Good morning, Sergeant," I said. "Officer."

"Let's clink him for interfering in a police investigation," suggested Fister. His long upper lip was skinned back to his gums, exposing teeth the shade of old plaster.

Blake ignored him. "You're screwing around with your license, Walker."

"Not technically, since I'm not working for anyone."

Fister said. "The law ain't in books, pal. It's here standing in front of you."

"Don't let us walk on your heels a second time," the sergeant said evenly. "We'll bend you till you break."

He walked around me into the office, followed a half-second later by his trained dog.

Four

The foreman's name was Lawler. I tried his home number from a booth, got no answer, and called the county dispatcher's office, where a dead-voiced secretary informed me Lawler was due at a road construction site on Dequindre at two. That gave me three hours. I coaxed my heap up Woodward to the Detroit Public Library and spent the time in the microfilm room reading copies of the *News* and *Free Press* for the dates Gooding had worked flagging cars. No major robberies or hits had taken place in those vicinities at the time. So much for the theory that he had seen someone driving through whom he was better off not seeing. Rubbing floating type out of my eyes, I put a hamburger out of its misery at a lunch counter on Warren and took the Chrysler north to Dequindre. On the way I flipped on the radio in the middle of a news report on the bombing outside my office building. The announcer managed to get my name right, but that was about all.

A crew of eight were taking turns shoveling gravel and Elmer's Glue into a single pothole the size of a dimple at Remington. They would tip the stuff into the hole, pat it down, then walk half a block back to the truck for another load. Even then it didn't look as if they could make the job last until quitting time, but you never know. A hardhat crowding 50, with a great firm belly and sleeves rolled back past thick forearms burned to a dark cherry color, stood with one work shoe propped on the truck's rear bumper, eyes like twin slivers of blue glass watching the operation through the smoke of his cigarette. They didn't move as I pulled my car off to the side a safe distance from the county vehicle and got out. "Mr. Lawler?"

His only reaction was to reach up with a crusted forefinger and flick ash off his cigarette without removing it from between his lips. Since the gesture seemed more positive than negative, I gave him a look at my license photostat and told him what I was doing there. "Gooding ran interference for your crew," I wound up. "What can you tell me about him?"

"He knew which side of the sign said STOP and which said SLOW."

"Anything else?"

"Anything meaning what?" He still wasn't looking at me.

You run into him in every profession, the one bee in the hive who would rather sting than make honey. "Look," I said, "I'm just earning a living, like you and the lightning corps here. You look like someone who's talked to investigators; you know what I want. How did the old man get along with the other workers? Did you notice if there were any he was especially friendly with, or especially not friendly with? Did you overhear one of them saying something like, 'Gooding, I don't like you and I'm going to blow you up in your car'? Little things like that."

He flicked off some more ash. "I talked to investigators," he acknowledged. "Two years ago I seen a car run a stop sign on Jefferson and knock down a kid crossing the street. When I was getting set to testify against the driver his lawyer hired a detective to follow me from bar to bar and prove in court I was a drunk and an unreliable witness. Yeah," he said, spitting out the butt, "I talked to investigators."

He walked away to look down into the pothole. I stood there for a moment, peeling cellophane off a fresh pack of Winstons. When he didn't return I put one in my mouth and went back to my car. A lanky black with a scar on his jaw and his hardhat balanced precariously on the back of his head climbed into the passenger's seat.

"I heard you talking to Lawler, mister," He talked through a sunny grin that brightened the interior. "He's not a bad dude; he's just had a run of bad luck."

"Must be tough." I touched a match to my weed and shook it out. Waiting.

"I knew Emmett Gooding some, " he said.

I waited some more, looking at him. His grin was fixed. I got out my wallet and held up a ten-spot between the first and second fingers of my right hand. When he reached for it I pulled it back. He shrugged and sat back, still grinning.

"Not enough to say much more than 'Hello' to," he went on. "There's like a wall around those old men, you know? Except to Jamie."

"Jamie?"

"James Dunrather, I think his right name was. White dude, about twenty-two. Long greasy blond hair and pimples. Lawler canned him a couple of weeks back for selling dope on the job." He shook his head. "Ugly scene, man. He kept screaming about how he could get Lawler killed. Lawler just laughed."

I scraped some dust off the dash with the edge of the bill. "Dunrather and Gooding were friends?"

"Not friends. Jamie had a way of talking at you till you had to say something back just to get him to stop. I seen him talking at the old man that way on lunch break. Not the old man exclusive, mind you, just anybody close. Gooding was the only one that didn't bother to up and walk away."

"What'd he talk about?"

"Mostly he bragged about what a bad dude he was and all the bad dudes he knew. What you expect to hear from a part-time pusher. Then Gooding got sick and quit. But he come back."

"To work?"

He shook his head again. "He come to where we was tearing up pavement on Eight Mile. It was about a week before Jamie got canned. Man, Gooding looked about a hundred, leaning on them canes. He talked to Jamie for maybe ten minutes and then left in that beat-up Pontiac of his. Rest of us might've been in Mississippi for all the notice he took of us."

"You didn't hear what they were talking about?"

"Man, when that Rotomill starts ripping up asphalt—"

"Yeah," I said. "Where can I find this Dunrather?"

He shrugged, eyeing the sawbuck in my hand. I gave it to him. "Hope that's worth the job." I nodded through the windshield at Lawler, watching us from beside the pothole. My angel grinned with one foot on the pavement.

"Affirmative Action, man," he said. "It's a sweet country."

Five

I made contact with Barry Stackpole at the *News,* who kept a personal file on street-level talent for his column. Jamie Dunrather had a record as long as Woodward Avenue for pushing pot and controlled substances, but no convictions, and an alias for each of his many addresses. Recent information had him living in a walkup over an adult bookstore on Watson. I promised Barry a dinner and tooled downtown.

There was a drunk snoring on the bottom step inside the street door with flies crawling on his face. I climbed over him and up a narrow squawking staircase with a gnawed rubber runner between mustard walls sprayed all over with words to live by. The upstairs hallway smelled of mold and thick paint that was fresh when Ford started paying five dollars a day. The building was as real as a stained Band-Aid on the floor of a YMCA pool. I rapped on Dunrather's door and flattened out against the wall next to the hinges, gripping the butt of my .38 in its belt clip. When no bullets splintered the panel I tried the knob. It gave.

Unclipping the gun, I pushed the door open slowly, going in with it to avoid being framed in the doorway. The shade was drawn over the room's only window, but enough light leaked in around it to fall on a ladderback chair mottled with old white paint, a dented table holding up a dirty china lamp and a portable TV, and a bed with a painted iron frame. The man dangling from the overhead fixture cast a gently drifting shadow as he twisted in the current of air stirring through the open door. He had a flexible wire like they hang pictures with sunk in the flesh of his neck, and his frog eyes and extended tongue were pale against his purple face. He was wearing faded jeans and track shoes and a red T-shirt with white letters that said MAKE ONLY BIG MISTAKES. You had to smile.

A floorboard sighed behind me while I was comparing the dead man's acned complexion and lank dishwater locks to my informant's description of Jamie Dunrather. I turned about a century too late. Later I thought I'd heard the swish, but all I was sure of was a bolt of white pain and a black mouth swallowing me.

Six

"Put this where it hurts and shut up."

I'd expected gentler words on my way through the gates, but after staring for a moment at the wet handkerchief folded on the dusty pink palm I accepted it. I found the sticky lump behind my left ear with no trouble and fought back fresh darkness when the cold damp cloth touched the pulpy mass. Bitter bile climbed my throat. My thick tongue made me think of Dunrather and thought of Dunrather made the bile rise. I swallowed, vaguely conscious of having spoken.

"Did I say anything worth holding against me?"

Sergeant Blake ignored the question. He was sitting on the ladderback chair with his hands on his knees and his face too far from the floor where I was lying for me to make out. But I recognized the suit. Now I became aware of movement around me, and spotted the white coats from the morgue. They had freed the body and were wrapping it. Fister stood by watching.

"Bag his hands," Blake told them. To me: "I'm betting the wire made those cuts on his palms. He wouldn't grab it that tight unless he was trying to save his life. It wasn't suicide."

I said, "The guy who slugged me must've been hiding behind the door. He had to go past the drunk on the stairs on his way out. Maybe the drunk saw something."

"The drunk's at Headquarters now. But he was as gone as you, and the guy took the service stairs out back when he heard us coming. We found this on the steps. He tossed my wallet onto my chest. "It's been dusted. He wore gloves. If he didn't know who you were before, he knows now. Feed it to me."

I fed it to him, starting with what I'd learned at the road construction site. From past experience I didn't try to sit up. A pillow from the iron bed was under my head, which was full of bass fiddles tuning up.

"I say clink him," Fister put in. "It's his putzing around scared the killer into icing Dunrather."

"Unless Dunrather killed Gooding," I said.

Blake said, "No, it's good business not to clog up an investigation with too many killers. We got the same information you did by threatening to take Lawler downtown, and traced Dunrather through the computer. On our way up here we heard a street door slam on the other side of the building. Those new security places with no fire exits to speak of spoiled us; we didn't think to look for a back way."

I turned the handkerchief around to the cool side. "The bombing story hit the airwaves this afternoon. He's mopping up. Dunrather was a braggart, a poor risk."

"Everything about this case screams contract." The sergeant considered. "Except Gooding. There's no reason a pro would bother with an old man like that, and he couldn't have expected anyone but Gooding to blow up in Gooding's car."

I said, "He's too sloppy for a pro anyway. If a seasoned heavyweight wanted Dunrather's death to look like suicide he wouldn't have let him cut up his hands that way."

"Now that he knows who you are and how close you are, whoever he is, I guess maybe we saved your butt by coming in when we did."

"You never get a flat tire when you need one," Fister growled.

Blake leaned his forearms on his knees. "Cop killings are messy, Walker. Third parties tend to stop lead. It doesn't matter much to the guy who stops it whether it came from a Saturday Night Buster or a Police Special. Fister will type up your statement and we'll collect your signature later. You want a ride home?" He stood.

"My crate's parked around the corner," I said, sitting slowly. The fiddles were louder in that position. "And your good cop, bad cop number's wasted on me."

"You're cluttering up the murder scene, Hot Wit." He held out my dented hat and gun, retrieved from the floor.

Seven

You can't live on the edge all the time, check behind all the doors and under all the beds and still be the sort of man who reads *Playboy*. But if you're lucky enough not to and live, it makes you alert enough next time to spot things like a cigarette end glowing like a single orange eye in the gloom behind your office window on your way to the front door of your building. I did, and forced my echoing skull to remember if I'd locked the inner sanctum. Then I decided remembering didn't matter, because people who don't mean harm don't smoke in strange rooms while dusk is gathering without turning on a light.

I mounted the stairs like anyone else returning to his place of business just before closing, but slower than usual, thinking. You get a lot of thinking done in three flights. By the time I reached my floor I was pretty sure why Emmett Gooding had been marked for death, though I didn't know by whom, and none of it made sense anyway. It rarely does outside Nero Wolfe.

I walked right past the outer office and through the one next to that, closing it behind me. My neighbor that week was a travel agent with one telephone and one desk and posters of places that looked nothing like Detroit on the walls. The agent's narrow sad brown face lit up when I entered, fell when he recognized me and registered curiosity when I lifted his receiver and dialed Police Headquarters.

Sergeant Blake had returned. When his voice finally came on the line I said, "How sure are you that Emmett Gooding left no survivors?"

"Why?" Suspicion curled like smoke out of the earpiece.

"Because someone had to be named beneficiary on his life insurance policy."

"Who told you he had one?"

"You just did. Who is it?"

"I'm reading the report now. Twenty-five thousand goes to a girl out on the Coast, the daughter of an old friend who worked with Gooding on the line at Dearborn till he died nine years ago. But she hasn't left San Francisco this year."

"Double indemnity," I pressed. "Fifty grand if he died by accident or mayhem."

"Why ask me if you know? And how do you know?" I told him I was a detective. After a pause he said, "Anything else, or can I go home and introduce myself to my wife?"

"Do that. On the way you might stop by and pick up your cop-killer. He's waiting for me in my office."

The pause this time was longer. "Where are you?"

I told him.

"Okay, sit tight."

"What if he tries to leave?"

"Stop him." The line went dead.

I hung up and offered the travel agent a cigarette, but he wasn't seeing the pack. He'd overheard everything. I lit one for myself and asked him if he'd sent anyone anywhere lately.

"Just my ex-wife and her boyfriend," he replied, coming out of it. "To Tahiti. On my alimony."

I grinned, but he could see my heart wasn't in it. The conversation flagged. I smoked and waited.

There had to be and insurance policy for Gooding to have done what he did. It had been done before, but the victims were always family men and any half-smart cop could wrap it up in an hour. Single men like my almost-client who had outlived whatever family or friends they'd had tended to throw off everyone but hunch-players like me and tireless pros like Blake who touched all the bases no matter how hopeless.

At two minutes past five I heard the door to my outer office close softly. Swearing quietly, I killed my butt in the travel agent's ashtray and advised him to climb under his desk. I didn't have to tell him twice. I moved out into the hallway with gun in hand.

His skinny back, clad in an army fatigue shirt, long black hair spilling to his shoulders, was just disappearing down the stairwell. I strode to the top of the stairs and cocked the .38. The noise made echoes. He started to turn. The overhead light painted a streak along the .45 automatic in his right hand.

"Uh-uh," I cautioned.

He froze in mid-turn. He wasn't much older than Dunrather, with a droopy moustache that was mostly fuzz and a bulbous lower lip like a baby's. He was a third of the way down the flight.

"Junior button man," I sneered. "What'd Gooding pay you, a hundred?"

"Five hundred." His voice was as young as the rest of him. "He said it was all he had."

"He wasted it. He was a sick old man with nothing to look forward to but a nursing home. So like a lot of other sick old men he decided to go for the fast burn. But suicide would've voided his insurance and he wanted his dead friend's daughter to get something out of his death. The stroke made up his mind. He remembered Jamie Dunrather bragging about all the bad cats he knew, got your name from him, and paid you to take him out."

"I didn't want to get mixed up in no cop-killing," he said. "Who knew the old man was going to conk and someone else would eat that charge I stuck under his hood?"

"So when you heard about it you started covering your tracks. You cooled Dunrather and you would have cooled me too if the cops hadn't interrupted you." His thick lower lip dropped a millimeter. I pressed on. "You didn't know it was the cops, did you? You knew Gooding had been to see me, you thought he'd told me everything, and you figured that by waiting for me back here you could ambush me and be in the clear."

"Why not? When you didn't show by quitting time I decided to hit you at home. You was all I had to worry about, I thought."

"Pros give the cops more credit than that," I said. "But you'll never be a pro."

The air freshened in the stairwell, as if someone had opened the street door. I was talking to draw his attention from it. His knuckles whitened around the automatic's grip, and I saw he was wearing transparent rubber gloves.

"What'd he want to come see you for anyway?" he demanded.

"He changed his mind. When it came down to it he didn't really want to die. When he couldn't find you to call it off he was going to hire me to look for you. He read my name in the paper and that gave him the idea."

He made a thin keening sound between his teeth and twisted around the rest of the way, straightening his gun arm.

"Police! Drop it!"

A pro would have gone ahead and plugged me, then tended to Blake on the second landing, but I was right about him. He swung back to fire down the stairs. Blake and I opened up at the same time. The reports of our .38s battered the walls. The man in the fatigue shirt dropped his .45 clattering down the steps, gripped the banister, and slid three feet before sliding off and piling into a heap of army surplus halfway down the flight.

In the echoing silence that followed, Officer Fister, who had entered the building a second behind his partner, bounded past Blake and bent to feel the man's neck for a pulse. He straightened after a moment. "He's killed his last cop."

"The hell with him," said the sergeant, holstering his gun under his left arm. Smoke curled spastically up the stairwell.

The dead man's name turned out to be Jarvis, and he had been questioned and released in connection with three unsolved homicides in the past year and a half. I didn't know him from Sam's cat. You can live in a city the size of Detroit a long time and never get to know all the killers if you're lucky.

Dead Soldier

Nha Nelson's Oriental face was shaped like an inverted raindrop, oval with a chin that came to a point. She just crested five feet and ninety pounds in a tight pink sweater and a black skirt that caught her legs just below the knees. Her eyes slanted down from a straight nose and her complexion was more beige than ivory. She was as Vietnamese as a punji stick.

I said, "My name's Amos Walker. I think we spoke on the telephone about a package I have for Mr. Nelson." I held up the bottle in the paper sack.

"Come in." She gave every consonant its full measure.

Carrying my wine like a party goer, I followed her into a neat living room where two men sat watching television. One rose to grasp my hand. Reed Nelson was my height and age—just six feet and on the wrong side of 30—but he had football shoulders under his checked shirt and wore his brass-colored hair cut very close. His brittle smile died short of his eyes. "My neighbor, Steve Minor."

I nodded to the other man, fortyish and balding, who grunted back but kept his seat. He was watching the Lions lose to Pittsburgh.

"Nha said a private detective called." Nelson's eyes went to the bottle. "It's about the tontine, isn't it?"

I said it was. He asked Steve Minor to excuse him, got a grunt in reply, and we adjourned to a paneled basement. Hunting prints covered the walls. Rifles and handguns occupied two glassed-in display cases, and a Browning automatic lay in pieces on a workbench stained with gun oil and crowded with cartridge-loading paraphernalia. My host cleared a stack of paper targets off one of a pair of crushed-leather armchairs and we sat down.

"Expecting someone?" I asked.

He smiled the halfway smile. "Friend of mine owns a range outside Dearborn. I was a sharpshooter in the army and I'd rather not lose the edge. If I were you I wouldn't smoke; you're sitting on a case of black powder."

I looked down at the edge of a carton stenciled EXPLOSIVE sticking out between the legs of my chair and put away my pack of Winstons.

"David Kurch hired me to find you and deliver the bottle," I said. "He's the lawyer you and the others left it with when you formed the tontine."

"I remember. He was an ARVN then, stationed in Que Noc." Nelson's expression turned in on itself. "That was only twelve years ago. It's hard to believe they're all dead."

"They are, though. Chuck Dundas stepped on a mine two feet shy of the DMZ in 'seventy. Albert Rule was MIA for seven years and has been declared dead. Fred Burlingame shot himself in New York last year, and Jerry Lynch died of cancer in August. Congratulations." I handed him the bottle.

He slid it out of the sack, fondled it. "It was bottled in some Frenchman's private vineyard in 'thirty-seven. Al found it in a ruined cellar near Hue, probably left behind when the French bugged out. The tontine was Fred's idea. The last man left was supposed to get the bottle. Were you over there?"

"Two years."

"Then you know how preoccupied we were with death. But, hell, I forgot all about this till you showed up. When I saw the package I remembered."

I passed him my receipt pad with a pen clipped to it. "If you'll sign this I'll shove off."

He read it swiftly and scribbled his name. "How'd you find me? I just moved to Detroit from Southfield, and my number's unlisted." He gave back the pad and pen.

"Kurch said you were an engineer at General Motors. I got it from Personnel."

"They have a hell of a nerve, after I just got fired."

"They cutting back again?"

He moved his head from side to side, but his eyes stayed on me. "They said I was a poor risk from a psychiatric standpoint."

"Are you?"

"You were in Nam. What do you think?"

I let that ride and got up. Crowd noise filtered down from the TV set upstairs. Someone had just made a touchdown. Nelson said, "You drink?"

I sat back down. "Do they make cars in Toyko?" This time his smile made it all the way. He turned his head and called, "Nha? Two glasses, please."

"What about your neighbor?" I asked.

"He'll understand. Steve and I aren't all that close. I only invite him over because I knew him slightly in Nam and he put me on to this house, not that that was such a favor with this mortgage staring at my throat. He introduced me to my wife."

On cue, Nha appeared, set a pair of stemmed glasses down on the workbench, and withdrew. She seemed flushed. Nelson scooped a

Swiss Army knife out of a drawer in the bench and used the corkscrew to unstop the bottle. When the glasses were full of dark red liquid, he handed one over and raised his. "Chuck, Al, Fred, and Jerry. Four among the fifty thousand."

We sipped. It was good, but nothing beats twelve-year-old scotch. "Were you married over there?"

He nodded. "She was working in a Saigon orphanage. Grew up there, after her parents got napalmed in 'sixty-five. You like being a private eye?"

We drank wine and sold each other our biographies. There wasn't much to tell beyond the gaping hole of Vietnam. After an hour or so, the noise upstairs ceased abruptly. Steve Minor had switched off the set. Nelson replaced the cork in the bottle, which was now half empty. "There's another afternoon's drinking in here," he said, rising.

I was already on my feet. "Share it with your wife, or with someone else close."

"She's a teetotaler. And if there were anyone else close, do you think I'd be wasting it on a shamus I don't even know?" His eyes pleaded.

I said I'd call him. Upstairs, Nha saw me out without speaking. Minor had left.

Two

It was three weeks before I made it back. I had spent much of that time following a city councilman's wife from male friend to male friend while her husband was on a junket to Palm Springs. Nelson greeted me at the door, explaining that Nha was out shopping. We killed the bottle in near-silence. He hadn't found a job and he wasn't talking much. It looked as if the novelty had worn off our relationship. We parted.

The rest of the month died painlessly. The Lions blew a late-season rally just before the play-offs. Snow was on the ground most other places. Detroit's streets were clogged with brown slush. Reed Nelson called me at the office on a Saturday and asked me to meet him somewhere for lunch.

"I've got a job interview in Houston next week," he said, when we were sharing a table in my favorite restaurant, one where the chef wore a shirt and didn't swat flies with his spatula. "Only the bank ate my last unemployment check and the savings account is down to double figures. When I applied for a loan, the manager of my friendly dependable finance company snickered and called in his assistant because he said he needed cheering up."

I blew on a spoonful of steaming chili. "What about old Steve? Army buddies are usually good for a few bucks."

"The hell with him."

I glanced up at Nelson's face. He'd lost weight. His cheeks were shadowed and there were purple thumbprints under his eyes. "How's Nha?" I asked.

"She's fine." The words cracked out like shots from a .22.

We ate. I said, "I'll give you two hundred for the Browning."

He hesitated. "It's not worth that. The trigger mechanism's sloppy and the barrel needs bluing."

"I always was a rotten businessman. We'll stop at my bank on the way back to the office. I'll come by later and pick up the automatic."

"Thanks, Amos. You ever need anything, just name it. "

"Pass the salt."

Three

I returned from a tail job early Monday afternoon. Whoever said travel is broadening never followed a possibly larcenous salesman clear to Toledo and sat up all night in a freezing car. I hadn't eaten since Sunday. Nursing the crick in my neck, I turned on the TV in my living room and lurched into the kitchen to find something to defrost. The volume was too high. When the sound came on, the name "Steven Minor" pasted me to the ceiling.

The picture was just blossoming on when I got back in. Floodlights illuminated two paramedics sliding a stretcher into the back of an ambulance. Then the camera cut to a male model in an overcoat standing in front of a house I recognized with a microphone in one hand. Police flashers throbbed sullenly in the street nearby.

"Police aren't saying yet what may have caused Nelson to shoot his neighbor and barricade himself in his house. But evidence suggests that the tragedy of Vietnam has just claimed another victim." The model identified himself and his grim face disappeared, to be replaced by a smiling one back at the Eyewitness News Desk. I left the set running and got out of there.

Four

John Alderdyce was the lieutenant in charge of the investigation. He spoke to a big sergeant from the Tactical Mobile Unit, who reluctantly let me through the cordon. John's black and has been a friend since childhood, or as much of one as a plastic badge can hope to find among the blue brotherhood.

"What's your billing in this?" he demanded when we were inside Nelson's house.

"Friend of the family." I scuffed a sole on a red stain on the carpet. It was still fresh, and it wasn't wine. The room was a shambles of overturned furniture and broken crockery. "When did Minor die?"

"He was DOA at Detroit Receiving." Alderdyce's face fluttered. "Damn it, who told you he's dead?"

"I'm a detective. Rumor has it you're with Homicide." I fed my face a butt. "What did I miss?"

"Right now it looks like this guy Nelson popped his cap, plugged his neighbor with a thirty-two auto, then locked· himself in, holding his wife hostage. Hostage Negotiations people talked him into surrendering. He's wearing handcuffs in the basement. Vietnam vet, certified psycho, unemployed. They ought to print up a form report for this kind of thing with blanks where we can fill in the names, save on overtime."

"Any witnesses?"

"Don't need 'em. Nelson confessed. We're just waiting for the press to clear out so we can take him downtown and get it on tape. He and Minor were talking downstairs when he flipped. You ought to see that gun room. I guess you have." He nailed me. "Since when are you anybody's friend?"

"Even the garbageman rates a cup of coffee now and then. What's Nha say? That's his wife."

"I met her. Pretty. Did I ever tell you I had a crush on Nancy Kwan before I was married? She was hysterical when I got here. Nelson's wife, not Nancy. We called her doctor. He just left. She's in the bedroom, under sedation."

"I wonder how she got along without it when they burned her parents to death." I blew smoke. "Can I see Nelson?"

Alderdyce's eyes glittered in narrow slits. "As what? Friend or representative?"

I said friend. He considered, then nodded as if agreeing with himself and started for the stairs. I dogged his heels. Drops of blood mottled the steps. I halted.

"Where'd Minor get it?" I asked.

"In the right lung." The lieutenant looked back up at me from the bottom step. "He staggered up the stairs, bounced off some furniture on his way through the living room, and collapsed by the front door. Hospital says he drowned in his own blood. Anything wrong with that?"

"Are you asking as a friend or a policeman?"

He made a rude noise and resumed moving. A cop in uniform and a plainclothesman I didn't know were guarding the prisoner, who was sitting in the chair I had occupied on my two visits, manacled wrists dangling between his knees. His shirt was soaked through with sweat. When I entered, he looked up and a tired smile tugged at the corners of his mouth. His features were cadaverous.

"I used your gun," he said. "Sorry."

"What's he mean, your gun?" snapped Alderdyce.

"Private joke," I said. "What happened, Reed?"

"They're saying I killed Steve. I was shooting at Charlie."

"Charlie?" Alderdyce's brow puckered.

"Viet Cong." I ditched my cigarette in an ashtray on the workbench. "Shrinks call it Vietnam Flashback. Years after a vet leaves the jungle, something triggers his subconscious and he suddenly thinks he's back there surrounded by the enemy. He reacts accordingly."

"Oh yeah, that. As if murderers didn't have enough loopholes to squirt through as it was."

The telephone rang upstairs. Alderdyce jerked his head at the uniform, who went up to answer it.

"It's a legitimate dodge," I said. "Only not in this case, right, Reed? Steve Minor was the target all along."

The uniform's feet on the stairs were very loud in the silence that followed. "It's for you, Lieutenant," he said. "The lab."

Alderdyce pointed at me. "Hold that thought." He left us.

Five minutes later he returned. His eyes were very bright. "Blow your diminished capacity plea a kiss quick, Nelson. We're going Mur-, der One."

Five

"The D.A. won't buy it," said the plainclothesman, after a moment.

"Bet me. The lab found powder burns on Minor's shirt, but guess what? There weren't any around the wound. I called the hospital and checked."

"Proving?" I asked.

"Proving he wasn't wearing it when he was shot. Someone held it up and fired a bullet through it, then put it on him while he was dying upstairs to make us think otherwise. We know you were at Metro Airport an hour before the shooting, Nelson, and that the airline lost your reservation on a flight to Houston. Was Minor in bed with your wife when you came home, or did you just have time to take off his shirt?"

The prisoner leaped to his feet, but was shoved back into it by the other two officers. He opened his mouth, then closed it. Slouched.

"Neighbors reported only one shot, Lieutenant," the plainclothesman pointed out. "And there was just one cartridge gone from the gun."

"They didn't hear the first because it was fired in the basement. And don't you think a man smart enough to know we'd question a chest wound without a corresponding hole in the shirt and then make up that psycho story to cover himself is smart enough to replace one of the spent shells? I want a crew here to search every inch of this house until they find where that second bullet went." He nailed me. "You knew Minor was the target. How? Did you know about him and Nelson's wife?"

"No, and I still don't," I said. "You're zero for two. Nelson never shot anyone. Not in this hemisphere, anyway."

Nelson glanced at me, then away. I continued before Alderdyce could ask any more questions.

"Reed was a sharpshooter over there. Still is; he told me he keeps in practice. There's no way, if he thought Minor was a Viet Cong, that he'd miss the heart at this range and give Charlie a chance to retaliate. And if it was Minor he wanted to kill, he would've made sure his victim didn't hang around long enough to talk. It's my guess he was shot before Reed got here."

"No! I killed him!" This time the cops held the prisoner in his chair.

"His car was parked in the driveway when the neighbors heard the gun go off," Alderdyce snarled. The skin on his face was drawn so tight it shone blue, as it often did when I was speaking.

"You said yourself it was the second shot they heard," I reminded him. "That one was his, to keep anyone from wondering why Minor didn't have his shirt on in his neighbor's house, and he did it upstairs because he knew it wasn't safe to pull a trigger in the basement with so much black powder lying around. Just one other person could have fired the fatal bullet. Just one other person was in the house at the time." I breathed some air. "What were Nha and Steve Minor to each other back in Vietnam, Reed?"

"Prostitute and pimp."

Alderdyce and I turned. Nha Nelson, barefoot in a Chinese house dress, her hair down and disheveled, was leaning against the wall at the bottom of the stairwell. Her face was streaked and puffy.

"Don't, Nha," pleaded her husband.

"I should not have let it come this far." She spoke slowly, like a record winding down. The doctor's sedative had furred the fine edge. "Minor made money on the side running prostitutes in Saigon. I was one of six. When his tour ended, he introduced us all to GIs he knew, hoping some of us would marry and he could blackmail the husbands later by threatening to tell all their friends and business associates what their wives used to do for a living.

"Reed was an engineer for a large corporation, the perfect victim. But he lost his job before Minor could begin squeezing him. Then he blackmailed me, but not for money. He was a depraved man. He said if I did not have sex with him he would tell Reed I lied about my past. I agreed."

Her eyes filled and ran over. Nelson said her name. She acted as if she hadn't heard. "I love my husband. I was afraid he would leave me if he knew the truth. Minor waited until Reed left for the airport and then he came over to collect. But I could not do it. I had done it many times, with many men, but that was in Vietnam, before I had Reed. I excused myself while Minor was undressing and came down here for a gun. I wanted only to scare him, to make him leave. He suspected something and followed me. When I heard him on the stairs I panicked. I turned and—" Bitter tears strangled her.

I gave her my handkerchief. She wiped her eyes and nose. Nelson was weeping too, his face buried in his hands, the chain dangling between the wrists. Quiet rolled in and sat down. Alderdyce booted it out. "Do you have the names of the other five women?"

"Three of them," she said. "The other two didn't marry the men Minor wanted them to. I even know the husbands' names and what cities they lived in. He bragged to me about how he had traveled around the country all this time, setting up shop wherever a victim was. That's what he called it, 'setting up shop.'"

The uniform took her elbow gently and steered her around as if she were a sleepy child. Nelson stood.

"Thanks for nothing, Walker."

I said, "I'll be surprised if the D.A. presses charges. If he does he'll lose."

"So what? I'm going to end up in the nut ward sooner or later. My way it counted for something. Why'd you have to take that away from me? We were friends for a while."

I had nothing to throw at that. The plainclothesman prodded him forward and up the steps.

Alderdyce hung back. He had spotted the empty wine bottle, standing in a back corner of the workbench behind a can of gun stock refinisher. "That looks out of place here. Maybe I should have it dusted."

"Forget it." I picked it up and chucked it into the wastebasket. "Dead soldier."

Eight Mile and Dequindre

The client was a no-show, as four out of ten of them tend to be. She had called me in the customary white heat, a woman with one of those voices you hear in supermarkets and then thank God you're not married, and arranged to meet me someplace not my office and not her home. The bastard had been paying her the same alimony for the past five years, she'd said, and she wanted a handle on his secret bank accounts to prove he was making twice as much as when they split. In the meantime she'd cooled down or the situation had changed or she'd found a private investigator who worked even cheaper than I did, leaving me to drink yellow coffee alone at a linoleum counter in a gray cinderblock building on Dequindre at Eight Mile Road. I was just as happy. Why I'd agreed to meet her at all had to do with a bank balance smaller than my IQ, and since talking to her I'd changed my mind and decided to refer her to another agency anyway. So I worked on my coffee and once again considered taking on a security job until things got better.

A portable radio behind the counter was tuned to a Pistons game, but the guy who'd poured my coffee, lean and young with butch-cut red hair and a white apron, didn't look to be listening to it, whistling while he chalked new prices on the blackboard menu on the wall next to the cash register. Well, it was March and the Pistons were where they usually were in the standings at that time and nobody in Detroit was listening. I asked him what the chicken on a roll was like.

"Better than across the street," he said, wiping chalk off his hands onto the apron.

Across the street was a Shell station. I ordered the chicken anyway; unless he skipped some lines it was too far down on the board for him to raise the price before I'd eaten it. He opened a stainless steel door over the sink and took the plastic off a breaded patty the color of fresh sawdust and slapped it hissing on the griddle.

We'd had the place to ourselves for a while, but then the pneumatic front door whooshed and sucked in a male customer in his thirties and a sportcoat you could hear across the street, who cocked a hip onto a stool at the far end of the counter and asked for a glass of water.

"Anything to go with that?" asked Butch, setting an amber tinted tumbler in front of him.

"No, I'm waiting for someone."

"Coffee, maybe."

"No, I want to keep my breath fresh."

"Oh. That kind of someone." He wiped his hands again. "It's okay for now, but if the place starts to fill up you'll have to order something, a Coke or something. You don't have to drink it."

"Sounds fair."

"This ain't a bus station."

"I can see that."

Nodding, Butch turned away and picked up a spatula and flipped the chicken patty and broke a roll out of plastic. The guy in the sportcoat asked how the game was going, but Butch either didn't hear him or didn't want to. The guy gave up on him and glanced down the counter at me.

"You waiting for someone too?"

"I was," I said. "Now I'm waiting for that bird."

"Stood you up, huh? That's tough."

"I'm used to it."

He hesitated, then got down and picked up his glass and carried it to my end and climbed onto the stool next to mine. Up close he was about 30, freckled, with a double chin starting and dishwasher hair going thin in front. A triangle of white shirt showed between his belt buckle and the one button he had fastened on the jacket. He had prominent front teeth and looked a little like Howdy Doody. "This girl I'm waiting for would never stand anyone up," he said. "She's got manners."

"Yeah?"

"No, really. Looks too. Here's her picture." He took a fat curved wallet out of his hip pocket and showed me the head and torso of a blond in a red bandana top, winking and grinning at the camera. She stank professional model.

"Nice," I said. "What's she do?"

"Waitress at the Peacock's Roost. That'll change when we're married. I don't want my wife to work."

"The girls in steel-rimmed glasses and iron pants will burn their bras on your lawn."

"To hell with them. Rena won't have anything to do with that kind. That's her name, Rena."

"I think it's dead now," I told Butch.

He landed the chicken patty on one half of the roll and planted the other half on top and put it on a china saucer and set the works on the linoleum. Howdy Doody finished putting away his wallet and stuck his right hand across his body in front of me. "Dave Tillet."

"Amos Walker." I shook the hand and picked up the sandwich. As it turned out I couldn't have done any worse across the street at the Shell station.

Tillet sipped his water. "That clock right?"

Butch looked up to see which clock he meant. There was only one in the place, advertising Stroh's beer on the wall behind the counter. "Give or take a minute."

"She ought to be here now. She's usually early."

"Maybe she stood you up after all," I said.

"Not Rena."

I ate the chicken and Tillet drank his water and the guy behind the counter picked up his chalk and resumed changing prices and didn't listen to the basketball game. I wiped my mouth with a cheesy paper napkin and asked Butch what the tariff was. He said "Buck ninety-five." I got out my wallet.

"Maybe I better call her," said Tillet. "That phone working?"

Butch said it was. Tillet drained his glass and went to the pay telephone on the wall just inside the door. I paid for the sandwich and coffee. "Well, good luck," I told Tillet on my way past him.

"What? Yeah, thanks. You too." He was listening to the purring in the earpiece. I pushed on the glass door.

Two guys were on their way in and I stepped aside and held the door for them. They were wearing dark windbreakers and colorful knit caps and when they saw me they reached up with one hand apiece and rolled the caps down over their faces and the caps turned into ski masks. Their other hands were coming out of the slash pockets of the windbreakers and when I saw that I jumped back and let go of the door, but the man closest to it caught it with his arm and stuck a long-barreled .22 target pistol in my face while his partner came in past him and lamped the place quickly and then put the

.22's twin almost against Tillet's noisy sportcoat. Three flat reports slapped the air. Tillet's mouth was open and he was leaning one shoulder against the wall and he hadn't had time to start falling or even know he was shot when the guy fired again into his face and then deliberately moved the gun and gave him another in the ear. The guy's buddy wasn't watching. He was looking at me through the eyeholes in his mask and his eyes were as flat and gray as nickels on a pad. They held no more expression than the empty blue hole also staring me in the face.

Then the pair left, Gray Eyes backing away with his gun still on me while his partner walked swiftly to a brown Plymouth Volare and around to the driver's side and got in and then Gray Eyes let himself in the passenger's side and they were rolling before he got the door closed.

Tillet fell then, crumpling in on himself like a gas bag deflating, and folded to the floor with no more noise than laundry makes skidding down a chute. Very bright red blood leaked out of his ear and slid into a puddle on the gray linoleum floor.

I ran out to the sidewalk in time to see the Plymouth take the corner. Forget about the license number. I wasn't wearing a gun. I hardly ever needed one to meet a woman in a diner.

When I went back in, the counterman was standing over Tillet's body, wiping his hands over and over on his apron. His face was as pale as the cloth. The telephone receiver swung from its cord and the metallic purring on the other end was loud in the silence following the shots. I bent and placed two fingers on Tillet's neck. Nothing was happening in the big artery. I straightened, picked up the receiver, worked the plunger, and dialed 911. Standing there waiting for someone to answer I was sorry I'd eaten the chicken.

Two

They sent an Adam and Eve team, a white man and a black woman in uniform. You had to look twice at the woman to know she was a woman. They hadn't gotten around to cutting uniforms to fit them, and her tunic hung on her like a tarpaulin. Her partner had baby fat in his cheeks and a puppy moustache. His face went stiff when he saw the body. The woman might have been looking at a loose tile on the floor for all her expression gave up. Just to kill time I gave them the story, knowing I'd have to do it all over again for the plainclothes team. Butch was sitting on one of the customers' stools with his hands in his lap and whenever they looked at him he nodded in agreement with my details. The woman took it all down in shorthand.

The first string arrived ten minutes later. Among them was a black lieutenant, coarse-featured and heavy in the chest and shoulders, wearing a gray suit cut in heaven and a black tie with a silver diamond pattern. When he saw me he groaned.

"Hello, John," I said. "This is a hike north from Headquarters."

John Alderdyce of Detroit Homicide patted all his pockets and came up with an empty Lucky Strikes package. I gave him a Winston from my pack and took one for myself and lit them both. He squirted smoke and said, "I was eight blocks from here when I got the squeal. If I'd known you were back of it I'd have kept driving."

John and I had known each other a long time, a thing I admitted to a lot more often than he did. While I was recounting the last few minutes in the life of Dave Tillet, a police photographer came in and took pictures of the body from forty different angles and then a bearded black Homicide sergeant I didn't know tugged on a pair of surgical gloves and knelt and started going through Tillet's clothes. Butch had recovered from his shock by this time and came over to watch. "Them gloves are to protect the fingerprints, right?" he asked.

"Wrong. Catch." The sergeant tossed him Tillet's wallet.

Butch caught it against his chest. "It's wet."

"That's why the gloves. "

Butch thought about it, then dropped the wallet quickly and mopped his hands on his apron.

"Can the crap," barked Alderdyce. "What's inside?"

Still chuckling, the sergeant picked up the wallet and went through the contents. He whistled. "Christ, it's full of C-notes. Eight, ten, twelve—this guy was carrying fifteen hundred bucks on his hip."

"What else?"

The celluloid windows gave up a Social Security card and a temporary driver's license, both made out to David Edward Tillet, and the picture of the blonde.

"That Rena?" Alderdyce asked.

I nodded. "She waits tables at the Peacock's Roost, Tillet said."

Alderdyce told the sergeant to bag the wallet and its contents. To me: "You saw these guys before they pulled down their ski masks?"

"Not enough before. They were just guys' faces. I didn't much look at them till they went for the guns. The trigger was my height, maybe ten pounds to the good. His partner gave up a couple of inches, same build, gray eyes." I described the getaway car.

"Stolen," guessed the sergeant. He stood and slid a glassine bag containing the wallet into the side pocket of his coat.

Alderdyce nodded. "It was a market job. The girl was the finger. She's smoke by now. Dope?"

"That or numbers," said the sergeant. "He's a little pale for either one in this town, but the rackets are nothing if not an equal opportunity employer. Nobody straight carries cash any more."

"I still owe a thousand on this building." Butch's upper lip was folded over his chin. "I guess I'd be dumb to pay it off now."

"The place is made," the sergeant told him.

"Yeah?" The counterman looked hopefully at Alderdyce, who grunted.

"The Machus Red Fox is booked into next year and has been ever since Hoffa caught his last ride from in front of it."

"Yeah?"

The lieutenant was still looking at me. "When can you come down and sign a statement?"

"Whenever it's ready. I'm not exactly swamped."

"Five o'clock, then." He paused. "Your part in this is finished, right?"

"When I work, I get paid," I said.

"How come that doesn't comfort me?

I said I'd see him at five.

The morgue wagon was just creaking its brakes in front when I came out into the afternoon sunlight and walked around the blue-and-white and a couple of unmarked units and a green Fiat to my heap. I was about to get in behind the wheel when I stopped and looked again at the Fiat. The girl Dave Tillet had called Rena was sitting in the driver's seat, staring at the blank cinderblock wall in front of the windshield.

Three

I opened the door on the passenger side and got in next to her. She jumped in the seat and looked at me quickly. Her honey-colored hair was caught in a clasp behind her neck, below which a kind of pony-tail hung down her back, and she was wearing a tailored navy suit over a cream-colored blouse open at the neck and jet buttons in her ears, but I recognized her large smoky eyes and the just slightly too-wide mouth that was built for grinning, although she wasn't grinning. The interior of the little car smelled of car and sandalwood.

She snatched up a blue bag from the seat and her hand vanished inside. I caught her wrist. She struggled, but I applied pressure and her face went white and she stopped struggling. I relaxed the hold, but just a little.

"Dave's dead," I said. "You can't help him now."

She said nothing. On "dead," her head jerked as if I'd smacked her. I went on.

"You don't want to be here when the cops come out. They've got your picture and they think you fingered Dave."

"That's stupid." Her voice came from just in back of her tongue. I didn't know how it was normally.

"It's not stupid. He was expecting you and got five slugs from a twenty-two. The cops know where you work and pretty soon they'll know where you live and when they find you they'll book you as a material witness and change it to accessory to the fact later."

"You talk like you're not one of them."

"Get real, lady. If I were we wouldn't be sitting here talking. On the other hand, if you set up Dave deliberately you wouldn't be here at all. It could just be you're someone who could use some help."

Her lips twisted. "And it could just be you're someone who could give it."

"We're talking," I reminded her. "I'm not hollering cop."

"Who the hell are you?"

I told her. Her lips twisted some more.

"A cheap snooper. I should have guessed it would be something like that."

I said, "It's a buyer's market. I don't set the price."

"What's the price?"

"Some truth. Not right now, though. Not here. Let's go somewhere."

"You go," she said. "I've got a pistol in this purse and when I pull the trigger it won't much matter whether it's inside or outside."

I didn't move. "Guns, everybody's got 'em. After a killer's screwed one in your face the rest aren't so scary."

We sat like that for a while, she with her hand in the purse and turned a little in the seat so that one silken knee showed under the hem of her pleated skirt while a cramp crawled across the palm I had clenched on her wrist. The morgue crew came out the front door of the diner wheeling a stretcher with a zipped bag full of Dave Tillet on it and folded the works into the back of the wagon. Rena didn't look at them. Finally I let go of her and got out one of my cards and a pen. I moved slowly to avoid attracting bullets.

"I'll just put my home address and telephone number on the back," I said, writing. "Open twenty-four hours. Just ring and ask for Amos. But do it before the cops get you or I'm just another spent shell."

She said nothing. I tucked the card under the mirror she had clamped to the sun visor on the passenger side and got out and into my crate and started the motor and swung out into the street and took off with my cape flying behind me.

Four

I made some calls from the office, but none of the security firms or larger investigation agencies in town had anything to farm out. I bought myself a drink from the file drawer in the desk and when that was finished I bought myself another, and by then it was time to go to Police Headquarters at 1300 Beaubien, or just plain 1300 as it's known in town. The lady detective who announced me to John Alderdyce was too much detective not to notice the scotch on my breath but too much lady to mention it. Little by little they are changing things down there, but it's a slow process.

In John's office I gave my story again to a stenographer while Alderdyce and the bearded sergeant listened for variations. When the steno left to type up my statement I asked John what he'd found out.

"Tillet kept the books for Great Lakes Importers. Ever hear of it?"

"Front for the Mob."

"So you say. It's worth a slander suit if you say it in public, they're that well screened with lawyers and holding corporations." He broke open a fresh pack of Luckies and fired one up with a Zippo. I already had a Winston going. "Tillet rented a house in Southfield. A grand a month."

"Any grand jury investigations in progress?" I asked.

"They're hard on the bookkeeping population."

He shook his head. "We got a call in to the feds, but even if they get back to us we'll still have to go up to the mountain to get any information out of those tight-mouthed clones. We're pinning our hopes on the street trade and this woman Rena. Especially her."

"What'd you turn on her?"

"She works at the Peacock's Roost like you said, goes by Rena Murrow. She didn't show up for the four P.M. shift today. She's got an apartment on Michigan and we have men waiting for her there, but she's empty tracks by now. Tillet's landlady says he's been away someplace on vacation. Lying low. Whoever wanted him out in the open got to Rena. By all accounts she is a woman plenty of scared accountants would break cover to meet.

"Maybe someone used her?"

He grinned that tight grin that was always bad news for someone. "Your license to hunt Dulcineas still valid?"

"Everyone needs a hobby," I said. "Stamps are sissy."

"Safer, though. According to the computer, this damsel has two priors for soliciting, but that was before she started bumming around with one Peter Venito. 'Known former associate,' it says in the print-out. Computers have no romance in their circuits."

I smoked and thought. Peter Venito, born Pietro, had come up through the Licavoli mob during Prohibition and during the old Kefauver Committee hearings had been identified as one of the five dons on the board of governors of that fraternal organization the Italian Anti-Defamation League would have us believe no longer exists.

"Venito's been dead four or five years," I said.

"Six. But his son Paul's still around and a slice off the old pizza. His secretary at Great Lakes Importers says he's in Las Vegas. Importing."

"Anything on the street soldiers?"

"Computer got a hernia sorting through gray eyes and the heights and builds you gave us. I'd go to the mugs but you say you didn't get a long enough hinge at them without their masks, so why go into golden time? Just sign the statement and give my eyes a rest from your ugly pan."

The stenographer had just returned with three neatly typewritten sheets. I read my words and wrote my name at the bottom. "I have it on good authority I'm a heartbreaker," I told Alderdyce, handing him the sheets.

"What's a Dulcinea, anyway?" asked the sergeant.

Five

The shooting at Eight Mile and Dequindre was on the radio. They got my name and occupation right, anyway. I switched to a music station and drove through coagulating dusk to my little three-room house west of Hamtramck, where I put my key in a door that was already unlocked. I'd locked it when I left that morning.

I went back for the Luger I keep in a special compartment under the dash, and when I had a round in the chamber I sneaked up on the door with my back to the wall and twisted the knob and pushed the door open at arm's length. When no bullets tore through the opening I eased the gun and my face past the door frame. Rena was sitting in my one easy chair in the living room with a .32 Remington automatic in her right hand and a bottle of scotch and a half-full glass standing on the end table on the other side.

"I thought it might be you," she said. "That's why I didn't shoot."

"Thanks for the vote of confidence. "

"You ought to get yourself a dead-bolt lock. I've known how to slip latches since high school."

"All they taught me was algebra." I waved the Luger.

"Can we put up the artillery? It's starting to get silly."

She laid the pistol in her lap. I snicked the safety into place on mine and put it on the table near the door and closed the door behind me. She picked up her glass and sipped from it.

"You buy good whisky. Keyhole-peeping must pay pretty good."

"That's my Christmas bottle."

"Your friends must like you."

"I bought it for myself." I went into the kitchen and got a glass and filled it from the bottle.

She said, "The cops were waiting for me at my place. One of them was smoking a pipe. I smelled it the minute I hit my floor."

"The world's full of morons. Cops come in for their share." I drank.

"What's it going to cost me to get clear of this?"

"How much you got?"

She glanced down at the blue bag wedged between her left hip and the arm of the chair. It was a nice hip, long and slim with the pleated navy skirt stretched taut over it. "Five hundred."

I shrugged.

"All of it?"

"It'd run you that and more to put breathing space between you and Detroit," I said. "It wouldn't buy you a day in any of the safe houses in town."

"What will I eat on?"

"On the rest of it. You knew damn well I'd set my price at whatever you said you had, so I figure you knocked it down by at least half."

She twisted her lips in that way she had and opened the bag and peeled three C-notes and four fifties off a roll that would choke a tuba. I accepted the bills and riffled through them and stuck the wad in my inside breast pocket.

"How's Paul?" I asked.

"He's in Vegas," she answered automatically. Then she looked up at me quickly and pursed her lips. I cut her off.

"The cops know about you and old Peter Venito, may he rest in peace. The word on the street is young Paul inherited everything."

"Not everything. "

I was lighting a cigarette and so didn't bother to shrug. I flipped the match into an ashtray. "Dave Tillet."

"I liked Dave. He wasn't like the others that worked for Paul. He wanted to get out. He was all set to take the CPA exam in May."

"He didn't just like you," I said. "He was planning to marry you."

She raised her eyebrows. They were darker than her hair, two inverted commas over eyes that I saw now were ringed with red under her make-up. "I didn't know," she said quietly.

"Who dropped the dime on him?"

Now her face took on the hard sheen of polished metal. "All right, so you tricked me into admitting I knew Paul Venito. That doesn't mean I know the heavyweights he hires."

"You've answered my question. When a bookkeeper for the Mob starts making leaving noises, his employers start wondering where he's going with what he knows. What'd Venito do to get you to set up Dave?"

"I didn't set him up!"

I smoked and waited. In the silence she looked at the wall behind me and then at the floor and then at her hands on the purse in her lap and then she drained her glass and refilled it. The neck of the bottle jingled against the rim. She drank.

"Dave went into hiding a week ago because of some threats he said he got over his decision to quit," she said. "None of them came from Paul, but from his own fellow workers. He gave me a number where he could be reached and told me to memorize it and not write it down or give it to anyone else. I'd gone with Paul for a while after old Peter died and Paul knew I was seeing Dave and he came to my apartment yesterday and asked me where he could reach Dave. I wouldn't give him the number. He said he just wanted to talk to him and would I arrange a meeting without saying it would be with Paul. He was afraid Dave's fellow workers had poisoned him against the whole operation. He wanted to make Dave a cash offer to keep quiet

about his, Paul's, activities and that if I cared for him and his future
I'd agree to help. I said okay. It sounded like the Paul Venito I used
to know," she added quickly. "He would spend thousands to avoid
hurting someone; he said that was bad business and cost more in the
long run."

"Who picked the spot?"

"Paul did. He called it neutral territory, halfway between Dave's
place in Southfield and Paul's office downtown."

"It's also handy to expressways out of the city," I said. "So you set
up the parley. Then what?"

"I called Paul's office today to ask him if I could sit in on the
meeting. His secretary told me he left for Las Vegas last night. That's
when I knew he had no intention of keeping his appointment, or of
being anywhere near the place when whoever was keeping it for him
went in to see Dave. I broke every law driving here, but—"

The metal sheen cracked apart then. She said "Damn" and dug
in her purse for a handkerchief. I watched her pawing blindly
through the contents for a moment, then handed her mine. If it was
an act it was sweet.

"Did anyone follow you here?" I asked.

She wiped her eyes, blew her nose as discreetly as a thing like that
can be done, and looked up. Her cheeks were smeared blue-black.
That was when I decided to believe her. You don't look like her and
know how to turn the waterworks on and off without knowing how
to keep your mascara from running too.

"I don't think so," she said. "I kept an eye out for cops and parked
around the corner. Why?"

"Because if what you told me is straight, you're next on Venito's
list of Things To Do Today. You're the only one who can connect
him to that diner. Have you got a place to stay?"

"I guess one of the girls from the Roost could put me up. . ."

"No, the cops will check them out. They'll hit all the hotels and motels too. You'd better stay here."

"Oh." She gave me her crooked smile. "That plus the five hundred, is that how it goes?"

"I'll toss you for the bed. Loser gets the couch."

"You don't like blondes?"

"I'm not sure I ever met one. But it has something to do with not going to the bathroom where you eat. Give me your keys and I'll stash your car in the garage. Cops'll have a BOL out on it by now."

She was reaching inside her purse when the door buzzer blew us a raspberry. Her hand went to the baby Remington. I touched a finger to my lips and pointed at the bedroom door. She got up clutching her purse and the gun and went into the bedroom and pushed the door shut, or almost. She left a crack. I retrieved my handkerchief stained with her make-up from the chair and put it in a pocket and picked up the Luger and said, "Who is it?"

"Alderdyce."

I opened the door. He glanced down at the gun as if it were a loose button on my jacket and walked around me into the living room. "Expecting trouble?"

"It's a way of life in this town." I safetied the Luger and returned it to the table.

"You alone?" He looked around.

"Who's asking, you or the department?"

He said nothing, circling the living room with his hands in his pockets. He stopped near the bedroom door and sniffed the air. "Nice cologne. A little feminine."

"Even detectives have a social life," I said.

"You couldn't prove it by me."

I killed my cigarette butt and fought the tug to reach for a replacement. "You didn't come all this way to do Who's On First with me."

"We tracked down Paul Venito. I thought you'd want to know."

"In Vegas?"

He moved his large close-cropped head from side to side slowly. "At Detroit Metropolitan Airport. Stiff as a stick in the trunk of a stolen Oldsmobile."

Six

The antique clock my grandfather bought for his mother knocked out the better part of a minute with no competition. I shook out my last Winston and smoothed it between my fingers. "Shot?"

"Three times with a twenty-two. Twice in the chest, once in the ear. Sound familiar?"

"Yeah." I speared my lips with the cigarette and lit up. "How long's he been dead?"

"That's up to the M.E. Twelve hours anyway. He was a cold cut long before Tillet bought it."

"Which means what?"

He shook his head again. His coarse face was drawn in the light of the one lamp I bad burning.

"My day rate's two-fifty," I said. "If you're talking about consulting."

"I'm talking about withholding evidence and obstruction of justice. The Murrow woman is getting to be important, and I think you know where she is."

I smoked and said nothing.

"It's this tingly feeling I get," he said. "Happens every time a case involves a woman and Amos Walker too."

"Christ, John, all I did was order the chicken on a roll."

"I hope that's all you did. I sure hope."

We watched each other. Suddenly he seized the knob and pushed open the bedroom door, scooping his Police Special out of his belt holster. I lunged forward, then held back. The room was empty.

He went inside and looked out the open window and checked the closet and got down in push-up position to peer under the bed. Rising, he holstered the .38 and dusted his palms off against each other. "Perfume's stronger in here," he observed.

"I told you I was a heartbreaker. "

"Make sure that's all you're breaking."

"Is this where you threaten to trash my license?"

"That's up to the state police," he said. "What I can do is tank you and link your name to that diner shoot for the reporters until little old ladies in Grosse Pointe won't trust you to walk their poodles."

On that chord he left me. John and I had been friendly a long time. But no matter how long you are something, you are not that something a lot longer.

Seven

So far I had two corpses and no Rena Murrow. It was time to punt. I dialed Great Lakes Importers, Paul Venito's legitimate front, but there was no answer. Well, it was way past closing time; in an orderly society even the crooks keep regular hours. I thawed something out for supper and watched an old Kirk Douglas film on television and turned in.

The next morning was misty gray with the bitter-metal smell of rain in the air. I broke out the foul-weather gear and drove to the Great Lakes building on East Grand River.

The reception area, kept behind glass like expensive cigars in a tobacco shop, was oval-shaped with passages spiking out from it, decorated in orange sherbet with a porcelain doll seated behind a curved desk. She wore a tight pink cashmere sweater and a black skirt slit to her ears.

"Amos Walker to see Mr. Venito," I said.

"I'm sorry. Mr. Venito's suffered a tragic accident." Her voice was honey over velvet. It would be.

"Who took his place?"

"That would be Mr. DeMarco. But he's very busy."

"I'll wait." I pulled a Thermos bottle full of hot coffee out of the slash pocket of my trenchcoat and sat down on an orange couch across from her desk.

The porcelain doll lifted her telephone receiver and spoke into it. A few minutes later, two men in tailored blue suits came out of one of the passages and stood over me, and that was when the front crumbled.

"Position."

I wasn't sure which of them had spoken. They looked alike down to the scar tissue over their eyes. I screwed the top back on the Thermos and stood and placed my palms against the wall. One of them ricked my feet apart and patted me down from tie to socks, removing my hat last and peering inside for atomic devices. I wasn't carrying. He replaced the hat.

"Okay, this way."

I accompanied them down the passage with a man on either side. We went through a door marked P. VENITO into an office the size of Hart Plaza with green wall-to-wall carpeting and one wall that was all glass, before which stood a tall man with a fringe of gray hair and a neat Van Dyke beard. His suit was tan and clung like sunlight to his trim frame.

"Mr. Walker?" he said pleasantly. "I'm Fred DeMarco. I was Mr. Venito's associate. This is a terrible thing that's happened."

"More terrible for him than you," I said.

He cocked his head and frowned. "This office, you mean. It's just a room. Paul's father had it before him and someone will have it after me. I recognized your name from the news. Weren't you involved in the shooting of this Tillet person yesterday?"

I nodded. "If you call being a witness involved. But you don't have to call him 'this Tillet person.' He worked for you."

"He worked for Great Lakes Importers, like me: I never knew him. The firm employs many people, most of whom I haven't had the chance to meet."

"My information is he was killed because he was leaving Great Lakes and someone was afraid he'd peddle what he knew."

"We're a legitimate enterprise, Mr. Walker. We have nothing to hide. Tillet was let go. Our accounting department is handled mostly by computers now and he elected not to undergo retraining. Whatever he was involved with outside the firm that led to his death bas nothing to do with Great Lakes."

"For someone who never met him you know a lot about Tillet," I said.

"I had his file pulled for the police."

"Isn't it kind of a big coincidence that your president and one of your bookkeepers should both be shot to death within a few hours of each other, and with the same caliber pistol?"

"The police were here again last night to ask that same question,"

DeMarco said. "My answer is the same. If, like Tillet, Paul had dangerous outside interests, they are hardly of concern here."

I got out a Winston and tapped it on the back of my hand. "You've been on the laundering end too long, Mr. DeMarco. You think you've gotten away from playing hardball. Just because you can afford a tailor and a better barber doesn't mean you aren't still Freddy the Mark, who came up busting heads for Peter Venita in the bad old days."

One of the blue suits backhanded the cigarette out of my mouth as I was getting set to light it. "Mr. DeMarco doesn't allow smoking."

"That's enough, Andy." DeMarco's tone was even. "I was just a boy when Prohibition ended, Walker. Peter took me in and almost adopted me. I learned the business and when I got back from the war and college I showed him how to modernize, cut expenses, and increase profits. For thirty years I practically ran the organization. Then Peter died and his son took over and I was back to running errands. But for the good of the firm I drew my pay and kept my mouth shut. We're legitimate now and I mean for it to stay that way. I wouldn't jeopardize it for the likes of Dave Tillet."

"I think you would do just that. You remember a time when no one quit the organization, and when Tillet gave notice and you found out young Paul had arranged to buy his silence instead of making dead sure of it, you took Paul out of the way and then slammed the door on Tillet."

"You're fishing, Walker."

"Why not? I've got Rena Murrow for bait."

The room got quiet. Outside the glass, fourteen floors down, traffic glided along Grand River with all the noise of fish swimming in an aquarium.

"She set up the meet with Tillet for Venito," I went on. "She can tie Paul to that diner at Eight Mile and Dequindre and with a little work the cops will tie you to that trunk at Metro Airport. She can finger your two button men. Looking down the wrong end of life in Jackson, they'll talk."

"Get him out of here," DeMarco snarled.

The blue suits came toward me. I got out of there. I could use the smoke anyway.

Eight

I was closing my front door behind me when Rena came out of the bedroom. She had fixed her make-up since the last time I had seen her, but she had on the same navy suit and it was starting to look like a navy suit she had had on for two days.

I said, "You remembered to relock the door this time."

She nodded. "I stayed in a motel last night. The cops haven't got to them all yet. But I couldn't hang around. They get suspicious when you don't have luggage."

"You can't stay here. I just painted a bull's-eye on my back for Fred DeMarco." I told her what I'd told him.

"I can't identify the men who killed Dave," she protested.

"Freddy the Mark doesn't know that." I lifted the telephone. "I'm getting you a cab ride to Police Headquarters and then I'm calling the cops. Things are going to get interesting as soon as DeMarco gets over his mad."

The doorbell buzzed. This time I didn't have to tell her. She went into the bedroom and I got my Luger off the table and opened the door on a man who was a little shorter than I, with gray eyes like nickels on a pad. He had traded his Windbreaker for a brown leather jacket but it looked like the same .22 target pistol in his right hand.

Without the ski mask he looked about my age, with streaks of pre-mature gray in his neat brown hair.

I waved the Luger and said, "Mine's bigger."

"Old movie line," he said with a sigh. "Take a gander behind you."

That was an old movie line too. I didn't turn. Then someone gasped and I stepped back and moved my head just enough to get the corner of my eye working. A man a little taller than Gray Eyes, with black hair to his collar and a handlebar moustache, stood behind Rena this side of the bedroom door with a squat .38 planted against her neck. His other hand was out of sight and the way Rena was standing said he had her left arm twisted behind her back. He too had ditched his Windbreaker and was in shirtsleeves. The lighter cal-iber gun he had used on Tillet and probably on Paul Venito would be scrap by now.

It seemed I was the only one who needed a key to get into my house.

"Two beats one, Zorro." Gray Eyes' tone remained tired and I figured out that was his normal voice. He stepped over the thresh-old and leaned the door shut. "Let's have the Heine." He held out his free hand.

"Uh-uh," I said. "I give it to you and then you shoot us."

"You don't, we shoot the girl first. Then you."

"You'll do that anyway. This way maybe I shoot you too."

Moustache shifted his weight. Rena shrieked. My eyes flickered that way. Gray Eyes swept the barrel of the .22 across my face and grasped the end of the Luger. I fired. The report gulped up all the sound in the room. Moustache let go of Rena and swung the .38 my way. She knocked up his arm and red flame streaked ceilingward. Rena dived for her blue bag on the easy chair. Moustache aimed at her back. I swung the Luger, but Gray Eyes was still standing and fired the .22. Something plucked at my left bicep. The front window exploded then, and Moustache was lifted off his feet and flung backwards against the wall, his gun flying. The nasty cracking report followed an instant later.

I looked at Gray Eyes, but he was down now, his gun still in his hand but forgotten, both hands clasped over his abdomen with the blood dark between his fingers. I relieved him of the weapon and put it with the Luger on tile table. Rena was half-reclining in the easy chair with her skirt hiked up over one long leg and her .32 Remington in both hands pointing at Moustache dead on the floor. She hadn't fired.

"Walker?"

The voice was tinny and artificially loud. But I recognized it.

"We're all right, John," I called. "Put down that bullhorn and come in." I told Rena to drop the automatic. She obeyed, in a daze.

Alderdyce came in with his gun drawn and looked at the man still alive at his feet and across at the other man who wasn't and at Rena. I introduced them. "She didn't set up Tillet," I added. "Fred DeMarco bought the hit, not Venito. This one will get around to telling you that if you stop gawking and call an ambulance before he's done bleeding into his belly."

"For you too, maybe." Alderdyce picked up the telephone.

He'd seen me grasping my left arm. "Just a crease," I said. "Like in the cowboy pictures."

"You're lucky. I know you, Walker. It's your style to set yourself up as the goat to smoke out a guy like DeMarco. I had men watching the place and had you tailed to and from Great Lakes. When the girl broke in we loaded the neighborhood. Then these two showed—" He broke off and started speaking into the mouthpiece.

I said, "My timing was off. I'm glad yours was better."

The bearded black sergeant came in with some uniformed officers, one of whom carried a 30.06 rifle with a mounted scope. "Nice shooting," Alderdyce told him, hanging up.

"What's your name?"

"Officer Carl Breen, Lieutenant." He spelled it.

"Okay. "

I let go of my arm and wiped the blood off my hand with my handkerchief and got out my wallet, counting out two hundred and fifty dollars, which I held out to Rena. "My day rate's two-fifty."

She was sitting up now, looking at the money. "Why'd you ask for five hundred?"

"You had your mind made up about me. It saved a speech."

"Keep it. You earned it and a lot more than I can pay."

I folded the bills and stuck them inside the outer breast pocket of her navy jacket. "I'd just blow it on cigarettes and whisky."

"Who's the broad?" demanded the sergeant.

I thought of telling him that's what a Dulcinea was, but the joke was old. We waited for the ambulance.

The surviving gunman's name was Richard Bledsoe. He had two priors in the Detroit area for ADW, one conviction, and after he was released from the hospital into custody he turned state's evidence and convicted Fred Demarco on two counts of conspiracy to commit murder. DeMarco's appeal is still pending. The dead man went by Austin Grant and had done seven years in San Quentin for second degree homicide knocked down from Murder One. The Detroit Police worked a deal with the Justice Department and got Rena Murrow relocation and a new identity to shield her from DeMarco's friends. I never saw her again.

I never ate in Butch's diner again, either. These days you can't get in the place without a reservation.

I'm In the Book

When I finally got in to see Alec Wynn of Reiner, Switz, Galsworthy, & Wynn, the sun was high over Lake St. Clair outside the window behind his desk and striking sparks off the choppy steel-blue surface with sailboats gliding around on it cutting white foam, their sharkfin sails striped in broad bright bikini colors. Wynn sat with his back to the view and never turned to look at it. He didn't need to. On the wall across from him hung a big framed color photograph of bright-striped sailboats cutting white foam on the steel-blue surface of Lake St. Clair.

Wynn was a big neat man with a black widow's peak trimmed tight to his skull and the soft gray hair at his temples worn long over the tops of his ears. He had on aviator's glasses with clear plastic rims and a suit the color and approximate weight of ground fog, that fit him like no suit will ever fit me if I hit the Michigan Lottery tomorrow. He had deep lines in his Miami-brown face and a mouth that turned down like a shark's to show a bottom row of caps as white and even as military monuments. It was a predator's face. I liked it fine. It belonged to a lawyer, and in my business lawyers mean a warm feeling in the pit of the bank account.

"Walker, Amos," he said, as if he were reading roll call. "I like the name. It has a certain smoky strength."

"I've had it a long time."

He looked at me with his strong white hands folded on top of his absolutely clean desk. His palms didn't leave marks on the glossy surface the way mine would have. "I keep seeing your name on reports. The Reliance people employ your services often."

"Only when the job involves people," I said. "Those big investigation agencies are good with computers and diamonds and those teeny little cameras you can hide in your left ear. But when it comes to stroking old ladies who see things and leaning on supermarket stock boys who smuggle sides of beef out the back door, they remember us little shows."

"How big is your agency?"

"You're looking at it. I have an answering service," I added quickly.

"Better and better. It means you can keep a secret. You have a reputation for that, too."

"Who told?"

"The humor I can take or let alone." He refolded his hands the other way. "I don't like going behind Reliance's back like this. We've worked together for years and the director's an old friend. But this is a personal matter, and there are some things you would prefer to have a stranger know than someone you play poker with every Saturday night."

"I don't play poker," I said. "Whoops, sorry." I got out a cigarette and smoothed it between my fingers. "Who's missing, your wife or your daughter?"

He shot me a look he probably would have kept hooded in court. Then he sat back, nodding slightly. "I guess it's not all that uncommon."

"I do other work but my main specialty is tracing missing persons. You get so you smell it coming." I waited.

"It's my wife. She's left me again."

"Again?"

"Last time it was with one of the apprentices here, a man named Lloyd Debner. But they came back after three days. I fired him, naturally."

"Naturally."

A thin smile played around with his shark's mouth, gave it up and went away. "Seems awfully Old Testament, I know. I tried to be modern about it. There's really no sense in blaming the other man. But I saw myself hiding out in here to avoid meeting him in the hall, and that would be grotesque. I gave him excellent references. One of our competitors snapped him up right away."

"What about this time?"

"She left the usual note saying she was going away and I was not to look for her. I called Debner but he assured me he hadn't seen Cecelia since their first fling. I believe him. But it's been almost a week now and I'm concerned for her safety."

"What about the police?"

"I believe we covered that when we were discussing keeping secrets," he said acidly.

"You've been married how long?"

"Six years. And, yes, she's younger than I, by fourteen years. That was your next question, wasn't it?"

"It was in there. Do you think that had anything to do with her leaving?"

"I think it had everything to do with it. She has appetites that I've been increasingly unable to fulfill. But I never thought it was a problem until she left the first time."

"You quarreled?"

"The normal amount. Never about that. Which I suppose is revealing. I rather think she's found a new boyfriend, but I'm damned if I can say who it is."

"May I see the note?"

He extracted a fold of paper from an inside breast pocket and passed it across the desk. "I'm afraid I got my fingerprints all over it before I thought over all the angles."

"That's okay. I never have worked on anything where prints were any use."

It was written on common drugstore stationery, tinted blue with a spray of flowers in the upper right-hand corner. A hasty hand full of sharp points and closed loops. It said what he'd reported it had said and nothing else. Signed with a C.

"There's no date."

"She knew I'd read it the day she wrote it. It was last Tuesday."

"Uh-huh."

"That means what?" he demanded.

"Just uh-huh. It's something I say when I can't think of anything to say." I gave back the note. "Any ideas where she might go to be alone? Favorite vacation spot, her hometown, a summer house, anything like that? I don't mean to insult you. Sometimes the hardest place to find your hat is on your head."

"We sublet our Florida home in the off-season. She grew up in this area and has universally disliked every place we've visited on vacation. Really, I was expecting something more from a professional."

"I'm just groping for a handle. Does she have any hobbies?"

"Spending my money. "

I watched my cigarette smoke drifting toward the window. "It seems to me you don't know your wife too well after six years, Mr. Wynn. When I find her, if I find her, I can tell you where she is, but I can't make her come back, and from the sound of things she may not want to come back. I wouldn't be representing your best interests if I didn't advise you to save your money and set the cops loose on it. I can't give guarantees they won't give."

"Are you saying you don't want the job?"

"Not me. I don't have any practice at that. Just being straight with a client I'd prefer keeping."

"Don't do me any favors, Walker."

"Okay. I'll need a picture. And what's her maiden name? She may go back to it."

"Collier." He spelled it. "And here." He got a wallet-size color photograph out of the top drawer of the desk and skidded it across the glossy top like someone dealing a card.

She was a redhead, and the top of that line. She looked like some-one who would wind up married to a full partner in a weighty law firm with gray temples and an office overlooking Lake St. Clair. It would be in her high school yearbook under Predictions.

I put the picture in my breast pocket. "Where do I find this Debner?"

"He's with Paxton and Ring on West Michigan. But I told you he doesn't know where Cecelia is."

"Maybe he should be asked a different way." I killed my stub in the smoking stand next to the chair and rose. "You'll be hearing from me."

His eyes followed me up. All eight of his fingers were lined up on the near edge of his desk, the nails pink and perfect. "Can you be reached if I want to hear from you sooner?"

"My service will page me. I'm in the book."

Two

A Japanese accent at Paxton & Ring told me over the telephone that Lloyd Debner would be tied up all afternoon in Detroit Recorder's

Court. Lawyers are always in court the way executives are always in meetings. At the Frank Murphy Hall of Justice a bailiff stopped spitting on his handkerchief and rubbing at a spot on his uniform to point out a bearded man in his early thirties with a mane of black hair, smoking a pipe and talking to a gray-headed man in the corridor outside one of the courtrooms. I went over there and introduced myself.

"Second," he said, without taking his eye off the other man. "Tim, we're talking a lousy twenty bucks over the fifteen hundred. Even if you win, the judge will order probation. The kid'll get that anyway if we plead Larceny Under, and there's no percentage in mucking up his record for life just to fatten your win column. And there's nothing saying you'll win."

I said, "This won't take long."

"Make an appointment. Listen, Tim—"

"It's about Cecelia Wynn," I said. "We can talk about it out here in the hall if you like. Tim won't mind."

He looked at me then for the first time. "Tim, I'll catch you later."

"After the sentencing." The gray-headed man went into the courtroom, chuckling.

"Who'd you say you were?" Debner demanded.

"Amos Walker. I still am, but a little older. I'm a P.I. Alec Wynn hired me to look for his wife."

"You came to the wrong place. That's all over."

"I'm interested in when it wasn't."

He glanced up and down the hall. There were a few people in it, lawyers and fixers and the bailiff with the stain that wouldn't go away from his crisp blue uniform shirt. "Come on. I can give you a couple of minutes."

I followed him into a men's room two doors down. We stared at a guy combing his hair in front of the long mirror over the sinks until he put away his comb and picked up a brown leather briefcase and left. Debner bent down to see if there were any feet in the stalls, straightened, and knocked out his pipe into the sink. He laid it on a soap canister to cool and moved his necktie a centimeter to the right.

"I don't see Cecelia when we pass on the street," he said, inspecting the results in the mirror. "I had my phone number changed after we got back from Jamaica so she couldn't call me."

"That where you went?"

"I rented a bungalow outside Kingston. Worst mistake I ever made. I was headed for a junior partnership at Reiner when this happened. Now I'm back to dealing school board presidents' sons out of jams they wouldn't be in if five guys ahead of me hadn't dealt them out of jams just like them starting when they were in junior high."

"How'd you and Cecelia get on?"

"Oh, swell. So good we crammed a two-week reservation into three days and came back home."

"What went wrong?"

"Different drummers." He picked up his pipe and blew through it.

"Not good enough," I said.

He grinned boyishly. "I didn't think so. To begin with, she's a health nut. I run and take a little wheat germ myself sometimes—you don't even have to point a gun at me—but I draw the line at dropping vitamins and herb pills at every meal. She must've taken sixteen capsules every time we sat down to eat. It can drive you blinkers. People in restaurants must've figured her for a drug-addict."

"Sure she wasn't?"

"She was pretty open about taking them if she was. She filled the capsules herself from plastic bags. Her purse rattled like a used car."

A fat party in a gray suit and pink shirt came in and smiled and nodded at both of us and used the urinal and washed his hands. Debner used the time to recharge his pipe.

"Still not good enough," I said, when the fat party had gone. "You don't cut a vacation short just because your bed partner does wild garlic."

"It just didn't work out. Look, I'm due back in court."

"Not at half-past noon." I waited.

He finished lighting his pipe, dropped the match into the sink where he'd knocked his ashes, grinned around the stem. I bet that melted the women jurors. "If this gets around I'm washed up with every pretty legal secretary in the building."

"Nothing has to get around. I'm just looking for Cecelia Wynn."

"Yeah. You said." He puffed on the pipe, took it out, smoothed his beard, and looked at it in the mirror. "Yeah. Well, she said she wasn't satisfied."

"Uh-huh. "

"No one's ever told me that before. I'm not used to complaints."

"Uh-*huh*."

He turned back toward me. His eyes flicked up and down. "We never had this conversation, okay?"

"What conversation?"

"Yeah." He put the pipe back between his teeth, puffed.

"Yeah."

We shook hands. He squeezed a little harder than I figured he did normally.

Three

I dropped two dimes into a pay telephone in the downstairs lobby and fought my way through two secretaries before Alec Wynn came on the line. His voice was a full octave deeper than it had been in person. I figured it was that way in court too.

"Just checking back, Mr. Wynn. How come when I asked you about hobbies you didn't tell me your wife was into herbs?"

"Into *what*?"

I told him what Debner had said about the capsules. He said, "I haven't dined with my wife in months. Most legal business is conducted in restaurants."

"I guess you wouldn't know who her herbalist is, then."

"Herbalist? "

"Sort of an oregano guru. They tell their customers which herbs to take in the never-ending American quest for a healthy body. Not a few of the runaways I've traced take their restlessness to them first."

"Well, I wouldn't know anything about that. Trina might. Our maid. She's at the house now."

"Would you call her and tell her I'm coming?"

He said he would and broke the connection.

Four

It was a nice place if you like windows. There must have been fifty on the street side alone, with ivy or something just as green crawling up the brick wall around them and a courtyard with a marble fountain in the center and a black chauffeur with no shirt on washing a blue Mercedes in front. They are always washing cars. A white-haired Puerto Rican woman with muddy eyes and a faint moustache answered my ring.

"Trina?"

"Yes. You are Mr. Walker? Mr. Wynn told me to expect you."

I followed her through a room twice the size of my living room, but that was designed just for following maids through, and down a hall with dark paintings on the walls to a glassed-in porch at the back of the house containing ferns in pots and lawn chairs upholstered in floral print. The sliding glass door leading outside was ajar and a strong chlorine stench floated in from an outdoor crescent-shaped swimming pool. She slid the door shut.

"The pool man says alkali is leaking into the water from an underground spring," she said. "The chlorine controls the smell."

"The rich suffer too." I told her what I wanted.

"Capsules? Yes. Mrs. Wynn has many bottles of capsules in her room. There is a name on the bottles. I will get one."

"No hurry. What sort of woman is Mrs. Wynn to work for?"

"I don't know that that is a good question to answer."

"You're a good maid, Trina." I wound a five-dollar bill around my right index finger.

She slid the tube off the finger and flattened it and folded it over and tucked it inside her apron pocket. "She is a good employer. She says please and does not run her fingers over the furniture after I have dusted, like the last woman I worked for."

"Is that all you can tell me?"

"I have not worked here long, sir. Only five weeks."

"Who was maid before that?"

"A girl named Ann Foster, at my agency. Multi-Urban Services. She was fired." Her voice sank to a whisper on the last part. We were alone.

"Fired why?"

"William the chauffeur told me she was fired. I didn't ask why. I have been a maid long enough to learn that the less you know the more you work. I will get one of the bottles."

She left me, returning a few minutes later carrying a glass container the size of an aspirin bottle, with a cork in the top.

It was half full of gelatin capsules filled with fine brown powder. I pulled the cork and sniffed. A sharp, spicy scent. The name of a health foods store on Livernois was typewritten on the label.

"How many of these does Mrs. Wynn have in her bedroom?" I asked.

"Many. Ten or twelve bottles."

"As full as this?"

"More, some of them."

"That's a lot of capsules to fill and then leave behind. Did she take her clothes with her?"

"No, sir. Her closets and drawers are full."

I thanked her and gave her back the bottle. It was getting to be the damnedest disappearing act I had covered in a long, long time.

The black chauffeur was hosing off the Mercedes when I came out. He was tall, almost my height, and the bluish skin of his torso was stretched taut over lumpy muscle. I asked him if he was William.

He twisted shut the nozzle of the hose, watching me from under his brows with his head down, like a boxer. Scar tissue shone around his eyes. "Depends on who you might be."

I sighed. When you can't even get their name out of them, the rest is like pulling nails with your toes. I stood a folded ten-spot on the Mercedes' hood. He watched the bottom edge darken as it soaked up water. "Ann Foster," I said.

"What about her?"

"How close was she to Cecelia Wynn?"

"'I wouldn't know. I work outside."

"'Who fired her, Mr. or Mrs. Wynn?"

He thought about it. Watched the bill getting wetter. Then he snatched it up and waved it dry. "She did, Mrs. Wynn."

"Why?"

He shrugged. I reached up and plucked the bill out of his fingers. He grabbed for it but I drew it back out of his reach. He shrugged again, wringing the hose in his hands to make his muscles bulge. "They had a fight of some kind the day Ann left. I could hear them screaming at each other out here. I don't know what it was about."

"Where'd she go after she left here?"

He started to shrug a third time, stopped. "Back to the agency, maybe. I don't ask questions. In this line—"

"Yeah. The less you know the more you work." I gave him the ten and split.

Five

The health foods place was standard, plank floor and hanging plants and stuff you can buy in any supermarket for a fraction of what they were asking. The herbalist was a small, pretty woman of about 30, in a gypsy blouse and floor-length denim skirt with bare feet poking out underneath and a bandana tied around her head. She also owned the place. She hadn't seen Mrs. Wynn since before she'd turned up missing. I bought a package of unsalted nuts for her trouble and ate them on the way to the office. They needed salt.

I found Multi-Urban Services in the Detroit metropolitan directory and dialed the number. A woman whose voice reminded me of the way cool green mints taste answered.

"We're not at liberty to give out information about our clients."

"I'm sorry to hear that," I said. "I went to a party at the Wynn place in Grosse Pointe about six weeks ago and was very impressed with Miss Foster's efficiency. I'd heard she was free and was thinking of engaging her services on a fulltime basis."

The mints melted. "I'm sorry, Miss Foster is no longer with this agency. But I can recommend another girl just as efficient. Multi-Urban prides itself—"

"I'm sure it does. Can you tell me where Miss Foster is currently working?"

"Stormy Heat Productions. But not as a maid."

I thanked her and hung up, thinking about how little it takes to turn mint to acid. Stormy Heat was listed on Mt. Elliott. Its line was busy. Before leaving the office, I broke the Smith & Wesson out of the desk drawer and snapped the holster onto my belt under my jacket. It was that kind of neighborhood.

Six

The outfit worked out of an old gymnasium across from Mt. Elliott Cemetery, a scorched brick building as old as the eight-hour day with a hand-lettered sign over the door and a concrete stoop deep in the process of going back to the land. The door was locked. I pushed a sunken button that grated in its socket. No sound issued from within. I was about to knock when a square panel opened in the door at head level and a mean black face with a beard that grew to a point looked into mine.

"You've got to be kidding," I said.

"What do you want?" demanded the face.

"Ann Foster."

"What for?"

"Talk."

"Sorry." The panel slid shut.

I was smoking a cigarette. I dropped it to the stoop and crushed it out and used the button again. When the panel shot back I reached up and grasped the beard in my fist and yanked. His chest banged the door.

"You white—!"

I twisted the beard in my fist. He gasped and tears sprang to his eyes. "Joe sent me," I said. "The goose flies high. May the Force be with you. Pick the password you like, but open the door."

"Who—?"

"Jerk Root, the Painless Barber. Open."

"Okay, okay." Metal snapped on his side. Still hanging on to his whiskers, I reached down with my free hand and tried the knob. It turned. I let go and opened the door. He was standing just inside the threshold, a big man in threadbare jeans and a white shirt open to the navel Byron-fashion, smoothing his beard with thick fingers. He had a Colt magnum in his other hand pointed at my belt buckle.

"Nice," I said. "The nickel plating goes with your eyes. You got a permit for that?"

He smiled crookedly. His eyes were still watering. "Why didn't you say you was cop?" He reached back and jammed the revolver into a hip pocket. "You got paper?"

"Not today. I'm not raiding the place, I just want to talk to Ann Foster."

"Okay," he said. "Okay. I don't need no beef with the law. You don't see nothing on the way, deal?"

I spread my hands. "I'm blind. This isn't an election year."

There was a lot not to see. Films produced by Stormy Heat were not interested in the Academy Award or even feature billing at the all-night grindhouses on Woodward Avenue. Its actors were thin and ferretlike and its actresses used powder to fill the cavities in their faces and cover their stretch marks. The lights and cameras were strictly surplus, their cables frayed and patched all over like old garden hoses. We walked past carnal scenes, unnoticed by the grunting performers or the sweat-stained crews, to a scuffed steel door at the rear that had originally led into a locker room. My escort went through it without pausing. I followed.

"Don't they teach you to knock in the jungle?"

I'd had a flash of a naked youthful brown body, and then it was covered by a red silk kimono that left a pair of long legs bare to the tops of the thighs. She had her hair cut very short and her face, with its upturned nose and lower lip thrust out in a belligerent pout, was boyish. I had seen enough to know she wasn't a boy.

"What's to see that I ain't already seen out on the floor?" asked the Beard. "Man to see you. From the Machine."

Ann Foster looked at me quickly. The whites of her eyes had a bluish tinge against her dark skin. "Since when they picking matinee idols for cops?"

"Thanks," I said. "But I've got job."

We stared at the guy with the beard until he left us, letting the door drift shut behind him. The room had been converted into a community dressing room, but without much conviction. A library table littered with combs and brushes and pots of industrial strength make-up stood before a long mirror, but the bench on this side had come with the place and the air smelled of mildew and old sweat. She said, "Show me you're a cop."

I flashed my photostat and honorary sheriff's star. "I'm private. I let Lothar out there think different. It saved time."

"Well, you wasted it all here. I don't like rental heat any more than the other kind. I don't even like men."

"You picked a swell business not to like them in."

She smiled, not unpleasantly. "I work with an all-girl cast."

"Does it pay better than being a maid?"

"About as much. But when I get on my knees it's not to scrub floors."

"Cecelia Wynn," I said.

Her faced moved as if I'd slapped her. "What about her?" she barked.

"She's missing. Her husband wants her back. You had a fight with her just before you got fired. What started it?"

"What happens if I don't answer?"

"Nothing. Now. But if it turns out she doesn't want to be missing, the cops get it. I could save you a trip downtown."

She said, "Hell, she's probably off someplace with her lawyer boyfriend like last time."

"No, he's accounted for. Also she left almost all her clothes behind, along with the herbs she spent a small country buying and a lot of time stuffing into capsules. It's starting to look like leaving wasn't her idea, or that where she was going she wouldn't need those things. What was the fight about?"

"I wouldn't do windows."

I slapped her for real. It made a loud flat noise off the echoing walls and she yelled. The door swung open. Beard stuck his face inside. Farther down the magnum glittered.

"What?"

I looked at him, looked at the woman. She stroked her burning cheek. My revolver was behind my right hipbone, a thousand miles away. Finally she said, "Nothing."

"Sure?"

She nodded. The man with the beard left his eyes on me a moment longer, then withdrew. The door closed.

"It was weird," she told me. "Serving dinner this one night I spilled salad oil down the front of my uniform. I went to my room to change. Mrs. Wynn stepped inside to ask for something, just like you walked in on me just now. She caught me naked."

"So?"

"So she excused herself and got out. Half an hour later I was canned. For spilling the salad oil. I yelled about it, as who wouldn't? But it wasn't the reason."

"What was?"

She smoothed the kimono across her pelvis. "You think I don't know that look on another woman's face when I see it?"

We talked some more, but none of it was for me. On my way out I laid a twenty on the dressing table and stood a pot of mascara on top of it. I hesitated, then added one of my cards to the stack. "In case something happens to change your mind about rental heat," I said. "If you lose the card, I'm in the book."

Back in civilization I gassed up and used the telephone in the service station to call Alec Wynn at his office. I asked him to meet me at his home in Grosse Pointe in twenty minutes.

"I can't," he said. "I'm meeting a client at four."

"He'll keep. If you don't show you may be one yourself." We stopped talking to each other.

Seven

Both William the chauffeur and the Mercedes were gone from the courtyard, leaving only a puddle on the asphalt to reflect the win-

dow-studded façade of the big house. Trina let me in and listened to
me and escorted me back to the enclosed porch. When she left I slid
open the glass door and stepped outside to the pool area. I was there
when Wynn came out five minutes later. His gray suit looked right
even in those surroundings. It always would.

"You've caused me to place an important case in the hands of an
apprentice," he announced. "I hope this means you've found Cecelia."

"I've found her. I think."

"What's that supposed to signify? Or is this the famous Walker
sense of humor at work?"

"Save it for your next jury, Mr. Wynn. We're just two guys talking. How long have you been hanging on to your wife's good-bye
note? Since the first time she walked out?"

"You're babbling."

"It worried me that it wasn't dated," I said. "A thing like that
comes in handy too often. Being in corporate law, you might not
know that the cops have ways now to treat writing in ink with chemicals that can prove within a number of weeks when it was written."

His face was starting to match his suit. I went on.

"Someone else knew you hadn't been able to satisfy Cecelia sex-
ually, or you wouldn't have been so quick to tell me. Masculine pride
is a strong motive for murder, and in case something had happened
to her, you wanted to be sure you were covered. That's why you hired
me, and that's why you dusted off the old note. She didn't leave one
this time, did she?"

"You have found her."

I said nothing. Suddenly he was an old man. He shuffled blindly
to a marble bench near the pool and sank down onto it. His hands
worked on his knees.

"When I didn't hear from her after several days I became frightened," he said. "The servants knew we argued. She'd told Debner of my—shortcomings. Before I left criminal law, I saw several convictions obtained on flimsier evidence. Can you understand that I had to protect myself?"

I said, "It wasn't necessary. Debner was just as unsuccessful keeping her happy. Any man would have been. Your wife was a lesbian, Mr. Wynn."

"That's a damn lie!" He started to rise. Halfway up, his knees gave out and he sat back down with a thud.

"Not a practicing one. It's possible she didn't even realize what her problem was until about five weeks ago, when she accidentally saw your former maid naked. The maid is a lesbian and recognized the reaction. Was Cecelia a proud woman?"

"Intensely."

"A lot of smoke gets blown about the male fear of loss of masculinity," I said. "No one gives much thought to women's fears for their femininity. They can drive a woman to fire a servant out of hand, but she would just be moving temptation from her path for the moment. After a time, when the full force of her situation struck home, she might do something more desperate."

"She would be too proud to leave a note."

Wynn had his elbows on his knees and his face in his hands. I peeled cellophane off a fresh pack of Winstons.

"The cops can't really tell when a note was written, Mr. Wynn. I just said that to hear what you'd say."

"Where is she, Walker?"

I watched my reflection in the pool's turquoise-colored surface, squinting against the chlorine fumes. The water was clear enough to see through to the bottom, but there was a recessed area along the north edge with a shelf obscuring it from above, a design flaw that would trap leaves and twigs and other debris that would normally be exposed when the pool was drained. Shadows swirled in the pocket, thick and dark and full of secrets.

Bodyguards Shoot Second

"A. Walker Investigations."

"Amos Walker?"

The voice on the other end of the line was male and youthful, one of those that don't change from the time they crack until the time they quake. I said, "This is he."

"Huh?"

"Grammar," I said. "It gets me business in Grosse Pointe. But not lately. Who's speaking?"

"This is Martin Cole. I'm Billy Dickerson's road manager."

"Okay."

"No, really."

"I believe you, Mr. Martin. How can I make your life easier?"

"Cole. Martin's my first name. Art Cradshaw recommended you. He said you were the best man for what you do in Detroit."

"Sweet of him. But he still owes me for the credit check I ran for his company six months ago."

"That's hardly my business. I need a man."

I parked the receiver in the hollow of my shoulder and lit a Winston.

"Walker?"

"I'm here. You need a man."

"The man I need doesn't pick his teeth with his thumbnail and can wear a dinner jacket without looking as if he was strapped in waiting for the current, but doesn't worry about popping a seam when he has to push somebody's face in. He's a good enough shot to light a match at thirty paces on no notice, but he carries himself as if he thought the butt of a gun would spoil the lines of his suit. He can swear and spit when called upon but in polite conversation wouldn't split an infinitive at knifepoint."

I said, "I wish you'd let me know when you find him. I could use someone like that in the investigation business."

"According to Art Cradshaw you're that man."

"I don't own a dinner jacket, Mr. Dickerson."

"Cole. Dickerson's the man I represent. The jacket's no problem. We have a tailor traveling with us and he'll fix you up in a day."

"I didn't know tailors traveled. But then I don't know any tailors. What business are you and Mr. Dickerson in?"

Pause. "You're kidding, right?"

"Probably not. I don't have a sense of humor."

"Billy Dickerson. The singer. Rock and Country. He's opening at the Royal Tower in Dearborn tomorrow night. Don't tell me you've never heard of him."

"My musical appreciation stops around nineteen sixty-two. What sort of work do you have in mind for this cross between Richard Gere and the Incredible Hulk?"

"Protection. Billy's regular bodyguard has disappeared and he can't leave his suite here at the Tower without someone to stand between him and his adoring fans. Too much adoration can be fatal."

"I don't do that kind of work, Mr. Cole. Bodyguards shoot second. If at all."

"We're paying a thousand. For the week."

I hesitated. Habit. Then: "My daily's two-fifty: That comes to seventeen-fifty for seven days."

"We'll go that."

"Can't do it, Mr. Cole. I'm sitting on retainer for a local union just now. They could call me anytime. Try Ned Eccles on Michigan; security's his specialty. Infinitives don't last too long around him, but he's hard and fast and he knows how to tie a bow."

"I don't know. Art said you were the guy to call."

"Cradshaw's in the tool design business. He doesn't know a bodyguard from a right cross."

"I thought you guys never turned down a job."

I said, "It's not a thing I'd care to get good at. Tell Ned I sent you."

"Will he give me a discount?"

"No. But he might give me one next time I farm something out to him." I wished him good luck and we were through talking to each other.

The union rep didn't call that day or the next, just as he hadn't called for a week, not since the day I'd accepted his retainer. Meanwhile I was laying in a hundred and a half every twenty-four hours just for paying solitaire within reach of the telephone. I closed the office at five and drove home. It was November. The city was stone-colored under a gray sky and in the air was the raw-iron smell that comes just before a snow.

Out of long habit I flipped on the television set the minute I got in the door and went into the kitchen, stripping off my jacket and tie as I went. When I came out opening a can of beer the picture had come on but not the sound and I was looking at a studio shot of Ned Eccles' fleshy moustached face.

". . . died three hours later at Detroit Receiving Hospital," came on the announcer's voice, too loud. I jumped and turned down the volume. Now they were showing film of a lean young man in a gold lame jumpsuit unzipped to his pelvis and stringy blond hair to his shoulders striding down a stage runway, shouting song lyrics into a hand mike while the crowd jammed up against the footlights screamed. The announcer continued.

"Dickerson, shown here during his last appearance at the Royal Tower two years ago, was shoved out of the line of fire by a member of his entourage after the first shot and was unharmed. The slain bodyguard has been identified as Edward Eccles, forty-five, a Detroit private investigator with a background in personal security. Police have no leads as yet to the man who fired the shots." After a short pause during which the camera focused on the announcer's grave face, he turned his head and smiled. "How are the Lions doing, Steve?"

I changed channels. There was a commercial for a woman's hygiene product on the next local station and a guy in a chef's hat showing how to make cheese gooey on the last. I turned off the set and sipped beer and thought. The telephone interrupted my thinking.

"Walker?"

"Yeah."

"This is Carol Greene. You heard?"

Carol Greene was Ned Eccles' business partner. I said, "I just caught a piece of it. What happened?"

"Not on the phone. Can you come to Ned's office?"

"What for?"

"I'll tell you when you get here." After a beat: "You owe Ned. You got him killed."

"Don't hang that on me, Carol. I just made a referral. He didn't have to take the job. Give me twenty minutes." I hung up and retrieved my tie and jacket.

Two

Eccles Investigations and Security worked out of a storefront off Cadillac Square, with an oak railing separating Carol's desk in front from Ned's in back and a lot of framed photographs on the walls of Ned shaking hands with the mayor and the governor and various presidential candidates whose faces remained vaguely familiar long after their names were faded on old baled ballots. The place had a friendly, informal, unfussy look that had set its owners back at least three grand. The basement vault where the firm's files were kept had cost more than the building. I went through a swinging gate in the railing to Ned's desk where Carol was supporting herself on her small angular fists.

"Give some guys twenty minutes and they'll take forty," she greeted.

"The rush hour got me by the throat. You look the same as always."

"Don't start." She put the cigarette she was holding between thumb and forefinger to her lips, bit off some smoke, and tipped it down her throat in a series of short, jerky movements like a bird bolting grain. She was a small, wiry woman in a man's flannel shirt and jeans with gray-streaked blond hair cut very short and unadorned glasses with underslung bows. She had been Ned Eccles' junior partner for ten years. Whatever else she might have been to him wasn't my business today or ever.

"How much do you know about what happened to Ned?" she asked.

"Just that he was killed. Apparently by someone trying to get Billy Dickerson."

She nodded jerkily, ate some more cigarette, ground it out in a glass ashtray full of butts on the desk. "Dickerson stopped to sign an autograph in front of the service elevator on the way up to his suite at the Royal Tower. Ned had told him to avoid the lobby. He'd told him not to stop for anyone either, but I guess Billy-boy didn't hear that part. The guy ducked Ned and stuck a pad in Dickerson's hand and while Dickerson was getting out a pen he pulled a piece. Ned saw it and got between them just in time to get his guts drilled. That was about noon. He spent the afternoon dying. I just got back from the hospital."

Her eyes were a little red behind the cheaters. I said, "Who saw this?"

"Dickerson's manager, Martin Cole. Dickerson. Some gofer, Phil something. I talked to them at the hospital. While they were busy getting the Music Man out of the way of the bullets, the gunny lit out through the rear entrance. Six feet, a hundred and eighty, thirties, balding. Dark zipper jacket. That's as good as it gets. The croakers dug two thirty-eight slugs out of Ned's insides."

"Say something before he died?"

She shook her head, firing up a fresh cigarette from a butane lighter whose flame leaped halfway to the ceiling. "Outside of cussing a blue streak. That why you turned Cole down? You had dope on the shoot?"

"I was in the clutch when he called."

"Yeah."

I said, "Ned and I didn't get along, that's yesterday's news. We had different ideas about how the investigating business should be run. But I didn't put him in front of those bullets."

"Yeah. I guess not." She tossed the cold lighter atop a stack of Manila file folders on the desk. Then she looked at me. "I'll go your full rate to look into Ned's death."

"Ned's death was an accident."

"Maybe. Either way you get paid."

"You've got a license."

"I make out the books, trace an occasional skip. That's all I've done for ten years. Ned was the detective. You do this kind of thing all the time."

"Wrong. Mostly I look for missing persons."

"The guy who killed Ned is missing."

"He's cop meat," I said. "Save your money and let them do their job."

"Cops. First Monday of every month I hand an envelope to our department pipeline, a night captain. A thing like that can shake your faith. You still in the clutch?"

I nodded. "Retainer. I sit by the telephone."

"You've got an answering service to do that. Look, I won't beg you." She made a face and killed the butt, smoked only a third down. "I know everyone thought I was sleeping with Ned, including that slut of a wife of his, who should know about that kind of thing. I haven't cared what people thought of me since my senior prom. For the record, though, I wasn't. He was my friend and my partner and I have to do this one thing for him before I can go back to what I was doing. If you won't take the job I'll find someone else. The Yellow Pages are lousy with plastic badges."

"I'll look into it. Courtesy rate, two hundred a day and expenses. Couple of days should tell if I'm wasting your money."

She wrote out a check for five hundred dollars and gave it to me. "That should see you through. If it doesn't, come back here. With an itemized list of expenses. No whisky."

"You keep the books, all right." I folded the check and stuck it in my wallet. "One question. Don't hit me with the desk when I ask it."

"Ask."

"Did you ever know Ned to be the kind of a bodyguard who would throw himself between a gun and its target, even if the target was the person he was guarding?"

"No," she said quickly. "No, I didn't know him to be that kind of bodyguard."

"Neither did I."

Three

I cashed the check at my bank, deposited all but a hundred of it, and drove the four miles to Dearborn. The sky was low and the heater took ten minutes to chase the chill out of the upholstery. I parked in the lot behind the Royal Tower. A uniformed cop stopped me at the main entrance to the hotel.

"Excuse me, sir, but are you a guest here?"

"No, I'm here to see someone. "

"No one goes in without a room key, sorry. We had some excitement here earlier."

I handed him one of my cards. "Would you see that Martin Cole gets that? He's with Billy Dickerson. It's important."

The cop called over another uniform, gave him the card, and told him to take it up. Ten minutes later the second officer returned. "Lieutenant says okay." To me: "Three-oh-six."

More uniforms and a group of men in suits greeted me in the hall when I stepped off the elevator. One of the latter was an inch shorter than I but half again as broad through the shoulders. It would have been a long time since he had gone through a doorway any way but sideways. His skin was pale to the point of translucence, almost albino, but his eyes were blue. He combed his short blond hair forward over a retreating widow's peak.

"Walker? I'm Gritch, homicide lieutenant with the Dearborn Police." He flashed his badge in a leather folder. "Cole says to let you through, but we got to check you for weapons."

"I'm not carrying," I said, but stood for the frisk by a black officer with hands like Ping-Pong paddles. Gritch meanwhile looked through the credentials in my wallet. He handed it back.

"Okay. We got to play it tight. The description of the guy that tried to kill Dickerson fits you as good as it fits a thousand other guys in this town."

"Anything new?" I put the crease back in my topcoat.

"Now, would I be earning your tax dollars if I answered that, after going to so much trouble to keep the public off the premises?"

"Nothing new," I said. "I thought so. Where's three-oh-six?"

"Right in front of you, Sherlock." He stepped away from it.

Before I could knock, the door was opened by a young man in shirt-sleeves and stockinged feet. His hair was brown and wavy and combed behind his ears, his face clean-shaven, and his eyes as lifelike as two stones. He had a nine millimeter automatic pistol in his right hand.

"Let him in, Phil."

The man who spoke was smaller than Lieutenant Gritch but not so small as Carol Greene, with a great mane of styled black hair and a drooping moustache and aviator's glasses with rose-tinted lenses. He wore a dark European-looking jacket with narrow lapels and a pinched waist over yellow-and-red checked pants. His shoes were brown leather with tassels, and he had a yellow silk scarf knotted at his throat.

"Walker, is it? I'm Martin Cole. Decent of you to stop in."

At first glance, Cole was as youthful as his voice, but there were hairline fissures around his eyes and pouches at the comers of his mouth that his moustache couldn't hide. I took the moist warm hand he offered and entered the suite. The room was plushly carpeted and furnished as a living room, with a sofa and easy chairs, but folding metal chairs had been added. Cole caught me looking at them.

"For the press," he said. "We're holding a conference as soon as the police finish downstairs. Billy Dickerson, Amos Walker."

I looked at the man seated on the end of the sofa with a small barrel glass of copper-colored liquid in one hand. In person he was older and not so lean as he appeared on television. His skin was grayish against the long open collar of his white jumpsuit, and a distinct roll showed over his wide brown tooled-leather belt with an ornate gold buckle. His long yellow hair was thinning at the temples. He glanced at me, drank from his glass, and looked at Cole, "He the best you could do?"

"Walker came on his own, Billy," the manager said.

Quickly he introduced the man with the gun as Phil Scabarda.

I said, "He must have a permit for that or he wouldn't be waving it around with the cops so close. That doesn't mean he can point it at me."

Cole gestured at the young man, who hesitated, then hung the pistol on a clip on the back of his belt. "Phil is Billy's driver and companion. These days that requires courses in racing and weaponry."

"Ned Eccles' partner hired me to look into the shooting," I said. "I appreciate your seeing me."

"Ah. I thought maybe you wanted his job after all. I'd rather hoped."

"You've got police protection now. What happened in front of the service elevator?"

"Well, we were standing there waiting for the doors to open when this guy came out from behind the elevator and asked Billy for his autograph. As soon as he got rid of the pad he pulled a gun from under his jacket. Eccles stepped in and took both bullets."

"Was Eccles armed?"

Cole nodded. "A revolver of some kind. I don't know from guns. It was still in his shoulder holster when the police came. There wasn't time to get it out."

"What was Phil doing while all this was going on?"

"Hustling Billy out of the way, with me. Meanwhile the guy got away." He gave me the same description he'd given Carol.

"If he was after Dickerson, why'd he leave without scratching him?"

"He panicked. Those shots were very loud in that enclosed space. As it was he barely got out before the place was jammed with gawkers."

"What happened to the pad?"

"Pad?"

"The pad he handed Dickerson for his autograph. Fingerprints."

"I guess Billy dropped it in the scramble. Some souvenir hunter has it by now."

I got out a cigarette and tapped it on the back of my left hand. "Anyone threaten Dickerson's life lately?"

"The police asked that. He gets his share of hate mail like every other big-name entertainer. They don't like his hair or his singing or his politics. That kind of letter is usually scribbled in Crayola on ruled paper with the lines an inch apart. I called Billy's secretary in L.A. to go through the files and send the most likely ones by air express for the police to look at. But she throws most of them away."

"What's the story on this bodyguard that disappeared?"

"Henry?" Carefully plucked eyebrows slid above the tinted glasses. "Forget him. He was a drunk and he got to wandering just when we needed him most. Flying in from L.A. day before yesterday we changed planes in Denver and he was missing when we boarded for Detroit. Probably found himself a bar and he's drying out in some drunk tank by now. If he hadn't ducked out we'd have fired him soon anyway. He was worse than no protection at all."

"Full name and description." I got out my notebook and pencil.

"Henry Bliss. About your height, a little over six feet. Two hundred pounds, sandy hair, fair complexion. Forty. Let's see, he had a white scar about an inch long on the right side of his jaw. Dropped his guard, he said. Don't waste your time with him. He was just an ex-pug with a taste for booze."

"It's my client's time. Any reason why someone would want to kill Dickerson? Besides his hair and his singing and his politics?"

"Celebrities make good clay pigeons. They're easier to get at than politicians, but you can become just as famous shooting them."

"Everyone's famous today. It's almost worth it to get an obscure person's autograph." I flipped the notebook shut.

"Can I reach you here if something turns up?"

"We're booked downstairs for two weeks."

"Except for tonight."

"We're opening tonight as scheduled. Look, you can tell Ned's partner how sorry we are, but—"

"The show must go on. "

Cole smiled thinly. "An ancient tradition with a solid mercenary base. No one likes giving refunds."

"Thanks, Mr. Cole. You'll be hearing from me."

"You know," he said, "I can't help thinking that had you been on the job, things would have gone differently today."

"Probably not. Ned knew his business. Your boy's alive. That's what you paid for."

As I closed the door behind me, Lieutenant Gritch came away from his crew next to the elevator. "What'd you get?" he demanded.

"Now, would I be earning my client's money if I answered that after going to so much trouble to keep the cops out of my pockets?"

His pale face flushed for a moment. Then the color faded and he showed his eyeteeth in a gargoyle's grin, nodding.

"Okay. I guess I bought that. We'll trade. You go."

I told him what I'd learned. He went on nodding.

"That's what we got. There's nothing in that autograph pad. Even if it had liftable prints, which nothing like that ever does, they'll have someone else's all over them by now. We Telexed this Henry Bliss's name and description to Denver. It won't buy zilch. This one's local and sloppy. If we get the guy at all it'll be because somebody unzipped his big yap. Give me a pro any time. These amateurs are a blank order."

"What makes him an amateur?"

"You mean besides he got the wrong guy? The gun. We frisked the service area and the parking lot and the alley next door. No gun. A pro would've used a piece without a history and then dumped it. He wouldn't take a chance on being picked up for CCW. You got a reference?"

The change of subjects threw me for a second. Then I gave him John Alderdyce's name in Detroit Homicide. He had a uniform write down the name in his notebook.

"Okay, we'll check you out. You know what the penalty is for interfering with a murder investigation."

"Something short of electrocution, " I said. "In this state, anyway."

"Then I won't waste breath warning you off this one. You get anything—anything—you know where to come." He handed me one of his cards.

I gave him one of mine. "If you ever have a rug that needs looking under."

"I'd sooner put my gun in my mouth," he said. But he stuck the card in his pocket.

Four

The sun had gone down, sucking all the heat out of the air. It still smelled like snow. On my way home I stopped at the main branch of the Detroit Public Library on Woodward, where I knew the security guard. I spotted him a ten to let me in after closing and browsed through the out-of-town directories until I found a list of detective agencies in Denver and copied some likelies into my notebook.

Colorado is two hours behind Michigan. Calling long-distance from home I found most of the offices still open.

The first two I called didn't believe in courtesy rates. The third took down the information I had on Henry Bliss the wandering bodyguard and said they'd get back to me. I hung up and dialed my service for messages. I had a message. I got the union executive I was working for at home. He had a tail job for me, a shop steward suspected of pocketing membership dues.

"What am I looking for?" I asked.

"Where he goes with the money." The executive's tone was as smooth as ice. No lead pipes across his throat like in the old days. "He's not depositing it and he's not investing it. Follow him until it changes hands. Get pictures."

The job would start in the morning. I took down the necessary information, pegged the receiver, slid a TV tray into the oven, and mixed myself a drink while it was heating up. I felt like a pretty, empty-headed girl with two dates for Saturday night.

In the morning after breakfast I rang up Barry Stackpole at the Detroit *News*. While waiting for him to answer I watched the snow floating down outside the window turn brown before it reached the ground.

"Amos the famous shamus," said Barry, after I'd announced myself. "What can I do you for this lovely morning?"

"You must be in St. Tropez. I need a name on a pro heavyweight." I described Ned Eccles' killer. Barry wrote a syndicated column on organized crime and had a national reputation and an artificial leg to show for it.

"Offhand I could name twenty that would fit," he said. "Local?"

"Maybe. More likely he was recruited from somewhere else."

"Make that a hundred. I can get a list to your office by special messenger this afternoon. What's the hit?"

"A P.I. named Eccles. You wouldn't know him. He ate that lead that was meant for Billy Dickerson yesterday."

"That was a hit?"

"I don't know. But the cops are following the amateur theory and that leaves this way open. I step on fewer official toes."

"When did you get religion?"

"I'm duplicating them on one thing, a previous bodyguard that got himself lost out West. The cops don't put much faith in it. I wouldn't be earning my fee if all I did was sniff their coattails. What's this list going to run me?"

"A fifth of Teacher's."

"Just one?"

"I'm cutting down. Hang tight."

After he broke the connection I called my service and asked them to page me if Denver called. Then I dug my little pen-size beeper out of a drawer full of spent cartridges and illegible notes to myself and clipped it to my belt and went to work for the union.

The shop steward lived a boring life. I tailed his Buick from his home in Redford Township to the GM Tech Center in Warren where he worked, picked him up again when he and two fellow workers walked downtown for lunch, ate in a booth across the restaurant from their table, and followed them back to work. One of the other guys got the tab. My guy took care of the tip. On my way out I glanced at the bills on the table. Two singles. He wasn't throwing the stuff away, that was sure.

During the long gray period before quitting time I found a public booth within sight of the Buick in the parking lot and called my service. There were no messages from Denver or anywhere else. I had the girl page me to see if the beeper was working. It was.

I followed the steward home, parked next to the curb for two hours waiting to see if he came out again, and when he didn't I started the engine and drove to the office. Opening the unlocked door of my little waiting room I smelled cop.

The door to my private office, which I keep locked when I'm not in it, was standing open. I went through it and found Gritch sitting behind my desk looking at a sheet of typing paper. His skin wasn't any more colorful and he looked like a billboard with the window at his back. My scotch bottle and one of my pony glasses stood on the desk, the glass half full.

"Pour one for me," I hung up my hat and coat.

He got the other glass out of the file drawer and filled it. His eyes didn't move from the paper in his left hand. "You got better taste in liquor than you do in locks," he said, leveling off his own glass.

"I'm working. I wasn't when I bought the lock," I put down my drink in one installment and waited for the heat to rise.

"This is quite a list you got. Packy Davis, yeah. Benny Boom-Boom Bohannen, sure. Lester Adams, don't know him." His voice trailed off, but his lips kept moving. Finally he laid the sheet on the desk and sat back in my swivel-shrieker and took a drink, looking at me for the first time.

"It isn't quite up to date. Couple of those guys are pulling hard time. Two are dead, and one might as well be, he's got more tubes sticking out of him than a subway terminal."

"You know lists. They get old just while you're typing them up." I bought a refill.

"Some smart kid in a uniform brought it while I was waiting for you. I gave him a quarter and he looked like I bit his hand. Who sent it?"

"A friend. You wouldn't know him. He respects locks."

His marblelike face didn't move. He'd heard worse. "This to do with the Eccles burn?"

I said nothing. Drank.

"Yeah, Alderdyce said you could shut up like an oyster. I called him. We had quite a conversation about you. Want to know what else he said?"

"No, I want to know what brings you to my office when everyone else's office who has any brains is closed."

"Your client won't answer her phone. Her office is closed too, but it's been closed all day and her home isn't listed. And you're harder to get hold of than an eel with sunburn. I didn't feel like talking to the girl at your service. She sounds like my aunt that tells fortunes. I got to find out if there was any connection between Eccles and Henry Bliss, Dickerson's old bodyguard."

A little chill chased the whisky-warmth up my spine, like a drop of cold water running uphill. "How come?"

"No reason. Except the Denver Police fished a floater out of the South Platte this morning, with two holes in the back of its skull. We got the Telex two hours ago. The stiff fits Bliss's description down to the scar on his chin."

Five

I struck a match, cracking the long silence, and touched the flame to a Winston. Gritch watched me. He said:

"Dunked stiffs surface after three days. That puts him in the river just about the time Dickerson and Cole and their boy Phil noticed him missing."

"Meaning?" I flipped the dead match into the ashtray on the desk and cocked a hip up on one corner, blowing smoke out my nostrils.

"Meaning maybe yesterday's try on Dickerson, if that's what it was, wasn't a backyard job after all. Meaning maybe the same guy that dusted Bliss dusted Eccles. Meaning that seeing as how the two hits were a thousand miles apart and seeing as how the guy that did it didn't leave tracks either time, he's pro after all."

"Slugs match up?"

He shook his fair head without taking his eyes off my face. "Nothing on that yet. But they won't. Major leaguers never use the same piece twice. What I want to know—"

"You said they didn't take their pieces away with them either."

"What I want to know," he went on, "is how it happens I come here looking to talk to you and your client about Eccles' being a mechanic's job and find a list of mechanics all typed up nice and neat before I'm here five minutes."

"Just touching all bases," I said. "Like you. You didn't send a flyer to Denver looking for some local nut that doesn't like loud music. "

"That's it, huh."

I said it was. He sipped more scotch, made a face, rubbed a spot at the arch of his ribcage, and set the glass down. I never knew a cop that didn't have something wrong with his back or his stomach. He said, "Well, I got to talk to Carol Greene."

"I'll set up a meet. What makes it Bliss and Eccles were connected?"

"Nothing. But if it's Dickerson this guy was after, he's a worse shot than I ever heard of."

"Why make the bodyguards targets?"

"That's what I want to ask the Greene woman." He got up, rubbing the spot. The hound's-tooth overcoat he had on was missing a few teeth. "Set it up. Today. I get off at eight."

"How'd Dickerson do last night?"

He opened the door to the outer office. "Capacity crowd. But he don't have the stuff he had when the wife was a fan. When no one shot at him they left disappointed."

He went out. I listened to the hallway door hiss shut behind him against the pressure of the pneumatic device. Thinking.

Six

I finished the cigarette and pulled the telephone over and dialed Carol's number. She answered on the third ring.

"Lieutenant Gritch wants to talk to you," I told her, after the preliminaries. "You're better off seeing him at Headquarters. That way you can leave when you want to."

"I already talked to him once. What is it this time?" Her tone was slurred. I'd forgotten she was an alcoholic. I told her about Bliss. After a pause she said, "Ned never mentioned him. I'd know if they ever did business."

"Tell Gritch that."

"You got anything yet?"

"A shadow of a daydream of an idea. I'll let you know. Take a cab to Dearborn."

Next I got the Denver P.I. on the telephone. He said he was still working on the description I'd given him of Henry Bliss. I told him that was all wrapped up and I'd send him a check. Then I called Barry Stackpole.

"That list all right?" he asked.

"A little out of date, according to the cops. I may not need it. Who's on the entertainment desk today?"

"Jed Dutt. I still get my Teacher's, right?"

"If you switch me over to Dutt I'll even throw in a bottle of tonic water."

"Don't be blasphemous." He put me on hold.

"Dutt," announced a rusty old wheeze thirty seconds later.

"My name's Walker," I said. "I'm investigating the attempt on Billy Dickerson's life yesterday. I have a question for you."

"Shoot."

"Very funny," I said.

"Sorry. "

I asked him the question. His answer was the first time I got more than one word out of him. I thanked him and broke the connection. The telephone rang while my hand was still on the receiver. It was the man from the union.

"I'm still working on it," I told him. "No money changed hands today."

He said, "Keep an eye on him. He isn't swallowing it or burying it in the basement. I made some inquiries and found out the house across the street is for rent. Maybe you ought to move in."

"Round-the-clock surveillance costs money."

"Name a figure."

I named one. He said, "Can you move in tomorrow?"

I said that was short notice. He said, "Your retainer buys us that right. Shall I make the rental arrangements?"

"I'll let you know," I said.

I smoked a cigarette, looking at the blonde in the bikini on the calendar on the wall opposite the desk. Then I ground out the stub and made one more call. It took a while. When it was finished I got up and unpegged my hat and coat. Before going out I got the Smith & Wesson out of my top drawer of the desk and checked it for cartridges and snapped the holster onto the back of my belt under my jacket. I hate forcing a case.

Seven

No cops stopped me on my way into the Royal Tower this time, no one was waiting to frisk me when I stepped off the elevator on the third floor. I felt neglected. I rapped on 306.

"What do you want?"

I grinned at Phil. There was no reflection at all in his flat dark eyes. The automatic pistol was a growth in his fist.

"This is for the grown-ups," I said. "Any around?"

"You got a lot of smart mouth."

"That makes one of us."

"Phil, who is it?"

The voice was Martin Cole's. It sounded rushed and breathless.

"That snooper," answered Phil, his eyes still on me.

"Tell him to come back later."

"You heard." The man with the gun smiled without opening his lips, like a cat.

A sudden scuffling noise erupted from inside the room. Someone grunted. A lamp was turned over with a thud, slinging lariats of shadow up one wall. Phil turned his head and I chopped downward with the edge of my left hand, striking his wrist at the break. He cursed and the gun dropped from his grip. When he stooped to catch it I brought my right fist scooping up, catching him on the point of the chin and closing his mouth with a loud clop. I stepped back to give him room to fall. He used it.

I got the automatic out from under his unconscious body and stepped over him holding it in my sore right hand. I'd barked the knuckles on his obelisk jaw. It was a wasted entrance. Nobody was paying me any attention.

Billy Dickerson, naked but for a pair of blue jockey shorts with his pale belly hanging over top, was on his knees on the floor astraddle a scarcely more dapper-looking Martin Cole. The manager's tailored jacket was torn and his neatly styled hair hung cockeyed over his left ear. It was the first I knew he wore a wig. Dickerson was holding a shiny steel straight razor a foot from Cole's throat and Cole had both hands on the singer's wrist trying to keep it there. Dickerson's eyes bulged and his lips were skinned back from long white teeth in a depraved rictus. His breath whistled. Through his own teeth Cole said, "Phil, give me a hand."

Phil wasn't listening. I took two steps forward and swept the butt of the automatic across the base of Dickerson's skull. The singer whimpered and sagged. Falling, the edge of the razor nicked Cole's cheek. It bled.

A floor lamp had been toppled against a chair. I straightened it and adjusted the shade.

"Most people watch television at this time of evening," I said.

The manager paused in the midst of pushing himself free to look at me. Automatically a hand went up and righted his wig. Then he finished rolling the singer's body off his and got up on his knees, listening with head cocked. A drop of blood landed on Dickerson's naked chest with a plop. The manager sat back on his heels,. "He's breathing. You hit him damn hard."

"Pistol-whipping isn't an exact science. What happened?"

"D.T.'s. Bad trip. Maybe a combination of the two. He usually doesn't get this violent. When he does, Phil's usually there to get a grip on him and tie him up till it's over." He glanced toward the man lying in the open doorway. "Jeez, what'd you do, kill him?"

"It'd take more than an uppercut to do that. How long's he been like this?"

"Who, Billy? Couple of years. The last few months, though, he's been getting worse. The drugs pump him up for his performances, the booze brings him back down afterwards. But lately it's been affecting his music."

"Not just lately," I said. "It's been doing that for the past year anyway. That's how long attendance at his concerts has been falling off, according to the entertainment writer I spoke to at the *News.*"

He had picked up his tinted eyeglasses from the floor and was polishing them with a clean corner of the silk handkerchief he had been using to staunch the trickle of blood from his cut cheek. He stopped polishing and put them on. "Your friend's mistaken. We're sold out."

"They came to see if history would repeat itself and someone would make a new try on Dickerson. Just as you hoped they would."

"Explain."

"First get your hands away from your body."

He smiled. The expression reminded me of Phil's cat's-grin. "If I were armed, do you think I'd have wrestled Billy for that razor barehanded?"

"You would have. He's too valuable to kill. Get 'em up."

He raised his hands to shoulder level. I unholstered my .38 and put the nine-millimeter in my topcoat pocket. Go with the weapon you know.

"There was no hit man," I said, "no attempt on your boy's life. The man you intended to get killed got killed. It was going to be Henry Bliss, but in Denver something went wrong and you had to dump him without trumpets. What did he do, find out what you had planned for him and threaten to go to the law?"

He was still smiling. "You're out of it, Walker. If there was no hit man, who killed Ned Eccles?"

"I'm coming to that. You've got a lot of money tied up in Dickerson, but he's depreciating property. I'm guessing, but I'd say a man with your expensive tastes has a lot of debts, maybe to some people it's not advisable to have a lot of debts with. So you figured to squeeze one more good season out of your client and get out from under. Attempted assassination is box office. A body gives it that authentic touch. After disposing of Bliss you shopped around. I looked pretty good. Security isn't my specialty, my reflexes might not be embarrassingly fast. Also I'm single, with no attachments, no one to demand too thorough an investigation into my death. But I turned you down. Ned Eccles wasn't as good. He was married. But his marriage was sour—you'd have found that out through questioning, as keeping secrets was not one of Ned's specialties—and being an experienced shield he'd have been looking for trouble from outside, not from his employers.

"I called Art Cradshaw a little while ago. That was a mistake, Cole, saying he recommended me. He wasted some of my time being evasive, but when he found out I wasn't dunning him for what he owes me he was willing to talk. He remembered especially how pleased you were to learn I have no family."

Dickerson stirred and groaned. His manager ignored him. Cole wasn't smiling now. I went on.

"What'd you do, promise to cut Phil in on the increased revenue, or just pay him a flat fee to ventilate the bodyguard?"

"Now I know you're out of it. If Phil shot him, where's the gun? His is a nine-millimeter. Eccles was shot with a thirty-eight."

"You were right in front of the service elevator. One of you stepped inside and ditched it. Probably Phil, who was more reliable than Dickerson and tall enough to push open one of the panels on top of the car and stash it there. The cops had no reason to look there, because they were after a phantom hit man who made his escape through the back door."

"You're just talking, Walker. None of it's any good."

"The gun is," I said. "I think you have it hidden somewhere in this suite. The cops will find it. They've been sticking too close to you since the shooting for you to have had a chance to get rid of it. Until now, that is. Where are they?"

"I pulled them off."

The voice was new. I jumped and swung around, bringing the gun with me. I was pointing it at Lieutenant Gritch. He was holding his own service revolver at hip level. Phil lay quietly as ever on the floor between us.

"Put it away," Gritch said patiently. "I don't want to add threatening a police officer to the charge of interfering in an official investigation. Too much paperwork."

I leathered the Smith & Wesson. "You pulled them off why?"

"To give Cole and Scabarda here breathing space. I didn't have enough to get a warrant to search the suite. I had a plainclothes detail in the lobby and near the back entrance ready to follow them until they tried to ditch the piece. Imagine my surprise when one of my men called in to say he saw you going up to the third floor."

"You knew?"

He said, "I'm a detective. You private guys forget that sometimes. I had to think who stood the most to gain from two dead bodyguards. What tipped you?"

"Cole's story of what happened downstairs. Ned Eccles wouldn't have stopped a bullet meant for his mother. But it didn't mean anything until you said what you did in my office about Dickerson's fans paying to see him get killed."

"Yeah, that's when it hit me too."

"Couple of Sherlocks, " I said.

And then the muzzle of Gritch's revolver flamed and the report shook the room and if there had been a mirror handy I'd have seen my hair turn white in that instant. The wind of his bullet plucked at my coat. Someone grunted and I turned again and looked at Cole kneeling on the floor, gripping his bloody right wrist in his left and. A small automatic gleamed on the carpet between him and Billy Dickerson, the King of Country Rock.

"Circus shooting," Gritch said, disgusted. "If my captain asks, I was aiming for the chest. I got suspended once for getting fancy. Oh, your client's waiting out in the parking lot, shamus. I was questioning her when the call came in. Couldn't talk her out of going. Three sheets to the wind she's still one tough broad. You'd better see her before she comes up here."

"Yeah," I agreed. "She might kick Cole's head in."

"Guess I'll be able to get that warrant now. You going to be handy for a statement?"

I wrote the address of the shop steward's house in Redford Township on the back of a card and gave it to him. "Don't try to reach me there. I'll be staying in the place across the street for a while starting tomorrow."

"How long?"

"Indefinitely."

"I got a sister-in-law trying to get out of Redford," he said. "I feel sorry for you."

"Like hell you do."

He grinned for the first time since I knew him.

The Prettiest Dead Girl in Detroit

No one sat in the lobby of the Hotel Woodward anymore. The ceiling was too high, the brass balls on the banister posts were too big, the oak paneling on the walls was carved too deep. The dark red crushed-leather chairs and sofa ached to wrap themselves around someone's thighs, and when I stepped through the front door and closed it against an icy gust, the potted fern that occupied the spot on the Persian rug where Theodore Roosevelt had stood to register stirred its dusty fronds like an old man raising his face to the sun. In six months it was all coming down to make room for a ladies' gym.

A geezer with a white moustache growing straight out of his nostrils moved his lips over my ID on the front desk and directed me to Room 212. I climbed a staircase broad enough to roll a rajah's dead elephant down and paused outside an open door with cigarette smoke curling through it. The girl lying on the floor was looking straight at me, but she didn't invite me in. She had learned her lesson the last time. She was a redhead, which I don't guess means much of anything these days, but the red was natural and would look blonde in some lights. She had a tan the shade of good brandy covering her evenly from hairline to pink-polished toenails without a bikini line anywhere. It was the only thing covering her. Her body was slim and sleekly muscled, a runner's body. Her eyes were open and very blue. The dark bruises on her throat where the killer's thumbs had gone were the only blemishes I could see.

The investigation business was the same as ever. All the beautiful women I meet are either married or guilty or dead. There were three men in the room with her, not dead. One was tall and fifty with crisp gray hair to match his suit and very black features carved along the coarse noble lines of a Masai warrior chief. Standing next to him, almost touching him, was a smaller man, fifteen years younger, with dark hair fluffed out on the sides to draw your eyes down from his thinning top to a handlebar moustache someone else trimmed for him and one of those outfits you grin at in magazine ads—plaid jacket over red vest over diamond-patterned sweater over shirt over pink silk scarf with red cherries on it. He looked very white next to the other man. The third man, also white, was very broad across the shoulders, bought his suit in Sears, and combed his hair with a rake. His age had leveled off somewhere between the others'. Guess which one of these men is the hotel dick.

He spotted me first and walked around the body, transferring his cigarette to his lips to take my hand. He had a grip like a rusted bolt. "Amos Walker? Trillen, security officer. I'm the one who called you."

"What seems to be the problem?"

He started a little and looked at me closely. He had gray eyes with all the depth of cigarette foil. "Yeah, I heard you were a comic. The night man, Applegate, gave me your name. You helped him clear up an employee matter a few months back before it got to the papers."

I remembered the case. One of the hops had been letting himself into rooms with a passkey and taking pictures of people who would rather not have had their pictures taken together in hotel rooms.

One night he went into 618 looking to Allen-Funt a city councilman with his male aide and got me.

"This is Charles Lemler," Trillen said. "He's with the mayor's press corps. I'll let him tell it."

"Everyone calls me Chuck. Amos, right?" The moustached man in the noisy outfit grasped the hand Trillen had finished with. Afterward I left it out to dry. "The woman was here when we checked in, just as you see her. The clerk offered to move Mr. De Wolfe to another room before the police got here, but it's going to get out anyway that he registered the day a dead body turned up in the hotel. Trillen suggested you by way of putting some kind of face on this before we call in the authorities."

"Mr. De Wolfe?"

"I'm sorry. Clinton De Wolfe, Amos Walker."

The tall black man standing with his back to the body inclined his head a tenth of an inch in my direction. Well, I'd had my hand wrung enough for one morning.

"Mr. De Wolfe is a former Chicago bank officer," Chuck Lemler explained. "He's the mayor's choice for city controller here."

"Ah."

" 'Ah' means what?" snapped De Wolfe.

"That my mouth is too big for my brain. Sorry. Can I look at the body?"

They made room for me. I checked the face and forehead for bruises and the hair for clotting, found nothing like that, spread my fingers to measure the marks on her neck. The spread was normal and while the dark spots were bigger than my thumbtips they weren't the work of an escaped orangutan or Bigfoot. It takes less strength to strangle a healthy woman than you might think. There was some darkening along her left thigh and under her fingernails. I did a couple of ungallant things with the body and then stood up. My hands felt colder for the contact with her skin.

"Cover her."

"You don't like 'em boned?" asked Trillen.

"Trillen, for God's sake!" Lemler's moustache twisted.

"Yeah, yeah." The dick strolled into another room and came back carrying a hotel bedspread under one arm. I took an end and we covered the body. I asked if anyone knew her.

Trillen shook his shaggy head and squashed out his butt in a glass ashtray atop the television set. Well, he'd hear about that from someone. "Just another night rental. I hustle 'em out the back door and they come in again through the side and prowl the bar for fresh meat. This one's new."

"This isn't just another fifty-a-pop career girl," I said. "It takes income to maintain an all-over tan in Michigan in November and the body stinks exclusive health club. Also she didn't die here, or if she did someone moved her. She was lying on that thigh until not too long ago."

"I'd heard politics were rotten in this town," said DeWolfe.

"That's just the sort of knee-jerk assumption we've been fighting for years," Lemler snapped. To me: "There's some opposition to Mr. De Wolfe's choice as controller. But they wouldn't go this far."

"You mean trash a hooker and stash the body in his suite to stir up bad press. It's been done." I shook a Winston out of my pack but stopped short of lighting it. Why later. "My consulting fee's two-fifty, same as my day rate." Lemler nodded. I said, "There's a lieutenant in Homicide named Alderdyce. If you ask him to sit on it he'll do it till it sprouts feathers. But only if you ask him."

De Wolfe glared. "That's your professional advice? Call the police?"

"Not the police. John Alderdyce."

"It's the same thing."

"I just got through telling you it isn't."

Lemler said, "We'll think about it."

I said, "You'll do it. Or I will. Maybe this is common practice at the City-County Building, but on Woodward Avenue it's failure to report a homicide. I have a license to stand in front of."

Trillen said, "Tell him to keep the name of the hotel out of it too."

"That's for the newspapers to decide when it breaks. And whether you advertise with them heavily enough to make it worth deciding."

"Will you stay on the case regardless?" Lemler asked.

"The sooner this gets squared away the better for us, but we can't throw the city's weight behind an ordinary homicide investigation without drawing flies."

"I'll stay as long as the two-fifty holds out. Or until Alderdyce orders me off it," I added.

Lemler produced a checkbook from an inside pocket and began writing. "Will a thousand buy a week of your services?"

"Four days. Not counting expenses."

"The mayor will howl."

"Tell him to make his new raise retroactive to August instead of July."

Trillen called the number I gave him for Alderdyce from downstairs. I was smoking my cigarette in the hall outside when they came, the lieutenant towing a black photographer with a beard like a shotgun pattern and a pale lab man with a shrinking hairline and a young Oriental carrying a black metal case. Alderdyce stopped in front of me. He's my generation, built heavy from the waist up, with facial features hacked out of a charred tree stump blindfolded.

"You didn't burn any tobacco in there?" he demanded. I shook my head. "Thank Christ for small miracles." The group swept in past me. I killed my stub in a steel wall caddy and brought up the rear.

Chuck Lemler broke off a conversation with Clinton De Wolfe to greet the newcomers. But Trillen intercepted Alderdyce and their clasped hands quivered grip for grip until the hotel dick surrendered. Alderdyce wasn't even looking at him. "The body was covered like that when it was found?"

Trillen said no. The lieutenant barked at the lab man to take some fiber samples from the blanket and subtract them from whatever else was found on the corpse. He lifted one corner of the blanket.

"Damn."

"Jesus," said the photographer, and took a picture.

I said, "Yeah."

Alderdyce flipped aside the blanket. "Bag her hands," he told the lab man. "There's matter under her fingernails."

"Blood and skin," I said. "She branded somebody."

He looked at me. "I guess you better feed me all of it."

"Strangulation maybe," said the young Oriental, before I could speak. He was down on one knee beside the body with his case open on the floor, prying one of the dead eyelids farther open with a thumb in a surgical glove. "Maybe OD. I'll say what when I get her open."

"No tracks," said Alderdyce, glancing at her wrists and legs.

I said, "There's scar tissue between her toes. I checked."

"Damn nice of you to think to call us in, Walker."

I let that one drift.

"Get some Polaroids," Alderdyce told the photographer. "Last time the shots were three days coming back from the lab." He stopped looking at the body and pointed at the used ashtray. "Careful with that butt. The girl's wearing lipstick. It isn't."

"Uh, that's mine," said Trillen.

The lieutenant swore.

The rest was routine. Under questioning Trillen revealed that the suite had been cleaned the afternoon before and that no one had been inside between then and when the body was found. There were enough passkeys floating around and keys that had gone off with former guests to spoil that angle, and while Lemler maintained that De Wolfe's arrival and the number of his suite had been kept confidential, Trillen admitted that there was no standing on the staff grapevine. Meanwhile the lab man quartered the carpet for stray paperclips, and the photographer, having traded the camera he'd been using for another strung around his neck, took more pictures of the body and laid them on the telephone stand to finish developing. I palmed a good one and let myself out while Alderdyce was politely grilling De Wolfe.

Two

Barry Stackpole came out of the YMCA showers scrubbing his sandy hair with a towel, hesitated when he saw me by the lockers, then grinned and lowered the towel to cover his lower body modestly. Only it wasn't his nakedness that embarrassed him, just his Dutch leg. I said, "Doesn't that warp or something?"

He shook his head, reaching for his pants. "Fiberglass. I could've used you out on that handball court a few minutes ago."

"No, you couldn't. I was watching you."

I've known Barry since we shared a shell crater in Cambodia, years before he started his column on organized crime for the Detroit *News* and got his leg and two fingers blown off for his syntax. Someone at the paper had told me I'd find him creaming a Mob attorney on the courts. I held the Polaroid I'd swiped in front of his face while he was tying his shoes. He whistled. "Actress?"

"Prostitute," I said. "Maybe. Know her?"

"Not on my salary. Who squiffed her?"

"Why I'm here. Can you float it among your friends on the well-known Street, put a name to the face? It wouldn't have stayed so pretty very long if she wasn't connected."

He finished drawing on his shirt and put the picture in the breast pocket. "User?"

"Yeah. Either someone throttled her unconscious and then shot too much stuff to her or shot too much stuff to her and couldn't wait. While you're at it, feed Clinton De Wolfe to your personal computer and see what it belches out."

"I know that name."

"If you do you heard it from your guy on city government. He'll be fine-tuning the books if the mayor gets his way."

"That isn't it. When I remember what it was I'll get back to you." He took down a bottle of mouthwash from the shelf in his locker and unscrewed the cap. "How rich does this little errand stand to make me?"

"A century, if I like what I hear, Otherwise seventy-five."

"Century either way. Plus a fifth of Jack Daniel's."

"I thought you were on the wagon."

"It's a cold dry ride." He hoisted the mouthwash. "Cold steel."

"Hot lead," I returned. The joke toast was as old as the last Tet offensive and the stuff in the bottle smelled like rye. I left him.

Three

My office waiting room was full of no customers. I unlocked the door to the brain trust, forward-passed a sheaf of advertising circulars I found under the mail slot to the wastebasket, pegged my hat and coat, and set the swivel behind the desk to squeaking while I broke the scotch out of the deep drawer. There was frost on the window, frost on my soul. I guessed Barry had found my breath sweet enough not to need help. As the warmth crawled through my veins I dialed my service. John Alderdyce had tried to reach me twice. I knew why. I asked the girl to hold any further calls from him and thumbed down the plunger and tried another number from memory. A West Indies accent answered on the third ring, cool and female.

"Iris, this is Amos."

"Amos who?"

"It's a funny hooker," I said dryly. "I'm trying to identify a lady who might have been in your line. Five-six and a hundred and ten, red and blue, Miami tan, about thirty. She showed up dead in a suite in the Woodward this morning. Drugs and strangulation. She wasn't a stranger to the drugs."

"Sounds a little rich for the street."

"You get around."

"In Blacktown. You're talking Grosse-Pointe chic. Try the escort services."

"The real ones or the fronts?"

"There's a difference?"

"That's all you can tell me, huh."

"Every one of us don't know everyone else," she retorted, her class slipping. "Amos?"

I'd started to peg the receiver. I raised it again and said yeah. After a pause she said, "I'm going home."

"Home where?"

"Home where. Home the island. I'm going back to live with my mother."

"I'm glad," I said after a moment. "It's what you've been wanting."

"That's all? I thought maybe you'd try to talk me out of it."

"I don't have any hold on you, Iris."

"No. I guess you don't."

"Have a good flight." I was speaking into a dead line.

I looked at the calendar on the wall across from my framed investigator's license. Then I looked at a pigeon shivering alone on the ledge of the apartment house facing my building. Then I looked at the calendar again to see what the date was. I winched the Yellow Pages out of the top drawer and looked up Escorts.

I tried the display advertisements first and got three possibles. Then I tried the cheaper listings and lucked out on the first call.

"I need an escort for a business party Friday night," I told the woman who answered, by rote. "What I'm interested in is a specific redhead I saw with a friend of mine in the restaurant of the Hotel Woodward recently. I didn't get her name but I think she's with your service." I described her.

"That sounds like Myra Langan," said the woman. "But she doesn't work here anymore."

"Did she resign?"

"I'm not at liberty to say."

"That means she was fired."

"I'm not—"

"Can I talk to you about her in person? It's important."

"We have another redhead," she started to say. I told her I'd pay for her time. She hesitated, then said, "Our regular escort fee is a hundred dollars." I said that sounded fair and agreed to meet her in the office at three. "Ask for Linda."

It was just past noon. I thought about the woman's voice. She sounded pleasant and young. You can't always get the accent you want. I skipped lunch and drove to a downtown theater where an old Robert Mitchum detective film was playing in revival. I took notes. In the lobby afterward I used the pay telephone to call Barry Stackpole's private number at the *News*.

"Nobody I showed the picture to knows her from Jane Fonda," he told me. "Could be I'm working the wrong level. All the *capos* are browning their bellies at Cannes this time of year."

"Try Myra Langan. I've got an appointment today with a woman she worked with at a legit floss rental firm." I named the place.

"Our guy on cophouse might turn something. It means bringing him in."

"Cut the best deal you can." I took the instrument away from my ear.

"Don't you want to hear what I found out about Clinton De Wolfe?"

I paused. "I'm on pins and noodles."

"I get an exclusive when this breaks, right?"

"Feed it to me. "

"I finally remembered where I'd heard the name and hooked a snitch," he said. "De Wolfe is on the books as having resigned his vice-presidency at a Chicago bank in September. The dope is he was forced out for making unsecured loans to a Mob subsidiary in Evanston and accepting repayment in cash skimmed from the tables in Vegas."

I looked at a stiff face reflected in the telephone's shiny steel cradle. "Laundering?"

"Yeah. They let him quit to duck bad press. Good?"

"Listen, I'm on my way to your office with a C-note and a fifth of JD. Have that picture ready, okay?"

"Bring a glass for yourself." He broke the connection.

Four

It was a quick stop and a quicker drink. From there I drove down-river to a low yellow brick building between a beauty salon and a hairpiece emporium with the escort firm's name etched in elegant script across the front. Inside was an office decorated like a living room with a white shag rug and ivory curtains and a lot of blond furniture, including a tall occasional table with turned legs and a glass top, but it didn't fool me. I know a desk when I see one. A brunette with her hair piled atop her head in blue waves and the kind of cheeks girls used to have their back teeth hauled out to get sat behind it wearing a black dress with a scoop neck and pearl buttons in her ears. I took off my hat and asked for Linda.

"You're Mr. Walker?" I said I was. "I'm Linda."

I glanced around. The room took up the entire ground floor and we were the only ones in it. "Who was I supposed to ask?"

"I wanted to get a look at you. In this business we have to go out with whoever has the price and no bloodstains on his necktie. When I get the chance to choose I leap on it. Are you a daylighter or a sun-downer?" I must have looked as stupid as I felt, because she said, "A sundowner waits for darkness before he'll take a drink. It's dark in England."

"My father's family was English."

She smiled and rose. "I'll get my coat and purse."

We went to a place down the street with a blue neon cocktail glass on the roof and took a booth upholstered in red vinyl around a table the size of a hubcap. She ordered something green. I took scotch and when the waitress left I slid the Polaroid shot I had gotten back from Barry across the table. Linda's nostrils whitened when she glanced down at it. Then she looked at me:

"You're not a policeman. Your eyes are too gentle."

"I'm a private investigator." I tapped the picture. "Myra Langan?"

"It's her. Are you looking for her murderer?"

"Who said murderer?"

"She was the kind of a girl who would wind up murdered or suicided. Did she kill herself?"

"Not unless she found a way to strangle herself bare-handed. What kind of a girl is the kind that would wind up murdered or suicided?"

She sipped her drink and set it down. After a beat I passed her two fifties. With what I'd given Barry, that left me just fifty from the first day of my retainer. I was on the wrong end of the information business.

"Myra got fired for her action on the side," said Linda, snapping shut her purse. "The police keep a tight eye on the escort business for just that. It was can her or risk a raid."

"Who snitched on her?"

"Another girl, Susan. They were at the same party and Susan overheard Myra discussing terms with her escort. Myra tried to cut her in but she wasn't having any."

"Myra got canned on just her word?"

"The boss lady ran a check. Her brother's a retired cop. He interviewed some of Myra's regular customers. The same pimp put six of them on her scent."

"What'd he interview them with, a Louisville Slugger?"

"He's retired like I said." She licked a drop off the end of her swiz-zle stick, eyeing me. "Married?"

"Not recently. Was she using when she worked for the firm?"

"You mean drugs? She couldn't have been. A complete physical is part of the screening process for new employees."

"Could've happened after she was hired. She worked there how long?"

"She was there when I came. A year, maybe. You think the pimp turned her on to get a handle on her?"

"It's not new. Looks like hers run high in executive circles. He have a name?"

"Probably. Talk to Max Montemarano. That's the boss lady's brother. He's a day guard at Detroit Bank and Trust. The main branch."

I got up and left money on the table for the drinks.

"Thanks. I have to see a man."

"Me, too." She swung a mile of silk-paved leg out from under the table. "What do you do when you're not detecting?"

I watched her stand up. Some women know how to get out of a booth. I asked her if she'd ever lived on an island.

"What? No."

"Okay, thanks again."

On my way out a man in a blue suit seated near the door looked from me to the woman in the black dress standing by the booth and then back to me. I agreed with him.

Five

I called the bank from an open-air booth outside a service station. A receptionist got me Montemarano, who explained in a hard fat man's voice that his shift didn't change for another hour but agreed to stop by my office on his way home for a quick fifty. The expenses on this one had just caught up with my fee.

A kid in a plaid overcoat stood in the foyer of my building reading the sign on the building super's door. The sign read MANAGER. He was still studying when I reached the second-floor landing. He might as well have worn a uniform.

I found Lieutenant John Alderdyce sitting on the bench in my waiting room learning about the Man of some other Year from a copy of *Time* he'd unstuck from the coffee table. He had on a tan jacket and a red knit tie over a champagne-colored shirt. Since I knew him he'd dressed from nowhere closer to the street than J. L. Hudson's second floor. "This year it's a computer," he said, flicking his fingers at the photograph on the cover. "What do you think about a machine making the cover of *Time?*"

"Electricity's cheap. You and I run on tobacco and alcohol."

I unlocked the inner office door. "Someone should enroll your boy in the lobby in a remedial reading course."

"He's on loan from the commissioner's office. His Police Positive has an ivory handle." He got up and followed me inside, where I shed my outerwear and sat down and got an old bill from under the desk blotter and pretended to check the arithmetic. He thumped his hand down on the desk, palm up. "The photog used up a twelve-pack of Polaroid film at the Woodward. He wound up with eleven pictures."

I started to reach for my inside breast pocket, then remembered I'd left the picture of Myra Langan on the table where I'd had drinks with Linda. "I'll stand the department to a new pack tomorrow."

"You wouldn't be prowling around in an open homicide investigation," he said. "Not you."

"It happens we're both working for the city this one time. Check with Lemler."

"No thanks. Every time I look at that guy's clothes and shut my eyes I see spots. What'd you turn?"

I watched him. He had sad eyes. Cops do, and it doesn't mean anything more than a croc's smile. Finally I said, "Her name was Myra Langan. She worked for an escort service downtown till they booted her for soliciting." I told him which service and gave him Linda's name. I didn't mention Max Montemarano or the pimp. It weighed light without them and Alderdyce saw it. He said, "I guess you stopped here on your way to Headquarters."

"More or less."

"More less than more. You passed Headquarters on your way here."

"I wanted to see if I had customers. "

"No good. Go again."

"I'm a small guy in a small business, John. I don't have your resources."

"Resources. The redhead—Myra?—rode the springs with some guy not long before she was killed, the M.E. said. He took a smear and the type matches the blood we found under her fingernails. She was alive until four this morning. I've got men knocking on doors in the hotel looking for busted lamps and shaving cuts that don't fit a razor and scouting up the night staff, which by now is scattered between here and Ann Arbor. It's a big hotel, Walker. It has a big staff and lots of rooms. If I could put the squad on it I'd have the answers

I need in an hour. But police reporters notice when the squad's missing and start asking questions. I've got Junior downstairs and one other detective and two uniforms borrowed from Traffic. I can't even get priority at the lab because someone who knows the number of one of this town's three TV stations might be looking."

He stuck his brutal face inches from mine. "Those are my resources, Walker. Four men, and the mayor's dresser asking me every five minutes when I'm going to arrest someone. You're a detective. Does it look to a detective like I need a keyholer playing Go Fish with me too?"

"I'm waiting to hear it," I said.

"Hear what?"

"'Get off my foot or I'll jerk your license.'"

Alderdyce lifted weights when he wasn't sifting leads. He gave the desk a shove and it struck me in the solar plexus and I rolled backward on squealing casters and came to a rest pinned against the window. He leaned on the desk.

"We've never mixed it up, you and me," he said. "You'd lose."

We stayed like that for a long moment, he resting his weight on the desk, I trying to breathe with the edge pressing my sternum and cold from the window glass soaking clammily through my jacket and shirt to my back. Then he pushed off and turned around and left. The door drifted shut against the pressure of the pneumatic closer.

John and I had played together as kids, a million years ago.

Max Montemarano found me straightening the furniture in the office a few minutes later. He wasn't fat at all, just large and slope-shouldered with a civilian overcoat over his gray guard's uniform and a visored cap on the back of his white head. His face was broad and ruddy, and burst blood vessels etched purple tributaries on his cheeks. "Colder'n a witch's tit," he said by way of greeting.

I blew dust out of a pair of pony glasses and filled them with scotch. He managed to snatch one up without spilling anything, lifted it in a sort of toast, and knocked it back the way they used to do in westerns. When the glass came down empty I poked a fifty-dollar bill into it. "Myra Langan," I said.

He looked down at the bill without touching it. "What about her?"

"You followed up another girl's complaint about her for your sister. She had a pimp. He had a name."

He set the glass down on the desk and drew himself up, squaring his visor. "I'm not a cop anymore. She ain't working for my sister now. I never dipped a finger in twenty-three years on the force and I ain't about to start now."

I said, "She's dead. There's a better than even chance her pimp killed her or knows who did."

He hesitated. I uncapped the bottle again and moved it toward his glass. He scooped out the bill and straightened it between his fingers and folded it and put it in his breast pocket and snapped the flap shut. I poured. He put down half.

"He was a regular customer of Myra's until he stopped coming in," he said. "That was about the time the first john was approached." A brow got knitted. "Wilson. Jim Wilson."

"Fat, short, tall, skinny, black, white, what?"

"White. Not fat. Thick like me. He had the widest shoulders for his height of any man I ever seen. Wider than yours. Wore cheap suits."

I was lighting a Winston. I avoided burning any fingers putting out the flame. "Shaggy head? A smoker?"

"Like a stack at the River Rouge plant. And if the guy combed his hair at all—"

I came around the desk and aimed him toward the door. "Thanks for coming in."

"My drink."

I handed him the glass and the bottle and held the door. "Happy Thanksgiving."

After the outer door closed on Montemarano I made a call and then unlocked the top drawer of the desk, checked my Smith & Wesson for cartridges, and clipped the holster to my belt under the tail of my jacket. It was heavier than a rabbit's foot but felt just as good.

Six

The same geezer was sorting mail into the pigeonholes behind the desk at the Woodward when I strode past heading for the stairs. The letters might have come Pony Express. I knocked at 212 and Trillen opened the door. The hotel dick was alone in the suite with a chalk outline on the carpet where the dead girl had been lying. I asked him where Chuck Lemler and Clinton De Wolfe were.

"Coming. De Wolfe changed hotels. What's it about?"

I walked around, poking my head into the other rooms. The air smelled of cigarettes and there were three butts in the ashtray on the television set, all Trillen's brand. He'd been waiting there since taking my call. "Applegate offered me a job nightside," I said. "The pay stunk. Head of security pay any better?"

"Not much. It ain't open anyway."

"Not yet."

De Wolfe and Lemler arrived fifteen minutes later. The black controller-to-be looked tall and gaunt in a dark overcoat and gray scarf. Lemler had on a horse blanket and one black glove and the other in his fist posing as a riding crop.

"I hope you have something," Lemler demanded. "The mayor wants to avoid identifying Mr. De Wolfe with this hotel any more than is absolutely necessary."

"I agree. It's bad enough he's identified with his old bank."

De Wolfe measured me out some of his icy glare.

I said, "You took early retirement. The board of directors was all for it. If the stockholders found out you'd been using bank funds to launder Mob money they'd clear the executive offices."

"You're drunk!" Lemler was paler than usual.

"It was a frame," said De Wolfe. "A good vice-president makes enemies. It was the only way they could get rid of me."

"It's probably true or you would've let it go to court," I said. "But it rules out the theory that your opponents here dumped a body in your suite to embarrass you. They have access to my information; the publicity from that Mob tie-in alone would have been enough to take you out of the running for city office. They didn't have to commit murder too." I turned to Lemler. "Chuck, I owe you five hundred from the retainer you gave me. I spent two-fifty. I'll eat the price of the whisky. "

"I didn't pay you to fork up dirt on my employer's choice for controller." He was twisting his glove.

"No, you paid me to find out who killed Myra Langan. That was the name of the murdered girl.

"Someone thought she was too pretty to throw away on old men at dinner parties in Birmingham and Grosse Pointe," I went on. "This someone started seeing her as a customer of the escort service she worked for and when he had her confidence he hooked her on drugs to make her easier to steer. He was in a line of work that put him in contact with useful people on every level. When it came time to collect for the stuff he was supplying her, he put her to work. Some men would pay two hundred dollars for twenty minutes with a girl like Myra. For a time it was sweet. But one night something tilted, as things will in business relationships of that nature, and she became a liability. As her pimp he was used to favors other than money; he picked an intimate moment to strangle her senseless and then load her with enough dope to send her over. It would look like accidental death or suicide. Only he hadn't counted on her throat showing the bruises his fingers made after death. He'd forgotten how strong his hands were."

It was warm in the room, but none of us who were wearing overcoats had moved to take his off. Trillen, wearing the same baggy gray suit I had met him in, hadn't stirred at all. I put my hands in the pockets of my coat and said, "But pimps are nothing if not resourceful. It happened that a political big gun was stopping at the hotel later that morning. If her body were found in his suite it would change the whole complexion of the investigation. This particular pimp had access to the service elevator and the authority to see to it that all the employees that might be prowling the halls at four in the morning were in another part of the hotel when he moved the corpse. The bare chance that a stray guest might spot him was worth taking. Bringing in a P.I. later to muck things up worse didn't hurt.

"How's the back, Wilson?" I asked Trillen. "You ought to get iodine on those scratches before they infect."

The hotel dick's mouth smiled. "You're just stirring ashes. No proof."

"Applegate, the night man, will remember you were in the hotel this morning hours before your shift started. Whatever excuse you made won't stand. You're wearing Myra's marks and I spoke to a man today who will identify you as her pimp. Take a fellow sleuth's advice and plead guilty to second-degree. The city will want to get this one under glass in a hurry. Am I right, Chuck?"

"I'll advise the mayor," said Lemler. He and De Wolfe were staring at Trillen, who was moving his huge shoulders around under his jacket. The dick said: "I didn't hook her. She was shooting between her toes when I met her. Whatever croaker gave her the nod at the escort place wasn't thorough. It was business all the way with us; I got her the stuff, she wiggled her tail at conventions and sometimes for me."

"What was she doing, moonlighting on you?" I asked.

"That wouldn't have been so bad, but she started doing it here where I work. I like this job and I busted my butt to get it. I left something here last night and when I came in for it I found her working the bar. She tried to sugar me out of my mad in one-ten. I went crazy in the middle of it. I thought she was dead. I OD'd her to make it look like an accident, but then the bruises started to show. Well…" He put a hand behind his back as if to stretch and brought it around with a gun in it.

"Let it go."

Trillen swung toward the new voice, bringing the gun with him. John Alderdyce, standing in the open door to the hallway, crouched with his .38 stretched out in front of him in both hands. The hotel man dropped his weapon and threw his palms into the air.

"Okay," called the lieutenant.

The kid in the plaid overcoat entered from the bedroom with his gun drawn. He holstered it, frisked Trillen against a wall, cuffed him, and started droning from a printed card he carried in his shirt pocket.

"Fire escape," explained Alderdyce, tucking away his own gun. "Junior was still in your building when Montemarano came out. We questioned him. I figured you'd come straight here. You should have called me."

"I had to earn my fee first," I said.

"You cut it fine."

"Not so fine." I pulled my right hand out of my coat pocket wrapped around the butt of the Smith & Wesson and returned it to its holster.

We shook hands.

De Wolf said, "Lieutenant, may I go now? I just have time to book the evening flight back to Chicago."

Lemler was standing by the window with his face on the floor. I went over there. "We didn't know about De Wolfe." he said.

"I believe you. Look on it as a break. The opposition would have run it up the nearest flagpole. Everybody crapped out on this one. The mayor lost an appointee, De Wolfe lost a good job, Trillen's out the next ten to twenty, and Myra Langan's behind one life. She was too pretty to live."

"You're the only one better off than he was this morning," Lemler said.

I looked out the window. My lone pigeon or one like it had followed me there and was perched on the ledge between gimcracks, looking cold and dirty and miserable and like the only pigeon in the whole world.

"Yeah, I'm way ahead."

Blond and Blue

Ernest Krell's aversion to windows was a legend in the investigation business. It was a trademark, like his gunmetal tie clasp made from a piece of shrapnel the army surgeons had pried out of his hip in Seoul and his passion for black suits with discreet patterns to break up their severity. During his seventeen years with the Secret Service he had spent so many public hours warning presidential candidates' wives away from windows that when it came time to open his own detective agency he dug into his wife's inheritance to throw up a building that didn't have any. Narrow vertical slits set eight feet apart let light into a black marble edifice that looked like a blank domino from anywhere along the Detroit river.

A receptionist with blue stones in her ears and that silver complexion that comes free with fluorescent lights took my hat and left me alone in Krell's office, a bowling alley of a room carpeted in black and brown and containing oak-and-leather chairs and an antique desk in front of a huge Miró landscape, lots of blues and reds, to make up for the lack of a window. The walls were painted two shades of cinnamon, darker on the desk side of the office to keep customers where they belonged. A lot of framed citations, Krell's license, and a square black-on-white sign reading RELIANCE—*"Courtesy, Efficiency, Confidentiality"* took care of the bare spots.

There were no ashtrays, so I took a seat near a potted fern and lit a cigarette, tipping my ashes into the pot. After five puffs the man himself came in through a side door and scowled at the curling smoke and then at me and said, "There's no smoking in this building."

"I didn't see any signs," I said.

"You don't see any ashtrays either." He ran a hand under the edge of the desk. A second later, the silver-skinned receptionist came in carrying an ashtray made just for putting out smokes in and I did that. I couldn't decide if it was the way he had pushed the button or if I just had the look of a guy that would light up in the boss's office. When she left carrying my squashed butt the man extended his hand and I rose to take it. His grip was cool and firm and as personal as a haberdasher's smile.

"Good to meet you, Walker. I don't think I've had the pleasure."

"This is the first time I've gotten any higher than the fourth floor," I said.

Krell chuckled meaninglessly. He was six-three and two hundred, a large pale man with black hair that looked dyed and wrinkles around his eyes and mouth from years of squinting into the sun looking for riflemen on rooftops. It was orange today, orange stripes on his black suit and jaunty orange sunbursts on his silk tie to pick it up. It softened the overall effect of his person like a bright ribbon tied to a buffalo's tail made you forget he was standing on your foot. The famous tie clasp was in place.

He waved me back into my chair but remained upright at parade rest with his hands folded behind him. "I spent last night reading the files on the cases you assisted us with," he said. "Despite the fact that you're anything but the Reliance type"—his gaze lit on my polyester gabardine—"you show a certain efficiency I admire. Also you spend more time and effort on each client than a Reliance operative could afford."

"You can do that when they only come into your office one at a time," I volunteered.

"Yes." He let the word melt on his tongue, then pressed on. "The reason I asked you to come down today, we have a client who might best benefit from your rather unorthodox method. A delicate case and a highly emotional one. Frankly, I'd have referred her to another agency had she not come recommended by one of our most valued clients."

"She?"

"You'll meet her in a moment. It's a missing persons situation, which I believe is your specialty. Her son's been kidnapped."

"That's the FBI's specialty."

"Only in cases where ransom is demanded. On the statutes it's abduction, which would make it a police matter except that her ex-husband is the suspected culprit. The authorities consider that a domestic problem and approach it accordingly."

"Meaning it gets spiked along with the butcher's wife who threw a side of pork at her husband," I said. "'How old is the boy?'"

"Seven." He quarter-turned toward the desk and drew a type-written sheet from a folder lying open on top. "Blond and blue, about four feet tall leaning to pudgy, last seen April third wearing a blue-and-white striped T-shirt, red corduroy shorts, and dirty white sneakers. Answers to Tommy. One minute he was playing with a toy truck in the front yard of his mother's home in Austin, Texas, and the next there was just the truck. Neighbor thought he saw him on the passenger's side of a low red sports car going around the corner. The ex-husband owns a red Corvette."

"That's April third this year?" I asked. It was now early May.

"I know it's a long time. She's been to all the authorities here and in Texas."

"Why here?"

"A relative of the mother's is sure she saw the father at the Tel-Twelve Mall in Southfield three weeks ago. She flew in right after. Staying at the relative's place there."

"What makes it too hot to touch?"

He stroked the edge of the sheet with a meaty thumb, making a noise like a cricket. "The ex-husband is an executive with a finance corporation I sometimes do business with. If it gets out I'm investigating one of its employees—"

"Last stop for the money train," I finished. "What's to investigate? She should've gone back to court to start, put the sheriffs on his neck."

"His neck is gone and so is he. He took a leave of absence from his company, closed out his apartment in Austin, and vanished, boy and all. He probably had all his bags packed in the Corvette's trunk when he picked up Tommy and just kept driving. It's all here." He put the sheet back inside the folder and handed the works to me.

It ran just five pages, triple-spaced and written in Reliance's terse patented preliminary-report language, but on plain paper without the distinctive letterhead. Very little of it was for me. The ex-husband's name was Frank Corcoran. He was a house investments counselor for Great Western Loans and Credit, with branch offices in seventeen cities west of the Mississippi. There were two numbers to call for information there. The name and number of the witness who had seen his car at the time of the boy's disappearance were there too, along with the 'Vette's serial number and license plate. It was long gone by now or the cops in Austin or Detroit would have had it in on a BOL weeks ago. I folded the report into quarters anyway and put it in a pocket and gave back the empty folder. "Can I talk to the mother?"

"Of course. She's in the other office."

I followed him through the side door into a room separate from the one where the receptionist sat, a chamber half the size of Krell's decorated in muted warm colors and containing a row of chairs with circular backs, like the room in a funeral home where the family receives visitors. "Charlotte Corcoran, Amos Walker," said Krell.

The woman seated on the end chair raised a sunken face to look at me. Her jaw was too long to be pretty, but it had been an attractive face before she started losing weight, the bones sculpted, not sharp like now, the forehead high and broad instead of jutting and hollow at the sides. The little bit of lipstick she wore might have been painted on the corpse in that same funeral home. Her hair was blond and tied back loosely with wisps of gray springing loose around her ears. Her dress was just a dress and her bare angular legs ended in bony feet thrust into low-heeled shoes a size too large for her. She was smoking a cigarette with a white filter tip. I peered through the haze at Krell, who moved a shoulder and then flipped a wall switch that started a fan humming somewhere in the woodwork. The smoke stirred and began twisting toward a remote corner of the ceiling. I got out a Winston and sent some of my own after it.

"My boy Tommy turned seven last week," Charlotte Corcoran told the wall across from her. "It's the first birthday I missed."

Her speech had an east Texas twang. I twirled another chair to face hers and sat down. The connecting door clicked shut discreetly behind Krell. It was the only noise he made exiting. "Tell me about your husband," I said.

She snicked some ash into a tray on the chair next to her and looked at me. Seeing me now. "I could call him a monster. I'd be lying. Before this the worst thing he did was to call a half hour before supper to say he was working late. He did that a lot; it's part of why I divorced him. That's old news. I want my son back."

"What'd the police in Austin say?"

"They acted concerned until I told them he'd been kidnapped by his father. Then they lost interest. They said they'd put Tommy's picture on the bulletin board in every precinct, and maybe they did. They didn't give it to the newspapers or TV the way they do when a child's just plain missing. I got the same swirl of no action from the police here. Kidnapping's okay between relatives, I guess." She spat smoke.

"Skipping state lines should've landed it in the feds' lap," I said.

"I called the Houston office of the FBI. They were polite. They test high on polite. They said they'd get it on the wire. I never saw any of them."

"So far as you know."

It was lost on her. She mashed out her butt, leaving some lipstick smeared on the end. "I spent plenty of time at Police Headquarters here and back home," she said. "They showed me the door nice as you please, but they showed me the door. They wouldn't tell me what they'd found out."

"That should have told you right there."

Her expression changed. "Can you find them, Mr.—I've forgotten."

"Walker," I said. "A lot rests on whether they're still here. And if they were ever here to begin with."

"Frank was. My cousin Millie doesn't make mistakes."

"That's Millicent Arnold, the relative you're staying with?" She nodded. "I'll need a picture of Tommy and one of Mr. Corcoran."

"This should do it." From her purse she drew a 5x7 bureau shot and gave it to me. "I took it last summer on a trip to Corpus Christi. Tommy's grown several inches since. But his face hasn't changed."

I looked at the man with dark curly hair and a towheaded boy standing in swim trunks on a yellow beach with blue ocean behind them. "His father didn't get that build lifting telephone receivers."

"He worked out at a gym near his office. He was a member."

I pocketed the photograph next to the Reliance report and stood up. "I'll be in touch."

"I'll be in."

Krell was on the intercom to his receptionist when I reentered his office. I waited until he finished making his lunch reservation, then:

"How much of a boost can I expect from Reliance on this one?"

"You already have it," he said. "The situation is—"

"Delicate, yeah. I'll take my full fee, then. Three days to start."

"What happened to professional courtesy?"

"It went out of style, same as the amateur kind. What about it? You're soaking her five bills per day now."

"Four-fifty." He adjusted his tie clasp. "I'll have Mrs. Marble draw you a check."

"Your receptionist has access to company funds?"

"She's proven herself worthy of my trust."

I didn't say it. My bank balance was stuck to the sidewalk as it was.

Two

The report had Mrs. Corcoran in contact with a Sergeant Grandy in General Service, missing persons detail. I deposited half of the Reliance check at my bank, hanging on to the rest for expenses, and drove down to Police Headquarters, where a uniform escorted me to a pasteboard desk with a bald head behind it. Grandy had an egg salad sandwich in one hand and a Styrofoam cup of coffee in the other and was using a blank arrest form for a placemat. He wore a checked sportcoat and a moustache healthy enough to have sucked all the hair from his scalp.

"Corcoran, yeah," he said, after reading my card and hearing my business. "It's in the works. You got to realize it don't get the same priority as a little boy lost. I mean, somebody's feeding him."

"Turn anything yet?"

"We got the boy's picture and the father's description out."

"That's what you've done. What've you got?"

He flicked a piece of egg salad off his lapel. "What I got is two Grosse Pointe runaways to chase down and a four-year-old girl missing from an apartment on Watson I'll be handing to Homicide soon as she turns up jammed in a culvert somewhere. I don't need part-time heat too."

We were getting started early. I set fire to some tobacco. "Who's your lieutenant?"

"Winkle. Only he's out sick."

"Sergeant Grandy, if I spent an hour here, would I walk out any smarter than I was when I came in?"

"Probably not."

"Okay. I just wondered if you were an exception."

I was out of there before be got it.

On the ground floor I used a pay telephone to call the Federal Building and explained my problem to the woman who answered at the FBI.

"That would be Special Agent Roseman, Interstate Flight," she said. "But he's on another line."

I said I'd wait. She put me on hold. I watched a couple of prowl-car cops sweating in their winter uniforms by the Coke machine. After five minutes the woman came back on. "Mr. Roseman will be tied up for a while. Would you like to call back?"

I said yeah and hung up. Out on Beaubien the sidewalks were throwing back the first real heat of spring. I rolled down the window on the driver's side and breathed auto exhaust all the way to my office building. You have to celebrate it somehow.

Three

The window in my thinking parlor was stuck shut. I strained a disc heaving it open a crack to smell the sweet sun-spread pavement three stories down. Then I sat down behind the desk—real wood, no longer in style but not yet antique—and tried the FBI again. Roseman was out to lunch. I left my number and got out the Reliance report and dialed one of the two numbers for the firm where Frank Corcoran worked in Austin.

"Great Western." Another woman. They own the telephone wires.

I gave her my name and calling. "I'm trying to reach Frank Corcoran. It's about an inheritance."

"I'm sorry, Mr. Corcoran is on indefinite leave."

"Where can I reach him?"

"I'm sorry."

I thanked her anyway and worked the plunger. I wasn't disappointed. It's basic to try the knob before you break out the lock picks. I used the other number, and this time I got a man.

"Arnold Wilson, president of Thornbraugh Electronics in Chicago," I said. Thornbraugh Heating & Cooling put out the advertising calendar tacked to the wall across from my desk. "We're building a new plant in Springfield and Frank Corcoran advised me to call Great Western for financing. Is he in?"

"What did you say your name was?" I repeated it. "One moment."

I had enough time to pluck out a cigarette before he came back on the line. "Are you the private investigator who spoke to my partner's secretary about Mr. Corcoran a few moments ago?" His tone had lost at least three layers of silk.

"What's the matter, you don't have any walls in that place?"

I was talking to myself. As I lowered the dead receiver I could hear the computers gossiping among themselves, trashing my credit rating. The laugh was on them; I didn't have one.

Four

My next trip was through the Yellow Pages. There were at least fifty public gymnasiums listed within a half hour of downtown Detroit, including Southfield, any one of which would suit Corcoran's obsession with a healthy body. We all have our white whales. I made a list of the bigger, cleaner places. It was still long. Just thinking about it made my feet throb.

I tried the number of the place where Charlotte Corcoran was staying in Southfield. A breathy female voice answered, not hers.

"Millicent Arnold?"

"Yes. Mr. Walker? Charlotte told me she spoke to you earlier. She's napping now. Shall I wake her?"

"That's okay. It's you I want to talk to. About the man you saw who looked like Frank Corcoran."

"It was Frank. I spent a week in their home in Austin last year and I know what he looks like."

"Where did you see him at the mall? In what store?"

"He was coming out of the sporting goods place. I was across the corridor. I almost called to him over the crowd, but then I remembered. I thought about following him, see where he went, but by the time I made up my mind he was lost in the crush. I went into the store and found the clerk who had waited on him. He'd paid cash for what he bought, didn't leave a name or address."

"What'd he buy, barbell weights?" Maybe he was working out at home and I could forget the gyms.

"No. Something else. Sweats, I think. Yes, a new sweatsuit. Does that help?"

"My feet will give you a different answer. But yeah. Thanks, Miss Arnold."

"Call me Millie. Everyone does."

I believed her. It was the voice.

After saying good-bye I scowled at the list, then raised my little electronic paging device from among the flotsam in the top drawer of the desk and called my answering service to test the batteries. They were deader than the Anthony dollar. I said I'd call in for messages and locked up.

The office directly below mine was being used that month by a studio photographer, five foot one and three hundred pounds, with a Marlboro butt screwed into the middle of a face full of stubble. I went through the open door just as he finished brushing down the cowlick of a gap-toothed ten-year-old in a white shirt buttoned to the neck and blue jeans as stiff as aluminum siding and waddled around behind the camera, jowls swinging. "Smile, you little," he said, squeezing the bulb on the last part. White light bleached the boy's face and the sky-blue backdrop behind.

When the kid had gone, following the spots in front of his eyes, I handed the photographer the picture Charlotte Corcoran had given me of her ex-husband and their son. "How much to make a negative from this and run off twenty-five prints?" I asked.

He held the shot close enough to his face to set it afire if his stub were burning. "Eighty-seven fifty."

"How much for just fifteen?"

"Eighty-seven fifty."

"Must be the overhead." I was looking at a rope of cobwebs as thick as my wrist hammocking from the ceiling.

"No, you just look like someone that wants it tomorrow."

"Early." I gave him two fifties and he changed them from a cigar box on a table cluttered with lenses and film tubes and wrote me out a receipt.

I used his telephone to call my service. There were no messages. I tried the Federal Building again. Special Agent Roseman had come in and gone out and wasn't expected back that day. He had the right idea. I went home and cooked a foil-wrapped tray for supper and watched the news and a TV movie and went to bed.

Five

I was pulling a tail.

Leaving the diner I let fix my breakfast those mornings I can't face a frying pan, I watched a brown Chrysler pull out of the little parking area behind me in the rearview mirror. Three turns later it was still with me. I made a few more turns to make sure and then nicked the red light crossing John R. The Chrysler tried the same thing but had to brake when a Roadway van trundled through the intersection laying down horn.

I was still thinking about it when I squeezed into the visitors' lot outside Police Headquarters. My next alimony payment wasn't due for a month and I hadn't anything to do with the Sicilian boys' betterment league all year.

Sergeant Grandy had a worried-looking black woman in a ratty squirrel coat in the customer's chair and was clunking out a missing persons report with two fingers on a typewriter that came over with Father Marquette. I asked him if Lieutenant Winkle was in today.

"What for?" He mouthed each letter as he typed.

"Corcoran, same as yesterday."

"Go ahead and talk to him. I had a full head of hair before people started climbing over it."

I followed his thumb to where a slim black man in striped shirtsleeves and a plain brown tie was filling a china mug at the coffee maker. He wore a modest Afro and gray-tinted glasses. I gave him a card.

"I've been hired by Charlotte Corcoran to look for her ex-husband and their boy Tommy," I said. "The sergeant wasn't much help."

"Told you to walk off the dock, right?" His eyes might have twinkled over the top of the mug, but you can never be sure about cops' eyes.

"Words to that effect."

"Grandy's gone as high as he's going in my detail," he said. "No diplomacy. You have some identification besides a card?"

I showed him the chintzy pastel-colored ID the state hands out. He reached into a pocket and flipped forty cents into a tray full of coins next to the coffee maker. "Let's go into the cave."

We entered an office made of linoleum and amber pebbled glass, closing the door. He set down his mug, tugged at his trousers to protect the crease, and sat on the only clear corner of his desk. Then he pulled over his telephone and dialed a number.

"Hello, Miss Arnold? This is Lieutenant Winkle in General Service. . . Millie, right. Is Mrs. Corcoran in? Thank you." Pause. "Mrs.

Corcoran? No, I'm sorry, there's nothing new. Reason I called, I've got a private investigator here named Walker says he's working for you…Okay, thanks. Just wanted to confirm it."

He hung up and looked at me. "Sorry. Department policy."

"I'm unoffendable," I said. "How many telephone numbers you keep in your head at a given time?"

"Last month I forgot my mother's birthday." He drowned his quiet smile in coffee. "We have nothing in the Corcoran case."

"Nothing as in nothing, or nothing you can do anything with?"

"Nothing as in zip. We run on coffee and nicotine here. When we get a box full of scraps we can hand over to the feds we don't waste time trying to assemble them ourselves. The FBI computer drew a blank on Corcoran."

"Not unusual if he doesn't have priors."

"It gets better. Because of the exodus from Michigan to Texas over the past couple of years a lot of local firms have been dealing with finance companies out there, so when it landed back in our lap we fed Great Western Loans and Credit into the department machine. Still nothing on Corcoran, because only the officers are on file. But the printout said the corporation invests heavily in government projects. As investments counselor, Frank Corcoran should have shown up on that FBI report. He'd have had to been screened one time or another."

"Some kind of cover-up?"

"You tell me. The word's lost a lot of its impact in recent years."

I opened a fresh pack of Winstons. "So why keep Mrs. Corcoran in the dark?"

"Don't worry, it's not rubbing off on us," he said. "We're just holding her at arm's length till we get some answers back from chan-

Nels. These things take time. Computer time, which is measured in Christmases."

nels. These things take time. Computer time, which is measured in Christmases."

"So why tell me?"

He smiled the quiet smile. "When Sergeant Grandy gave me your card I did some asking around the building. If you were a bulldog you'd have what the novelists call 'acquisitive teeth.' Quickest way to get rid of you guys is to throw you some truth."

"I appreciate it, Lieutenant." I rose and offered him my hand. He didn't give it back as hastily as some cops have.

"Oh, what would you know about a brown Chrysler that was shadowing me a little while ago?"

"It wasn't one of mine," he said. "I'm lucky to get a blue-and-white when I want to go in with the band."

I grasped the doorknob. "Thanks again. I guess you're feeling better."

"Than what? Oh, yesterday. I called in sick to watch my kid pitch. He walked six batters in a row."

I grinned and left. That's the thing I hate most about cops. Find one that stands for everything you don't like about them and then you draw one that's human.

Six

The job stank, all right. It stank indoors and it stank on the street and it stank in the car all the way to my building. I had the window closed this trip; the air was damp and the sky was throwing fingers whether to rain or snow. Michigan. But it wouldn't have smelled any better with the window down.

The pictures came out good, anyway. It must be nice to be in a business where if they don't you can trace the problem to a bad filter or dirt in the chemicals, something definite and impersonal that you can ditch and replace with something better. I left the fat photographer developing nude shots for a customer on Adult Row on Woodward and went upstairs.

I lock the waiting room overnight. I was about to use the key when the door swung inward and a young black party in faded overalls and a Pistons warm-up jacket grinned at me. He had a mouth built for grinning, wide as a Buick with door-to-door teeth and a thin moustache squared off like a bracket to make it seem even wider. "You're late, trooper," he said. "Let's you come in and we'll get started."

"Thanks, I'll come back," I said, and back-pedaled into something hard. The wall was closer this morning. A hand curled inside the back of my collar and jerked my suitcoat down to my elbows, straining the button and pinning my arms behind me.

Teeth drew a finger smelling of marijuana down my cheek. Then he balled his fist and rapped the side of my chin hard enough to make my own teeth snap together.

"Let's you come in, trooper. Unless you'd rather wake up smiling at yourself from your bedside table every morning."

I kicked him in the crotch.

He said, "Hee!" and hugged himself. Meanwhile I threw myself forward, popping the button and stripping out of my coat. My left arm was still tangled in the sleeve lining when I pivoted on my left foot and swung my right fist into a face eight inches higher than mine. I felt the jar clear to my shoulder. I was still gripping the keys in that hand.

The guy I hit let go of the coat to drag the back of a hand the size of a platter under his nose and looked at the blood. Then he took hold of my shirt collar from the front to steady me and cocked his other fist, taking aim.

"Easy, Del. We ain't supposed to bust him." Teeth's voice was a croak.

Del lowered his fist but kept his grip on my collar. He was almost seven feet tall, very black, and had artificially straightened hair combed into a high pompadour and sprayed hard as a brick. In place of a jacket he wore a full-length overcoat that barely reached his hips, over a sweatshirt that left his navel and flat hairy belly exposed.

Behind me Teeth said, "Del don't like to talk. He's got him a cleft palate. It don't get in his way at all. Now you want to come in, talk?"

I used what air Del had left me to agree. He let go and we went inside. In front of the door to my private office Teeth relieved me of my keys, unlocked it, and stood aside while his partner shoved me on through. Teeth glanced at the lock on his way in.

"Dead bolt, yeah. Looks new. You need one on the other door too."

He circled the room as he spoke and stopped in front of me. I was ready and got my hip out just as he let fly. I staggered sideways. Del caught me.

"That's no way to treat a client, trooper," Teeth said. "It gets around, pretty soon you ain't got no business."

"Client?" I shook off the giant's hand. My leg tingled.

Teeth reached into the slash pocket of his Pistons jacket and brought out a roll of crisp bills, riffling them under my nose. "Hundreds, trooper. Fifty of them in this little bunch. Go on, heft it. Ain't no heavier'n a roll of quarters, but, my oh my, how many more miles she draws."

He held it out while I got my coat right side in. Finally his arm got tired and he let it drop. I said, "You came in hard for paying customers. What do I have to forget?"

"We want someone to forget something we go rent a politician," he said. "Twenty-five hundred of this pays to look for somebody. The other twenty-five comes when the somebody gets found."

"Somebody being?" Knowing the answer.

"Same guy you're after now. Frank Corcoran."

"That standard for someone who's already looking for him for a lot less?"

"There's a little more to it," he said.

"Thought there might be."

"You find him, you tell us first. Ahead of his wife."

"Then?"

"Then you don't tell her."

"I guess I don't ask why."

His grin creaked. "You're smart, trooper. Too smart for poor."

"I'll need a number," I said.

"We call you." He held up the bills. "We talking?"

"Let's drink over it." I pushed past him around the desk and tugged at the handle of the deep drawer. Teeth's other hand moved and five inches of pointed steel flicked out of his fist. "Just a scotch bottle," I said.

He leaned over the corner to see down into the drawer. I grabbed a handful of his hair and bounced his forehead off the desk. The switchblade went flying. Del, standing in front of the desk, made a growling sound in his chest and lurched forward. I yanked open the top drawer and fired my Smith & Wesson .38 without taking it out. The bullet smashed through the front panel and buried itself in the wall next to the door. It didn't come within a foot of hitting the big man. But he stopped. I raised the gun and backed to the window.

"A name," I said. "Whose money?"

Teeth rubbed his forehead, where a purple bruise was spreading under the brown. He stooped to pick up the currency from the floor and stood riffling it against his palm. His smile was a shadow of a ghost of what it had been. "No names today, trooper. I'm fresh out of names."

I said, "It works this way. You tell me the name. I don't shoot you."

"You don't shoot. Desks and walls, maybe. Not people. It's why you're broke and it's why I get to walk around with somebody else's five long ones on account of it's what I drop on gas for my three Cadillacs."

"What about a Chrysler?"

"I pay my dentist in Chryslers," he said. "So long, trooper. Maybe I see you. Maybe you don't see me first. Oh." He got my keys out of his slash pocket and flipped them onto the desk. "We're splitting, Del."

Del looked around, spotted my framed original *Casablanca* poster hanging on the wall over the bullethole, and swung his fist. Glass sprayed. Then he turned around and crunched out behind his partner, speckling my carpet with blood from his lacerated fingers.

The telephone rang while I was cleaning the revolver. When I got my claws unhooked from the ceiling I lifted the receiver. It was Lieutenant Winkle. He wanted to see me at Headquarters.

"Something?" I asked.

"Everything," he said. "Don't stop for cigarettes on the way."

I reloaded, hunted up my holster, and clipped the works to my belt. No one came to investigate the shot. The neighborhood had fallen that far.

On Beaubien I left the gun in the car to clear the metal detectors inside. Heading there I walked past a brown Chrysler parked in the visitors' lot. There was no one inside and the doors were locked.

Seven

The lieutenant let me into his office, where two men in dark suits were seated in mismatched chairs. One had a head full of crisp gray hair and black-rimmed glasses astride a nose that had been broken sometime in the distant past. The other was younger and looked like Jack Kennedy but for a close-trimmed black beard. They stank federal.

"Eric Stendahl and Robert LeJohn." Winkle introduced them in the same order. "They're with the Justice Department."

"We met," I said. "Sort of."

Stendahl nodded. He might have smiled. "I thought you'd made us. I should have let Bob drive; he's harder to shake behind a wheel. But even an old eagle likes to test his wings now and then." The smile died. "We're here to ask you to stop looking for Frank Corcoran."

I lit a Winston. "If I say no?"

"Then we'll tell you. We have influence with the state police, who issued your license."

"I'll get a hearing. They'll have to tell me why."

"That won't be necessary," he said. "Corcoran was the inside man in an elaborate scheme to bilk Great Western Loans and Credit out of six hundred thousand dollars in loans to a nonexistent oil venture in Mexico. He was apprehended and agreed to turn state's evidence against his accomplices in return for a new identity and relocation for his protection. You're familiar with the alias program, I believe."

"I ran into it once," I looked at Winkle. "You knew?"

"Not until they came in here this morning after you left," he said. "They've had Mrs. Corcoran under surveillance. That's how they got on to you. It also explains why Washington turned its back on this one."

I added some ash to the fine mulch on the linoleum floor.

"Not too bright, relocating him in an area where his ex-wife's cousin lives."

Stendahl said, "We didn't know about that, but it certainly would have clinched our other objections at the time. He spent his childhood here and had a fixation about the place. The people behind the swindle travel in wide circles; we couldn't chance his being spotted. Bob here was escorting Corcoran to the East Coast. He disappeared during the plane change at Metro Airport. We're still looking for him."

"It's a big club," I said. "We ought to have a secret handshake. What about Corcoran's son?"

LeJohn spoke up. "That's how he lost me. The boy was along. He had to go to the bathroom and he didn't want anyone but his father in with him. I went into the bookstore for a magazine. When I got back to the men's room it was empty."

"The old bathroom trick. Tell me, did Corcoran ever happen to mention that the boy was in his mother's custody and that you were acting as accomplices in his abduction?"

"He seemed happy enough," said LeJohn, glaring. "Excited about the trip."

His partner laid manicured fingers on his arm, calming him. To me: "It was a condition of Corcoran's testimony that the boy go with him to his new life. Legally, our compliance is indefensible. Morally—well, his evidence is expected to put some important felons behind bars."

"Yeah," I tipped some smoke out of my nostrils. "I guess you got too busy to clue in Mrs. Corcoran."

"That was an oversight. We'll correct it while we're here."

"What did you mean when you said it was a big club?" LeJohn pressed me. "Who else is looking for Corcoran?"

I replayed the scene in my office. Lieutenant Winkle grunted. "Monroe Boyd and Little Delbert Riddle," he said.

"I had one or both of them in here half a dozen times when I was with C.I.D. Extortion, suspicion of murder. Nothing stuck. So they're jobbing themselves out now. I'll put out a pickup on them if you want to press charges."

"They'd be out the door before you finished the paperwork. I'll just tack the price of a new old desk and a picture frame on to the expense sheet. The bullethole's good for business."

"How'd they know you were working for Mrs. Corcoran?" Stendahl asked.

"The same way you did, maybe. Only they were better at it."

He stood. "We'll need whatever you've got on them in your files, Lieutenant. Walker, you're out of it."

"Can I report to Mrs. Corcoran?"

"Yes. Yes, please do. It will save us some time. You've been very cooperative."

He extended his hand. I went on crushing out my cigarette in the ashtray on Winkle's desk until he got tired and lowered it. Then I left.

Eight

Millicent Arnold owned a condominium off Twelve Mile Road, within sight of the glass-and-steel skyscrapers of the Southfield Civic Center sticking up above the predominantly horizontal suburb like new teeth in an old mouth. A slim brunette with a pageboy haircut answered the bell wearing a pink angora sweater over black harem pants and gold sandals with high heels on her bare feet. Charlotte Corcoran might have looked like her before she had lost too much weight.

"Amos Walker? Yes, you are. My God, you look like a private eye. Come in."

I kept my mouth zipped at that one and walked past her into a living room paved with orange shag and furnished in green plush and glass. It should have looked like hell. I decided it was Millie Arnold standing in it that made it work. She hung my hat on an ornamental peg near the door.

"Charlotte's putting herself together. She was asleep when you called."

"She seems to sleep a lot."

"Her doctor in Austin prescribed a mild sedative. It's almost the only thing that's gotten her through this past month. You said you had some news." She indicated the sofa.

I took it. It was like sitting on a sponge. "The story hangs some lefts and rights," I said.

She sat next to me, trapping her hands between her knees. She wasn't wearing a ring. "My cousin and I are close," she said. "More like sisters. You can speak freely."

"I didn't mean that, although it was coming. I just don't want to have to tell it twice. I didn't like it when I heard it."

"That bad, huh?"

I said nothing. She tucked her feet under her and propped an elbow on the back of the sofa and her cheek in her hand. "I'm curious about something. I recommended Reliance to Charlotte. She came back with you."

"The case came down my street. Krell said she was referred to him by one of his cash customers."

She nodded. "Kester Clothiers on Lahser. I'm a buyer. I typed Charlotte's letter of reference on their stationery. The chain retains Reliance for security, employee theft and like that."

"I guess the hours are good."

"I'm off this week. We're between seasons." She paused. "You know, you're sort of attractive."

I was looking at her again when Charlotte Corcoran came in. She had on a maroon robe over a blue nightgown, rich material that bagged on her and made her wrists and ankles look even bonier than they were. Backless slippers. When she saw me her step quickened. "You found them? Is Tommy all right?"

I took a deep breath and sat her down in a green plush chair with tassels on the arms and told it.

"Wow," said Millie after a long silence.

I was watching her cousin. She remained motionless for a moment, then fumbled cigarettes and a book of matches out of her robe pocket. She tried to strike a match, said "Damn!" and threw the book on the floor. I picked it up and struck one and held the flame for her. She drew in a lungful and blew a plume at the ceiling. "The bastard," she said. "No wonder he never had time for me. He was too busy making himself rich."

"You didn't know about his testifying?" I asked.

"He came through with his child support on time. That's all I heard from him. It explains why he never came by for his weekends with Tommy." She looked at me. "Is my son in danger?"

"He is if he's with his father. Boyd and Riddle didn't look like lovers of children. But the feds are on it."

"This is the same federal government that endowed a study to find out why convicts want to escape prison?"

"Someone caught it on a bad day," I said.

"How much to go on with the investigation, Mr. Walker?"

"Nothing, Mrs. Corcoran. I just wanted to hear you say it."

She smiled then, a little.

"What progress have you made?" asked Millie.

"I'm chasing a lead now. If it gets any slimmer it won't be a lead at all. But it beats reading bumps." I got the package of prints out of my coat pocket, separated the original of Corcoran and Tommy from the others, and gave it back to Mrs. Corcoran. "I've got twenty-five more now, and at least that many places to show them. When I run out I'll try something else."

She looked at the picture. Seeing only one person in it. Then she put it in her robe pocket. "I think you're a good man, Mr. Walker."

Millie Arnold saw me to the door. "She's right, you know," she said, when I had it open. "You are good."

Attractive, too.

Nine

There was a gymnasium right around the corner on Greenfield. No one I talked to there recognized either of the faces in the picture, but I left it with the manager for seed along with my card and tried the next place on my list. I had them grouped by area with Southfield at the top. I hit two places in Birmingham, one in Clawson, then swung west and worked my way home in a loop through Farmington and Livonia. A jock in Redford Township with muscles on his T-shirt thought Corcoran looked familiar but couldn't finger him.

"There's fifty bucks in it for you when you do," I said. He flexed his trapezius and said he'd work on it.

I'd missed lunch, so I stopped in Detroit for an early supper, hit a few more places downtown, and went back to the office to read my mail and call my service for messages. I had none and the mail was all bills and junk. I locked up and went home. That night I dreamed I was Johnny Appleseed, but instead of trees every seed I threw sprang up grinning Monroe Boyds and hulking Delbert Riddles.

Ten

My fat photographer neighbor greeted me in the foyer of my building the next morning. He was chewing on what looked like the same Marlboro remnant and he hadn't been standing any closer to his razor than usual. "Some noise yesterday," he said. "Starting a range up there or what?"

"No, I shot a shutterbug for asking too many questions."

I passed him on the stairs, no small feat.

With my gun drawn, I entered my office, felt stupid when I found it unoccupied, then saw the shattered glass from the poster frame and felt a little better. I swept it up and called my service. I had a message.

"Walker?" asked a male voice at the number left for me.

"Tunk Herman, remember?"

"The guy in Redford," I said.

"Yeah. That fifty still good?"

"What've you got?"

"I couldn't stop thinking about that dude in the picture, so I went through the records of members. Thought maybe his name would jump out at me if I heard it, you know? Well, it did. James Muldoon. He's a weekender. I don't see him usually because I don't work weekends except that one time. I got an address for him."

I drew a pencil out of the cup on my desk. It shook a little.

Eleven

It was spring now and no argument. The air had a fresh damp smell and the sun felt warm on my back as I leaned on the open-air telephone booth, or maybe it was my disposition seeping through from inside. Charlotte Corcoran answered on the eighth ring. Her voice sounded foggy.

"Walker, Mrs. Corcoran," I said. "Come get your son."

"What did you say? I took a pill a little while ago. It sounded—"

"It wasn't the pill. I'm looking at him now. Blond and blue, about four feet—"

The questions came fast, tumbling all over one another, too tangled to pull apart. I held the receiver away from my ear and waited. Down the block, on the other side of Pembroke, a little boy in blue overalls with a bright yellow mop was bouncing a ball off the wall of a two-story white frame house that went back forever. While I was watching, the front door came open and a dark-haired man beckoned him inside. Corcoran's physique was less impressive in street clothes.

"Tommy's fine," I said, when his mother wound down. "Meet me here." I gave her the address. "Put Millie on and I'll give her directions."

"Millie's out shopping. I don't have a car."

"Take a cab."

"Cab?"

"Forget it. You've got too much of that stuff in your pipes to come out alone. I'll pick you up in twenty minutes."

It was all of that. The road crews were at work and everyone who had a car and no job was out enjoying the season. I left the engine running in front of the brick complex and bounced up the wrought-iron steps to where Millie's door stood open. I rapped and went inside. Charlotte Corcoran was sitting on the sofa in the robe and nightgown.

"That's out of style for the street this year," I said. "Get into something motherly."

"Plenty of time for that."

I felt my face get tired at the sound of the voice behind me. I turned around slowly. Millie Arnold was standing on the blind side of the door in a white summer dress with a red belt around her trim waist and a brown .32 Colt automatic in her right hand pointing at me.

"You don't look surprised." She nudged the door shut with the toe of a red pump.

"It was there," I said, raising my hands. "It just needed a kick. I had to wonder how Boyd and Riddle got on to me so fast. They couldn't have been following Mrs. Corcoran without Stendahl and LeJohn knowing. Someone had to tell them."

"It goes back farther than that. I made two calls to Texas after spotting Frank at the mall. The first was to his old partners. I can't tell you how much they appreciated it. If I did I'd be in trouble with the IRS. Then I called Charlotte. Throw the gun down on the rug, Mr. Walker. It made an ugly dent in my sofa when you were here yesterday."

I unholstered the .38 slowly. It hit the shag halfway between us with a thump. "Then, when Mrs. Corcoran arrived, you talked her into hiring the biggest investigative firm you knew. You figured to let them do the work of finding Corcoran. It probably meant a discount on Boyd and Riddle's fee."

"It also guaranteed me a bonus when Frank got dead," she said. "Krell giving the case to you threw me, but it worked out just fine. When I got back from shopping and Charlotte gave me the good news I just couldn't wait to call our mutual friends and share it."

"My cousin," said Mrs. Corcoran.

Millie showed her teeth. Very white and a little sharp. "You married a hundred-thou-a-year executive. I'd have settled for that. But if it wasn't enough for him, why should what I make be enough for me? I met his little playmates that time I visited you in Austin. I remembered them when it counted."

"What happens to us?" I asked.

"You'll both stay here with me until that phone rings. It'll be Boyd giving me thumbs up. I'll have to lock you in the bathroom when I leave; but you'll find a way out soon enough. You can have the condo, Charlotte. It isn't paid for."

"The boy had nothing to do with Corcoran's scam," I said. "You're putting him in front of the guns too."

"Rich kid. What do I owe him?"

"They won't hurt Tommy." Mrs. Corcoran got up.

"Sit down." The gun jerked.

But she was moving. I threw my arm in front of her. She knocked it aside and charged. Millie squeezed the trigger. It clicked. Her cousin was all over her then, kicking and shrieking and clawing at her eyes. It was interesting to see. Millie was healthier, but she was standing between a mother and her child. When the gun came up to clap the side of Mrs. Corcoran's head I tipped the odds, reversing ends on the Smith & Wesson I'd scooped up from the rug and tapping Millie behind the ear. Her knees gave then and she trickled through her cousin's grasp and puddled on the floor.

I reached down and pulled back her eyelids. "She's good for an hour," I said. "Call nine-one-one. Give them the address on Pembroke."

While she was doing that, breathing heavily, I picked up the automatic and ran back the action. Millie had forgotten to rack a cartridge into the chamber.

Twelve

Approaching Pembroke we heard shots.

I jammed my heel down on the accelerator and we rounded the corner doing fifty. Charlotte Corcoran, still in her robe, gripped the door handle to stay out of my lap. Her profile was sharp against the window, thrust forward like a mother hawk's.

There was no sign of the police. As we entered Corcoran/Muldoon's block, something flashed in an open upstairs window, followed closely by a hard flat bang. A much louder shot answered it from the front yard. There, a huge black figure in an overcoat too short for him crouched behind a lilac bush beside the driveway. His .44 magnum was as long as my thigh but looked like a kid's water pistol in his great fist.

"Hang on!" I spun the wheel hard and floored the pedal.

The Olds's engine roared and we bumped over the curb, diagonaling across the lawn. Del Riddle straightened at the noise and turned, bringing the magnum around with him. I saw his mouth open wide and then his body filled the windshield and I felt the impact. We bucked up over the porch stoop and suddenly the world was a deafening place of tearing wood and exploding glass. The car stopped then, although my foot was still pasted to the floor with the accelerator pedal underneath and the engine whining. The rear wheels spun shrilly. I cut the ignition. A piece of glass fell somewhere with a clank.

I looked at my passenger. She was slumped down in the seat with her knees against the dash. "All right?"

"I think so." She lowered her knees.

"Stay here."

The door didn't want to open. I shoved hard and it squawked against the buckled fender. I climbed out behind the Smith & Wesson in my right hand. I was in a living room with broken glass on the carpet and pieces of shredded siding slung over the chairs and sofa. Riddle lay spread-eagled on his face across the car's hood and windshield, groaning. His legs dangled like broken straws in front of the smashed grille.

"Lose the piece, trooper."

My eyes were still adjusting to the dim light indoors. I focused on Monroe Boyd baring his teeth in front of a hallway running to the back of the house. He had one arm around Tommy Corcoran's chest under the arms, holding him kicking above the floor. His other hand bad a switchblade in it with the point pressing the boy's jugular.

"Tommy!" Charlotte Corcoran had gotten out on the passenger's side. She took a step and stopped. Boyd bettered his grip.

"Mommy," said the boy.

"What about it, trooper? Seven or seventy, they all bleed the same."

I relaxed my hold on the gun.

A shot slammed the walls and a blue hole appeared under Boyd's left eye. He let go of Tommy and lay down. Twitched once.

I looked up at Frank Corcoran crouched at the top of the staircase to the second story. His arm was stretched out full length with a gun at the end of it, leaking smoke. He glanced at Tommy. "I told you to stay upstairs with me."

"I left my ball here." The boy pouted, then spotted Boyd's body. "Funny man."

Mrs. Corcoran flew forward and knelt to throw her arms around her son. Corcoran saw her for the first time, said "Charlotte?" and looked at me. The gun came around.

"Stop waving that thing," his ex-wife said, hugging Tommy. "He's with me."

Corcoran hesitated, then lowered the weapon. He surveyed the damage. "What do I tell the rental agent?"

I heard the sirens then.

Bloody July

The house was a half-timbered Tudor job on Kendall, standing on four acres fenced in by a five-foot ornamental stone wall. It wasn't the only one in the area and looked as much like metropolitan Detroit as it tried to look like Elizabethan England. A bank of lilacs had been allowed to grow over the wall inside, obstructing the view of the house from the street, but from there inward the lawn was bare of foliage, after the fashion of feudal estates to deny cover to intruders.

I wasn't one. As instructed previously, I stopped in front of the iron gate and got out to open it and was on my way back to the car when something black hurtled at me snarling out of the shrubbery. I clambered inside and shut the door and rolled up the window just as the thing leaped, scrabbling its claws on the roof and clouding the glass with its moist breath.

"Hector!"

At the sound of the harsh voice, the beast dropped to all fours and went on clearing its throat and glaring yellow at me through the window while a small man with a white goatee walked out through the gate and snapped a leash onto its collar. He wore a gray sportcoat and no tie.

"It's all right, Walker," he said. "Hector behaves himself while I'm around. You are Amos Walker."

I cranked the window down far enough to tell him I was, keeping my hand on the handle and my eye on the dog.

"You're Mr. Blum?"

"Yeah. Drive on up to the house. I'll meet you there."

The driveway looped past an attached garage and a small front porch with carriage lamps mounted next to the door. I parked in front of the porch and leaned on the fender smoking a cigarette while Leonard Blum led the dog around back and then came through the house and opened the door for me. The wave of conditioned air hit me like a spray of cold water. It was the last day of June and the second of the first big heat wave of summer.

"You like dogs, Walker?"

"The little moppy noisy kind and the big gentle ones that lick your face."

"I like Dobermans. You can count on them to turn on you someday. With friends you never know." He ushered me into a dim living room crowded with heavy furniture and hung with paintings of square-riggers under full sail and bearded mariners in slick sou'westers shouting into the bow-wash. A varnished oak ship's wheel as big around as a hula hoop was mounted over the fireplace.

"Nautical, I know," said Blum. "I was in shipping a long time back. Never got my feet wet, but I liked to pretend I was John Paul Jones. That wheel belonged to the *Henry Morgan,* fastest craft ever to sail the river. In my day, anyway."

"That doesn't sound like the name of an ore carrier."

"It wasn't."

I waited, but he didn't embroider. He was crowding eighty if it wasn't stuck to his heels already, with heavy black-rimmed glasses and a few white hairs combed diagonally across his scalp and white teeth that flashed too much in his beard to be his. There was a space there when we both seemed to realize we were being measured, and then he said:

"My lawyer gave me your name. Simon Weintraub. You flushed out an eyewitness to an accident last year that saved his client a bundle."

"I'm pretty good." I waited some more.

"How are you at tracing stolen property?"

"Depends on the property."

He produced a key from a steel case on his belt, hobbled over to a bare corner of the room, and inserted the key in a slot I hadn't noticed. The wood paneling opened in two seconds, exposing a recessed rectangle lined in burgundy plush and tall enough for a man to stand in.

"Notice anything?" he asked.

"Looks like a hairdresser's casket."

"It's a gun cabinet. An empty gun cabinet. Three days ago there wasn't enough room to store another piece in it."

"Were you at home when it got empty?"

"My wife and I spent the weekend on Mackinac Island. I've got a place there. Whoever did it, it wasn't his first job. He cut the alarm wires and picked the locks to the front door and the cabinet slick as spit."

"What about Hector?"

"I put him in a kennel for the weekend."

"Are you sure someone didn't just have a key?"

"The only key to this cabinet is on my belt. It's never out of my sight."

"Who else lives here besides your wife?"

"No one. We don't have servants. Elizabeth's at her CPR class now. I've got a heart I wouldn't wish on an Arab," he added.

"What'd the police say?"

"I didn't call them."

I was starting to get the idea. "Have you got a list of the stolen guns?"

He drew two sheets folded lengthwise out of his inside breast pocket, holding it back when I reached for it. "When does client privilege start?"

"When I pick up the telephone and say hello."

He gave me the list. It was neatly typewritten, the firearms identified by make, caliber, patent date, and serial number.

Some handguns, four high-powered rifles, a few antiques, two shotguns. And a Thompson submachine gun. I asked him if he was a dealer.

"No, I'm in construction."

"Non-dealers are prohibited from owning full automatic weapons," I said. "I guess you know that."

"I wanted a lecture I'd have gone to the cops to start."

"Also a warrant for your arrest. Are any of these guns registered, Mr. Blum?"

"That's not a question you get to ask," he said.

I handed back the list. "So long, Mr. Blum. I've got some business up in Iroquois Heights, so I won't charge you for the visit."

"Wait, Walker."

I had my back to him when he said it. It was the way he said it that made me turn around. It didn't sound like the Leonard Blum I'd been talking to.

"Nothing in the collection is registered," he said. "The rifles and shotguns don't have to be, of course, and I just never got around to doing the paper on the handguns and the Thompson. I've never been fingerprinted."

"It's an experience no one should miss," I said.

"I'll take your word for it. Anyway, that's why I didn't holler cop.

For a long time now I've lived for that collection. My wife lays down for anything with a zipper; she's almost fifty years younger than me and it's no more than I have any right to expect. But pleasant memories are tied up with some of those pieces. I've seen what happens to old friends when they lose all interest, Walker. They wind up in wheelchairs stinking of urine and calling their daughters Charlie. I'd splatter my brains before I'd let that happen to me. Only now I don't have anything to do it with."

I got out one of my cards, scribbled a number on the back, and gave it to him. "Call this guy in Belleville. His name's Ben Perkins. He's a P.I. who doubles in apartment maintenance, which as lines of work go aren't so very different from each other. He's a cowboy, but a good one, which is what this job screams for. But I can't guarantee he'll touch it."

"I don't know." He was looking at the number. "Weintraub recommended you as the original clam."

"This guy makes me look like a set of those wind-up dime store dentures." I said so long again and let myself out, feeling cleansed. And as broke as a motel room chair.

Two

The Iroquois Heights business had to do with a wandering wife I never found. What I did find was a deputy city prosecutor living off the town madam and a broken head courtesy of a local beat officer's monkey stick. The assistant chief is an old acquaintance. A week after the Kendall visit I was nursing my headache and the office fan with pliers and a paperclip when Lieutenant John Alderdyce of Detroit Homicide walked in. His black face glistened and he was breathing like a rhinoceros from the three-story climb. But his shirt and Chinese silk sportcoat looked fresh. He saw what I was doing and said, "Why don't you pop for air conditioning?"

"Every time I get a fund started I get hungry." I laid down my tools and plugged in the fan. The blades turned, wrinkling the thick air. I lifted my eyebrows at John.

He drew a small white rectangle out of an inside pocket and laid it on my desk, lining up the edges with those of the blotter. It was one of my business cards. "These things turn up in the damnedest places," he said. "So do you."

"I'm paid to. The cards I raise as best as I can and then send them out into the world. I can't answer for where they wind up."

He flipped it over with a finger. A telephone number was written on the back in a scrawl I recognized. I sighed and sat back.

"What'd he do," I asked, "hang himself or stick his tongue in a light socket?"

He jumped on it with both feet. "What makes it suicide?"

"Blum's wife was cheating on him, he said, and he lost his only other interest to a B-and-E. He as much as told me he'd take the back way out if that gun collection didn't find its way home."

"Maybe you better throw me the rest of it," he said.

I did, starting with my introduction to Blum's dog Hector and finishing with my exit from the house on Kendall. Alderdyce listened with his head down, stroking an unlit cigarette. We were coming up on the fifth anniversary of his first attempt to quit them.

"So you walked away from it," he said when I was through. "I never knew you to turn your back on a job just because it got too illegal."

I said, "We'll pass over that on account of we're so close. I didn't like Blum. When he couldn't bully me he tried wheedling, and he caught me in the wrong mood. Was it suicide?"

"It plays that way. Wife came home from an overnight stay with one of her little bridge partners and found him shot through the heart with a thirty-eight automatic. The gun was in his right hand and the paraffin test came up positive. Powder burns, the works. No note, but you can't have music too."

"Thirty-eight auto. You mean one of those Navy Supers?"

"Colt Sporting Pistol, Model Nineteen-Oh-Two. It was discontinued in nineteen twenty-eight. A real museum piece. The same gun was on a list we found in a desk drawer."

"I know the list. He said everything on it had been stolen."

"He lied. We turned your card in a wastebasket this morning. We tried to reach you."

"I was up in the Heights getting a lesson in police work, Warner Brothers style. Check out the wife's alibi?"

He nodded, rolling the cold cigarette along his lower lip.

"A pro bowler in Harper Woods. You'd like him. Muscles on his elbows and if his IQ tests out at half his handicap you can have my pension. Blum started getting cold around midnight and she was at Fred Flintstone's place from ten o'clock on. She married Blum four years ago, about the time he turned seventy-five and handed over the operation of his construction firm to his partners. We're still digging."

"He told me he used to be in shipping." Alderdyce shrugged. I said, "I guess you called Perkins."

"The number you wrote on the card. Blum didn't score any more points with him than he did with you. I'm glad we never met. I wouldn't want to know someone who wasn't good enough for two P.I.'s with cardboard in their shoes."

I lit a Winston, just to make him squirm. "What I most enjoy paying rent on this office for is to provide a forum for overdressed fuzz to run down my profession. Self-snuffings don't usually make you this pleasant. Or is it the heat?"

"It's the heat," he said. "It's also this particular self-snuffing. Maybe I'm burning out. They say one good way of telling is when you find yourself wanting to stand the stiff on its feet and ask it a question."

"As for instance?"

"As for instance, 'Mr. Blum, would you please tell me why before you shot yourself you decided to shoot your dog?'"

I said nothing. After a little while he broke his cigarette in two and flipped the pieces at my wastebasket and went out.

Three

I finished my smoke, then broke out my Polk Administration Underwood and cranked a sheet into it and waited for my report to the husband of the runaway wife to fall into order. When I got tired of that I tore out the blank sheet and crumpled it and bonged it into the basket. My head said it was time to go home.

"Mr. Walker?"

I was busy locking the door to my private office. When I turned I was looking at a slender brunette of about thirty standing in the waiting room with the hall door closing on its pneumatic tube behind her. She wore her hair short and combed almost over one eye and had on a tailored black jacket that ran out of material just below her elbows, on top of a ruffled white blouse and a tight skirt to match the jacket. Black purse and shoes. The weather was too hot for black, but she made it look cool.

I got my hat off the back of my head and said I was Walker. She said, "I'm Andrea Blum. Leonard Blum is—was my husband."

I unlocked the door again and held it for her. Inside the brain room she glanced casually at the butterfly wallpaper and framed *Casablanca* poster and accepted the chair I held for her, the one whose legs were all the same length. I sat down behind the desk and said I was sorry about Mr. Blum.

She smiled slightly. "I won't pretend I'm destroyed. It's no secret our marriage was a joke. But you get used to having someone around, and then when he's not—" She spread her hands. "Leonard told me he tried to hire you to trace his stolen guns and that you turned him down."

"I'd have had to tell the police that a cache of unregistered firearms was loose," I said. "Three out of five people in this town carry guns. They'd like to keep the other two virgin."

"Don't explain. I was just as happy they were taken. Guns frightened me. Anyway, that's not why I'm here. The police think Leonard's death was self-inflicted."

"You don't."

She moved her head. The sunlight caught a reddish thread in her black hair. "The burglary infuriated him. After that other detective refused to take the case he was determined to find one that would. He was ready to do it himself if it came to that. Do people shoot themselves when they're angry, Mr. Walker?"

"Never having shot myself I can't say."

"And he wouldn't have killed Hector," she went on. "He loved that dog. Besides, where could he have gotten the gun? It was one of those missing."

"Could be the burglars overlooked it and he just didn't tell you. And it wouldn't be the first time a suicide took something he loved with him. Generally it's the wife. You're lucky, Mrs. Blum."

"That he cared less for me than he did for his dog? I deserve that, I guess. Marrying an old man for his money gets boring. All those other men were just a diversion. I loved Leonard in my way." She lined up her fingers primly on the purse in her lap. The nails were sharp and buffed to a high gloss, no polish. "He didn't kill himself. Whoever killed him shot the dog first when it came at him."

I offered her a cigarette from the deck. When she shook her head I lit one for myself and said, "I've got a question, but I don't want one of those nails in my eye."

"Insurance," she said. "A hundred thousand dollars, and I'm the sole beneficiary. It's worth more than twice the estate minus debts outstanding. And yes, if suicide is established as cause of death the policy is void. But that's only part of why I'm here, though I admit it's the biggest part. At the very least I owe it to Leonard to find out who murdered him."

"Who do you suspect?"

"I can't think of anyone. We seldom had visitors. He outlived most of his friends and the only contact he had with his business partners was over the telephone. He was in semiretirement."

She gave me the name of the firm and the partners' names. I wrote them down. "What did your husband do before he went into construction?" I asked.

"He would never tell me. Whenever I asked he'd say it didn't matter, those were dead days. I gather it had something to do with the river but he never struck me as the sailor type. May could tell you. His first wife. May Shinstone, her name is now. She lives in Birmingham."

I wrote that down too. "I'll look into it, Mrs. Blum. Until the cops stop thinking suicide, anyway. They frown on competition. Meanwhile I think you should find another place to stay."

"Why?"

"Because if Mr. Blum was murdered odds are it was by the same person who stole his guns, and that person sneezes at locks. If you get killed I won't have anyone to report to."

After a moment she nodded. "I have a place to stay."

I believed her.

Four

When she had left, poorer by a check in the amount of my standard three-day retainer, I called Ben Perkins. We swapped insults and then I drew on a favor he owed me and got the number of a gun broker downtown, one who wasn't listed under Guns in the Yellow Pages. Breaking the connection I could almost smell one of the cork-tipped ropes Perkins smokes. When he lit one up in your presence you wouldn't have to see him pull it out of his boot to know where he keeps them.

Eleven rings in, a voice with a Mississippi twang came on and recited the number I had just dialed.

"I'm a P.I. named Walker," I said. "Ben Perkins gave me your number."

He got my number and said he'd call back. We hung up. Three minutes later the telephone rang. It was Mississippi.

"Okay, Perk says you're cool. What?"

"I need a line on some hot guns," I said.

"Nix, not over the squawker. What's the tag?"

"Fifty, if you've got what I want."

"Man, I keep a roll of fifties in the crapper. Case I run out of Charmin, you know? A hunnert up front. No refunds."

"Sixty-five. Fifty up front. Nothing if I don't come away happy."

"Sevenny-five and no guarantees. Phone's gettin' *heavy*, man."

I said okay. We compared meeting places, settling finally on a city parking lot on West Lafayette at six o'clock.

My next call was to Leonard Blum's construction firm, where a junior partner referred me to Ed Klagan at a building site on Third.

Klagan's was one of the names Andrea Blum had given me. I asked for the number at the building site.

"There aren't any phones on the twenty-first floor, mister," the junior partner told me.

An M. Shinstone was listed in Birmingham. I tried the number and cradled the receiver after twenty rings. It was getting slippery. I got up, peeling my shirt away from my back, stood in front of the clanking fan for a minute, then hooked up my hat and jacket. The thermometer at the bank where I cashed Mrs. Blum's check read 87°, which was as cool as it had been all day.

It was hotter on Third Street. The naked girders straining up from the construction site were losing their vertical hold in the smog and twisting heat waves, and the security guard at the opening in the board fence had sweated through his light blue uniform shirt. I shouted my business over the clattering pneumatic hammers. At length he signaled to a broad party in a hardhat and necktie who was squinting at a blueprint in the hands of a glistening half-naked black man. The broad party came over, getting bigger as he approached until I was looking up at his Adam's apple and three chins folded over it. The guard left us.

"Mr. Klagan?"

"Yeah. You from the city?"

"The country, originally." I showed him my ID. "Andrea Blum hired me to look into her husband's death."

"I heard he croaked himself."

"That's what I'm being paid to find out. What was his interest in the construction firm?"

"Strictly financial. Pumped most of his profits back into the business and arranged an occasional loan when we were on the shorts, which wasn't often. He put together a good organization. Look, I got to get back up on the steel. The higher these guys go the slower they work. And the foreman's a drunk."

"Why don't you fire him?"

He uncovered tobacco-stained teeth in a sour grin. "Local two-two-six. Socialism's got us by the uppers, brother."

"One more question. Blum's life before he got into construction is starting to look like a mystery. I thought you could clear it up."

"Not me. My old man might. They started the firm together."

"Where can I find him?"

"Mount Elliott. But you better bring a shovel."

"I was afraid it'd be something like that," I said.

"All I know is Blum came up to the old man in January of 'thirty-four with a roll of greenbacks the size of a coconut and told him he looked too smart to die a foreman. He had the bucks, Pop had the know-how."

He showed me an acre of palm and moved off. I smoked a cigarette to soothe a throat made raw by yelling over the noise and watched him mount the hydraulic platform that would take him up to the unfinished twenty-first floor. Thinking.

Six

The parking lot on West Lafayette was in the shadow of the *News* building; stepping into it from the heat of the street was like falling headfirst into a pond. I stood in the aisle, mopping the back of my neck with my soaked handkerchief and looking around. My watch read six on the nose.

A horn beeped. I looked in that direction. The only vehicle occupied was a ten-year-old Dodge club cab pickup parked next to the building with Michigan cancer eating through its rear fenders and a dull green finish worn down to brown primer in leprous patches. I went over there.

The window on the driver's side came down, leaking loud music and framing a narrow, heavy-lidded black face in the opening. "You a P.I. named Walker?"

I said I was. He reached across the interior and popped up the lock button on the passenger's side. The cab was paved with maroon plush inside and had an instrument-studded leather dash and speakers for a sound system that had cost at least as much as the book on the pickup, pouring out drums and electric guitars at brain-throbbing volume. He'd had the air conditioner on recently and it was ten degrees cooler inside.

My eardrums had been raped enough for one day. I shouted to him to turn down the roar. He twirled a knob and then it was just us and the engine ticking as it cooled.

My host was a loose tube of bones in a red tank top and blue running shorts. And alligator shoes on his bare feet. He caught me looking at them and said, "I got an allergy to everything but lizard. You carrying?"

When I hesitated he showed me the muzzle of a nickel-plated .357 magnum he had lying face down on his lap. I didn't think he was the *Ebony* type. I took the Smith &Wesson out of its belt holster slowly and handed it to him butt first. His lip curled.

"Police Special. Who you, Dick Tracy? I got what you want here." He laid my revolver on his side of the dash and snaked an arm over the back of the seat into the compartment behind. After some rummaging he came up with a chromed Colt Python as long as my forearm. "Man, you plug them with this mother, the lead goes through them, knocks down a light pole across the street."

"I've got no beef with Detroit Edison."

He dropped his baggy grin, put the big magnum back behind the seat and its little brother on the dash next to my .38, and held out his palm. I laid seventy-five dollars in it. He folded the bills and slid them under a clip on the sun visor. "You after hot iron."

"Just its history." I recited Blum's list so far as I remembered it. "They came up gone from a house on Kendall a little over a week ago," I added. "Unless someone's hugging the ground they should be on the market by now. Some of those pieces are pretty rare. You'd know them."

"Ain't come my way. I can let you have a forty-five auto Army, never issued. Two hunnert."

"How many notches?"

"Man, this is a virgin piece. The barrel, anyway."

"The guns," I said. "You'd hear if they were available. It's a lot of iron to hit the streets all at one time."

"When S 'n' W talks, people listen. Only I guess it missed me."

"Okay, hang your ears out. I've got another seventy-five says they'll show up soon." I gave him my card.

"Last week a fourteen-year-old kid give me that much for a Saturday night banger I don't want to be in the same *building* with when it goes off. Listen, I can put you behind a Thompson Model Nineteen Twenty-One for a thousand. The Gun That Won Chicago. Throw in a fifty-round drum."

I looked back at him with my hand on the door handle. I'd clean forgotten that item on Blum's list. "You've got a Thompson?"

His eyes hooded over. "Could be I know where one can be got."

I peeled three fifties off the roll in my pocket and held them up.

"I trade you a thousand-dollar piece for a bill and a half? Get out of my face, turkey white meat." He turned on the sound system. The pickup's frame buzzed.

"Ooh, jive," I said, turning it off. "You keep the gun. All I want is the seller's name. There's a murder involved."

He hesitated. I skinned off another fifty. He put his fingers on them. I held on. "I call you, man," he said.

I tore the bills in two and gave him half. "You know the speech."

"Ain't no way to treat President Grant." But he clipped the torn bills with the rest and gave me back my gun, tipping out the cartridges first. There's no more trust in the world.

Seven

Shadows were lengthening downtown, cooling the pavement without actually lowering the temperature. I caught a sandwich and a cold beer at a counter and used the pay telephone to try the Birmingham number again. A husky female voice answered.

"May Shinstone?"

"Yes?"

I told her who I was and what I was after. There was a short silence before she said, "Leonard's dead?"

I made a face at the snarl of penciled numbers on the wall next to the telephone. "I'm sorry, Mrs. Shinstone. I got so used to it I forgot everyone didn't know."

"Don't apologize. It was just a surprise. It's been two years since I've seen Leonard, and almost that long since I've thought about him. I don't know how I can help you."

"Just now I'm sweeping up whatever's lying around. I'll sort it out later. I need some stuff on his life before January nineteen thirty-four."

"That isn't a story for the telephone, Mr. Walker."

There was something in her tone. I played around with it for a second, then poked it into a drawer. "If you have a few minutes this evening I'd like to come talk to you about it," I said.

"How big is your car trunk?"

"Would you say that again, Mrs. Shinstone? We have a bad connection."

"I'm giving up the house here and moving to an apartment in Royal Oak. I have one or two things left to move. If your trunk's big enough I can dismiss the cab I have waiting." She gave me her address.

I said, "I'll put the spare tire in the back seat."

I paused with my hand on the receiver, then unhooked it again and used another quarter to call my service. Lieutenant Alderdyce had tried to reach me and wanted me to call him back. I dialed his extension at Headquarters.

"I spoke to Mrs. Blum a little while ago," he said. "You're fired."

"Funny, you don't sound like her."

"She'll tell you the same thing. Blum's death is starting not to look like suicide and that means you can go back to your bench and leave the field to the first string."

"How much not like suicide is it starting to look?"

"Just for the hell of it we ran Blum's prints. We got a positive."

"He told me he'd never been printed."

"He must've forgot," Alderdyce said. "We didn't mess with the FBI. They destroy their records once a subject turns seventy. We got a match in a box of stuff on its way to the incinerator because it was too old to bother feeding into the computer. There is no Leonard Blum. But Leo Goldblum got to know these halls during Prohibition, whenever the old rackets squad found it prudent to round up the Purple Gang and ask questions."

"Blum was a Purple?"

"Nice kids, those. When they weren't gunning each other down and commuting to Chicago to pull off the St. Valentine's Day Massacre for Capone they found time to ship bootleg hooch across the river from Canada. That was Goldblum's specialty. He was arrested twice for transporting liquor from the Ecorse docks and drew a year's probation in 'twenty-nine on a Sullivan rap. Had a revolver in his pocket."

"Explains why he never registered his guns," I said. Licenses aren't issued to convicted felons. "That was a long time ago, John."

"Yeah, well, there's something else. Ever hear of Bloody July?"

"Sounds like the name of a punk rock group. No, wasn't that when they killed Jerry Buckley?"

"The golden boy of radio. Changed his stand on the mayor's recall on July twenty-second, nineteen thirty, and a few hours later three Purples left him in a pool of blood in the lobby of the Hotel LaSalle. And during the first two weeks of the month the gang got frisky and put holes in ten of their Mob playmates. It was a good month not to be a cop."

"All this history is leading someplace, I guess."

"Yeah. We got a lot of eager young uniforms here. One of them spent a couple of hours after his shift was over pawing through dusty records in the basement and matched the bullet that killed Blum with the ballistics report on the shooting of one Emmanuel Eckleberg, DOA at St. Mary's Hospital July sixth, nineteen thirty."

"Yesterday was July sixth," I said. "You're telling me someone waited all these years to avenge Manny Whatsizname on the anniversary of his death with the same gun that was used to kill him?"

"Eckleberg. You want someone to tell you that, call Hollywood. I just read you what we've got. You're walking, right?"

"Give me some time to square away a couple of things for my report."

He might have said "Uh-oh." I can't be sure because I was hanging up. It was getting to be a hell of a case, all right.

Eight

The address I wanted in Birmingham belonged to a small crackerbox with blue aluminum siding and a rosebush that had outgrown its bed under the picture window. My watch read seven-thirty and the sky showed no signs of darkening. You get a lot more for your money by hiring a private investigator in the summertime.

My knock was answered by a tall slim woman in sweats with blond streaks in her gray hair drawn up under a knotted handkerchief. She had taken the time to put on lipstick and rub rouge into her cheeks, but she really didn't need it. She had to be in her early seventies but looked twenty years younger. Her eyes were flat blue.

She smiled. "You look like you were expecting granny glasses and a ball of yarn."

"I was sort of looking forward to it," I said, taking off my hat. "No one seems to knit any more except football players."

"I never could get the knack. Come in."

The place looked bigger inside, mainly because there was hardly any furniture in it and the walls and floor were bare. She led me to a heavy oak table with the round top removed and leaning against the pedestal base. "Will it fit?" she asked.

"Search me. I flunked physics." I put my hat back on and got to work.

It was awkward, but the top eventually slid onto the ledge where the spare belonged and the pedestal fit diagonally into the well. She carried out a carton of books and slid it onto the back seat. "Take Telegraph down to Twelve Mile," she said, getting in on the passenger's side in front.

On the road I asked if Mr. Shinstone was waiting for her in Royal Oak.

"He died in 'seventy-eight. I would have sold the place then, but my sister got sick and I took her in. She passed away six weeks ago."

I said I was sorry. She shrugged. "You were married to Leonard Blum when he was Leo Goldblum?" I asked.

She looked at me, then untied her handkerchief and shook her hair loose. She kept it short. "You've been doing your homework. Have you got a cigarette?"

I got out two, lit them from the dash lighter, and gave her one. She blew smoke into the slipstream outside her window.

"I started seeing him when I was in high school," she said. "He was twenty and very dashing. They all were; handsome boys in sharp suits and shiny new automobiles. We thought they were Robin Hoods. Never mind that people got killed, it was all for a good cause. The right to get hung over. The world was different then."

"Just the suits and automobiles," I put in. "Prohibition was repealed in December nineteen thirty-three. In January nineteen thirty-four, Goldblum shortened his name and invested his bootlegging profits in construction."

"He and Ed Klagan, Sr., had a previous understanding. I don't know how many buildings downtown are still being held up by people Leo didn't get on with. Mind you, I only suspected these things at the time."

"Was Manny Eckleberg one of them?"

"Who was he?"

I told her as much as I knew. We were stopped at a light and I was watching her. She was studying the horizontal suburban scenery. "I think I remember it. It was during that terrible July. Leo and some others were questioned by the police. Somebody was convicted for it. Abe Somebody; my sister dated him once or twice. Leo and I were married soon after and I remember hoping it wouldn't mean a postponement."

"Why was he killed?"

"A territorial dispute, I suppose. It was a long time ago."

"Did you divorce Blum because of his past?"

"I could say that and sound noble. But I just got tired of being married to him. That was twenty years ago and he was already turning into an old crab. From what I saw of him during the times I ran into him since I'd say he never changed. Turn right here."

She had three rooms and a bath in the back half of a house on Farnum. I carried the table inside and set both pieces down in the middle of a room full of cartons and furniture. She added the box of books to the pile. "Thank you, Mr. Walker. You're a nice man."

"Mrs. Shinstone," I said, "can you tell me why Blum might have been killed by the same gun that killed Manny Eckleberg?"

"Heavens, no. You said he was killed by a gun from his collection, didn't you?" I nodded. "Well, I guess that tells us something about the original murder then, doesn't it? Not that it matters."

She let me use her telephone to call my service. I had a message. I asked the girl from whom.

Nine

"He wouldn't leave his name, just his number." She gave it to me. I recognized it. This time it rang fourteen times before the voice came on.

"What've you got for me, Mississippi?" I asked.

"They's a parking lot on Livernois at Fort," he said. "Good view of the river."

"No more parking lots. Let's make it my building in half an hour."

I broke the connection, thanked Mrs. Shinstone, and got out of her new living room.

The sky was purpling finally when I stepped into the foyer of my office building. A breeze had come up to peel away the smog and humidity. I mounted the stairs, stopping when something stiff prodded my lower back.

"Turn around, turkey white meat."

The something stiff was withdrawn and I obeyed. The lanky gun broker had stepped out from behind the propped open fire door and was standing at the base of the stairs in his summer running outfit and alligator shoes. His right hand was wrapped around the butt of a lean automatic.

"Bang, you dead." He flashed a grin and reversed the gun, extending the checked grip. "Go on, see how she feels. Luger. Ninety bucks."

I said, "That's not a Luger. It's a P-thirty-eight."

"Okay, eighty-five. 'Cause you discerning."

"Keep the gun. I'm getting my fill of them." I produced my half of the hundred I'd torn earlier, holding it back when he reached for it.

He moved a shoulder and clipped the pistol under his tank top. "He goes by Shoe. I don't know his right name. White dude, big nose. When he turns sideways everything disappears but that beak. Tried to sell me the tommy gun and some other stuff on your list. Told him I had to scratch up cash. He says call him here." He handed me a fold of paper from the pocket of his shorts. "Belongs to a roach hatchery at Wilson and Webb."

"This better be the square." I gave him the abbreviated currency.

"Hey, I deal hot merchandise. I got to be honest."

Ten

They had just missed the hotel putting through the John Lodge and that was too bad. It was eight stories of charred brick held together with scaffolding and pigeon-splatter. An electric sign ran up the front reading O LPON C. After five minutes I gave up wondering what it was trying to say and went inside. A kid in an Afro and army BVD undershirt looked up from the copy of *Bronze Thrills* he was reading behind the desk as I approached. I said, "I'm looking for a white guy named Shoe. Skinny guy with a big nose. He lives here."

"If his name ain't Smith or Jones it ain't in the register."

He laid a dirty hand on the desk, palm up.

I rang the bell on the desk with his head and repeated what I'd said.

"Twenty-three," he groaned, rubbing his forehead. "Second floor, end of the hall."

It had been an elegant hall, with thick carpeting and wainscoting to absorb noise, but the floorboards whimpered now under the shiny fabric and the plaster bulged over the dull oak. I rapped on 23. The door opened four inches and I was looking at a smoky brown eye and half a nose the size of my fist.

"I'm the new house man," I said. "We got a complaint you've been playing your TV too loud."

"Ain't got a TV." He had a voice like a pencil sharpener.

"Your radio, then."

The door started to close. I leaned a shoulder against it. When it sprang open I had to change my footing to keep my face off the floor. He was holding a short-barreled revolver at belly level.

A day like that brought a whole new meaning to the phrase Detroit iron.

"You're the dick, let's see your ID."

I held it up.

"Okay. I'm checking out tonight anyway." The door closed.

I waited until the lock snapped, then walked back downstairs, making plenty of noise. I could afford to. I'd had a good look at Shoe and at an airline ticket folder lying on the lamp table next to the door.

I passed the reader in the lobby without comment and got into my crate parked across the street in front of a mailbox. While I was watching the entrance and smoking a cigarette, a car rolled up behind mine and a fat woman in a green dress levered herself out to mail a letter and scowl at me through the windshield. I smiled back.

The streetlights had just sprung on when Shoe came out lugging two big suitcases and turned into the parking lot next door. Five minutes later a blue Plymouth with a smashed fender pulled out of the lot and the light fluttered on a big-nosed profile. I gave him a block before following.

We took the Lodge down to Grand River and turned right onto Selden. After three blocks the Plymouth slid into a vacant space just as a station wagon was leaving it. I cruised on past and stopped at the next intersection, adjusting my rearview mirror to watch Shoe angle across the street on foot, using both hands on the bigger of the two suitcases. He had to set it down to open a lighted glass door stenciled ZOLOTOW SECURITIES, then brace the door with a foot while he backed in towing his burden.

I found a space around the corner and walked back. Two doors down I leaned against the closed entrance to an insurance office, fired a Winston, and chased mosquitoes with the glowing tip while Shoe was busy striking a deal with the pawnbroker.

He was plenty scared, all right.

It was waiting time, the kind you measured in ashes. I was on my third smoke when a blue-and-white cut into the curb in front of Zolotow's and a uniform with a droopy gunfighter's moustache got out from behind the wheel.

The glass door opened just as the cop had both feet on the pavement. He drew his side arm and threw both hands across the roof of the prowl car. "Freeze! Police!"

Empty-handed, Shoe backpedaled. The cop yelled freeze again, but he was already back inside. The door drifted shut.

A second blue-and-white wheeled into the block, and then I heard sirens. A minute crawled past. I counted four guns trained on the door. Blue and red flashers washed the street in pulsing light. Then the door flew open again and Shoe was on the threshold cradling a Chicago typewriter.

Someone hollered, "Drop it!"

Thompsons pull to the left and up. The muzzle splattered fire, its bullets sparking off the first prowl car's roof and pounding dust out of the granite wall across the street and shattering windows higher up, tok-tok-tok-tok-tok.

The return shots came so close together they made one long roar. Shoe slammed back against the door and slid into a sitting position spraddle-legged in the entrance, the submachine gun in his lap.

As the uniforms came forward, guns out, an unmarked unit fishtailed into the street. Lieutenant Alderdyce was out the passenger's side while it was still rocking on its springs. He glanced down at the body on the sidewalk, then looked up and spotted me in the crowd of officers. "What the hell are you doing here?"

"Mainly, abusing my lungs," I said. "How about you?"

"Pawnbroker matched the guns this clown was selling to the hot sheet. He made an excuse and called us from the back."

I said, "He was running scared. He had a plane ticket and he checked out of the hotel where he was living. He was after a getaway stake."

"The murder hit the radio tonight. When his suicide scam went bust he rabbited."

The plainclothesman who had come with Alderdyce leaned out the open door of the pawnshop. Shoe was acting as a doorstop now. "He had all the handguns in the suitcase except one or two, John."

"Hey, this guy's still alive."

Everyone looked at the uniform down on one knee beside Shoe. The wounded man's chest rose and fell feebly beneath his bloody shirt. Alderdyce leaned forward.

"It's over," he said. "No sense lying your way deeper into hell. Why'd you kill Blum?"

Shoe looked up at him. His eyes were growing soft. After a moment his lips moved. On that street with the windows going up on both sides and police radios squawking it got very quiet.

Eleven

It was even quieter on Farnum in Royal Oak, where night lay warm on the lawns and sidewalks and I towed a little space of silence through ratcheting crickets on my way to the back door of the duplex. The lights were off inside. I rang the bell and had time to smoke a cigarette between the time they came on and when May Shinstone looked at me through the window. A moment later she opened the door. Her hair was tousled and she had on a blue robe over a lighter blue nightgown that covered her feet. Without make-up she looked older, but still nowhere near her true age.

"Isn't it a little late for visiting, Mr. Walker?"

"It's going to be a busy night," I said. "The cops will be here as soon as they find out you've left the place in Birmingham and get a change of address."

"I don't know what you're talking about, but come in. When I was young we believed the night air was bad for you."

She closed the door behind me. The living room looked like a living room now. The cartons were gone and the books were in place on the shelves. I said, "You've been busy."

"Yes. Isn't it awful? I'm one of those compulsive people who can't go to sleep when there's a mess to be cleaned up."

"You can't have gotten much sleep lately, then. Leaving Shoe with all those guns made a big mess."

"Shoe? I don't—"

"The cops shot him at the place where he tried to lay them off. When he found out he was mired up in murder he panicked. He made a dying statement in front of seven witnesses."

She was going to brazen it out. She stood with her back to the door and her hands in the pockets of her robe and a marble look on her face. Then it crumbled. I watched her grow old.

"I let him keep most of what he stole," she said. "It was his payment for agreeing to burgle Leo's house. All I wanted was the Colt automatic, the thirty-eight he used to kill Manny Eckleberg. Shoe— his name was Henry Schumacher—was my gardener in Birmingham. I hired him knowing of his prison record for breaking and entering. I didn't dream I'd ever have use for his talents in that area."

"You had him steal the entire collection to keep Blum from suspecting what you had in mind. Then on the anniversary of Eckleberg's murder you went back and killed him with the same gun. Pure poetry."

"I went there to kill him, yes. He let me in and when I pointed the gun he laughed at me and tried to take it away. We struggled. It went off. I don't expect you to believe that."

"It doesn't matter what I believe because it stinks first degree any way you smell it," I said. "So you stuck his finger in the trigger afterwards and fired the gun through the window or something to satisfy the paraffin test and make it look like suicide. Why'd you kill the dog?"

"After letting me in, Leo set it loose on the grounds. It wouldn't let me out the door. I guess he'd trained it to trap intruders until he called it off. So I went back and got the gun and shot it. That hurt me more than killing Leo, can you imagine that? A poor dumb beast."

"What was Manny Eckleberg to you?"

"Nothing. I never knew him. He was just a small-time bootlegger from St. Louis who thought he could play with the Purple Gang."

I said nothing. Waiting. After a moment she crossed in front of me, opened a drawer in a bureau that was holding up a china lamp, and handed me a bundle of yellowed envelopes bound with a faded brown ribbon.

"Those are letters my sister received from Abe Steinmetz when he was serving time in Jackson prison for Eckleberg's murder," she said. "In them he explains how Leo Goldblum paid him to confess to the murder. He promised him he wouldn't serve more than two years and that there would be lots more waiting when he got out. Only he never got out. He was stabbed to death in a mess room brawl six months before his parole.

"I was the one who was dating Abe, Mr. Walker; not my sister. I was seeing him at the same time I was seeing Leo. He swore her to secrecy in the letters, believing I wouldn't understand until he could explain things in person. The money would start our marriage off right, he said. But instead of waiting I married Leo."

She wet her lips. I lit a Winston and gave it to her. She inhaled deeply, her fingers fidgeting and dropping ash on the carpet. "My sister kept the secret all these years. It wasn't until she died and I opened her safety deposit box and read the letters—" She broke off and mashed out the cigarette in a copper ashtray atop the bureau. "Do I have time to get dressed and put on lipstick before the police arrive? They never even gave Leo time to grab a necktie whenever they took him in for questioning."

I told her to take as much time as she needed. At the bedroom door she paused. "I don't regret it, you know. Maybe I wouldn't have been happy married to Abe. But when I think of all those wasted years—well, I don't regret it." She went through the door.

Waiting, I pocketed the letters, shook the last cigarette out of my pack, and struck a match. I stared at the flame until it burned down to my fingers.

He had all the handguns in the suitcase except one or two. I dropped the match and vaulted to the bedroom door. Moving too damn slowly. I had my hand on the knob when I heard the shot.

Twelve

The temperatures soared later in the month, and with them the crime statistics. The weathermen called it the hottest July on record. The newspapers had another name for it, but it had already been used.

The Anniversary Waltz

I caught up with Judd Lindauer in the Detroit Free Republic of Nicotine Abuse, otherwise known as the parking lot behind the Frank Murphy Hall of Justice. The flag is a black lung on a field of tobacco leaves.

A big man of sixty beginning to stoop to a mere six-six, Lindauer left a crowd of litigants and judges and changed hands on his cigar to shake my hand. He had on a blue suit with flared lapels and a tan suede yoke over a snap-front shirt secured with a string tie. As far as I knew he'd never been west of Kalamazoo except when tracking a jump on a hundred-grand bail. He was a bail bondsman and a bounty hunter and enjoyed looking the part.

"Remember me on this one, Amos," he said when we were out of earshot of the others. "There's miles of press in it if you tear this one off. That can't be bad for a one-man band like yours."

I said, "Maybe I'll buy you a drink when I know what it's about. All my service told me is you wanted to see me."

"That's all I told them." He lowered his voice to a reverberating boom. "It's Adelaide Dix."

"The trunk murderess?"

"If you believe the tabloids. Personally I don't think she ever harmed a piece of luggage in her life, and I'm the one who went her bail."

"Which time? She escaped what, four times?"

"Four and a half. She got outside the wall up in Marquette six weeks after they transferred her from Jackson, but they kept that one out of the papers. They managed to hang on to her for two years after that; then she flushed herself down the sewer. That was eight years ago. Nobody's seen her since."

I plucked a Winston out of my pack and put it between my lips without lighting it. There was enough smoke drifting across the lot to cure a ham. "I heard she drowned in Lake Superior."

"I don't have any reason to doubt it. Superior never gives up its dead."

"So where is she?"

He handed me one of his cards, embossed in gold on white stock with a gold lariat in one corner. A telephone number was written on the back next to a name: G. Tolliver.

"The G stands for Geraldine," he said. "She's Adelaide's daughter. Her husband's Bert Tolliver, a building contractor. You get her, you get him too. But she does the talking. She says her mother's alive."

"Says to who, you? And why?"

"I put up bail when Adelaide got a new trial. She jumped—that was the first escape—and I brought her back. I flew with her from Denver to Detroit, first-class, no cuffs. I was the first person not to treat her like a tarantula. Geraldine was grateful. I'm the only member of the law enforcement community she thinks she can trust."

"Why tell anyone? Old lady getting too tough to care for?"

"Ask Geraldine. I didn't ask her any questions and I stopped her before she could give me any specific information. I'm an officer of the court; it's my license if I fail to report knowledge of a fugitive's whereabouts. I told her I was giving it to you and you're no gossip."

"I've got a license too," I said. "I didn't get this job drawing Sherlock Holmes off a matchbook."

"You've got the hot handle. What you do with it won't burn me." He blew a smoke ring big enough to snare me around the neck.

• • •

In 1985, Adelaide Dix had driven Iran-contra off the front pages when she was convicted of chopping up her second husband, packing him in an antique trunk, and stowing it in a corner of her Sterling Heights basement. A meter reader reported the smell and Adelaide got life. Her first escape while out on bail pending a new trial destroyed her defense; two more bought her a cell away up North in Marquette. She had an I.Q. of 160, fifty points higher than the average corrections officer, so another escape was inevitable. A set of size six footprints in the sand leading to Lake Superior convinced authorities she was dead, but that didn't prevent her from showing up at a McDonald's drive-through every couple of months with Elvis at the wheel.

A well-tended female voice, ratcheted a notch high for normal intercourse, provided an invitation and directions to a house in one of the newer suburbs, founded since white flight. It was a stack of trapezoidal boxes with passive solar windows—ornamental only in Michigan's cloudy climate—tucked between hills in a tract named after a tree that had been extinct in the area for three hundred years.

Geraldine Tolliver was small and compact, about twenty, with short red hair and a tiny waist in a tailored shirt and capri pants or whatever they're calling them this year. Her husband, Bert, was heavily muscled and sunburned in a polo shirt and khakis. He was a hand-mangler; two drinks and he'd be pounding my back. I avoided the sofa in case he decided to sit within range and settled into an Eames knockoff with a scotch and soda.

Mrs. Tolliver tasted her gin and tonic, set it down, and never returned to it. "Mr. Lindauer says you're a man one can confide in. Are you like a priest?"

"Only in that department."

"Honey, I think we'd better see some ID. We'd better see some ID," Bert Tolliver told me, over the top of a whiskey sour the size of a conga drum.

I showed them some ID.

"Mr. Walker, we need your word you'll tell no one about this," the woman said. "Not even your wife. Things have a way of getting back to Alvin Shrike. It's almost supernatural."

"I don't have a wife. Who's Alvin Shrike?"

"An icicle-pissing son of a bitch. Sorry, honey." Tolliver sat back in the sofa and drank.

Mrs. Tolliver gave him the fisheye and finished what she'd started to say. "Shrike's chief of police here. Bert's right about the rest. He was an officer in Sterling Heights fifteen years ago. The man my—the dead man in the trunk was his partner."

"That would be your father?"

"No. My father died of cancer when I was three months old. George Dix was a good-looking brute and a drunk who seduced my mother into marrying him and beat her up on a regular schedule. When he started in on me she did something about it."

"No one would argue with that."

"I don't remember much about that night. I remember he slapped me and the way my face was still burning when I woke up. When I was old enough to understand she told me she shot him

with his service revolver. I have no doubt she'd have been acquitted
if she'd stopped there. The dismemberment was a mistake."

"It usually is."

"She didn't want me to wake up and find a corpse in the house.
She was temporarily insane, of course, but the jury rejected that.
Calling her 'Adelaide the Axe' in the tabloids didn't help."

"'Slice-and-Dice Dix,'" put in Tolliver.

She closed her eyes. "That too. There were others. Why do people take such delight in grisly details?"

"It's a dark old world," I said. "Have you heard from your mother?"

"Once a year for eight years." She got up, opened a drawer in a
bleached oak table with a cordless telephone on top, and brought
over a picture postcard. There was no message on the back, just a
USPS postmark and the Tollivers' address block-printed with a black
felt-tipped pen. It had been mailed last week. The picture on the
other side was a color shot of Grand Traverse Bay.

"They always come before my birthday," Geraldine said. "Always a different scene, but always in Michigan. Mother's a native,
but like so many she never got around to visiting the local vacation
spots. We used to talk about going to all of them when she got out
of prison. This is as close as we can come to that as long as Shrike's
around."

I gave it back. "It's been fifteen years. Maybe he's put it behind him."

She shut the drawer on the postcard and stepped over to a window. "I want you to look at something."

When I joined her, she drew aside the curtain two inches. A gold
Chrysler four-door was parked on the corner across the street. I could
read the headline on the newspaper the driver had spread in front of
his face. "It isn't Shrike," she said. "Or maybe it is. The point is it
doesn't have to be, as long as he runs the police department in this

town. We have an escort every time we leave the house. I'd actually miss them if they weren't there."

"You could do a quarterback split and decoy him off."

"I'm sure there's a contingency plan. Anyway, where would we go? Mother's always been careful not to give any hints as to her whereabouts. You couldn't even prove in court she's the one who sends the cards. But I know."

We sat back down. I asked her what she wanted me to do.

"I want you to talk her into giving herself up. She can't run forever. I'm terrified someday I'll turn on the news and hear she's been shot down by Shrike or one of his officers. He said in court he wished Michigan would bring back the death penalty just for her."

"Traverse City's a good-size town. Even if it weren't, she's probably blown it by now, if she was ever there to begin with. You can buy postcards anywhere. I'd need a bigger comb than Shrike's got and I'd have to start in Little America."

"No, you wouldn't. She'll be at the cemetery in Sterling Heights the day after tomorrow."

I looked from her to Tolliver, who was watching me over his glass like someone who'd heard the joke before and was waiting to see the reaction. I disappointed him. I sipped scotch and soda and said, "What time? I'm going to a ball game that night."

Geraldine shook her head. "I can't tell you that because I don't know. The day after tomorrow is my parents' twenty-fifth wedding anniversary. It'll be their anniversary all day."

I was starting to get it. "That's where your father's buried? What makes you think she'll show?"

"Because when my father got sick and needed hope, my mother promised him they'd be together on their silver anniversary. She keeps her promises. And she never forgets a date." She tilted her head toward the drawer containing the postcard. "By now that officer outside has radioed in your license number and knows who you are, but I assume you're experienced in discouraging people from following you. We're not. We'd lead Shrike right to her."

"Okay, the Tigers can lose without me in the bleachers. My fee's five hundred for the day."

Tolliver made himself useful and put down his drink and wrote me a check. His wife took the back off a picture frame from the fireplace mantel and handed me a photo of a handsome middle-aged woman with sharply intelligent eyes.

"That's the latest we have. It was taken nine years ago. Every Christmas the inmates got to put on civilian clothes and pose for a professional photographer."

I got up and slid it into my inside breast pocket along with the folded check. "It wouldn't be an honest five hundred if I didn't tell you it's wasted. If your mother keeps that promise she isn't as smart as I'd heard, even if she's alive. Anyone could be sending you those postcards as a sick gag. You don't know who knows about your conversations."

"Thank you, Mr. Walker," Geraldine said. "It isn't wasted."

I went out and stopped to light a cigarette before getting into the car, because I needed it and because it let me get another look at the driver of the gold Chrysler. He was still reading the Lively Arts section, committing the opera times to memory.

I put five blocks behind me before I spotted the tail. Same make, different color, fresh from Dispatch. You didn't get to be chief of anyone's police by sitting around growing your whiskers.

•   •   •

The outer-office buzzer caught me thinking the next morning about climbing up and dumping the fly wings out of the bowl fixture above my desk. I decided they wouldn't be any deader an hour later, and opened the door for a square party a couple of inches below my height in a stiff gray suit with his tie snugged up to a chin that had begun to double and shards of silver glittering in his sandy crew cut. He looked like an unmarked car.

"I'm going out on a limb," I said. "Chief Shrike?"

"That obvious?" He smiled with his bottom teeth only and took my hand. His was one even Bert Tolliver couldn't mangle.

"Just the cop part. I was expecting the rest." I showed him the chair. He put his hands in his pockets and stayed where he was.

"What's a Detroit private cop got going with Adelaide Dix's daughter?"

I put my hands in my own pockets. It was like looking in a mirror from ten years in the future, if I didn't hurry up and take violin lessons. "Lizzie Borden was taken. What color's your Chrysler?"

"Blue. That was me, all right. I figured you were wise. You know that was my marriage Adelaide broke up with her set of Ginsus. Best partner I ever had. He saved my ass six ways from Sunday."

"Sundays he kicked his wife's."

"He had a temper. Lots of guys slap their women around. Lots of women don't cut them into easily manageable pieces and put them up like preserves."

"She's in a lake."

"I don't think so. Why go that direction? Once you're over the wall you got directions up the ass."

"So she drowned herself."

"She could've stopped her clock inside. Why go over the wall at all? She walked backwards in her own footprints and she's been walking ever since. Her daughter knows it. She just don't know where she is. That's why she hired you. I knew she'd crack if I leaned on her long enough."

"I'm looking for a hit-and-run vehicle. Hers was on the list."

"She told me you're working for her."

I laughed in his face.

He turned deep copper right up to his cropped hair. His hands came out fists. "I can pull you in right now as a material witness."

"To what? A drowning? She's dead. Marquette thinks it, the governor thinks it, the FBI thinks it, and so does the secretary who filled out the legal declaration of death. You're a one-man Flat Earth Society, Shrike."

"Wrong. There's three others. Adelaide Dix knows she's alive. So does Geraldine Tolliver. So do you. And I'm going to be on you like flies on a carp till you walk me right up to her."

After he left, I looked up at the dead wings in the fixture, but I didn't go after them. I appreciated the company.

•   •   •

I spent the rest of that day with Alvin Shrike. The blue Chrysler was with me when I wheeled my bucket out of its slot and it stayed three lengths behind except when it looked like I might lose it in traffic. It followed me around seventeen corners, across a vacant lot, and down both sides of a divided street as well as up and over the divider itself. Either he was one hungry fly or I was a pretty ripe carp. After we got both our cars washed on West Grand River I could see I would have to get rid of the horses.

I parked where the trucks go into the *Free Press,* where I could get a nice safe tow to the police garage, cut through the thundering pressroom on foot, and went out the front entrance past a surprised security guard. He probably did a double take when Shrike went out right behind. I thought I'd shaken the tail when I skipped across Washington directly in front of the streetcar, but when I stopped sprinting a couple of hundred yards later and looked behind me, he was legging his way along Fort. I got lucky and caught a cab two blocks over; Shrike got lucky too and flashed his badge at a motorist who turned out to be a solid citizen and they trailed me clear to Redford.

We had supper at a chain place with license plates and other assorted junk on the walls. I sent him a bottle of beer which he drank without even lifting it in acknowledgment.

We had a moment when we both called for cabs from adjacent pay telephones, but by then I was getting tired and couldn't raise a chuckle. I reached over and pushed down the lifter on his, breaking his connection. "Why don't we just share mine? All I'm going is home."

"I don't tip cabbies," he said. "You want to, go ahead."

When the Redtop came, I got in first. He pushed in fast in case I tried to jerk the door shut. I hit him with everything I had; he was hard for a desk cop, but his forward momentum helped and he sagged against me like a sack of ball bearings. I worked the door handle on my side and slid out from underneath him.

"Take my friend to the Wayne County Airport," I told the driver.

"Where's his luggage?" He was a big Jamaican with gold teeth.

"He doesn't have any. He's going to a nudist camp."

After the cab left I hightailed it to a Shell station, called another cab, and took it to my reporter friend Barry Stackpole's place to borrow his car. He has an artificial leg and the hand controls took getting used to, but they got me to a motel in Sterling Heights.

I wasn't taking chances. In the room I set the radio clock for 11:30 and called for a wake-up in case it wasn't working. If I were on the run from the law—which I was, but my situation was variant—

and I had to be somewhere tomorrow, I'd pick one minute past midnight. Before I caught some sleep I laid my Chief's Special on the floor in front of the door so I wouldn't forget it when I left. I was meeting Adelaide the Axe, and I hadn't thought to ask her daughter if she liked surprises.

• • •

At one minute past midnight I was leaning against the cool marble wall of a mausoleum in the Sterling Heights cemetery, wanting a cigarette and jerking my head around every time a nighthawk squirrel scampered up a tree. The temperature had dropped steeply after nightfall and there was a light ground mist rolling among the headstones like the dry ice in a Dracula movie. It and the squirrels were the only things that moved until dawn, by which time my back ached from standing and the clothes I'd had on for twenty-four hours felt like wet burlap. When it was light enough to burn tobacco I moved under a tree where the branches would break up the smoke. That was when I spotted Alvin Shrike striding between the posts that flanked the entrance to the cemetery.

He'd gotten it out of Geraldine Tolliver somehow, or more likely Bert, who seemed closer to the type who succumbed to the oldest kind of police persuasion. It had taken all night, and he'd started out mad; his face was the deep copper I'd seen earlier and his feet pounded dust out of the gravel path. There was a purple mark on his jaw left by my knuckles and his tie was no longer snug.

"Shrike."

His head swiveled in my direction. He saw my gun and stopped, his flush draining away, the pro adjusting to a familiar situation. His bottom teeth showed in that werewolf grin.

"Drop the weapon!"

This time I swiveled. The uniformed cop was a pro too. I hadn't known he existed until I saw him leveling a sniper's rifle at me across the top of the iron fence that enclosed the grounds. I dropped the Chief's Special and raised my hands. Shrike got his piece out and pulled me away from the tree and threw me up against the mausoleum and frisked and cuffed me in less time than it takes to tell.

"Aiding and abetting a fugitive and officer assault," he said. "If one don't stick the other will."

"What'd you do to the Tollivers?" The cuffs were cutting off circulation to my fingers. I worked them. I didn't want to forget how to make a fist.

"He'll be sucking his lunch through a straw for a while, but he'll live. Usually those muscle boys bend easy, but he did better than expected. Geraldine's the one who talked, to save him the rest of his teeth. She loves her old lady, but Bert was there and so was I. Okay, Kennedy. Put him in the car and be invisible."

Kennedy was tall and black and carried his rifle at rest as if it weighed no more than a cardboard roll. Fingers like pliers closed around my biceps and we walked out the entrance. The car, another unmarked Chrysler, was parked down the street in the shade of a tall hedge. One fender of Shrike's blue Chrysler or another just like it showed around the corner.

"Why two cars?" I asked

"Shut up." Kennedy shoved me into the backseat of the one by the hedge and got in behind the wheel, leaning his rifle against the door on the passenger's side. After we'd sat long enough he got talkative. "Chief said two cars. I don't ask how come."

I didn't like it. But there wasn't one thing about the way the day was starting out that I did like.

A quiet cemetery will draw some visitors even on a weekday. Half a dozen people came and went over the next several hours, including two couples. Nobody looked like Adelaide Dix in the picture in my pocket.

She came at high noon.

It was either a bonehead play or diabolically smart. She wasn't even in disguise, unless you counted the quietly tailored dress and simple hairstyle. She looked older than her picture, older than she was, but not as if she'd been eating and sleeping in ratty motels for eight years. She had a job and had probably arranged identification papers that would pass quick inspection. I decided on diabolically smart.

Until that day.

In front of the entrance she stopped and looked around, looked directly at us. But we were too far away, and the shade was too deep to see inside the car. Still she went on looking for a minute before she entered the cemetery. She was carrying long-stemmed yellow flowers wrapped in silver paper.

"She's coming, Chief" Kennedy had his microphone in his hand and an old front-and-profile mug of Adelaide Dix taped to the dashboard.

"Okay. Cover the gate." Shrike's voice from a handheld radio sounded thin and tight.

Kennedy hung up the mike and got out with his rifle. He positioned himself on the side of the car opposite the cemetery entrance, bumping the roof a couple of times as he leveled the long gun.

When Adelaide walked out five minutes later with her hands behind her and Shrike's hand on her shoulder, I took my fingers out of the seat cushion and worked blood back into them. The woman's face was pale but calmer than the chief's. His bottom-teeth smile was a rictus. He walked her right past us and around the corner and came back a minute later alone.

"Take this character's piece and lose it in the system."

He smacked my gun into Kennedy's palm. "I'll see you back in the barn."

"Great work, Chief She give you any heartache?"

"Tame as a kitten. No trunks close by."

He still sounded wound up tight. Most cops talk lazy after an arrest. The adrenaline leaks out fast once the job's done.

Two cars.

"Kennedy!" I shouted. "Go with him. If he gets in that car alone with her she'll never make it to the station alive."

"Get him the hell out of here," Shrike said. "Mirandize the son of a bitch and throw him in Holding. Throw him hard."

"Two cars Kennedy! No witnesses. Think about it."

"Shut up, you. See you there, Chief." Kennedy got back in and put up his rifle. Shrike walked back around the corner. The blue fender swung away from the curb and was gone.

· · ·

No charges were filed against me because the arresting officer never appeared. After twenty-four hours they got around to letting me go and I got my gun back finally at the end of a long strip of red tape.

Neither Adelaide the Axe nor Alvin Shrike made it to the police station. They found the blue Chrysler parked on a quiet residential street in Sterling Heights with a bullet from Shrike's revolver embedded in the backseat, clotted with his blood. No one could figure out what he'd been doing in the backseat to begin with. He wasn't around to tell whatever story he'd cooked up, and I wasn't asked. It had to happen close so he could say he shot her during a struggle for the gun. Only he forgot she'd outmaneuvered more than one cop and a couple of hundred prison guards.

Adelaide Dix wasn't seen again in Sterling Heights or anywhere else. It hasn't been a year yet, so Geraldine Tolliver hasn't gotten any more postcards.

When the cops searched the rest of the car, they found Chief Shrike. In the trunk.

Needle

The old man said his name was Doto. I don't know if it was short for something or if someone had hung it on him when he was a boy in Warsaw. There was no sign of it on his mail or in the string of names that appeared later with his picture in the paper or on local TV. For years I only spoke with him when the carrier put his mail in my box or I rescued his *Free Press* from a snowdrift.

When he came to my door it was spring, no snow for a week, and the mail hadn't run. I let him in and we sat down in the breakfast nook. I poured coffee from my second bucket of the morning.

My three-room hut stood on the Detroit side of the street facing his in Hamtramck, a suburb surrounded entirely by the city. The houses there resemble one another, not through the arbitrary vision of a designer of tract homes but because the people who built them had come from the same place and culture, and they had stood for most of the twentieth century, with an invisible line drawn between the Polish and Ukrainian neighborhoods by a sense-memory of Cossack wars. The cars in the driveways are held together by wire hangers and tape, but the lawns are cropped and the houses repainted every five years.

"Your coffee is strong, Mr. Walker. How do you sleep?"

"At night I cut it with bourbon. Would you like milk?"

"I would like bourbon."

I got the bottle down from the cabinet and topped off our cups. He put both hands around his and inhaled the fumes. He was in his seventies, with a low center of gravity and small features set out generously to take up space on his broad face. He needed a shave. His forearms were thick, and where a white thermal cuff was turned back over a plaid sleeve, the last two digits of a faded blue tattooed number showed.

He saw me looking and tugged down the cuff as if to hide a stain. "Treblinka," he said. "I was nine when I came. Nine hundred when I left. The odd thing is I remember best the way the needle stung like red ants."

I said nothing, which started the flow. He made no more mention of the Nazi concentration camp, but I found out about his two wives, one dead of fever during the crossing to America, the other dead of cancer twenty years ago. He'd worked at the Dodge Main plant until it was torn down in a conspiracy involving Mayor Young of Detroit, the Hamtramck city council, and General Motors to condemn the Poletown neighborhood for a Cadillac plant that was never built. I gathered he was some kind of artist who'd taken advantage of his enforced retirement to open a shop in Detroit, where he'd sold his work exclusively, but he'd retired from that as well and lived on Social Security. He had no children, and his silence on any other blood relations suggested they'd disappeared in the ovens of Treblinka and Auschwitz.

The Polish are emotional as a rule, not ashamed to shed tears in healthy bales, but he spoke in an even tone and his face never cracked. I didn't know the why of it, or why me, but he was old and alone and I hadn't anything pressing at the office, so I sipped and listened. The lost-diamond season was over, it was too early for stolen racehorses, and the credit-check business had gone the way of the dot-com bubble. Anyway, I was alone, too, and not young.

Then he surprised me.

"You are a detective?" he asked.

I nodded. "Private."

"What means private?"

"It means I work for one person at a time and pay my own hospital bills."

"It sounds expensive."

"So's health insurance."

"How much do you charge?"

When I told him, his face didn't change, but an opaque shadow slid across his wintry blue eyes.

"What do you need done?" I asked. "On simple jobs I charge by the hour."

He seemed to brighten at that. He slid off the seat, apologizing for not touching a drop of his spiked coffee. "I have good vodka at home," he said, "not that Stalin's piss they make in Russia."

"It's a little early for me. I was only joining you to be polite."

"You can be polite across the street."

It was as close to a command as I'd heard from him, in the tone he'd probably used as a foreman at Dodge. We went across the street.

He unlocked his front door and led me through a small, overstuffed living room, a dining room with piles of books and newspapers on the table, and a spotless kitchen, each stacked behind the other like plant rooms in a greenhouse. We stepped out onto a screened back porch, where I caught a puckery whiff of a stench I'd never liked. A twelve-gauge Remington shotgun leaned in a corner. It didn't mean anything. You don't have to register a shotgun in

Michigan, and in Detroit it's the self-defense weapon of choice, as well as a handy noisemaker on New Year's Eve.

It didn't mean anything, except longtime Detroiters know better than to keep them in a place as easy to break into as a screened porch. Especially when there's a ragged hole gaping in the nylon screen on the outside door.

I stepped over and leaned down to sniff at the barrel. I felt older then.

He pulled open the door against the pressure of the spring. The body on the winterkilled grass was a pile of limbs in a dirty T-shirt, filthy and tattered jeans, and a pair of athletic shoes run down thin as paper at the heels. It lay facedown. I picked up the shotgun, holding it by the middle to avoid smearing prints, and straddled the body, one foot on the wooden stoop, the other on the ground, to reach down and grope for a pulse in the thick vein on the side of its neck. There wasn't any. The skin felt cool.

"I heard scratching," Doto said. "It sounded like an animal trying to get in. It was still dark. I came out with the gun. The light hit him from the kitchen. I don't remember even raising the gun."

I straightened. "How long ago?"

"Five. Five thirty, maybe. I waited for the police. I thought someone would hear the shot and call. When the sun came up and they didn't come, I waited another hour. Then I got dressed and went across the street."

I tried to remember if I'd heard anything that early in the morning. It's the tool of the town, as I said, and a night without a long bang somewhere is as rare as virgin timber. "Know him?" I asked.

"I didn't see his face too clear."

I like turning over dead bodies as well as the next guy, and the cops are specific on where they stand on rearranging the centerpiece;

it's a union thing. But he'd come to me and told me his life story. No rigor yet, so I was able to turn the top half enough to see the face, patched purple where the blood had settled. The age surprised me; he looked seventeen or younger. His shaggy, dirty, fair hair had looked almost white from the back.

There was a mark on the right cheek that hadn't been made by post-mortem lividity. It was a swastika, etched delicately in turquoise-colored ink.

I told Doto he needed a lawyer, not a private detective, and he needed to call the police. They get woolly when you fail to report a gunshot corpse on day of issue.

"I can't afford a lawyer."

"The court will appoint one." I climbed back onto the porch, realized I was still holding the shotgun, and returned it to its corner. I'd seen there was a telephone in the living room, but I made him lead me to it.

"One question." I rested my hand on the receiver. "Did you see that swastika before you fired?"

"I don't remember. I told you, I don't even remember shooting."

"You might want to stick with that answer. The law's clear on defending yourself in your home with deadly force, but a hungry prosecutor can fog it up quicker than a doggie in the window. Right now your two best friends are that tattoo on your arm and the one on his cheek."

"I don't even know him."

"Better and better." I dialed 911.

• • •

The first uniforms on the scene were a sergeant and an officer, both black. The Hamtramck department used to be mostly Polish descent, but the established ethnic groups had been migrating to the suburbs since before we landed on the moon, leaving behind the senior citizens on fixed incomes and new faces from the Middle East and what remained of the Jim Crow South. The team took turns confirming there was a body, never leaving us alone on the porch. We could have skedaddled anytime after I made the call but you can't fight procedure with logic.

The officer shooed Doto into the house to question him. The sergeant stayed with me.

"You move the shotgun?"

"It's where I found it."

"That isn't what I asked."

I said I'd taken it with me when I went out to look at the corpse.

"That's called tampering."

"I call it being considerate. Two carcasses mean double the paperwork for you guys."

"You said you've been neighbors for years."

"We didn't speak ten words to each other that whole time. He told me he shot the man. In those circumstances I wouldn't turn my back on my long-lost brother with the weapon in the room."

"Prints!"

"If he left any they're still on the pistol grip and the forepiece. I took it by the middle."

"You one of those private guys used to be a cop?"

"I got in my thirty."

He lowered his lids. "You must've started young."

"Minutes. Not years."

"I got no time for this. I ought to put the bracelets on you for obstruction and interference."

"You've got as much time as it takes before the first squad shows up."

We got on like that until the plainclothes arrived, led by a lieutenant named Sandusky. He had short blond hair and the erect bearing of a Polish lancer, but the eyes in the fifty-year-old face were kind. He glanced at me a couple of times while the sergeant was reporting, then dismissed him and strolled over. He'd been to see the sight, which was now in the charge of the lab rats with their black metal cases.

"How long you live here, Walker?"

"Twenty-five years."

"It's not that big of a town. I'm surprised we never met."

"I live on the Detroit side. I've met plenty over there."

"So I heard. I checked you out with Thirteen Hundred. You've worn yourself quite a trough there."

Thirteen hundred is the street address of Detroit Police Headquarters on Beaubien. I said, "I'm taking a personal day today. Seems I can get into trouble even when I'm just doing the neighborly thing."

"Don't worry about Futterman. We call him Cop-a-tude downtown. I'd close this one today if they let me. My uncle survived the Warsaw ghetto. Best way to deal with these white supremacist pukes is to arm everyone who went through the Holocaust and put them on the scent."

"This kid's generation is barely aware we fought a war over there. Maybe he thought it was just a pretty tattoo."

"Same difference to a man like Doto. If I were his p.d., I wouldn't let a man or woman under seventy on the jury, and I'd try to smuggle in one or two with a concentration camp serial number on their arm. If he saw that swastika before he pulled off. He didn't seem sure."

"A man has a right to defend himself in his home if he feels threatened, whether it's by a Boy Scout or the Hitler Youth."

"Damn straight. He says the screen was hooked, and the techies found an open pocket knife when they turned the puke over; small for a weapon, but good for sticking between the door and the frame to slip the hook. But there's been a rash of accidental firearms deaths lately, and a lot of noise about keeping them out of civilian hands. The county prosecutor wants to be attorney general, the attorney general wants to be governor, and the governor wants to go to Washington."

"That's a lot of weight to put on the back of one little old man."

"Well, you saw what happened to the Detroit cops just for beating one rotten little recidivist to death with flashlights. We can't carry 'em that size anymore even here. Have to make do with guns and tasers and sap gloves and batons. We're going out there practically naked. What chance has a private citizen got?"

"Maybe the puke has a violent record."

"How can he not? That's not a Happy Face on his cheek."

The lieutenant cut me loose. Outside, Doto sat in the back of a police cruiser, staring through the grid separating him from the front seat. His head came barely level with the padded rest. He looked nine years old.

•   •   •

Sandusky's puke didn't have a violent record. He had almost no record at all, and the one he had told a story nearly as sad as Doto's.

His name was Ryan Lister. He was sixteen and, by all appearances, had been living on the street since his father had booted him out for not contributing to the household income. In February the manager of a Starbucks in Highland Park found him sleeping in a corner of the kitchen when he came in to open up, discovered the latch broken on the back door, and had him arrested for breaking and entering. He pleaded guilty to the lesser charge of illegal entry, spent six weeks in a juvenile detention center, and was released. That was the narrative on Lister's life of crime.

Doto's first lawyer, assigned by the public defender's office, stood up for him at his arraignment and was gone, replaced by an experienced criminal attorney retained by a Holocaust survivors' organization that had taken an interest in his case. When the prosecution proposed that Lister had merely sought shelter from the cold in Doto's house as he had in the Starbucks, the defense established that the temperature that night had not dropped below fifty, far warmer than on many of the nights the boy had slept in alleys.

Throughout the prosecution's part of the trial, the sides played badminton with the evidence:

—Surveillance records of all the area's known white supremacist groups contained no mention of Lister's ever having been a member or attended a meeting or rally;

—A medical examiner confirmed that the swastika had been tattooed on Lister's cheek quite recently—had not even had a chance to scab over—indicating that he was a new convert and therefore unknown to surveillance officers;

—Sergeant Futterman, one of the first Hamtramck police officers on the scene, testified that Doto had delayed reporting the shooting for more than two hours, suggesting the defendant had used the time to dress the scene and concoct his alibi;

—Amos Walker, neighbor, offered the defendant's explanation that he'd waited patiently for the police to arrive, expecting someone in his neighborhood to have called them to complain about hearing a shot. Yes, Doto hadn't been sure he'd seen the swastika, but under emotional pressure—(Objection; speculation).

And like that, back and forth.

The prosecution scored a hit when it seated a licensed psychotherapist whose sessions with Holocaust survivors had convinced him that the unremitting horror of life in the Nazi concentration camps had inured them to violence and human suffering, effectively turning them into psychopaths, without conscience or compunction about striking out against threateners real or perceived. In his opinion based on his research and interviews with the defendant, Doto had been a time bomb waiting for more than sixty years to explode.

The therapist's testimony infuriated groups representing survivors of Hitler's Final Solution, but the jury stirred and murmured and the judge tapped his gavel.

When the defense stepped up to bat, reporters speculated that a string of camp survivors would be called to confirm from their own experience that the sight alone of a swastika worn by an intruder was justifiable cause to act in one's own defense; disclosure records revealed that Doto's attorney had been interviewing dozens from the Polish community in Hamtramck alone with that purpose in mind. But he called only one witness.

On the stand Doto answered questions calmly, recounting, with the startling clarity of an old man's memory of past traumas, his experiences as a Jew imprisoned in Treblinka. The litany of humiliations and abuses climaxed with an account of his separation from his parents and his younger sister, and the certainty later that they'd been killed in gas chambers, their ashes shoveled from ovens and deposited among those of thousands of others spread for miles around the camp. When the Allies liberated him in 1945, the ten-year-old boy had weighed less than forty pounds.

He broke down only once, weeping softly when he described his last meeting with his family. After a brief recess, he took the stand and repeated what he had told me of the shooting, with one exception: he was now in no doubt that he'd seen the swastika before he fired. His own lawyer defused the prosecution's best cross-question by asking him why he'd told investigators he wasn't sure he'd seen it.

He replied that he'd been too upset by the attempted break-in and his own action in response to remember the details clearly at the time. When the shock passed, his memory had returned.

Summations were brief. The prosecutor recapped the therapist's testimony and reminded the jury that the defendant had changed his story about seeing the tattoo. Counsel for the defense delivered an impassioned plea for a lifelong victim driven at last to a violent act to defend himself and his home.

The jury deliberated for two nerve-wracking hours. County residents were sympathetic to the homeless in those first weeks following a severe winter, and Ryan Lister's lack of a serious criminal record was troublesome. But in the end that swastika swept up the last holdout. Doto was acquitted.

I offered him a ride home. On the way he remembered that bottle of Polish vodka we hadn't cracked. He kept it in the freezing compartment of his refrigerator; the liquor smoked when he poured it and tasted like an ice-cold cloud.

When he left the living room to refill our glasses, I opened a large green cloth-bound album lying on the coffee table. Of course there were no pictures from his childhood, and either his first wife had never been photographed or her successor, who was probably the one who'd assembled the album, had left her out from natural jealousy, but there was a rich record of the couple's American life, with vintage cars and fashions and extinct Detroit area landmarks throughout and vacations on the beach. Snapshots showed Doto in his Dodge coveralls with lunch pail; relaxing with friends around an old-fashioned beergarden table crowded with longnecks; retired at last from the daily scramble, posing proudly in the doorway of the shop where he'd peddled the product of his artistic talent downtown. I smiled in response to a grin I'd never seen on his face in person.

His remained; mine faded when I read the sign lettered on the plate-glass display window:

TATTOOS TO YOUR ORDER

I knew then, as clearly as if there was a picture there of the poleaxed expression on my face, how I'd come to be a part of it all. I'd helped bear witness to his uncertainty about the swastika on Lister's cheek, corroborating the testimony of the professionals on the scene. I'd done my part to saw a hole in the floor under the therapist's evidence on psychopathic behavior. Anyone can relate to shock. It's a human emotion after all, not the machinelike reaction of a cold-blooded killer. I'd been as useful a tool as the needle in the kit he'd hidden or destroyed after it had served its purpose. I could see him taking pains with his masterpiece, his last work, with no pesky resistance from his human canvas because it was incapable of flinching. Nevertheless, it required all his skill. It would have taken him every minute of the time before he called on me.

• • •

When I looked up from the album, Doto had returned. His face was flat as paint. He set down our glasses, took it gently from my hands, closed it, and slid it onto a shelf packed with mementos of his life in Hamtramck.

Cigarette Stop

One

My pack ran out two miles north of the village of Peck. I crumpled it into the ashtray and started paying attention to signs.

I was an hour and a half out of Detroit, following State Highway 19 through Michigan's Thumb area on my way to Harbor Beach and my first job in more than a week. It was a warm night in late May and the sky was overcast, with here and there a tattered hole through which stars glittered like broken glass at the scene of an accident. My dashboard clock read 10:50.

Up there, miles inland from the resort towns along the Lake Huron coastline, there are no malls or fast-food strips or modern floodlit truck stops complete with showers and hookers to order; just squat brick post offices and stores with plank floors and the last full-service gas stations left in the western world. I pulled into a little stop-and-rob on the outskirts of Watertown with two pumps out front and bought a pack of Winstons from a bleach job on the short side of fifty who had taken makeup lessons from the Tasmanian Devil. The kid was standing by my car when I came out.

He was a lean weed in dungarees, scuffed black oxfords, and a navy peacoat too heavy for the weather that hung on him the way they always do when you draw them from a quartermaster. His short-chopped sandy hair and stiff posture added to the military impression. Also the blue duffel resting on the pavement next to him with ABS C. K. SEATON stenciled on it in white.

"Lift, mister?"

I stripped the pack and speared a filter between my lips. He looked safe enough, clear-eyed and pink where he shaved. So had Richard Speck, Albert DeSalvo, and our own John Norman Collins.

"Where to?" I asked. "I'm headed up to Harbor Beach."

"That'll do. My folks are in Port Austin."

"Why aren't you traveling up Twenty-five? That's the coast highway."

"Why aren't you?"

"Seen one Big Boy, seen 'em all," I said.

"Me too."

"Hop in."

He threw his duffel into the backseat of the Mercury and climbed into the passenger's seat in front. Under the domelight he didn't look as fresh as I'd thought. His face was drawn and pale as a clenched knuckle and he was breathing hoarsely, as if he'd been running. Then I closed my door and darkness clamped down over us both.

Back on the road, with the broken white line flaring and fading in the headlamps, I made a comment or two about the lack of traffic—where I came from, only two cars in three miles meant nuclear war at the least—but he didn't respond and I shut up. Well, in my own hitching days I'd hoped for the company of drivers who didn't feel they had to entertain me. Somewhere between Elmer and Snover he slumped down in the seat with his knees up and his chin on his chest. He didn't miss anything.

In Argyle I stopped for gas at a place that might have been the twin of the one in Watertown. While the attendant was filling the tank I used the men's room and bought a Coke from a machine to douse the nicotine burn in my throat. I bought another one, paid for the gas, and stuck the second can through the open window on the passenger's side. When the kid didn't reach for it I shook him gently by the shoulder. He fell over the rest of the way, and that's when I saw the blood shining in the light mounted over the pumps.

• • •

The attendant, a tall strip of sandpapery hide in baggy suitpants and a once-white shirt with *Norm* stitched in red script over the pocket, bobbed his Adam's apple twice when I showed him the dead body in my car, then went inside to use the telephone. Just for the hell of it I groped again for the big artery on the side of my passenger's neck. It wasn't any busier than it had been the first time I'd checked. I located the source of the blood in a ragged gash between two ribs on his right side under his shirt. He'd bled to death quietly while I was remarking on the thin traffic.

I went through his pockets. Nothing, not even a wallet. Straightening, I looked at the attendant through the window of the little store, gesticulating at the receiver in his left hand. I opened the rear door and inspected the duffel. I found sailor's blues rolled neatly to avoid wrinkles, cooking utensils and related camping equipment, and thick sheaves of some kind of newsprint, there presumably to keep the stuff from rattling as he carried it. The only identification Able Bodied Seaman C. K. Seaton had had with him was his name stenciled on his one piece of luggage. If it was his name.

Norm was hanging up the telephone. I carried the duffel behind the car, unlocked the trunk, threw it in, and slammed the lid just as he came out. I had no idea why. I didn't know why I did a lot of the things I did, like picking up strange hitchhikers in downtown Nowhere.

"Raise anyone?" I asked Norm.

"State troopers. We ain't got no police in Argyle. You reckon somebody croaked him?" He was gaping through the passenger's window with his chin in his lap.

"If he shot himself he ditched the gun. And you can lay off the dialect. I was born in a town not much bigger than this one. We wore shoes and everything."

"Shit." He dealt himself a Marlboro out of the bottom of a box he kept in his shirt pocket and lit it with a throwaway lighter. "Thought you was one of them Detroiters come up here to the boonies to cheat us rustics out of our valuable antiques. Last month my boss sold a woman from Grosse Pointe a Coca-Cola sign he bought off a junkyard in Port Huron for ten bucks. She gave him fifty. It was the 'shucks' and 'you-alls' done it."

I consumed my Coke in place of the cigarette I really wanted; one of us lighting up that close to the pumps was plenty. "Where'd you graduate?" I asked him. "Jackson?"

His face squinched up. "Marquette. What gave me away?"

"You've got to start smoking them from the top of the pack if you don't want anyone to know you were inside. Out here we don't scramble for cigarettes when they fall out and scatter. Yet."

"You a cop?"

"Private." I showed him the ID.

"Amos Walker," he read. "I never heard of you."

"That doesn't make you special."

We were still going around like that a few minutes later when a blue-and-white pulled in off 19 and a blocky figure in a blue business suit climbed out of the right side. "Christ, it's Torrance," Norm said. "Do me a favor, okay? Don't tell him about Marquette. Nobody knows about that around here."

"Nobody has to," I said. "What did they take you down for, anyway?"

"I stuck up a gas station."

Two

Luther Torrance commanded the Cass City post of the Michigan State Police. He was square-built and shorter than they like them in that jurisdiction—which said something about what kind of cop he had to be to have made commander—with short brown hair and eyes that looked yellow in the harsh outdoor light, like a wolf's. The uniformed trooper who had driven him ran six-four and wore amber Polaroids. He stood around with his thumbs hooked inside his gun belt, in case Norm and I threw down a gum wrapper or something.

"Thirty-eight'd be my guess," said Torrance, stripping off a pair of rubber surgical gloves as he came away from the body in the Mercury. "Maybe nine-millimeter. It's still in there, so we won't be guessing long. You're the owner of the car?" He looked up at me.

I said I was and showed him the PI license. When he was through being impressed I told him what had happened, starting at the cigarette stop. He took it all down in a leather-bound notebook with a gold pencil.

"What's a private sleuth doing up here?" he asked.

"Does it matter?"

"Not if you're on vacation, which you aren't or you'd be a lot closer to the lake. Nobody comes through here unless he's lost or on his way someplace else. You don't look lost."

"Security job up in Harbor Beach."

"Judge Dunham's poker game." I must have reacted, because he showed me his bridgework. "Shoot, everybody in these parts knows about the judge's annual game. You don't shove a couple of hundred thousand back and forth across a table one weekend every spring and expect not to get talked about around here. That's why he needs security. Well, I'll check it out. This guy never introduced himself?"

I shook my head. "He said he had family in Port Austin."

"We'll send a man up there with a morgue shot. Any luggage?"

"No."

"Most hitchers have something. A backpack or something."

"This one didn't."

He tapped the gold pencil against his bridgework. Just then a county wagon pulled in and two attendants in uniform got out. He put away the pencil and notebook. "You heading straight up to Harbor Beach tonight?"

"Not this late. I thought I'd get a room and make a fresh jump in the morning. Any place you'd recommend?"

"The roaches all look alike up here. I got your address and number if we need you, or I can call the judge if we need you quick. We won't. I figure our boy got robbed and put up a fuss. Fact he didn't tell you he was wounded makes me think a dope deal went bad, something on that order. We get that, even here."

I said, "I guess there aren't any Mayberrys any more."

"There never were, except on television." He thanked me and walked back to take charge of the body. Norm, watching, was on his second pack of Marlboros. I noticed he'd opened this one on top.

Three

The motel I fell into a mile up 19 was a concrete bunker built in a square *U* with the office in the base. The manager, fat and hairless except for a gray tuft coiling over the *V* in his Hawaiian shirt, took my cash and registration card and handed me a key wired to the anchor from the *Edmund Fitzgerald*. My room, second from the end in the north leg of the *U*, stood across from an ice machine illuminated like an icon under a twenty-watt bulb. I had a double bed, a TV, and a shower stall with a dispenser full of pink soap that smelled like Madame Ling's Secrets of the East Massage Parlor on Gratiot. The TV worked like my plans for the evening.

Back at the convenience store in Argyle I'd placed a call to Judge Dunham, whose round courtroom-trained voice came on the line after two rings. I said I had car trouble and was stuck for the night. I didn't say the trouble had to do with a stiff in the front seat.

"No sweat," he said. "Senator Sullivan won't be here till morning and I never start without my worst poker player. Just steam on in come sunup."

I pulled my overnight case out of the car, then as an afterthought grabbed Seaton's duffel and carried them both into the room. I was too keyed up to sleep. I broke my flat pint of J&B out of the case, stripped the cellophane off the plastic glass in the bathroom, and went out for ice. Under the lights in the parking lot the blood on my front seat looked black as I passed it. I wondered if I could charge the cleaning to the judge.

I was about to plunge my plastic ice bucket into the machine when someone came strolling along the sidewalk on the other side of the lot. Most of the rooms were vacant—mine was one of only three cars parked inside the U—so he was worth watching. He was built along the lanky lines of Norm, but younger, and made no sound at all on sneakered feet. He had on a dark jacket and pants, but I couldn't make out his features at that distance. He was carrying something.

He paused in front of the door to my room and stood for a moment as if listening. Apparently satisfied, he stepped off the sidewalk and approached my car. A hand came out of one of his jacket pockets with something in it.

A Slim Jim.

He was nobody's amateur. After casting a glance up and down the row of rooms, he tried the door on the driver's side, then slid the flat hooked device between the closed window and the outside door panel and yanked it up decisively. I heard the click.

My gun was in the overnight case in the room. I hardly ever needed it to get ice. I used the only other weapon I had.

"Hey!"

He was a pro down to the ground. The Slim Jim jangled to the pavement and he went into a crouch I knew too well. I let go of the ice bucket and wedged myself between the machine and the block wall. He fired twice, the shots so close together I saw the yellow flame as one continuous spurt. Much closer to home I heard a twang and a thud as the first bullet ricocheted off the concrete behind me and the second penetrated the ice machine's steel skin. Then he took off running, his lanky legs eating up pavement two yards at a bite, back in the direction he'd come. He hadn't waited to see if he'd hit anything. They never do, except in submarine pictures.

I pried myself loose from cover. On the other side of the building an engine started, wound up, and faded down Highway 19, gearchanges hiccoughing. A pair of red tail-lamps flicked past the edge of the motel and on into darkness. I waited, but no lights came on behind any of the dark windows and nobody came out to investigate. Gunshots late at night were nothing unusual there in raccoon country.

At my car I picked up the Slim Jim and wandered around with my head down until something tiny caught the light in a yellow glint. I picked it up and looked for its mate, but it must have rolled into the shadows. I didn't need it. I'd been pretty sure because of the close spacing of the shots that the weapon was an automatic and that I'd find at least one of the spent shells it kicked out. I had to take it into the room to make out what had been stamped into the flanged end: .38 SUPER.

I pocketed it, unpacked the Smith & Wesson in its form-fitted holster, checked the cylinder for cartridges, and clipped it to my belt. The fact that he'd come armed told me my visitor had been prepared to search the room if whatever he was after wasn't in my car; a room he had every reason to believe was occupied by me. That kind of determination usually meant a return engagement.

Why was another matter. I wasn't the most promising robbery target around. The Mercury was the oldest car in the lot and a hell of a long way from the most flashy. My clothes wouldn't get me past the door of the Detroit Yacht Club. My overnight case had been in my family since the last Kiwanis Rummage Sale. As far as I knew, the only person worth shooting in those parts was already dead. Shot with a .38.

I dumped the contents of C. K. Seaton's duffel out onto the bed and took inventory. One canteen, half full of something that smelled like water. Two cans of C rations. A knife and fork. One of those hinged camp pans divided into sections. Sailor's blues, unrolling into sailor's blues, nothing hidden there. And the crumpled sheaves of coarse paper to prevent the mess from banging around.

In the lamplight I liked the paper. I liked it a lot.

There were two bales, two feet by eighteen inches and two inches thick. I hefted one, rubbed individual sheets between thumb and forefinger. Not newsprint. Rag paper. I held a sheet up to the light and looked at the threads running through it.

I sat in the room's only chair and smoked a Winston down to the filter. The frayed end when I ground it out resembled my brain. I stood and put everything back into the duffel except the papers. Those I combined in one stack. From the shelf in the bottom of the telephone stand I removed the county directory and took it out of its heavy vinyl advertising cover. I doubled over the blank sheets, slid them inside the cover, and inspected the result. It looked bloated. I returned it to the shelf and put the heavy telephone book on top of it. Better.

There is no place in a motel room you can hide something where someone hasn't thought to look. But you can buy time.

• • •

I was dead in my shoes. If my friend came back for his burglar tool he would just have to wait until I woke up. I returned the camping equipment to the duffel, laid it lengthwise on the bed, drew the blanket over it, and stretched out in the chair with the lamp off and the revolver in my lap. Between the makeshift dummy and the time it would take my visitor's pupils to adjust from the lighted parking lot, I might have the opportunity to teach him a lesson in target shooting.

Three gentle raps on the door pulled me out of a dream in which Frank Sinatra, Gene Kelly, and another guy, dressed up in sailor suits in the big city, got themselves gunned down by someone with a .38 automatic. The third guy was me.

The luminous dial of my watch read 2:11. Well, he *might* bother to knock. I got up, straightening the kinks, drew back the hammer on the Smith & Wesson, crab-walked to the door, and used the peephole. The fisheye glass made an avian caricature of the man standing alone under the light mounted over the door. He was a middle-aged number going to gravity in a porkpie hat and a powder-blue sport-coat on top of a shirt with a spread collar. His hands were empty. I unlocked the door and opened it a foot and leveled the muzzle at his belly. His liquid brown eyes took in the weapon and gave nothing back. "Mr. Walker?"

"That's half of it," I said. "Let's have the rest."

"My name's Hugh Vennable. I have some fancy identification in my pocket if you'll let me take it out."

I sucked a cheek. "What time is it?"

He hesitated, then looked at his watch. "Two-fifteen, why?"

It was strapped to his right wrist. "Take out your ID," I said. "Use your right hand."

"How'd you know I'm a lefty? Oh." His smile was shallow. "Pretty slick." He fished out a leather folder and showed me his picture on a card bearing the seal of the United States Navy.

"You're with Naval Intelligence?"

He was still smiling. "I avoid saying it. Sounds like something you learn sitting around admiring your belly-button. Can I come in?"

I elevated the revolver's barrel and let down the hammer, stepping away from the door. "By the way, your watch is two minutes fast."

"I doubt it." He came in, a soft-looking heavy man, light on his feet. His hair was fair at the temples under a cocoa straw hat—his eyebrows were almost invisible against a light working tan—and he had a roll of fat under his chin. His quick graceful movements said it was all camouflage; I knew a street tiger when I saw one. He looked around the room and sat on the edge of the bed, exposing briefly the square checked butt of a nine-millimeter Beretta in a speed holster on his belt.

I put away the Smith & Wesson. "I thought the navy issued Thirty-eight Supers."

"Phasing 'em out. Some prefer the old pieces, but I'm not one of them. Is that J and B?" He was looking at the pint bottle standing on top of the dresser.

"You're not on duty?"

"Sure, but I'm no fanatic."

I took the wrapper off another glass and poured two inches into it and the one I'd stripped earlier. I handed him one. "No ice, sorry. That trip's longer than you'd think."

"Never touch it." He made a silent toast and drank off the top inch. "The state police told me where to find you. You reported a dead man in Argyle?"

"Did you know him?"

"His name was Charles Seaton, U.S.N. I've been tracking him since Cleveland."

"Tracking him for what?" I sipped scotch.

"Federal robbery. You didn't tell the law about the duffel he was carrying."

"Was he?"

Vennable shook his head. "I'm not here to blow the whistle on you, son. I'd like a look in that bag."

"What would you expect to find?"

"A couple of reams of paper. Not just any paper. The kind they print currency on."

"What's a seaman doing with treasury paper?"

"Not U.S. currency; navy scrip. Negotiable tender on any naval base in the world. We change the design and ink color from time to time to screw the counterfeiters, but never the paper. It's a special rag bond, can't be duplicated. The amount Seaton stole is worth maybe a couple of million on the European black market. Last week he and a partner ripped off an armored car on its way to Washington from the mill in Cleveland where the paper's made. Earlier tonight we pulled the partner out of Lake Huron near Lexington. I guess they both got their licks in."

"That's not far from where I picked him up." I replaced the liquor he'd drunk.

"Thank you kindly. I figure they shot it out over the booty and Seaton won, sort of. Which means he'd have had the paper with him when you linked up."

"He could've ditched it somewhere."

"He wouldn't throw it away and he was hurt too bad to waste time looking for a good hiding place. He's got people in Port Austin. He'd have gone that way for his doctoring."

"What about the third partner?"

A pair of transparent eyebrows got lifted. "Our scuttlebutt says he was twins. Not triplets."

"Someone tried breaking into my car a couple of hours ago. When I yelled he shot at me." I took the shell out of my pocket and handed it to him.

"Super." He sniffed at the open end and gave it back. "One of the stick-up men used a thirty-eight auto. You get a look at him?"

"Not good enough for a court of law. But I'd know him."

"Another player? Well, maybe." He drained his glass and set it on the floor. "Where's the duffel?"

"Under the blanket."

He started, looked at the lump in the bed. "Thought you used pillows." He got up to pull back the covers and grope inside the sack. When he looked at me again I was pointing the Smith & Wesson at him.

"Hold on, son."

"That's just what I'm doing," I said. "You didn't find the paper because it isn't there. You killed Seaton rather than deal with him. Now you can deal with me."

Four

He stood with his hands away from his body. "Son, you're shouting down the wrong vent."

"Yeah, yeah, Popeye," I said. "It was a good hand, but you overplayed it. The state police didn't tell you where to find me. They didn't know I'd be putting in at this motel. Neither did I when I left them. You had to have followed me, just like the guy you sent to break into my car."

"You saw my bona fides."

"I saw them. They might even be genuine. Who better to make off with navy valuables than someone in Naval Intelligence? What happened, you get double-crossed by Seaton?"

"Seaton wouldn't know how to double-cross anyone. He was straighter than the Equator."

This was a new player. I'd inspected the bathroom window and decided it was too narrow to admit anything human, but I hadn't reckoned on the skimpy proportions of the gent I thought of as Slim Jim, after his calling card. He'd shed his jacket, and his rucked-up shirt told me it had been a snug fit, but here he was walking out of the bathroom with a nickel-plated .38 Super automatic in his right hand. He had a yellow complexion and a military buzz cut that helped his general resemblance to a skull.

Vennable didn't look at him. "I didn't make up much," he told me, "just changed the names around. We stuck up that armored car.

Seaton was one of the couriers we locked inside. He got out some-how, caught a ride, and jumped us down the road. Nick here shot him when he was picking up the paper we dropped. He lost his weapon, but he got into the car with the paper and the driver took off. We caught up with the car in Toledo. The driver said he'd stopped and refused to go any farther, so Seaton left on foot carry-ing the paper. That driver was full of talk when Nick did the asking."

"So he hitched another ride north and you tailed him and here you are," I said. "What about the dead man near Lexington?"

"A little invention to explain Seaton's wound." Vennable was smiling. "Shoot him, Nick. That paper's got to be in this room."

I'd been through the Detroit Police training course, and the sit-uation's covered: Go for your primary target and worry about the others later. The navy must have had a similar policy, because Vennable crouched and charged me, clawing for the Beretta on his belt, and that's why I shot him in the groin instead of the chest where I'd been aiming. He reeled in front of Nick. Nick changed positions to get a clear field. I shot him twice, once through his partner. Some-how he was still standing when the door splintered and Commander Torrance of the state police put a third one in him before he knew about the first. I don't know if he'd have fallen even then if he hadn't tripped over Vennable. These wiry boys are hell for stamina.

Five

"This one's still flopping." Straightening, the blocky commander jerked the Beretta from Vennable's holster and leathered his own Po-lice Special. Blood was pumping between the navy man's fingers where he lay moaning and clutching his crotch with both hands.

The second bullet had passed through his left arm. "Tell 'em not to bother about any sirens for the other one."

I finished giving the information to the 911 operator and hung up. "What brought you, the shots in the parking lot?"

"Folks up here get involved, they make calls. When I heard the name of the motel I thought you might've checked in here. What's the skinny?"

Sliding the telephone book cover from under the directory, I opened it and held up the thick sheaf of paper. "This is what they killed my hitchhiker to get their hands on," I said.

"What the hell is it?"

"The dreams that stuff is made of." I told him the rest. By the time he had it all, the first ambulance had arrived. The room was full of state troopers and paramedics now.

Torrance's wolf eyes never left my face. "Why didn't you just turn the duffel over to me to begin with?"

"Old habit. When I pick someone up on the road I'm offering him protection, even if he was beyond it when I met him, and way beyond anyone's when we parted company. That included finding out who killed him and why."

"Boy, that's the worst lie I ever heard."

"I've told worse." I breathed some air. "Maybe I just wanted to see how this one ended. It was a long dull trip otherwise."

"Better. Was it worth it?"

"Put it this way. Before I leave here in the morning I'm buying a pack of cigarettes off the manager so I won't have to make any more stops. That's how I fell into this mess."

"Better make it a carton," Torrance said.

Deadly Force

One

When I heard Redline Records had banned smoking everywhere in the renovated warehouse where it conducted business on Riopelle, I knew I'd find Ansel Albany sneaking a butt back in the stacks. He saw me coming between racks of inflammable 78 and 45 rpm records and squashed out a Camel under one of his size fifteens. At fifty he was white-haired and his complexion had faded from plum blue to medium gray, but he still looked like an old athlete. Following a disappointing season with the Pistons, the six-foot-nine Kettering graduate had joined the Detroit Police Department, where he served twelve years until he shot three suspects to death during an attempted liquor store robbery on Woodward. The first two passed at the inquiry, but an eyewitness testified that Albany had given the third man a ten-second head start, then drew and shot him in the back through the glass door. Albany got the boot.

Whether the report was true or not—Ansel swore it wasn't—there was nothing false about the sixteen-inch Colt Python he wore strapped to his ribs under his old plaid jacket. I caught a glimpse of it when he reached out to accept the mailer I'd brought. He slid out the videotape and examined both sides.

"Did you play it?"

"That's why the meet was in a video store," I said. "There might be copies, but I don't think you'll be hearing from them again."

"Rough 'em around, did you? Wish I could've been there to help."

"I told them next time you would be. It was easier on my knuckles."

He laughed once, a short deep bark, and slipped the tape back into the mailer and the mailer into his side pocket. "Management should've canned the little asshole when they found out he was into payola. But he's the front man and they're convinced he's another Barry Gordy."

"Here's two thousand back." I handed him a thick envelope. "They believed me when I told them Motown is dead and the local record business is depressed. All part of the service."

"I'd have shot the motherfuckers."

"Why didn't you?"

"I'm paid to end trouble, not start it. And they demanded an outsider. What do we owe you, Walker?"

"Simple buy-back, no complications. A C-note ought to do it."

"Hell." He drew two bills from the envelope and held them out. "Buy a new suit with the extra hundred. You'll never get the stink out of the one you're wearing." I took one of the bills. "We go back a long way, Ansel. Put it in your retirement fund."

"Who's retiring?"

I started to go. He called me back. His Masai features were unreadable. "If you won't accept tips, maybe you'll take work. A girl I know could use a break."

"What kind?"

"If I knew that I'd help her myself. Redline's got her on contract. Lately she's been missing sessions. Management was getting set to tout her as the new Diana Ross, but now they're talking about dropping her. She's got trouble but she won't say what."

I lit a Winston. "What's she to you?"

He drew himself up; all the way up, which was hard on my neck. "What's that mean?"

"Don't sweat it, Ansel. If she's your kid, swell. If she's your something on the side, that's swell, too, but it makes a difference in the way I approach her. You know that."

"Shit." He relaxed. "I've been around these corporate twerps so long I'm starting to *act* like a pimp. Sheilah's just a sweet kid, used to stop by security on her way to the studio and pass the time of day. When I brought up the rumors and asked her if I could help, she walked out. Now she won't even look at me on her way past. Maybe a young stud like you could get something out of her. Color doesn't matter any more, not in this business."

"Sheilah's her name?"

"With an H on the end. Sheilah Sorrell, that's the name on the label. You'll find her in Farmington Hills." He scribbled an address in his pocket pad and gave me the sheet. "She lives with Ronnie Madrid."

"The druglord?"

"Please. The entertainment mogul. He owns two comedy clubs in town and tried to buy this company."

"He can afford to. When his boys wiped out the Little Colombia mob he inherited the whole East Side."

"You got something against free enterprise? A girl can't help who she falls in love with."

"Who pays?"

"Redline Records, who else?"

"You mean you."

He leaned back against the brick wall. His jacket fell open, exposing the big shiny magnum.

"They pay me too much to keep out the pirates, and I'm too old to spend it on anything worthwhile."

"Like hell you are." I left.

Two

The neighborhood was made up of large homes with clean lines tucked between hills, not one of them more than twenty years old or worth less than three hundred thousand. The Madrid house was glass and brick with a red tile roof and a swimming pool that would have held my place in Hamtramck. Nice work for a kid who not so long ago was begging in the streets of Managua.

Ronnie Madrid, born Rafael Maldronado y Sanchez etcetera, had found a shortcut Horatio Alger had overlooked. The only survivor of a family of Nicaraguan rebels massacred by Sandanistas, he'd been brought to Detroit by a distant relative while still in short pants, gone to work running dope for the Colombians, and become a bodyguard at age nineteen for Luis "El Tigre" Rodriguez; but he wasn't too good at that, because six weeks later The Tiger turned up bound and gagged and shot full of holes in the trunk of his Excalibur at City Airport. A gutter war raged for months. When it ended, Ronnie was the Man to See east of Cadillac Square for everything from Mescaline to Mexican Brown. Twenty now, old enough to vote if he were a citizen but still too young to buy beer, he was using his good looks, streetwise charm, and drug connections in South America to gain a foothold in the local entertainment industry, assuring himself both a legitimate front and a place to launder his money to Uncle Sam's taste. Like the man said, only in America.

The doorbell chimed "Spanish Harlem," no kidding. A maid whose ironclad features suggested she would know "Der Horst Wessel Lied" better carried my card back into the house and returned five minutes later to tell me Miss Sorrell would see me.

I waited in the entryway. The floor tiles were Mexican. Spanish needles grew in ceramic pots on either side of a curving staircase. A framed poster advertised a bullfight in Spanish on one wall. Inside the curve of the staircase stood a suit of Japanese armor, looking abashed.

"Awful, isn't it? Ronnie insisted on buying it. I told him it wouldn't go with the rest of the house, but you don't tell Ronnie anything."

She had come up on me while I was staring at the armor. She was small, with fine Jamaican features and skin as light as mine, which may have been why she wore her hair in cornrows and dressed in a stiff white cotton robe with African symbols painted on it in primary colors. Unbelted, it left her collarbone bare and covered her feet.

"Maybe he thinks he needs a tin suit," I said. "They'd be a sellout in high school parking lots."

"I'm Sheilah Sorrell. Did Ansel send you, Mr. Walker?" I'd written his name on the back of my card.

"He's fresh out of kittens caught in trees. He thinks you're in some kind of jam."

"I'm not. He's kind of like an uncle, always looking out for me. Can I offer you a drink, or are you on duty?"

"I'm not that kind of detective."

"I've got gin, scotch—"

"Stop there."

She laughed in a way only singers can, turned, and lifting her robe the way they do in Victorian movies, led the way into something they probably don't call a living room in houses like that. It was done in blue and white with French doors looking out on the sparkling pool. There was a small bar and a wall full of audio equipment that looked like the computer in *2001*. Sheilah Sorrell stepped behind the bar.

"This is something I never let Greta do for Ronnie. I like mixing drinks. Water or ice?"

"A glass is fine."

She poured it from a cut-glass decanter, fixed herself something amber, and brought them over to a blue satin sofa. We sat down. She crossed a country block of smooth bare leg over the other and showed me a white leather sandal and coral polish on her toenails. "I'm sorry you wasted your time," she said. "Ansel's a mother hen."

"That mother hen was thrown out of the toughest police department in the country for misuse of deadly force." I drank. "Where's Ronnie?"

"Away on business. What did Ansel tell you?"

"He said you've been missing work."

"I'm a musician. I play a delicate instrument. My voice strains easily and I have to rest it. I don't expect a security man to understand that but Redline should."

"He says there's talk of letting you go."

"They can't do that. I've got a contract."

"I heard someone say once that in show business a signed contract is considered the beginning of the negotiating process."

She smiled then. The colors in the room faded in the light. Then her gaze shifted. "Yes, Greta."

"Telephone, missus." The maid was standing in the doorway.

"Who is it?"

"He would not say. It is important he said."

"I'll take it upstairs." She set her drink down untasted on the white coffee table and rose, "Excuse me, Mr. Walker. Play some music if you like." She went out, followed by Greta.

A cabinet contained several of Sheilah Sorrell's CDs. After a few minutes I figured out how to work the player—I haven't forgiven the music business for changing technologies just when I had amassed a collection of all my favorites on eight-track—and put on one, "Ev'ry Time We Say Goodbye." She ran Cole Porter through Motown and it came out like raw silk. I stood listening and looking at the pool for thirty seconds before the detective in me kicked in. The bar was stocked with wines and liquors I had only heard about. The carpet and drapes had been bought in New York. And Sheilah Sorrell had a pistol in the drawer of a blue lamp table.

It was a .22 magnum derringer, a two-shot and too delicate-looking for an *hombre de guerra* like Madrid: it was nickel-plated and the sidegrips were mother-of-pearl. The engraving on the backstrap read: "Your Ace in the Hole. Ronnie." "Ace in the Hole" was another Cole Porter song in Sheilah's CD cabinet. The muzzle gave off a vanilla-flavored whiff of powder solvent. I tipped light into the barrels and looked inside. No dust. A thorough job of cleaning for a woman, and very recent.

Three

I heard footsteps and returned the pistol to its drawer. The disc player was still making plaintive sounds in Sheilah's lost voice.

"Missus said she is sorry," the maid said. "She was called away."

"I didn't hear her leave."

"She is dressing. Call later," she said.

I drove around the corner and parked on the blind side of a bank of lilacs. Through the leaves I could see the front of the house. It was surrounded by a wrought-iron fence and the driveway was the only exit. For the neighbors' sake I pretended to be studying a road map. The map was of Arizona and I had no idea what it was doing in my glove compartment.

Somewhere between Flagstaff and Tucson a bottle green Jaguar chortled down the driveway with Sheilah Sorrell at the wheel. She turned left, directly in front of me. I slumped down until she passed, then threw aside the map, hit the ignition, and swung out behind. There were no other cars on the shady street and I gave the Jag two blocks.

We took Maple Road to Telegraph and points south, past West Bloomfield and neighborhoods that made Farmington Hills look like a welfare project—Ronnie Madrid's next stop on his way to Grosse Pointe, where the Spanish accents cut the grass and the residents thought a *contra* was a foreign convertible. Below Ten Mile Road the scenery broke down and became plain old Detroit. There the traffic was brisk and I closed up. On Seven Mile the Jaguar drifted into the parking lot of a Chinese restaurant and Sheilah got out and went inside. She had on a yellow cotton shift and dark glasses.

I found a space on the street and adjusted my rearview mirror to include the restaurant door. In a little while a burly black party in an electric blue suit walked past my car carrying a leather briefcase and entered the restaurant.

Things were getting interesting. I'd been visiting police headquarters the day they brought in Virgil Sweet for questioning in connection with a drive-by shooting at a crack house on Watson. Since then he'd gained about twenty pounds and several yards of expensive Italian tailoring. Two minutes after he went inside he came out and walked back the way he had come, without the briefcase.

Sheilah Sorrell had it. She came clicking back across the parking lot, threw the item onto the front seat of the Jaguar, and got in with it. She took off with a chirp of rubber. Of course I followed.

We went downtown. Afternoon rush hour was thirty minutes away and we could have driven on the sidewalks for all the pedestrians we would hit. Finally she parked behind a produce truck on Monroe and got out carrying the briefcase. I wedged my car into a loading zone and shadowed her on foot. We crossed into Greektown, where restaurateurs with thick arms and white aprons to their ankles were sweeping out their establishments in preparation for the dinner trade. But Sheilah had had her fill of restaurants, and turned into Trapper's Alley instead.

I almost lost her in the crowd that was a fixture in the vertical shopping mall. When I spotted her she was on the escalator halfway to the second level. She never looked around. I might have been tailing her in an army halftrack.

On the top level she stopped at a newsstand, bought a ticket for the People Mover, and went out on the tiled platform to wait. I bought one too and loitered among the magazines until the train came. We boarded with a small crowd. I hurried past her while she was settling herself on the molded bench under the windows and found a place to stand at the rear of the car.

The train slid out of the station, its motion as smooth as the graft that had built it. We stopped at Cadillac Center, Joe Louis Arena, Grand Circus. Some passengers got on, others left. Approaching Bricktown, the last stop before the station where we had boarded, Sheilah slid the briefcase under the bench and stood. When the doors opened, she stepped off. The briefcase remained behind. So did I.

I rode the circuit twice and started around again. Several stories below, the streets were thickening with traffic. Nobody touched the briefcase, hidden in the shadows. I had thought I knew what it contained, but when no one claimed it the trip started to look like a try-out, to see if Sheilah followed instructions. At Cadillac Center I got in with a knot of Japanese tourists waiting to alight and scooped up the case on my way through the doors. It felt heavy.

In the nearest men's room I tried to open the briefcase, but it was locked. There would be time enough to break into it later and remove the newspapers or whatever other useless items it held. I dropped a quarter into one of the telephones in the hallway outside and dialed John Alderdyce's number at police headquarters. A rumpled-looking business type in two-toned cordovans was using the other instrument. I turned my back on him.

"Walker, what's happenin'?" Alderdyce said. "I heard you died."

"That was three days ago. I'm back."

"What can I do for you, you blasphemous son of a bitch?" he asked brightly.

"What do you hear lately about Virgil Sweet?"

"Nothing good, and I read the obituaries every day. Word is he's partnered up with the Hispanics. Shooting kids on street corners is for the help. What about him?"

"Would one of those Hispanics be Ronnie Madrid?"

"That's the name I heard. We're looking for Ronnie, by the way. He missed an appointment."

"A hearing?"

"Prelim. Nobody's seen him in a duck's age. What's Sweet up to?"

I couldn't answer the question. I probably wouldn't have anyway. I saw movement reflected in the shiny black surface of the telephone. Then a purple light exploded in my skull and I didn't see anything for a while.

Four

I woke up to a white glare. Someone was moving a penlight back and forth between my pupils. I said, "Turn that off or I'll use it to take your temperature." That was the planned speech. It came out in some dead language.

"Dilation normal," muttered a voice I didn't know. "How many fingers am I holding up, son?"

"December 7th, 1941." That at least sounded like English, winched up from the bottom of a dusty shaft.

Someone else chuckled. I knew John Alderdyce's sinister mirth. I was lying on my back on the hard floor in the short passage outside the men's room at Cadillac Center. The man with the penlight and the fingers was supporting my head with one hand. He was a balding person with thick-rimmed glasses and a long tragic face that looked medical. Beyond this was John's brutal black features, gentling slightly as he spread into middle age. "I had your call traced," he said. "I almost arrested the doc here when I found him bending over you. I thought that 'Stand back, I'm a doctor' line went out with Louis B. Mayer."

I said, "The briefcase."

"What briefcase?"

"That answers one question. Got a light?" I sat up and patted my pockets. My head expanded like an airbag.

The doctor sat back on his heels. "You should check yourself into Emergency. You could be concussed."

"Walker bounces backhoes off his skull Saturdays." John speared a mentholated cigarette between my lips from the pack he was always quitting from and lit it off a disposable lighter. It tasted like Old Spice.

"In that case sign this." The doctor snapped open a folded sheet from a pocket and held it and a pen under my nose. It was a form releasing him from liability. I scribbled my name at the bottom and he was gone like Clayton Moore.

"What's new?" John asked.

I grabbed his arm and jacked myself vertical. My head kept expanding. It was going to hurt like hell when it finally burst. The small crowd we'd collected began to fade. "I make it Ronnie Madrid was kidnapped," I said, leaning against the wall. "Sheilah Sorrell, his squeeze, told me he was away on a buy, but someone called the house and she was in a lather to leave after that. She met Virgil Sweet in a Chinese place on Seven Mile and he gave her a briefcase. She left it on the People Mover. When nobody claimed it I figured it was a trial run, snatched the case myself, and called you. That's when the sky fell on me."

"Ronnie Madrid's dead."

I waited.

"Metro called just as I was leaving the office," he said. "Somebody put two in him and dumped him behind a video arcade on Michigan Avenue. Customers heard a car tearing away about five this afternoon."

"That was just about the time his girlfriend caught the train."

"They must've been pretty sure she'd deliver."

"Who do you like for it?" I asked.

"The guy was a dealer. Tomorrow morning I'll sit down with the city directory and check off the names of the ones I *don't* like for it."

He watched me crush out the cigarette. "You okay? Maybe the doc was right about having yourself looked at."

"It was just my head."

"Get a hinge at the sapper?"

"Just for a second. A legend died today; I didn't spot the tail when I left the train. He was waiting for me when I came out of the toilet, pretending to be making a call. He looked like a bad salesman." I described what I remembered, including the flashy cordovans.

"Pudge Capstone," John said. "Legbreaker and bag man. Does a little bodyguarding when he feels like being legit. He's got a thing for fancy footwear."

"How about a lift to my car? I'm sick of trains."

"Sure. I've only got a half-dozen homicides waiting for me back at the shop."

"Thanks, John. I was afraid I'd be imposing," I tested the pulpy spot on the back of my head. My finger didn't go in, so I was only half done. "Capstone ever do any body-guarding at Redline Records?"

"Maybe. Some of those rockers need protection. Why?"

Just a thought. You'd be surprised what a knock on the head does for the faculties of reason."

"In that case you must be the most reasonable guy in town," he said.

Five

The bell played several bars of "Spanish Harlem" before Sheilah Sorrell came to the door. She had on the African robe I'd seen before, as if she'd never been out of it.

"Where's Eva Braun?" I asked.

"If you mean Greta, it's her night off. I'm a little tired now, Mr. Walker. Call me tomorrow." She started to close the door. My shoulder got in the way.

"Tonight's better. By tomorrow the place will be crawling with cops."

She took a step back. I slid in through the opening and pushed the door shut behind me. The house looked the same, right down to the Oriental armor. I wondered if Ronnie had had time to regret leaving it at home.

"What is it, Mr. Walker?"

"I thought you might like to know there's an all-points out for Pudge Capstone. My guess is when they get him he'll talk. Murder's out of his line."

"I don't know anyone by that name."

"Sure you do. You hired him to take me down and grab the ransom you conned out of Virgil Sweet for Ronnie's release."

She looked at me, at the suit I'd wrinkled while napping on the floor at Cadillac Center. "You're drunk. Ronnie's in Miami."

"Ronnie's in formaldehyde and you know it. You put him there. The cops found him right where you had him dumped. Who did the dumping doesn't matter right now; it could have been anyone in pants. Men like to do you favors. Ask Ansel Albany."

She turned toward the living room. "I'm calling the police."

"Ask them what's keeping them," I said. "On my way here I stopped and left a message for a friend at headquarters. I was with him a little while ago and could have told him in person, but I wanted time with you first."

She turned back. "Maybe I'm the one who's drunk. I don't follow you."

"You should've ditched the gun after you shot Ronnie. Could be you clean and oil it as regularly as any good N.R.A. granny but I doubt it. You must have dirtied it recently. It's my hunch Pudge worked for Redline a time or two, and you found out he was good for the rough stuff. Why you killed Ronnie isn't important. Maybe it was an accident, because an ambitious young dealer like he was would be worth a lot more to you alive than any ransom as long as you could hold him. Maybe you found out you couldn't, and reacted badly. Anyway you made the most of it, stashed the stiff someplace while you convinced Virgil Sweet his partner had been kidnapped by a rival outfit and that they'd told you to deliver the ransom alone. Sweet came through with the cash today and you went through the motions of a drop because you knew I was watching. Pudge was already aboard the train when you and I got on. He hits hard."

Her face was like something carved from teak. "That's a lot to draw from a freshly cleaned gun. I mean, without a laboratory."

"The gun was just part of it. Things moved just a little too fast once I came in. I had the feeling the party was waiting for me to arrive before it heated up."

"Yes." It was just a word to fill the silence. Then the teak split. A tear slicked her cheek. "I didn't want him to hit me any more."

"Who, Ronnie?"

"He'd hit me so many times. I was so bruised I stayed home from the studio so I wouldn't have to show my face. I don't even remember what it was we were fighting about this time. He came at me and I used this." She drew the derringer out of the pocket of her robe and pointed it at me. "He gave it to me for protection."

"You don't need it now. You need a lawyer." Keep her talking.

"It was my ace in the hole. I shot him and he fell."

She gave me the gun.

"As anybody would, with two slugs in him." I put the two-shot in my coat pocket.

She said, "I only shot him once."

Six

He wasn't in his office, a crabbed little accident of a room created when two walls were improperly joined; warehouse architecture is not the UN Building. But I knew where to look.

The light shed by the ceiling funnels in the big echoing room where Redline stored its old recordings fell short of the floor, making the tall racks look as if they were floating on shadow. I could smell Ansel's tobacco smoke in the stale air. I called his name. No answer.

The racks were arranged like library stacks with wide aisles running between them. I walked along the ends. One, two, three aisles, all unoccupied. Four ...

Something clipped the corner of a record sleeve near my right ear, followed closely by a report that swallowed up all the air in the room. I jumped back, snapping my Smith & Wesson from its belt clip.

"Walker?"

Ansel's voice, at large somewhere in the big room.

Crouching behind the rack I said, "She could have used her one telephone call on a lawyer, but she called you. That's something, anyway."

"Go home, Amos. I don't have so many friends I can afford to start killing them off."

"Ansel, the cops are on their way. I just left John Alderdyce at Ronnie Madrid's house with Sheilah. Ronnie was shot twice, John said. Once with a twenty-two and once with a forty-four; a magnum from the way it penetrated. Why'd you do it?"

"You're telling it."

I had a hunch he was moving around. He was silent on his feet, but he wouldn't stay in the same place under those circumstances. I backed up, putting another rack between us. "The way I see it, you were aware of the situation between Ronnie and Sheilah and told her to call you the next time he threatened to beat her up," I said. "She did, but by the time you got there she'd plugged him once already. You finished the job."

"It wasn't the first time I killed a man to protect someone."

"I heard it was three men."

"No, that was another time. Can you blame me for this one?"

"Not so much for the kill. You shouldn't have tried to make a buck off it."

"The son of a bitch hid all his cash and he didn't have life insurance. If you charged him ten bucks for every one of Sheilah's bruises, he still came out ahead. Did you think I was going to take any of it for myself?"

"Where is it?"

In the little silence that followed I could hear the air moving, "Pudge was supposed to bring it straight to Sheilah. Didn't the cops find it at her place?"

"Not on the first search. I didn't hang around to watch them steam off the wallpaper."

"I don't have it. I was busy ditching the body." He laughed his short deep bark. "Who thought Pudge would have the brains to look inside the briefcase?"

"He's been a bag man a long time. Maybe he finally got curious."

The tip of a long shadow fluttered on the brick wall at the end of the aisle. Ansel was searching the aisles one by one. I looked at the record rack nearest me. It was solid, reinforced with angle irons and tiered like bookshelves. I holstered the revolver and began climbing.

"You should've left things as they fell." I raised my voice to cover the creaking. "It would've been self-defense for Sheilah and justifiable homicide for you. Framing a snatch makes it look like murder."

"Capping a druglord isn't murder." He was close now. His foot scuffed concrete two or three aisles over. When I was six feet above the floor I stretched a leg and gained a foothold on the rack across the aisle. Now I was straddling the space between. Reaching for my gun I almost lost my balance. I caught myself and double-handed the Smith & Wesson, training it a few feet up the wall. Through the space between two tiers of records I saw him coming around the corner into the next aisle, the glitter of the big .44 magnum.

"You used me, Ansel. You needed a reliable witness to report to the cops he saw the ransom drop, so you hired me to look in on Sheilah. You called her when you knew I was at her place, and when she ran out to meet Virgil Sweet you knew I'd be curious enough to follow. You set me up for a sapping so I wouldn't see too much. Every time I try to look at it your way my head starts hurting."

"It had to be your head," he said. "You were the only one I could count on to take the case that far. Tell you what. Since we're friends I'll give you five seconds to make a break for the door. If you get to it before I finish counting, I'll let you keep running."

"You gave that liquor-store bandit ten."

"I'm older now. I need the edge."

"It doesn't have to be this way, Ansel."

"Sure it does."

As he spoke he lunged around the end of the rack into my aisle. My voice must have told him I was there, because he squeezed off two quick shots that spanged off the brick wall behind me, at what would have been chest level if I were standing on the floor. Before he could adjust his aim upward I returned fire, smashing his forearm. The big shiny gun slammed to the floor.

He clutched the arm, staring up at me. He only had a minute before the pain and shock took away his speech. "That wasn't any kind of a fair chance."

"It's been a long day," I said, "I needed an edge too."

"That's how it starts." His knees started to bend.

Seven

They tried Sheilah Sorrell and Ansel Albany separately for murder and conspiracy to commit extortion. The jury hung on Sheilah—there were only four women and it was easy to figure which way they split— and the prosecution decided against retrial. The police in Romulus picked up Pudge Capstone at Detroit Metropolitan Airport with $200,000 in twenties and fifties in a carry-on bag and a ticket to Mexico City in his pocket. And every time my work takes me to Jackson I stop in at the state penitentiary to visit Ansel. I don't have so many friends I can afford to drop one just because he tried to kill me.

People Who Kill

"People who kill are different from you and me."

The guy doing the talking was a professor at the University of Detroit, one of the new breed with parlor hair pushed back behind his ears, a brown corduroy jacket, and a skinny tie like you see in early Dean Martin movies without Jerry Lewis. He had a gunfighter's droopy moustache that kept getting in his wine and a pair of those glasses that react to light in steel rims. He was a little drunk, but then so was everyone else in the party except me. I was working.

We were sitting at a big round table inside the red plush candy box of a downtown club; the professor and his trim wife and their guests, a former U.S. congressman and *his* wife, a lean woman in her fifties with very blonde hair and no flesh on her face, and me. The former congressman, a large, smiling bald man, was guest lecturing at the university. I was there to keep an eye on the string of matched pearls his wife wore around her skinny neck. My specialty as a private investigator is tracing missing persons, but the guard work would look good on my resume, and anyway my bank account could use the transfusion.

The professor's trim wife laughed quietly. The laugh fluttered at the hollow of her throat and her teeth showed liquid white against her red lipstick. I was watching her whenever I wasn't watching the other woman's pearls.

"How'd we get on the subject of killing?" asked the professor's wife.

"Sorry. I was just thinking about this fellow in tonight's *News*, who shot and killed the kid breaking into his house. The paper said the guy was popular in his neighborhood and had no criminal record. But he's old enough to be a veteran of World War II, and I'll lay you any odds that's where he was trained to kill. There are two kinds of killers, those who are born and those who undergo rigorous conditioning to overcome their natural inclination toward nonviolence. Which is why I'm saying that people who kill aren't like you and me."

"I'm not so sure," put in the congressman's wife. "If I ever found myself in this man's position, all alone late at night with an intruder trying to get in, I wouldn't hesitate to use a gun if I had one. The instinct for self-preservation runs deep."

The congressman said, "You surprise me, Ellen. I spent two terms fighting for stiffer gun laws."

The professor's smile was a paper cut over his glass. "You might want to pull the trigger, but wanting to and pulling it aren't the same. All that has been bred out of us. Assuming it was there to begin with."

"Well, I find the whole thing repugnant," said his wife. But her eyes glittered.

"Why are we arguing when we have an expert right here?" The congressman turned his beaming politician's face on me. "What about it, Amos? Are killers an aberration or part of the natural order?"

"Walker's an example on my side," said the professor. "He fought in Vietnam and has had to do with guns ever since."

His wife patted his hand. "Let him talk, Carl."

"I'm just the help."

"Don't be difficult," the congressman insisted. "With all respect to Carl, you're the only one here whose opinion counts in this case."

"I know of someone," I said, "but the story takes time."

"They don't lock up here until two," said the professor. They were all watching me. I moved a shoulder and got started.

"He was crowding sixty when this happened, a chunky little old guy with a lot of rumpled white hair. They called him Whitey back on Jefferson where he hung out in his old black overcoat, but his real name was Walter and he'd been married and raised a girl. The wife died and the girl moved out and never came back. He was deaf in one ear, by the way, a thing that kept him out of the military during the war, so he had no combat training. He was a retired cabinetmaker living on a small pension in an apartment house on Michigan until it went condo, and then he relocated in a condemned hotel on Jefferson. It came down later to make room for the Renaissance Center. Dillinger had stayed there once when Illinois got too hot, but the place had to go so they could put up another hotel where no one stayed.

"Anyway, Whitey checked out the rooms on the ground floor where he wouldn't have to climb any stairs, but derelicts and rats had claimed all those, and the only vacancies on the second were on the side facing the river and the wind from Windsor came cold as a ghost's breath through the broken panes. He settled finally for a room on the third with plywood over the window and empties insulating it on both sides. He had some blankets and a kerosene heater and there was a squirrel-chewed mattress on the floor, and as long as his monthly check kept coming care of General Delivery, he could afford to eat. A lot of old people with nice homes and relatives to look after them live worse.

"Whitey was a night person. Thirty years on the graveyard shift are hard to shake, and with no light to read by and nothing to read even if he had light, he started taking long walks after midnight, when the streets are safe only for poor people and muggers. His rounds usually took him behind furniture stores, where he rescued items he could use from the dumpsters: a chair with a broken rung, a table missing a leg, part of a bed frame— things he could carry up to his room and fix up for his own use, with worn-out tools he got from the same place, and sometimes sell back to the stores where he got them. This is how he spent his days when he wasn't sleeping. In four months of these nighttime scrounges, he was stopped only once, by a bored cop who wanted to know what he was doing carrying a rickety bookcase through the streets at one-thirty in the morning. The cop was probably too bored to hear the answer, and let him go. Being old and poor in this town is as good as being invisible.

"When you make a habit of being out at that hour, you tend to see a lot worth keeping to yourself, and Whitey soon learned the wisdom of keeping his feet moving and his eyes straight ahead. He never walked faster than when he was crossing the mouth of an alley or cutting through a sheltered parking lot. Not seeing things requires special skill, because you not only have to not see something but also *look* like you didn't see it in case someone sees you not seeing it. Am I making sense?" I looked at the professor.

"A great deal," he said. "But then I don't teach English."

I went on. "This night I'm talking about, Whitey dropped the ball. It was January, the wind chill was knocking around twenty below, and to avoid the icy air blasting between two buildings he ducked into an underground garage, carrying an end table with a wrinkled veneer, and found himself looking at four guys grunting and cursing between a pair of parked cars. One guy had another's arms pinned behind his back and the other two were putting it to the pinned guy with their fists and a galvanized pipe. Moonlight from the entrance replayed the whole thing in shadows on the concrete wall.

"Whitey couldn't just keep going without walking right past them, and not seeing something is difficult under those circumstances. He turned back the way he came, but forgot he was carrying the end table and hung up one of its legs on someone's bumper. He lost his grip and the table hit the floor with nothing near the racket a truck makes spilling off a haulaway trailer. Somebody yelled and Whitey took off running. Behind him the table made some more noise and someone cursed, but he didn't look back to see who had stumbled over it. He hit the street on the fly, galloped around the corner of the building the garage was under, clattered through an alley, vaulted a construction sawhorse, and half slid, half rolled down a hill being gouged out for another underground garage for guys like the ones chasing him to beat up other guys in. He landed running and didn't stop until his lungs tasted bloody in his throat. Remember that he was almost sixty and that he hadn't run more than half a block to catch a DSR bus since high school. When his heart slowed to twice its normal rate and he didn't hear footsteps behind him with his good ear, he wound his way back to his condemned hotel, hugging shadows and looking in every direction but up and down, contrary to his normal rules for survival. He stayed in his room all the next day and didn't go out the night after that. He didn't even leave to eat.

"He couldn't afford a daily paper and of course he didn't own a television set, so he had no way of knowing that the guy he had seen being worked over in the garage died the following morning at Detroit Receiving without regaining consciousness, or that the cops were questioning a local numbers chief that the dead guy had owed eight hundred dollars to. Seems the muscle that the chief had sent to remind him of his obligation had gotten a little too enthusiastic with the pipe. So about the time Whitey was figuring it was safe to venture out, the crew was busy canvassing the winos and the bag ladies downtown for a line on the only witness to their murder.

"About dusk on his second day indoors, Whitey heard loud voices and put his eye to the crack between the plywood and his window frame in time to see the three guys entering the building. The pipe man was a big black with a lot of jaw and an arrest record for ADW going back to before the riots, but only one conviction. His name was Leon something. His partners were a dead-eyed, long-haired, nineteen-year-old white named Chick and another black about the same age everyone called Sugar Ray on account of the scar tissue over his eyes, only he didn't get that in the ring but from his old man, who he put in the hospital when he got too big to knock down. What the cops call a salt-and-pepper team. Chick was the only one who had a gun, Sugar Ray preferring his fists and Leon his pipe. It was Chick who had been holding the victim that night in the garage.

"Another thing Whitey didn't know was that while the trio had succeeded in bribing and threatening his address out of Detroit's walking wounded, they still didn't know what room he was staying in. So Sugar Ray questioned the bums and degenerates on the ground floor, Chick got to work searching the building from the bottom up, and Leon climbed the stairs to the sixth floor and started working his way down with pipe in hand. Meanwhile, Whitey, thinking they were heading straight for his room, hid out in the vacant hole next door, hoping they'd think he was out and would go away. He crouched in a littered corner with his overcoat drawn over his head to shut out the cold and the noise of shouts and blows from downstairs.

"Chick was ten minutes kicking in doors on the first and second levels and pointing his gun at a lot of mold and cracked plaster. Whitey heard him mounting the squawking steps to his floor, heard more wood splintering as Chick zigzagged down the hall from room to room shattering locks that hadn't worked in years. Realizing his mistake, the old man backed into a closet and drew the door shut. When Chick got to Whitey's quarters he noticed the signs of occupancy and spent a little more time searching that one. He came up empty, but he'd seen the tools and the repaired furniture and must have remembered the abandoned table in the garage and known he was getting close. He poked his head through the empty doorway of the room opposite Whitey's, then strode kittycorner to the next one down. That was the one Whitey was hiding in.

"He reared back and threw a heel at the lock, but the door had a broken latch and when it swung open he had to wrestle with his momentum to keep his face off the floor. Just then he caught a movement out of the corner of his right eye. He spun and fired. Glass collapsed and something made a shrill boinging noise, and he felt a blow to his ribs and his feet were snatched out from under him and he landed hard on his chest, almost letting go of the gun. He felt moist warmth under him and he must have known at that moment that he'd been shot.

"What he probably never knew was that the movement he'd fired at was his own reflection in the bathroom mirror to the right of the door, and that his bullet had struck the tiles behind the mirror at an angle, ricocheted, skidded off the adjacent wall, and struck him. In the process the soft-nosed slug had changed its shape a couple of times, and that, together with its wobbling trajectory, had made a hole in him the size of a baby's fist, through which his blood was pumping at the rate of about a quart every three minutes. There are five quarts of blood in the body of a full-grown man, and, well, you figure it out.

"Whitey, of course, had no idea what was going on. He thought he was the one being shot at, and since there seemed no good reason to stay where he was, he piled out through the closet door and, seeing two legs sticking out of the open bathroom door, leaped over them and out the exit. He had a survivor's instinct for not stopping to ask himself questions he had no time to answer.

"By this time, having found the other tenants too far gone on drugs and rotgut to remember who Whitey was, much less where, Sugar Ray had taken up guard duty at the foot of the stairs. He heard the shot and thinking that Chick had got his man, headed on up to view the remains. He was rounding the second flight when he met Whitey coming down the third.

"The old man did an about-face while Sugar Ray was still trying to piece together what this meant in terms of Chick, and bounded back the other way, intending to go up past the third floor. But then he heard heavy footsteps further up and ran back down his own hallway instead. Sugar Ray, assimilated now, was taking the flight three steps at a time with his fists balled."

I stopped to light a cigarette and looked around at my audience. "I know what you're thinking. It would have been poetic if Sugar Ray and Leon the Pipe had met on the third-floor landing and seen to each other. But they weren't armed for that, and anyway Leon was stalled somewhere up above, probably trying to figure out at what level the shot had been fired.

"Getting back to Sugar Ray. He reached the hallway in time to see Whitey, the dark tail of his overcoat flying behind him, leaping into the shadows at the far end. It was getting dark now. The slugger had been wondering if the other man had a gun, but the fact that he was running instead of shooting reassured him and he thundered down that echoing old corridor as fast as his long legs would take him. At the end he ran out of floor and plunged kiyoodling down through three stories of dark cold nothing.

"Whitey had stopped just short of the empty elevator shaft he knew was there and flattened himself against the wall while Sugar Ray hurtled past and down, landing on his feet with the grace of a born athlete and driving his knees into his chin hard enough to snap his neck like a dry stick. For a long time after that, no doctor thought he would live, but you can visit him now at the State Forensics Center in Ypsilanti, where they feed him liquids and turn him over from time to time to prevent bedsores.

"While Ray was crumpled up down there groaning among the empty bottles and other scraps of garbage the building's tenants had been throwing into the shaft for years, Whitey tried again for the stairs. But Sugar Ray's cries had reached Leon, and once again the old man heard his tread, this time on the flight immediately above. It was as if some invisible force wouldn't let him leave; he was the Flying Dutchman of the third floor. Not trusting the elevator trick to work a second time, and that having been pretty much an accident anyway, he ducked through the nearest open door.

"He didn't know what room he was in. It was getting hard to see and he'd lost his bearings. He closed the door and in turning tripped over something on the floor. He landed on top of whatever it was and rolled off in a panic, because in that instant he realized it was Chick's body. He'd made a complete circle and ended up in the room where he'd started.

"Chick wasn't moving, and whether he was dead yet isn't important to the story. The floor was slippery under Whitey's hand. When he realized why, he jerked it away and barked his wrist on something hard that moved when he struck it. He closed his hand around it, and he was holding Chick's gun.

"Leon was in the hall now. A pale yellow oval slid under the door and Whitey shrank back with a gasp, but it sprang away and he knew the man with the pipe was swinging a flashlight beam from side to side in front of him as he crept through the darkness on the balls of his feet, softly calling Chick's and Sugar Ray's names. Whitey held his breath until the sighing of the floorboards under Leon's weight grew faint. Then he moved as quickly as he could without making a noise that would carry down the hall.

"Once you've got your coat off it isn't easy to put it on a man who's dead or dying. The arms aren't where you need them to be and the sleeve linings keep snagging on buttons and things. But he got it on the motionless man finally and got up and backed into the shadows, gripping the butt of the gun growing warm and slippery in his hand. He had never held one before and he was surprised at how heavy it was. He had heard about safeties and he hoped there was nothing like that on this gun because he wouldn't know how to take it off. He did know about cocking it, which he did with both thumbs. Shards from the broken mirror crunched under the thin soles of his shoes, but he wasn't worried about making noise now. He kept backing until his shoulder blades touched the tiles. There he waited with his heart bounding off his breastbone.

"By now Leon had had time to reach the end of the hall, but no one knows if he trained his light on the bottom of the shaft and saw Sugar Ray. His failure to raise either of his partners must have put him on his guard in any case. To Whitey it seemed a good hour before the squeak of an occasional hinge told him the pipe man was making his way back in Whitey's direction one room at a time, poking the flash into each dark empty cell with his weapon probably raised. Whatever small sounds the old man had made putting his coat on Chick and getting ready had apparently died at the door, although to him they had seemed loud enough to bring half the underworld crashing in on him. He stood in the cold moldy dark sweating into his collar and shoes and listening to the air dragging in and out of his lungs. His eyes had adjusted to the faint city glow leaking through the ventilator louvers over the toilet and he could see Chick's inert bulk in his own black overcoat on the floor. If he hadn't been dead before he certainly was now.

"A soft rubber sole kissed the sprung boards on the other side of the door, Whitey thought; but he had learned long ago not to trust his defective hearing. To calm himself he switched the gun from his right to his left hand and wiped his right palm down his thigh. Then he changed grips again and stopped breathing. The door to the hall was opening.

"It inched open as if pushed by the phantom beam that followed it into the room. The light nudged a smoky path through the blackness, prowled the area beyond the edge of the empty bathroom doorway, and attached itself to the dead man's feet sticking out over the threshold. Leon took his breath in sharply. Then the light touched the worn hem of Whitey's overcoat on the corpse and the intruder came in the rest of the way, the pipe dangling at the end of his right arm. Enough illumination came back up off the littered tile floor to expose a wolfish grin on Leon's face. The smell of spent cordite was still thick in the enclosed space, and he must have thought he was looking at Chick's handiwork. Which he was, but not in the way he thought.

"'Chick?' he said, and lifted the beam to take in the rest of the room.

"Whitey fired then, twice into the center of the light that was blinding him. The reports thudded massively against the tiles, the recoil vibrating up his arm and through his body, shaking loose what shreds of mirror glass remained on the wall he was touching.

"Something clanged under the echoing of the shots. Whitey stood unmoving while the choking smoke curled and twisted toward the ventilator and out. When it cleared he was prepared to fire again because there was still light in the room, but then he saw it bending along the floor from the abandoned flash lying against Chick's leg. He was alone with the dead man.

"Now he moved, stepping over the body but almost falling when something rolled out from under his foot. He caught himself against the jamb and knew without looking that the object was Leon's pipe. He left it there but picked up the flash. The fresh bloodstains on the floor looked black in the light. Leon was wounded.

"Whitey followed the dribbling trail out of the room and up the hall toward the stairs. The flashlight beam reflected off a big dark puddle on the landing. He could smell it now, sharp and musty in the icy air. The traces meandered down two flights, at the bottom of which the clear outline of one of Leon's waffle-patterned soles where he had stepped in his own leakage pointed toward the second-floor hallway. The light found no stains on the last flight before the ground. In his shock and panic Leon had miscounted his flights.

"There was nothing keeping the old man from leaving the building. Instead he turned and followed the stains. The gun was part of his hand now.

"Debris and great peeling sheets of wallpaper made bizarre shadows before the flash. The doors of most of the rooms on that floor had been kicked in by Chick, but he ignored them. The trail continued down the hall.

"He found Leon sitting on the floor with his back against the closed elevator doors that made the corridor a dead end, whimpering with both hands buried in the gaping black hole above his belt. His bowels were torn, their stench foul enough to have texture. He screwed up his slick face against the light in his eyes and said something unintelligible in a pleading tone.

"Whitey didn't make him wait. He snapped off the flash and there was an instant of darkness before the flame from the muzzle splattered it. Leon's body arched, the back of his head striking the elevator doors with a reverberating boom, and then his torso sagged and his big chin settled into the hollow of his right shoulder. Whitey was still standing there holding the weapon when the cops came."

I took advantage of the silence to lay in an inch of red wine in my glass. The congressman's wife was the first to speak.

"Is that a true story?"

I nodded, wetting my tongue. "I spent three weeks tracking down derelicts who were in the building that night and collecting affidavits for the public defender who represented Whitey at his trial. The rest of it came from the old man himself."

"What happened to him?" asked the professor.

"He pulled a year for third-degree murder knocked down from first. The coroner ruled death by misadventure on Chick, and Sugar Ray's testimony by closed-circuit television from his hospital room failed to incriminate Whitey, but the judge wouldn't go self-defense on Leon because the old man had his chance to flee after shooting him the first time. He's living in a convalescent home in Southfield now. The hearing in his other ear went finally, but he doesn't need it to fix furniture in the workshop for sale by the Salvation Army."

"I think that's nice," said the professor's wife.

Pickups and Shotguns

One

Fifty minutes after I arrived for my appointment five minutes early, Lawrence Otell's secretary—a tawny-haired angel whose placard read MS. ROLAND—hung up her telephone and told me I could go in. I left off studying an actuarial chart on the wall that informed me I'd been dead for two years, passed through the door marked PRIVATE, and shook the hand of the big square middle-aged type seated behind a desk shaped like a lima bean. He managed my name and indicated the chair on the customer's side, helping himself to a lump of hard candy from the jar on the desk without offering me one or apologizing for making me wait. I didn't give it much thought. I'd been working off and on for Midwest Confidential Life, Automobile, & Casualty for fifteen years and had yet to receive so much as a Christmas card from its headquarters in downtown Detroit.

"I see you've handled a number of assignments for us, Mr. Walker." Otell peered through a pair of black-rimmed readers at a file with my name lettered on the tab.

"You gave me the last six personally."

That upset him quite a bit. He glanced at me over the tops of his glasses, then closed the folder. "Have you ever investigated arson?"

"I went along on a couple of torch jobs. Is that the beef?"

"My usual man is out sick this week. He seems to be taken ill every year during the first week of deer hunting season. You don't hunt?"

"I used to, with my father. It isn't so much fun now that I do it for a living."

"I don't go in for blood sports myself. This case shouldn't be too complicated. The only reason I'm suspicious at all is the policy holder refused permission to the local fire department to investigate the premises. By law the investigators are required to ask permission. Otherwise they must seek a warrant. They're in the process of doing that now, but the circuit judge is away on a hunting trip and can't be reached."

"Can't they get another judge?"

"It's a small town, and it's Friday afternoon. They might not be able to locate another before

Monday, by which time the integrity of the scene may be violated. Of course, this could be simply a case of a disgruntled homeowner sticking his finger in the spokes just to cause trouble. Do you know the term 'pickups and shotguns'?"

I shook my head, which pleased him. Otell was a frustrated pedant.

"It's a phrase advertisers use when they divide the population into consumer groups. Huron's a small town in a farm community yielding slowly to suburban development. Pickups and shotguns outsell sportscars and cufflinks five to one."

"I was there once. You're overestimating sportscars and cufflinks."

He slid another folder out from under the one with my name on it and held it out. "This contains all the information you'll need to start. The commander of the sheriff's substation is Sergeant Early. You'll want to let him know what you're up to."

I didn't ask him why. It was hunting season, and there were bound to be a lot more shotguns circulating around the neighborhood than pickups.

Two

Huron had changed since my last visit. The local newspaper office was closed, probably having been wolfed down by a larger competitor and relocated. The restaurant was boarded up, real estate offices had taken over several of the retail stores in the business district, and the town had sprouted a tail along the main highway made up of chain department stores, fast-food franchises, and an antiques mall with all the old-world charm of a sperm bank. The twenty-first century was bearing down on Huron like an iron heel in an Air Jordan.

Sergeant Early was a solid-looking number with a military brush moustache in a cocoa-brown uniform with a sheriff's star embroidered on each sleeve. He looked at my credentials, then got up from behind his desk and rescued his cap off a peg. "Supreme Court ought to have its head examined. Why a private cop can go into a place where sworn authority is barred is the first question the shrink should ask."

"It's a waiver the policyholder signs when he applies for insurance," I said.

"He must've been drunk when he signed it. Mike Hopper won't even sign a traffic citation. But he's no insurance fraud."

Early accompanied me in my car to a plot just outside the village limits containing a small barn, a couple of other outbuildings, and a pile of charred timbers that had once been a house. He leaned against a fender while I pulled an old rubber raincoat and a pair of galoshes out of the trunk and put them on. "What do you look for, exactly?" he asked.

"Suspicious burn patterns, combustible materials where they don't belong, obvious evidence of arson. If they're not present I leave the actual cause of the fire to the experts. I'm just a troubleshooter."

"Well, you won't find any trouble here. Hopper's a pain in the butt. He's also one of the most honest men I know."

According to the file Lawrence Otell had given me, the Hopper family had sold its acreage short to developers years before, then watched the developers make back ten times the investment by subdividing, building houses, and selling the plots for a hundred thousand apiece. Meanwhile Mike, the last of the family, had become an independent trucker to survive. He had been alone at home, sleeping on the second story, when the fire broke out, and had escaped with only the pajamas he was wearing. The house was totally engulfed by the time the fire department arrived.

Sergeant Early remained outside while I waded through a muck of sodden ashes, turning over lumps of melted and half-burned furniture and shining my flashlight into corners made inaccessible by the piles of debris. The stench was one I could never get used to, which was why I didn't specialize in arson investigation. I'd only taken the job to remind Midwest Confidential I was still in business. The company had saved me from a negative balance more times than I could count.

I fished out a couple of bowling trophies, smeared with soot but undamaged, and a thick spiralbound book charred around the edges that upon opening I found to contain what looked like family snapshots going back to the thirties, judging by the cars and clothing that appeared in them. These items I wrapped in one of the kitchen trash bags I'd carried along to store evidence and laid atop what used to be a cabinet television. The sky looked like rain or snow, and such mementos are irreplaceable. That was it for the ground floor, as well as the second story, which had collapsed along with the rest of the house.

Finding the stairs to the basement I switched on my flash and descended, testing each step before I trusted my full weight to it. The half-cellar was dank and airless, and the stagnant water from the firemen's hoses came up almost to my boot tops on the concrete floor. Something nudged one of my calves. My light found a red plastic can, half-burned, that I might have thought was a watering can floating on the surface if it weren't just the kind of thing I was looking for. I picked it up by what was left of its handle and smelled the inside. Gasoline never smells like anything but what it is.

Advertised warnings to the contrary, a lot of people store gasoline in their cellars. I did some more looking. In a corner relatively untouched by the flames, I found two more cans just like it. Training the flashlight beam around the room, I spotted another floating object and waded over to it. It was a wooden dowel about two feet long, partially burned, with a husk of what might have been charred oilcloth wrapped around the end. On this end I smelled more gasoline. I carried the cans and the makeshift torch upstairs and showed them to Sergeant Early.

"It's not conclusive," I said. "Experts may be able to tell if the fire started in the basement, or maybe not. Right now it looks like someone doused the place with gas, then lit a torch and threw it in from the top of the stairs where he could get out before it got going."

Early took off his cap, ran his fingers back through his short thinning hair, and put it back on. "Mike's got enemies. One of 'em might have been sore enough to burn him out."

"If that's true, he did him a favor, at least financially. The place was insured for a lot more than he would have gotten for it on the market."

"Let's go talk to him."

Three

Mike Hopper's tractor-trailer, bearing his name on the cab, was parked behind a motel on an as yet undeveloped section of state highway, one of the old-fashioned kind with bungalows lined up on either side of the office. We were greeted at the door of No. 11 by a big man with narrow eyes, a reddish-brown beard and moustache that concealed his mouth completely, and a strip of untanned flesh at the top of his forehead where a cap would rest normally. He was shoeless and had on an undershirt and stained workpants. One of his big hands was wrapped around a beer can.

"Mike, this is Amos Walker. He's with your insurance company. We need to talk."

"I said I didn't want nobody snooping around my place. I was born there. Nobody goes in without an invite but family, and I'm all the family that's left."

"It's gone past that." I held up one of the gasoline cans. "Is this yours?"

"I sold my pickup for a down payment on my rig. It's diesel. I got no use for gas."

"What do you owe on your rig?" Early asked.

"I'm three payments behind, not that it's your damn business. What the hell goes on here?"

I read it like a primer. "You get much behind, the company repossesses your tractor-trailer. Without a rig you starve. That's what goes on here. Did you put a match to your place for the insurance?"

He almost caught me square on the jaw, but only because I thought he'd need more reaction time. As it was his fist clipped my left ear when I moved my head. The sergeant caught his wrist and twisted it behind his back, using Hopper's own momentum against him. "Hold on, Mike. Walker doesn't know you. Can you think of anybody you've had a run-in with who might want to set fire to your house?"

When the answer didn't come right away, Early twisted harder. "No! Jeez, Tom, who do you think I hang out with? I tee somebody off, he takes a swing at me. He don't come around in the middle of the night and try to fry me in my bed."

"Mike's right. His crowd isn't that original."

"In that case, Sergeant, I'm informing you that Midwest Confidential intends to press charges against Mr. Hopper for attempted fraud."

"You heard him, Mike. I'm going to have to put you in custody."

As he said it, Early gave me a black look that told me all I needed to know about which man he'd rather put handcuffs on.

Four

He was still wearing the look an hour later, when he returned to his desk in the substation after seeing Hopper off to the county lock-up in the back of a squad car. "I never had to arrest a friend before," he said. "I like it a lot, no, I don't."

I said, "I don't much like being the bad cop, but he knows you."

"I still don't think he did it."

"Neither do I."

He touched his moustache, watching me. I liked that way he had of waiting for answers to the questions he didn't ask. He had a lot of city cop in him for a glorified security officer.

I offered him a cigarette, and lit one for myself when he shook his head. "I wanted to get a look at him, just to see if he was the type who would throw away family treasures in return for the fast buck," I said, depositing the match in a clay ashtray that looked as if Early had a kid who went to summer camp. "He isn't. He was telling the truth when he said he didn't want anyone but family poking through the ashes of his birthplace. If he burned his own house, he might sacrifice his bowling trophies to make it look good, but he'd find some way to save family pictures. He almost lost an album full of memories in the flames. He didn't set that fire."

"Who do you think did?"

"I don't know. Maybe nobody. Maybe somebody sneaked in after the fire and planted the gasoline cans and the torch to make it look like arson."

"Somebody'd have to hate Mike a lot to try to frame him. He's got some enemies, but he's got a lot of friends too. I'd hate to think what they'd do to someone who'd sink that low. If you didn't buy it, why'd you have me arrest Mike?"

"If whoever it was thinks it worked, he may not be looking over his shoulder when we come up on him from behind. It would help if someone saw somebody hanging around the scene after the fire was out."

"That's a tough one. There are always gawkers. Pesky kids. Wait." He touched his moustache again. "Al Ludendorf—that's the fire chief—told me he caught Lloyd Golson skulking around the night after the fire. Golson's a petty thief. Al thought he might've been there to loot the place, but he searched him and didn't find anything on him. He ran him off."

"Where would I find Golson?"

Sergeant Early smiled for the first time since we'd met. "Hell, that's easy. I caught him shoplifting a circular saw out of the Huron Hardware yesterday. He's locked up in the same wing with Mike Hopper."

Five

I drove straight from the county seat to the Midwest Confidential building. Ms. Roland, Lawrence Otell's secretary, was putting on her coat when I stepped off the elevator into the reception area.

"Quitting time, sorry," she said. "Mr. Otell's busy clearing up some unfinished business."

"So am I. Got a minute?"

"Just about that." She glanced at the watch strapped to the underside of her wrist.

"I guess Mr. Otell's pretty valuable to the company."

"He holds the record for delivering the most policies with the fewest claims. He's the front runner for the president's job when Mr. Silverman retires."

"That's important, huh. I mean about his reporting the fewest claims against the policies he sold."

"Well, yes. For a while it looked like Jeff Knapp had the inside track because he sold more policies, but then he caught a bad break during fire season. It's kind of unfair when you think about it. No one can predict that."

"You don't know your boss as well as you think."

"I'm sorry?"

But I was already going through the door to the private office. Inside Otell looked up quickly from the paperwork spread across his desk. "Around here we knock," he said.

I said, "Things are a little less formal in Huron. I just spoke with Lloyd Golson."

His square face showed nothing. "Who's that?"

"You'll find him in company files. Midwest Confidential sold a lot of policies around Huron. Several burglary claims were filed. His name came up in four of them as a suspect in the break-ins. He was convicted twice. Is that why you decided to use him, because his name kept showing up in claim cases?"

"Naturally I don't know what you're talking about."

"Sure you do. You've got a shot at the presidency because you've made the company more money from policies than you've lost in claims. That would change if too many customers like Mike Hopper were paid off for their losses in fires. Tampering with the fire scene to make it look like Hopper torched his own house for the insurance would allow the company to reject his claim, preserving your record and your chances for advancement."

He pointed a finger. "Repeat that in front of witnesses and I'll sue you for character assassination."

"I can't kill what you don't have," I said. "Golson talked, Otell. He ratted you out to get a shoplifting charge dropped that would have imprisoned him for five years as a repeat offender. You called him the morning after the fire and offered him five hundred dollars to plant evidence implicating Hopper."

"A man like that would say anything to stay out of jail."

"Maybe. It's enough to make the authorities curious about other aborted claims against policies you sold. A man who would break the law once to improve his statistics would do it again. I'm guessing when they're finished taking a hard look you'll be facing several counts of interfering in criminal investigations and insurance fraud. You won't like prison any more than Golson. The pinstripes go the wrong way."

He thought about it a second, then opened the top drawer of his desk and brought out a revolver. That disappointed me.

"If you're going to shoot yourself, don't do it in your own office. That joke's too old."

"Who said anything about shooting myself?" He pointed the revolver at me.

Just then Ms. Roland came in. "Larry? Is everything—" She froze when she saw the gun.

Otell didn't. In a second he was on his feet and lunging. He grabbed her arm, pulled her off balance, and swept behind her, grabbing her around the waist and clapping the revolver's muzzle under her chin. "Don't move, Walker!"

"Well, that one's even older," I said. "I thought you didn't go in for blood sports." But I didn't move.

He backed through the open door, bringing her with him. I gave him a beat, then followed.

They were standing in front of the elevator. He took the gun from her throat long enough to push the button with his elbow, then replaced it. His expression was totally alien. The shock of a drop as long as the one from the president's office to the defendant's table affects many different people many different ways.

The doors slid open. He shoved the woman stumbling into the office and backed inside the elevator, swinging the gun from side to side. I stayed where I was. The doors closed and the car started down.

I helped Ms. Roland to her feet. "Are you going to call the police?" she asked.

"No." I went back into Otell's office. The wall behind the desk was made entirely of glass and looked down onto the street before the entrance to the underground garage where the employees parked. The secretary joined me.

"I called the parking attendant earlier," I said. "Otell drives a gray Mercedes?"

"Yes. Are the police waiting for him?"

"Not exactly."

A minute later a gray Mercedes nosed out into the street. It was waiting to turn when a battered Dodge pickup swept away from the curb and plowed into the door on the driver's side. After a pause the passenger's side door popped open and Otell piled out, waving his revolver. Just then a second pickup roared down the lane on that side and screeched to a halt. Both doors swung open and the occupants of the cab leveled shotguns across the tops. By then other pickups had appeared, ringing in the Mercedes and the man who had been driving it. All the drivers and passengers had shotguns except one.

Sergeant Early stepped down from a Ford Ranger, walked up to Otell, and took away his gun without a struggle.

The Crooked Way

One

You couldn't miss the Indian if you'd wanted to. He was sitting all alone in a corner booth, which was probably his idea but he hadn't much choice because there was barely enough room in it for him. He had shoulders going into the next county and a head the size of a basketball and he was holding a beer mug that looked like a shot glass between his horned palms. As I approached the booth he looked up at me—not very far up—through slits in a face made up of bunched ovals and a nose like the corner of a building. His skin was the color of old brick.

"Mr. Frechette?" I asked.

"Amos Walker?"

I said I was. Coming from him my name sounded like two stones dropped into deep water. He made no move to shake hands, but he inclined his head a fraction of an inch and I borrowed a chair from a nearby table and joined him. He had on a blue shirt buttoned to the neck and his hair, parted on one side and plastered down, was blue-black without a trace of gray. Nevertheless he was about fifty.

"Charlie Stoat says you track like an Osage," he said. "I hope you're better than that. I couldn't track a train."

"How is Charlie? I haven't seen him since that insurance thing."

"Going under. The construction boom went bust in Houston just when he was expanding his operation."

"What's that do to yours?" He'd told me over the telephone he was in construction.

"Nothing worth mentioning. I've been running on a shoestring for years. You can't break a poor man."

I signaled the bartender for a beer and he brought one over. It was a workingman's hangout across the street from the Ford plant in Highland Park. The shift wasn't due to change for an hour and we had the place to ourselves. "You said your daughter ran away," I said, when the bartender had left. "What makes you think she's in Detroit?"

He drank off half his beer and belched dramatically. "When does client privilege start?"

"It never stops."

I watched him make up his mind. Indians aren't nearly as hard to read as they appear in books. He picked up a folded newspaper from the seat beside him and spread it out on the table facing me. It was yesterday's Houston *Chronicle*, with a banner:

Boyd Manhunt Moves Northeast
Bandit's Van Found Abandoned in Detroit

I had read a related wire story in that morning's Detroit *Free Press*. Following the unassisted shotgun robberies of two savings and loan offices near Houston, concerned citizens had reported seeing 22-year-old Virgil Boyd in Mexico and Oklahoma, but his green van with Texas plates had turned up in a city lot five minutes from where we were sitting. As of that morning, Detroit Police Headquarters was paved with feds and sun-crinkled out-of-state cops chewing toothpicks.

I refolded the paper and gave it back. "Your daughter's taken up with Boyd?"

"They were high school sweethearts," Frechette said. "That was before Texas Federal foreclosed on his family's ranch and his father shot himself. She disappeared from home after the first robbery. I guess that makes her an accomplice to the second."

"Legally speaking," I agreed, "if she's with him and it's her idea. A smart DA would knock it down to harboring if she turned herself in. She'd probably get probation."

"She wouldn't do that. She's got some crazy idea she's in love with Boyd."

"I'm surprised I haven't heard about her."

"No one knows. I didn't report her missing. If I had, the police would have put two and two together and there'd be a warrant out for her as well."

I swallowed some beer. "I don't know what you think I can do that the cops and the FBI can't."

"I know where she is."

I waited. He rotated his mug. "My sister lives in Southgate. We don't speak. She has a white mother, not like me, and she takes after her in looks. She's ashamed of being half Osage. First chance she had she married a white man and got out of Oklahoma. That was before I left for Texas, where nobody knows about her. Anyway she got a big settlement in her divorce."

"You think Boyd and your daughter will go to her for a getaway stake?"

"They won't get it from me, and he didn't take enough out of Texas Federal to keep a dog alive. Why else would they come here?"

"So if you know where they're headed, what do you need me for?"

"Because I'm being followed and you're not."

The bartender came around to offer Frechette a refill. The big Indian shook his head and he went away. "Cops?" I said.

"One cop. J. P. Ahearn."

He spaced out the name as if spelling a blasphemy. I said I'd never heard of him.

"He'd be surprised. He's a commander with the Texas State Police, but he thinks he's the last of the Texas Rangers. He wants Boyd bad. The man's a bloodhound. He doesn't know about my sister, but he did his homework and found out about Suzie and that she's gone, not that he could get me to admit she isn't away visiting friends. I didn't see him on the plane from Houston. I spotted him in the airport here when I was getting my luggage."

"Is he alone?"

"He wouldn't share credit with Jesus for saving a sinner." He drained his mug. "When you find Suzie I want you to set up a meeting. Maybe I can talk sense into her."

"How old is she?"

"Nineteen."

"Good luck."

"Tell me about it. My old man fell off a girder in Tulsa when I was sixteen. Then I was fifty. Well, maybe one meeting can't make up for all the years of not talking after my wife died, but I can't let her throw her life away for not trying."

"I can't promise Boyd won't sit in on it."

"I like Virgil. Some of us cheered when he took on those bloodsuckers. He'd have gotten away with a lot more from that second job if he'd shot this stubborn cashier they had, but he didn't. He wouldn't hurt a horse or a man."

"That's not the way the cops are playing it. If I find him and don't report it I'll go down as an accomplice. At the very least I'll lose my license."

"All I ask is that you call me before you call the police." He gave me a high school graduation picture of a pretty brunette he said was Suzie. She looked more Asian than American Indian. Then he pulled a checkbook out of his hip pocket and made out a check to me for fifteen hundred dollars.

"Too much," I said.

"You haven't met J. P. Ahearn yet. My sister's name is Harriett Lord." He gave me an address on Eureka. "I'm at the Holiday Inn, room 716."

He called for another beer then and I left. Again he didn't offer his hand. I'd driven three blocks from the place when I spotted the tail.

Two

The guy knew what he was doing. In a late-model tan Buick he gave me a full block and didn't try to close up until we hit Woodward, where traffic was heavier. I finally lost him in the grand circle down- · town, which confused him just as it does most people from the greater planet earth. The Indians who settled Detroit were being far-sighted when they named it the Crooked Way. From there I took Lafayette to 1-75 and headed downriver.

Harriett Lord lived in a tall white frame house with blue shutters and a large lawn fenced by cedars that someone had bullied into cone shape. I parked in the driveway, but before leaving the car I got out the unlicensed Luger I kept in a pocket under the dash and stuck it in my pants, buttoning my coat over it. When you're meeting someone they tell you wouldn't hurt a horse or a man, arm yourself.

The bell was answered by a tall woman around forty, dressed in a khaki shirt and corduroy slacks and sandals. She had high cheekbones and slightly olive coloring that looked more like sun than heritage and her short hair was frosted, further reducing the Indian effect. When she confirmed that she was Harriett Lord I gave her a card and said I was working for her brother.

Her face shut down. "I don't have a brother. I have a half-brother, Howard Frechette. If that's who you're working for, tell him I'm unavailable." She started to close the door.

"It's about your niece Suzie. And Virgil Boyd."

"I thought it would be."

I looked at the door and got out a cigarette and lit it. I was about to knock again when the door opened six inches and she stuck her face through the gap. "You're not with the police?"

"We tolerate each other on the good days, but that's it."

She glanced down. Her blue mascara gave her eyelids a translucent look. Then she opened the door the rest of the way and stepped aside. I entered a living room done all in beige and white and sat in a chair upholstered in eggshell chintz. I was glad I'd had my suit cleaned.

"How'd you know about Suzie and Boyd?" I used a big glass ashtray on the Lucite coffee table.

"They were here last night."

I said nothing. She sat on the beige sofa with her knees together. "I recognized him before I did her. I haven't seen her since she was four, but I take a Texas paper and I've seen his picture. They wanted money. I thought at first I was being robbed."

"Did you give it to them?"

"Aid a fugitive? Family responsibility doesn't cover that even if I felt any. I left home because I got sick of hearing about our proud heritage. Howard wore his Indianness like a suit of armor, and all the time he resented me because I could pass for white. He accused me of being ashamed of my ancestry because I didn't wear my hair in braids and hang turquoise all over me."

"He isn't like that now."

"Maybe he's mellowed. Not toward me, though, I bet. Now his daughter comes here asking for money so she and her desperado boyfriend can go on running. I showed them the door."

"I'm surprised Boyd went."

"He tried to get tough, but he's not very big and he wasn't armed. He took a step toward me and I took two steps toward him and he grabbed Suzie and left. Some Jesse James."

"I heard his shotgun was found in the van. I thought he'd have something else."

"If he did, he didn't have it last night. I'd have noticed, just as I noticed you have one."

I unbuttoned my coat and resettled the Luger. I was getting a different picture of "Mad Dog" Boyd from the one the press was painting. "The cops would call not reporting an incident like that being an accessory," I said, squashing out my butt.

"Just because I don't want anything to do with Howard doesn't mean I want to see my niece shot up by a SWAT team."

"I don't suppose they said where they were going."

"You're a good supposer."

I got up. "How did Suzie look?"

"Like an Indian."

I thanked her and went out.

Three

I had a customer in my waiting room. It was a small angular party crowding sixty in a tight gray three-button suit, steel-rimmed glasses, and a tan snapbrim hat squared over the frames. His crisp gray hair was cut close around large ears that stuck out and he had a long sharp jaw with a sour mouth slashing straight across. He stood up when I entered. "Walker?" It was one of those bitter pioneer voices.

"Depends on who you are," I said.

"I'm the man who ought to arrest you for obstructing justice."

"I'll guess. J. P. Ahearn."

"*Commander* Ahearn."

"You're about four feet short of what I had pictured."

"You've heard of me." His chest came out a little.

"Who hasn't?" I unlocked the inner office door. He marched in, slung a look around, and took possession of the customer's chair. I sat down behind the desk without asking permission. He glared at me through his spectacles.

"What you did downtown today constitutes fleeing and eluding."

"In Texas, maybe. In Michigan there has to be a warrant out first. What you did constitutes harassment in this state."

"I don't have official status here. I can follow anybody for any reason or none at all."

"Is this what you folks call a Mexican standoff?"

"I don't approve of smoking," he snapped.

"Neither do I, but some of it always leaks out of my lungs." I blew some at the ceiling and got rid of the match. "Why don't let's stop circling each other and get down to why you're here?"

"I want to know what you and the Indian talked about."

"I'd show you, but we don't need the rain."

He bared a perfect set of dentures, turning his face into a skull. "I ran your plate with the Detroit Police. I have their complete co-operation in this investigation. The Indian hired you to take money to Boyd to get him and his little Osage slut to Canada. You delivered it after you left the bar and lost me. That's aiding and abetting and accessory after the fact of armed robbery. Maybe I can't prove it, but I can make a call and tank you for forty-eight hours on suspicion."

"Eleven."

He covered up his store-boughts. "What?"

"That's eleven times I've been threatened with jail," I said. "Three of those times I wound up there. My license has been swiped at fourteen times, actually taken away once. Bodily harm, you don't count bodily harm. I'm still here, six-feet-something and one-hun-dred-eighty-pounds of incorruptible P.I. with a will of iron and a skull to match. You hard guys come and go like phases of the moon."

"Don't twist my tail, son. I don't always rattle before I bite."

"What's got you so hot on Boyd?"

You could have cut yourself on his jaw. "My daddy helped run Parker and Barrow to ground in '34. *His* daddy fought Geronimo and chased John Wesley Hardin out of Texas. My son's a Dallas City patrolman and so far I don't have a story to hand him that's a blister on any of those. I'm retiring next year."

"Last I heard Austin was offering twenty thousand for Boyd's arrest and conviction."

"Texas Federal has matched it. Alive *or* dead. Naturally, as a duly sworn officer of the law I can't collect. But you being a private citizen."

"What's the split?"

"Fifty-fifty."

"No good."

"Do you know what the pension is for a retired state police commander in Texas? A man needs a nest egg."

"I meant it's too generous. You know as well as I do those rewards are never paid. You just didn't know I knew."

He sprang out of his chair. There was no special animosity in it; it would be the way he always got up.

"Boyd won't get out of this country even if you did give him money," he snapped. "He'll never get past the border guards."

"So go back home."

"Boyd's *mine.*"

The last word ricocheted. I said, "Talk is he felt he had a good reason to stick up those savings and loans. The company was responsible for his father's suicide."

"Bah!"

"Excuse me?"

"Bah!"

"That's what I thought you said. I never heard anyone actually say it before."

"If he's got the brains God gave a mad dog he'll turn himself in to me before he gets shot down in the street or kills someone and winds up getting the needle in Huntsville. And his squaw right along with him." He took a shabby wallet out of his coat and gave me a card. "That's my number at the Houston post. They'll re-route your call here. If you're so concerned for Boyd you'll tell me where he is before the locals gun him down."

"Better you than some stranger, that it?"

"Just keep on twisting, son. I ain't in the pasture yet."

After he left, making as much noise in his two-inch cowboy heels as a cruiserweight, I called Barry Stackpole at the Detroit *News.*

"Guy I'm after is wanted for Robbery Armed," I said, once the small talk was put away. "He ditched his gun and then his stake didn't come through and now he'll have to cowboy a job for case dough. Where would he deal a weapon if he didn't know anybody in town?"

"Emma Chaney."

"Ma? I thought she'd be dead by now."

"She can't die. The Detroit cops are third in line behind ATF and Customs for her scalp and they won't let her until they've had their crack." He sounded pleased, which he probably was. Barry made his living writing about crime and when it prospered he did too.

"How can I reach her?"

"Are you suggesting I'd know where she is and not tell the authorities? Got a pencil?"

I tried the number as soon as he was off the line. On the ninth ring I got someone with a smoker's wheeze. "Uh-huh."

"The name's Walker," I said. "Barry Stackpole gave me this number."

The voice told me not to go away and hung up. Five minutes later the telephone rang.

"Barry says you're okay. What do you want?"

"Just talk. It isn't cheap like they say."

After a moment the voice gave me directions. I hung up not knowing if it was male or female.

Four

It belonged to Ma Chaney, who greeted me at the door of her house in rural Macomb County wearing a red Japanese kimono with green parrots all over it. The kimono could have covered a Toyota. She was a five-by-five chunk with marcelled orange hair and round black eyes imbedded in her face like nailheads in soft wax. A cigarette teetered on her lower lip. I followed her into a parlor full of flowered chairs and sofas and pregnant lamps with fringed shades. A long strip of pimply blonde youth in overalls and no shirt took his brogans off the coffee table and stood up when she barked at him. He gaped at me, chewing gum with his mouth open.

"Mr. Walker, Leo," Ma wheezed. "Leo knew my Wilbur in Ypsi. He's like another son to me."

Ma Chaney had one son in the criminal ward at the Forensic Psychiatry Center in Ypsilanti and another on Florida's Death Row. The FBI was looking for the youngest in connection with an armored car robbery in Kansas City. The whole brood had come up from Kentucky when Old Man Chaney got a job on the line at River Rouge and stayed on after he was killed in a propane tank explosion. Now Ma, the daughter of a Hawkins County gunsmith, made her living off the domestic weapons market.

"You said talk ain't cheap," she said, when she was sitting in a big overstuffed rocker. "How cheap ain't it?"

I perched on the edge of a hard upright with doilies on the arms. Leo remained standing, scratching himself. "Depends on whether we talk about Virgil Boyd," I said.

"What if we don't?"

"Then I won't take up any more of your time."

"What if we do?"

"I'll double what he's paying."

She coughed. The cigarette bobbed. "I got a business to run. I go around scratching at rewards I won't have no customers."

"Does that mean Boyd's a customer?"

"Now, why'd that Texas boy want to come to Ma? He can deal hisself a shotgun at any K-Mart."

"He can't show his face in the legal places and being new in town he doesn't know the illegal ones. But he wouldn't have to ask around too much to come up with your name. You're less selective than most."

"You don't have to pussyfoot around old Ma. I don't get a lot of second-timers on account of I talk for money. My boy Earl in Florida needs a new lawyer. But I only talk after, not before. I start setting up customers I won't get no first-timers."

"I'm not even interested in Boyd. It's his girlfriend I want to talk to. Suzie Frechette."

"Don't know her." She rocked back and forth. "What color's your money?"

Before leaving Detroit I'd cashed Howard Frechette's check. I laid fifteen hundred dollars on the coffee table in twenties and fifties. Leo straightened up a little to look at the bills. Ma resumed rocking.

"It ain't enough."

"How much is enough?"

"If I was to talk to a fella named Boyd, and if I was to agree to sell him a brand new Ithaca pump shotgun and a P-38 still in the box, I wouldn't sell them for less than twenny-five hunnert. Double twenny-five hunnert is five thousand."

"Fifteen hundred now. Thirty-five hundred when I see the girl."

"I don't guarantee no girl."

"Boyd then. If he's come this far with her he won't leave her behind."

She went on rocking. "They's a white barn a mile north on this road. If I was to meet a fella named Boyd, there's where I might do it. I might pick eleven o'clock."

"Tonight?"

"I might pick tonight. If it don't rain."

I got up. She stopped rocking.

"Come alone," she said. "Ma won't."

On the way back to town I filled up at a corner station and used the pay telephone to call Howard Frechette's room at the Holiday Inn. When he started asking questions I gave him the number and told him to call back from a booth outside the motel.

"Ahearn's an anachronism," he said ten minutes later. "I doubt he taps phones."

"Maybe not, but motel operators have big ears."

"Did you talk to Suzie?"

"Minor setback," I said. "Your sister gave her and Boyd the boot and no money."

"Tight bitch."

"I know where they'll be tonight, though. There's an old auto court on Van Dyke between 21 and 22 Mile in Macomb County, the Log Cabin Inn. Looks like it sounds." I was staring at it across the road.

"Midnight. Better give yourself an hour."

He repeated the information.

"I'm going to have to tap you for thirty-five hundred dollars," I said. "The education cost."

"I can manage it. Is that where they're headed?"

"I hope so. I haven't asked them yet."

I got to my bank just before closing and cleaned out my savings and all but eight dollars in my checking account. I hoped Frechette was good for it. After that I ate dinner in a restaurant and went to see a movie about a one-man army. I wondered if he was available.

Five

The barn was just visible from the road, a moonlit square at the end of a pair of ruts cut through weeds two feet high. It was a chilly night in early spring and I had on a light coat and the heater running. I entered a dip that cut off my view of the barn, then bucked up over a ridge and had to stand the Chevy on its nose when the lamps fell on a telephone pole lying across the path. A second later the passenger's door opened and Leo got in.

He had on a mackinaw over his overalls and a plaid cap. His right hand was wrapped around a large-bore revolver and he kept it on me, held tight to his stomach, while he felt under my coat and came up with the Luger. "Drive." He pocketed it.

I swung around the end of the pole and braked in front of the barn, where Ma was standing with a Coleman lantern. She was wearing a man's felt hat and a corduroy coat whose sleeves came down to her fingers. She signaled a cranking motion and I rolled down the window.

"Well, park it around back," she said. "I got to think for you, too?"

I did that and Leo and I walked back. He handed Ma the Luger and she looked at it and put it in her pocket. She raised the lantern then and swung it from side to side twice.

We waited a few minutes, then were joined by six feet and 250 pounds of red-bearded young man in faded denim jacket and jeans carrying a rifle with an infrared scope. He had come from the direction of the road.

"Anybody following, Mason?" asked Ma.

He shook his head and I stared at him in the lantern light. He had small black eyes like Ma's with no shine in them. This would be Mace Chaney, for whom the FBI was combing the western states for the Kansas armored car robbery.

"Go on in and warm yourself," Ma said. "We got some time."

He opened the barn door and went inside. It had just closed when two headlamps appeared down the road. We watched them

approach and slow for the turn onto the path. Ma, lighting a cigarette off the lantern, grunted.

"Early. Young folks all got watches and they can't tell time."

Leo trotted out to intercept the car. A door slammed. After a
pause the lamps swung around the fallen telephone pole and came
up to the barn, washing us all in white. The driver killed the lamps
and engine and got out. He was a small man in his early twenties
with short brown hair and stubble on his face. His flannel shirt and
khaki pants were both in need of cleaning. He had scant eyebrows
that were almost invisible in that light, giving him a perennially surprised look. I'd seen that look in Frechette's Houston *Chronicle* and
in both Detroit papers.

"Who's he?" He was looking at me.

I had a story for that, but Ma piped up. "You ain't paying to ask
no questions. Got the money?"

"Not all of it. A thousand's all Suzie could get from the sharks."

"The deal's two thousand."

"Keep the P-38. The shotgun's all I need."

Ma had told me twenty-five hundred; but I was barely listening
to the conversation. Leo had gotten out on the passenger's side,
pulling with him the girl in the photograph in my pocket. Suzie
Frechette had done up her black hair in braids and she'd lost weight,
but her dark eyes and coloring were unmistakable. With that hairstyle and in a man's workshirt and jeans and boots with western heels
she looked more like an Indian than she did in her picture.

Leo opened the door and we went inside. The barn hadn't been
used for its original purpose for some time, but the smell of moldy
hay would remain as long as it stood. It was lit by a bare bulb swinging from a frayed cord and heated by a barrel stove in a corner. Stacks
of cardboard cartons reached almost to the rafters, below which Mace

Chaney sat with his legs dangling over the edge of the empty loft, the rifle across his knees.

Ma reached into an open carton and lifted out a pump shotgun with the barrel cut back to the slide. Boyd stepped forward to take it. She swung the muzzle on him. "Show me some paper."

He hesitated, then drew a thick fold of bills from his shirt pocket and laid it on a stack of cartons. Then she moved to cover me. Boyd watched me add thirty-five hundred to the pile.

"What's *he* buying?"

Ma said, "You."

"Cop!" He lunged for the shotgun. Leo's revolver came out. Mace drew a bead on Boyd from the loft. He relaxed.

I was looking at Suzie. "I'm a private detective hired by your father. He wants to talk to you."

"He's here?" She touched Boyd's arm.

He tensed. "It's a damn cop trick!"

"You're smarter than that," I said. "You had to be, to pull those two jobs and make your way here with every cop between here and Texas looking for you. If I were one, would I be alone?"

"Do your jabbering outside." Ma reversed ends on the shotgun for Boyd to take. He did so and worked the slide.

"Where's the shells?"

"That's your headache. I don't keep ammo in this firetrap."

That was a lie, or some of those cartons wouldn't be labeled C-4 EXPLOSIVES. But you don't sell loaded guns to strangers.

Suzie said, "Virgil, you never load them anyway."

"Shut up."

"Your father's on his way," I said. "Ten minutes, that's all he wants."

"Come on." Boyd took her wrist.

"Stay put."

This was a new voice. Everyone looked at Leo, standing in front of the door with his gun still out.

"Leo, *what* in the *hell*—"

"Ma, the Luger."

She shut her mouth and took my gun out of her right coat pocket and put it on the carton with the money. Then she backed away.

"Throw 'er down, Mace." He covered the man in the loft, who froze in the act of raising the rifle. They were like that for a moment.

"Mason," Ma said.

His shoulders slumped. He snapped on the safety and dropped the rifle eight feet to the earthen floor.

"You too, Mr. Forty Thousand Dollar *Re*ward," Leo said. "Even empty guns give me the jumps."

Boyd cast the shotgun onto the stack of cartons with a violent gesture.

"That's nice. I cut that money in half if I got to put a hole in you."

"That reward talk's just PR," I said. "Even if you get Boyd to the cops they'll probably arrest you too for dealing in unlicensed firearms."

"Like hell. I'm through getting bossed around by fat old ladies. Let's go, Mr. *Re*ward."

"No!" screamed Suzie.

An explosion slapped the walls. Leo's brows went up, his jaw dropping to expose the wad of pink gum in his mouth. He looked down at the spreading stain on the bib of his overalls and fell down on top of his gun. He kicked once.

Ma was standing with a hand in her left coat pocket. A finger of smoking metal poked out of a charred hole. "Dadgum it, Leo," she said, "this coat belonged to my Calvin, rest his soul."

Six

I was standing in front of the Log Cabin Inn's deserted office when Frechette swung a rented Ford into the broken paved driveway. He unfolded himself from the seat and loomed over me.

"I don't think anyone followed me," he said. "I took a couple of wrong turns to make sure."

"There won't be any interruptions, then. The place has been closed a long time."

I led him to one of the log bungalows in back. Boyd's Plymouth, stolen from the same lot where he'd left the van, was parked alongside it facing out. We knocked before entering.

All of the furniture had been removed except a metal bedstead with sagging springs. The lantern we had borrowed from Ma Chaney hung hissing from one post. Suzie was standing next to it. "Papa." She didn't move. Boyd came out of the bathroom with the shotgun. The Indian took root.

"Man said you had money for us," Boyd said.

"It was the only way I could get him to bring Suzie here," I told Frechette.

"I won't pay to have my daughter killed in a shoot-out."

"Lying bastard!" Boyd swung the shotgun my way. Frechette backhanded him, knocking him back into the bathroom. I stepped forward and tore the shotgun from Boyd's weakened grip.

"Empty," I said. "But it makes a good club."

Suzie had come forward when Boyd fell. Frechette stopped her with an arm like a railroad gate.

"Take Dillinger for a walk while I talk to my daughter," he said to me.

I stuck out a hand, but Boyd slapped it aside and got up. His right eye was swelling shut. He looked at the Indian towering a foot over him, then at Suzie, who said, "It's all right. I'll talk to him."

We went out. A porch ran the length of the bungalow. I leaned the shotgun against the wall and trusted my weight to the railing. "I hear you got a raw deal from Texas Federal."

"My old man did." He stood with his hands rammed deep in his pockets, watching the pair through the window. "He asked for a two-month extension on his mortgage payment, just till he brought in his crop. Everyone gets extensions. Except when Texas Federal wants to sell the ranch to a developer. He met the dozers with a shotgun. Then he used it on himself."

"That why you use one?"

"I can't kill a jackrabbit. It used to burn up my old man."

"You'd be out in three years if you turned yourself in."

"To you, right? Let you collect that reward." He was still looking through the window. Inside, father and daughter were gesturing at each other frantically.

"I didn't say to me. You're big enough to walk into a police station by yourself."

"You don't know Texas Federal. They'd hire their own prosecutor, see I got life, make an example. I'll die first."

"Probably, the rate you're going."

He whirled on me. The parked Plymouth caught his eye. "Just who the hell are you? And why'd you—" He jerked his chin toward the car.

I got out J. P. Ahearn's card and gave it to him. His face lost color. "You work for that headhunter?"

"Not in this life. But in a little while I'm going to call that number from the telephone in that gas station across the road."

He lunged for the door. I was closer and got in his way. "I don't know how you got this far with a head that hot," I said. "For once in your young life listen. You might get to like it."

He listened.

. . .

"This is Commander Ahearn! I know you're in there, Boyd. I got a dozen men here and if you don't come out we'll shoot up the place!"

Neither of us had heard them coming, and with the moon behind a cloud the thin, bitter voice might have come from anywhere. This time Boyd won the race to the door. He had the reflexes of a deer.

"Kill the light!" I barked to Frechette. "Ahearn beat me to it. He must have followed you after all."

We were in darkness suddenly. Boyd and Suzie had their arms around each other. "We're cornered," he said. "Why didn't that old lady have shells for that gun?"

"We just have to move faster, that's all. Keep him talking. Give me a hand with this window." The last was for Frechette, who came over and worked his big fingers under the swollen frame.

"There's a woman in here!" Boyd shouted.

"Come on out and no one gets hurt!" Ahearn sounded wired.

The window gave with a squawking wrench.

"One minute, Boyd. Then we start blasting!"

I hoped it was enough. I slipped out over the sill.

Seven

"The car! Get it!"

The Plymouth's engine turned over twice in the cold before starting. The car rolled forward and began picking up speed down the incline toward the road. Just then the moon came out, illuminating the man behind the wheel, and the night came apart like mountain ice breaking up, cracking and splitting with the staccato rap of handgun fire and the deeper boom of riot guns. Orange flame scorched the darkness. Slugs whacked the car's sheet metal and shattered the windshield. Then a red glow started to spread inside the vehicle and fists of yellow flame battered out the rest of the windows with a *whump* that shook the ground. The car rolled for a few more yards while the shooters, standing now and visible in the light of the blaze, went on pouring lead into it until it came to a stop against a road sign. The flame towered twenty feet above the crackling wreckage.

I approached Ahearn, standing in the overgrown grass with his shotgun dangling, watching the car burn. He jumped a little when I spoke. His glasses glowed orange.

"He made a dash, just like you wanted."

"If you think I wanted this you don't know me," he said.

"Save it for the Six O'clock News."

"What the hell are you doing here, anyway?"

"Friend of the family. Can I take the Frechettes home or do you want to eat them here?"

He cradled the shotgun. "We'll just go inside together."

We found Suzie sobbing in her father's arms. The Indian glared at Ahearn. "Get the hell out of here."

"He was a desperate man," Ahearn said. "You're lucky the girl's alive."

"I said get out or I'll ram that shotgun down your throat."

He got out. Through the window I watched him rejoin his men. There were five, not a dozen as he'd claimed. Later I learned that three of them were off-duty Detroit cops and he'd hired the other two from a private security firm.

I waited until the fire engines came and Ahearn was busy talking to the firefighters, then went out the window again and crossed to the next bungalow, set farther back where the light of the flames didn't reach. I knocked twice and paused and knocked again. Boyd opened the door a crack.

"I'm taking Suzie and her father back to Frechette's motel for looks. Think you can lie low here until we come back in the morning for the rent car?"

"What if they search the cabins?"

"For what? You're dead. By the time they find out that's Leo in the car, if they ever do, you and Suzie will be in Canada. Customs won't be looking for a dead bandit. Give everyone a year or so to forget what you look like and then you can come back. Not to Texas, though, and not under the name Virgil Boyd."

"Lucky the gas tank blew."

"I've never had enough luck to trust to it. That's why I put a box of C-4 in Leo's lap. Ma figured it was a small enough donation to keep her clear of a charge of felony murder."

"I thought you were some kind of corpse freak." He still had the surprised look. "You could've been killed starting that car. Why'd you do it?"

"The world's not as complicated as it looks," I said. "There's always a good and a bad side. I saw Ahearn's."

"You ever need anything," he said.

"If you do things right I won't be able to find you when I do." I shook his hand and returned to the other bungalow.

Eight

A week later, after J. P. Ahearn's narrow, jug-eared features had made the cover of *People,* I received an envelope from Houston containing a bonus check for a thousand dollars signed by Howard Frechette. He'd repaid the thirty-five hundred I'd given Ma before going home. That was the last I heard from any of them. I used the money to settle some old bills and had some work done on my car so I could continue to ply my trade along the Crooked Way.

Redneck

"**Don't take no pictures.** I ain't looking for evidence for no divorce court. I just want to know is she cheating." As he spoke, Billy Fred McCorkingdale polished off another rib and laid the bone across the ends of the other three in the latest layer. He had a respectable log cabin going.

The place was called Dem Bones and occupied a sheet-metal barn on Michigan Avenue in Ypsilanti—or Ypsitucky, as it's sometimes called, for the legions of skilled and unskilled workers who swarmed up Old 23 from Kentucky and points south after Pearl Harbor. They came to Detroit to build tanks and bombers and stayed on after Hiroshima. Billy Fred was a tinsmith at the General Motor's Powertrain plant nearby, and his raw hands and big forearms were just what you'd expect of someone who worked with tin snips all day. He had a gourd-shaped head, narrow at the top, small eyes set close, and a nose like a rivet punched way too far above his wide, expressive mouth. He shaved his hair around his ears, which stuck out enough without help.

"That's good," I said, "about the pictures. Because I'm not taking the job. I can recommend a couple of good divorce men."

"I got your name from a divorce man. He said you were the best shadow in *De*troit. I want to know where she goes when I'm at work and if she meets anyone. I don't need to know who he is. I can't work things out with her till I know what it is I'm dealing with."

For a second-generation native, he had a redneck accent as broad as the Ohio River.

"That's all?" I emptied my coffee cup and signaled for a refill. I'd been about to leave.

"I ain't been a good husband for a long time, Mr. Walker. I caught overtime fever: sixteen-hour days, holidays and weekends. I told myself the extra money was for her, but that don't cover the bar time I spent after work. It ain't her fault if she had to go looking for company. But I got to know."

The waitress refilled my cup. I sipped, studying Billy Fred's puppy-dog look. "My fee's five hundred a day," I said. "First three days up front."

He plucked a roll of bills from inside his coat, pulled off the rubber band, and counted fifteen hundred dollars in fifties and hundreds onto the table in front of me. My poker face must have slipped, because he said, "Overtime fever, remember? It ain't worth nothing without Lynne."

I put the bills in my wallet, wrote him out a receipt, and opened my notebook. "Tell me about Lynne."

•   •   •

Lynne McCorkingdale clerked in a Perry Drugs in Romulus, next door to Detroit Metropolitan Airport. All the shelves were equipped with horizontal bars like a boat's, to keep merchandise from falling off when 737s roared overhead. I bought a bottle of aspirin to get a look at her. She was several years younger than her husband, fine-boned and blond, with a short, breezy haircut and gray eyes—pretty in a fussed-over kind of way. She'd have looked better in less makeup, but I'm old-fashioned about such matters. She rang me up with barely a glance.

She drove a blue Chevy Cavalier, two years old, parked in a municipal lot a block from the store. I found a slot farther down the row and pulled the Cutlass into it. The store closed in twenty minutes. I watched a couple of seagulls fighting over half a Hostess cupcake; then Lynne came around the corner and got into the Cavalier and backed out. I gave her till the end of the row, then followed. The gulls took off.

I didn't expect anything the first night; nothing is what I got, not counting a necktie I bought from one of the floating stalls at Fairlane, Dearborn's largest shopping mall, while waiting for Lynne to come out of the Gap. She bought a blouse in Hudson's, a Clint Black CD in Recordtown, looked at a bra in Victoria's Secret without buying it, drank a Coke at Arby's, and went home, where nobody came or left until Billy Fred's Jimmy thundered into the garage at half-past ten. Thirty minutes later the lights went out. I hung around another hour just for the hell of it, but Lynne didn't shinny down the drainpipe. I clocked out.

The next day was Saturday, a half-day at the drugstore. She left at noon, drove to Detroit, and spent the afternoon in the library downtown, where she researched a paper for the night course she attended Tuesdays and Thursdays at Wayne State University. I interested myself in the out-of-town newspapers and tried not to feel guilty about spending Billy Fred's overtime dollars reading the box scores in the *Cleveland Plain Dealer*.

After the library closed, we had supper in a diner on Woodward. I sat at the end of the counter with the combined Saturday edition of the *News and Free Press*; she read a Danielle Steel paperback from her purse. So far she fit the profile of an errant wife as well as I qualified for a seat on the next space shuttle.

At eight o'clock she looked at her watch, put the book back into her purse, and paid for her meal at the cash register. I laid a ten-spot on the counter to cover my Reuben and the tip and went out behind her.

She took Woodward down to Jefferson and turned left. I closed in to avoid losing her in the homeward traffic from Belle Isle Park and the marinas on Lake St. Clair—too close to follow her when she swung left into a parking lot without signaling, unless I wanted to draw attention to myself. I continued for another eighth of a mile, then turned around in the driveway of an apartment complex and backtracked.

The parking lot belonged to the Alamo Motel: cable in every room and room service around the clock. Only they'd chopped up and sold the cable for the copper years ago, and the restaurant had closed at the request of the health department.

I thought at first she'd given me the slip—turned around and gone back the way she'd come while I was playing catch-up. Then I spotter her Cavalier in a slot behind the motel, next to the Dumpster. I drove back around to the front, got out, and went into the lobby.

It was clean enough. The linoleum had a fresh coat of wax, and the air smelled of Lysol and Raid. The clerk was a slender black in his early twenties, with thick glasses and his hair shaved down to stubble. He used a finger to mark his place in a textbook on abnormal psychology and asked me if I wanted a room.

I showed him the badge from the Wayne County Sheriff's Department. "Blond woman, about twenty-five. Five four, hundred and ten, short hair, gray eyes, pink sweater. What room's she in?"

"Can I see some ID?"

"Amos Walker." I gave him one of my cards. "The badge is a gag, I use it to serve papers."

"Then I guess I don't have to tell you anything."

I pointed at his textbook. "Wayne State?"

"U of D, third year."

"I hear tuition's stiff." I fished a twenty out of my wallet.

"I'm on scholarship."

"Basketball?"

"Academic. Four point 0, all four years at Mumford."

I pulled back the twenty and laid one of Billy Fred's fifties on the desk. He chewed the inside of his cheek. Then he took his finger out of the book, replaced it with the bill, found a registration card in the box on the desk, and slapped it down in front of me.

"Mr. and Mrs. Robert Brown," I read. "Bob showed up yet?"

"I wouldn't know. Nobody goes in through the lobby."

Room 112. I skidded the card back his way. "I guess *Smith* is out of style."

"I never ask." He opened his book again.

•   •   •

There were four outside entrances to the motel. Room 112 was at the opposite end of the hall from a door with a large number "1" flaking off the glass. A cigarette machine stood just inside. After a quick reconnoiter I went back to the Cutlass and smoked a cigarette. I smoked another, then turned on the radio and listened to the ball game. In the bottom of the seventh a black Ford Taurus came down the row and backed into a space three cars down from Lynne's Cavalier. A tall, fair-haired party in a sport shirt and slacks got out and went through Door Number One carrying a gym bag.

I trotted in behind him and busied myself with the cigarette machine while he walked down the hall and knocked at 112. The door opened, and Lynne McCorkingdale drew him into the room with her arms around his neck.

Back in the car I listened to the Tigers lose and then a couple of experts tell us why. I heard a call-in talk show and the same details of the same drive-by shootings, child abductions, and congressional investigations on three different news programs. By then it was after midnight, and neither Lynne nor her fair-haired companion had emerged. I went home.

• • •

Billy Fred and the customer's chair in my office were a snug fit. He sat hunched over, licking his big thumb and turning the pages of my typewritten report without comment, his lips moving. When he finished, he read it again. Then he carefully laid it on my desk, with an expression on his gourd-shaped face I can still see when I close my eyes.

"I wrote down the license number of the Taurus," I said. "I could have someone run it, if you're interested."

"I already told you I don't want to know his name."

I opened the safe that came with the office, took out five hundred dollars in cash, and put it on top of the report. "It only took two days. I'm returning the rest of your advance."

"I don't want it."

"You won't say that after the divorce."

"Who said I want a divorce?"

"Put it toward reconciliation, then," I said. "Dinner at the Whitney, flowers, a night in a hotel. Not the Alamo."

After a long time he got up and put the bills into a pocket of his coat. "You done your job."

I could have left it there. Nothing happened from then on was my business. "It's not the worst thing that can happen in a marriage."

"You married?"

"I was."

"She cheat?"

"Not how you think."

He shook his head. "I love Lynne. Nothing don't make sense without her."

Any way I dissected that sentence didn't please me. I clapped him on the shoulder, and he left.

Two nights later I got home from a tail job that ended in Toledo, slapped a slice of ham between two slices of bread, poured a glass of milk, and turned on the news. An EMS team appeared, pushing a pair of figures covered in sheets on stretchers into the back of a van. A sign in the background identified the Alamo Motel.

• • •

"Twelve-gauge shotgun, double-O buck, two rounds per customer fired at close range. You don't get any surer than that." The ugly words were coming out of an attractive face. Mary Ann Thaler, detective lieutenant, closed the file on the autopsy report on her desk at Felony Homicide and folded her slender hands on top of it She was wearing her light-brown hair short these days and had a white silk scarf around her throat.

"Recover the weapon?" I asked.

"We think. McCorkingdale had a twelve-gauge Ithaca pump in his bedroom and a box of double-O shells. Of course, you can't trace shotgun pellets like you can bullets. But the gun had been cleaned very recently. No dust inside the barrel."

"Everybody in Ypsilanti owns a shotgun. They won't sell you a house there if you don't."

"Excuse me, but wasn't it you who came in here two minutes ago and dropped this on my desk?" She slid a copy of the report I'd typed for Billy Fred from under the autopsy file.

'Just playing devil's advocate. It isn't every day I provide someone with a motive for double murder. "

"I'm not here to dispel your guilt complex. I've got a philandering wife and her lover, both shot to pieces. I've got the gun. And I've got the redneck cuckolded husband in an interrogation room with nothing to account for his whereabouts at the time of the shoot. If they were all this easy, I'd be an inspector by now."

"Any ID yet on the guy?"

She consulted her notebook. "Kenneth Brindle, thirty-three, single, apartment in Madison Heights. Pharmacist. Apparently he and Lynne met a couple of months ago when he filled in at the drug store in Romulus."

I got out my own notepad and read her the license number I'd gotten off the Taurus. She found the proper page in hers and nodded. "Shame," she said. "He had only two payments to go."

"I deliberately waited till the next day to tell Billy Fred. Didn't they know it was bad luck to go to the same place twice?"

"They probably got a hint at the end." She tapped her coral nails on the desk. "It wasn't your fault. He was bound to find out sooner or later and do what he did."

"I'm supposed to know a thing or two about people. I didn't figure him for that. I still don't."

Her telephone whirred. She picked up, said yes three times, and cradled the receiver. "That's a big ten four. McCorkingdale just confessed."

I felt my face sag. I pushed back my chair and stood. Thanks, Lieutenant. Let me know when you need a statement. I'll be in the unemployment line."

"People get killed every day," she said, "especially in this town. Somebody plugged 'Joey Bats' Battaglia this morning in front of the Michigan Central Depot. He's gasping out what's left of his life at Detroit Receiving."

"Wasn't me. Fingering lonely wives is more my speed."

Billy Fred got three inches of type in the *Free Press* city section Tuesday morning, bumped to page three by the front-page spread on Joseph 'Joey Bats' Battaglia, who was said to have been cutting a deal with the Justice Department on a labor-racketeering charge when his union brothers hung a price tag on him. He'd hoped to throw them off by taking a train to Miami instead of flying, but he was in the ICU at Detroit Receiving Hospital with his kidneys punctured and his ticket intact. His mistress, a local waitress and part-time professional singer, had been waiting inside the depot when Battaglia stepped out for a smoke. Cigarettes kill.

Not entirely, though.

The employee break room at the Powertrain plant was painted sunset orange and electric blue, probably as a respite from the grays and beiges in Assembly. I found Merle Ketch sitting at one of the trestle tables, reading a magazine and drinking from a can of Pepsi.

My badge impressed him more that it had the clerk at the Alamo. He laid down the magazine and sat up straight. "I put in my two hundred hours," he said. "I got the judge's signature on the papers at home." His redneck accent was even stronger than my former client's.

I sat down across from him. "Relax, Mr. Ketch. Personnel told me you work Billy Fred McCorkingdale's shift. I understand you're friends."

"We bowl and go see the Tigers. You can't get much friendlier than that. This about Lynne?"

"What did he tell you about Lynne?"

"I don't want to get him in trouble."

I dug out the good-old-boy grin. "He was arraigned yesterday in Recorder's Court on a charge of open murder. How much more trouble could he get in?"

Ketch went sullen. "They ought to pay him a bounty. If my Judy was ever to step out on me, I'd wring her neck."

"Not very nineties."

"Some things don't change."

"Did he tell you his wife was seeing anyone?"

"Like I said, we're friends. He hired some detective to follow her around. I told him just what I told you. All the boys on the shift are behind him. One or two of our granddaddies done the same thing down home. They none of 'em never saw the inside of a prison."

"You said all that?"

"Hell, yes. Man can only take so much."

"Did it occur to you that you might be putting ideas in his head?"

"What if I did? Billy Fred's a hero. Just like them boys that take just so much crap from their supervisors, then come in blasting with a big old AK-47. That's how this here country got started."

"I don't think there were any assault rifles at Valley Forge." I drew a doodle of a clown in my notebook. "Mind if I ask where you were Monday night?"

He drained the last of his Pepsi, then crushed the can. "Break's over."

"I thought you got fifteen minutes."

"I do. You just used up your last minute."

I left but didn't want to. I liked Merle. I hadn't liked anyone so much since the Ayatollah.

The young man behind the desk at the Alamo was still reading about abnormal psychology. I asked him if he was cramming for a final.

"Aced it yesterday. You'd be surprised how much of this applies to my job." His eyes were alert behind the thick spectacles. "I told the police you were asking about Mr. and Mrs. Brown before it happened. My statement's on the record."

"You're safe. I'm not a suspect. Lieutenant Thaler says you told her no one came in asking about them the night of the shooting. Anybody else come in that night?"

"Just Mrs. Brown, to pay for the room. Mondays are slow. I never did see Mr. Brown. Not that Mr. Brown."

"Get a lot of Browns, do you?"

"Like you said, *Smith*'s out of style."

"What I can't figure out is how McCorkingdale knew what room they were in if he didn't come in and ask."

"I'm no detective."

"You're a psych student. Pretend it's a pop quiz."

He smiled for the first time. He'd inherited the smile from every night clerk who had ever stood in the lobby of a hotel where the guests paid in cash. I laid a fifty dollar bookmark on the desk. This one went into his shirt pocket.

"She asked for the same room she had last Saturday night. It was vacant, so I gave it to her. Maybe her husband guessed she'd do that and went straight there without stopping to inquire."

"One night's pretty much like all the rest in this place. You're sure you didn't forget?" I handed him the photograph of Merle Ketch I'd gotten from the personnel manager at Powertrain.

The kid glanced at it, then handed it back. "I saw McCorking-dale on the news. This isn't him."

"I didn't say it was."

"Well, I didn't see him either."

"Or maybe he paid you up through next semester to forget you did."

He adjusted his glasses. "Education's expensive. Look, just because I have to do a little grifting doesn't mean I'd cover up for a killer."

I put away the photograph. "Okay."

"Okay?" His forehead wrinkled.

I pointed at the book. "I read the same text in college. They fight to update them every twenty years or so. Anyway, you missed."

I went out to my car, but I didn't drive away. I'd parked it at a discreet angle so I could see through the glass doors into the lobby. I was prepared for a very long wait. The clerk's kidneys were much younger than mine, and for all I knew he'd taken a break just before I arrived. But I had the whole night to see this through. And an empty coffee can for emergencies.

Luck smiled after twenty minutes. The clerk slid off his high stool, laid down the textbook, stretched and went through a door behind the desk. I was out of the car in less than five seconds. The box was on the shelf under the desk where he'd had it Saturday.

When he came back from the bathroom, he found me standing there scratching my chin with the corner of a registration card from Monday night.

I caught Mary Ann Thaler in the squad room, dunking a tea bag into a cup of hot water. It was the 8:00 P.M. to 4:00 A.M. shift, and we had the place all to ourselves. The lieutenant looked as fresh as the morning in a royal-blue silk blouse and a black skirt.

"I got the message you left this afternoon," she said. "We checked out Merle Ketch. He was drinking beer with some buddies in the Sidecar Tavern when the thing went down at the Alamo. That good a friend he wasn't. Sorry."

"I'm not interested in him anymore. I need a pass to see Billy Fred."

"Now? What've you got?"

"I'll tell you after I talk to him. "

"Withholding evidence, are we?"

"A hunch isn't evidence. What about it?"

"I don't guess it would hurt. I've got my hands full enough with Joey Bats without worrying about McCorkingdale."

"Any change?"

"His vitals have stabilized, whatever that means, but the news isn't good. These pro jobs don't leave much to go on."

"Talk to his mistress?"

She nodded. "She didn't see anything. She was inside the station reading a paperback."

"Ask her where she was Saturday night."

"Not without knowing why, I won't."

"I'll fill you in while you write out that pass."

The visitors' room I was shown into at the Wayne County Jail was drywalled and painted a not unpleasant shade of ivory, but it had no decorations or outside windows or features of any kind except the two doors that led into it and a table and two folding chairs. I was seated there thirty seconds when Billy Fred McCorkingdale came in, accompanied by a turnkey in a deputy's uniform who took a glance around, then departed, locking the door behind him. His slab face remained in the steel-gridded window.

Billy Fred sat down facing me. His eyes were sunken. I saw no recognition in them.

"Amos Walker," I reminded him. "You hired me last week."

"I know." His voice grated, as if he hadn't used it in days. He hadn't said a word at his arraignment.

"I talked to Merle Ketch," I said. "You got lousy taste in friends."

He shrugged and said, "Merle's company."

"You'd do better with a parakeet. I suppose he told you his grand-daddy wrung his wife's neck for straying, and the jury let him off."

"Cut her throat, he said."

"Things have changed since then. People don't walk on their knuckles. They don't hang their long johns in the backyard and almost never acquit wife murderers. Even when the wives are unfaithful."

He said nothing.

"Life in Jackson's ten times as long as life on the outside," I went on. "Those rednecks you work with will have plenty of time to forget all about what a hero you are, and you'll be in for another thirty years. Take back the confession."

He squeezed his eyes shut. Tears came out of the cracks. He raised his hands to his face. "I killed her," Billy Fred said. "I murdered Lynne."

"No, you didn't."

"It's my fault she's dead."

"Better, but still not accurate. It may be your fault she went looking for attention, but that's between you and a therapist. I know one, if you don't mind waiting for him to graduate. Lynne's dead and so is that poor slob Kenneth Brindle because some bottom feeder who didn't know either of them from Rembrandt kicked down the door of their room and blew them into kibble. And he's out there walking around while you're in here blubbering and being admired by that dirtbag Merle Ketch."

His face went blank but only for a moment. He was listening now.

"I sneaked a peek at the Alamo registration cards," I said. "I did it the same way the killer did Monday night—waited for the clerk to go to the bathroom and went in and rifled the box. Your wife and Brindle weren't the only couple who registered as Mr. and Mrs. Brown that night. There was one other."

His fingers made deep indentations in the table's padded vinyl top, but he kept quiet.

"The clerk at the Alamo scores tuition money for college the same way employees in ratty hotels the world over draw cash. He registered a party he recognized from TV and the newspapers and accepted a bribe to forget he ever saw him. *That* was the phony Brown the killer was looking for."

"Who?"

"I don't know the killer's name. I only know why he did it. He was hired to kill a man registered as Brown and the woman he had with him, to eliminate her as a witness. He was in a hurry. As soon as he found a card with that signature and a room number, he stopped looking. Once that door flew open, he didn't have time for a positive ID. He saw a man and a woman in bed, shot them both twice and took off. I doubt he knew he'd killed the wrong Browns until he saw the news later."

"Who?" he asked again, but it wasn't the same question,

"The other Browns? 'Joey Bats' Battaglia and his girlfriend. They hauled out of there after the big noise and before the cops arrived. That's why Joey was in such a hurry to leave town the next day. He wasn't so lucky that time. That time the shooter made up for his mistake."

"Like hell he did." He had his face in his hands again.

"All this is speculation so far," I said, "although the desk clerk's ready to talk. The cops figured they had their man—you—they never bothered to check the registration cards. They're talking to Battaglia's mistress now. If she confirms that she and Joey were at the Alamo Monday night, you'll have a defense. But you have to retract that confession."

"Sure." He was staring down at his hands: big hands, callused all over, with decades of dirt and steel shavings ground deep into the knuckles. "Poor Lynne."

I got up and signaled to the turnkey, who let himself in. Billy Fred rose. At the door to the cells he looked back over his shoulder. "I'm hiring you again. Trust me on the advance?"

"Hiring me for what?"

"You're the detective."

The guard followed him out and drew the door shut with a clink.

It looked as if I had underestimated Joey Bats's luck. On Thursday the head of surgery at Detroit Receiving Hospital announced at press conference that his team had managed to save one of the patient's kidneys. Arrangements had been made to transfer him to Hutzel Hospital for recovery as early as the weekend.

When the appointed day arrived, a crew consisting of a nurse and a pair of interns, with a uniformed police officer looking on, strapped their charge to a gurney and ferried him for security's sake through an exit normally reserved for mortuary cases. An intern held open the door to the ambulance while his partner and the nurse prepared to slide the patient inside.

Just as they lifted the stretcher, an ambulance bearing the logo of another company rolled around the corner, squished to a stop, and two men in ski masks piled out of the back. One of them covered the uniformed cop with an automatic pistol. His companion sprinted up to the gurney and swung up a shotgun with the stock and barrel sawed off. Before he could squeeze the trigger, the patient sat up and shot him in the chest with a .38 revolver. This startled the man with the pistol just long enough for the "nurse" to produce a nine-millimeter Beretta from the folds of her uniform.

"Police!" Mary Ann Thaler shouted. "Drop the weapon!"

He dropped the weapon. At this point the driver of the second ambulance floored the accelerator. Tires spun, and the vehicle took off. The uniformed officer drew his sidearm, crouched, and fired a single shot through the open door at the back of the ambulance. The vehicle veered sharply, jumped the curb, and slammed into a steel post holding up a sign calling for silence. The horn sounded in a long, irritating blast. It didn't stop until one of the "interns," a detective with Felony Homicide, grabbed the driver by his collar and pulled his dead body away from the steering wheel.

By the time I got free of the gurney, the uniform had Ski Mask Number One facedown on the ground with his wrists in cuffs. The second "intern," another plainclothesman, bent over Ski Mask Number Two with the shotgun in hand. "This one's still breathing, Lieutenant," he said.

Thaler knelt and stripped off the man's mask. He had one of those faces you couldn't have picked out of a lineup if you were married to him—young and unlined without a single distinguishing feature. I holstered my revolver under the paper gown I had on over my clothes and got down on one knee beside the lieutenant.

I said, "Joke's on you, fella. Joey died Thursday morning. The whole thing was a gag to bring you back for a third try."

"I just figured that out," he said. "Bonehead play. That's two this week," he said. "Stupid." Pink bubbles rippled between his lips.

I was tingling now, but I didn't have time to savor it. "What was the first?"

"The Alamo." He coughed and gurgled, or maybe it was an attempt to laugh. "Remember the Alamo—get it?"

"Got it," I said. And then he was gone.

Lieutenant Thaler and I stood. "Deathbed confession," she said, and put away her Beretta. "Looks like your client's off the hook."

"Yeah," I said. "Too bad it's not the one that counts."

Dogs

One

Elda Chase lived in an efficiency flat in Iroquois Heights with no rugs on the hardwood floor and the handsome furniture arranged in geometric patterns like a manor house maze. That day she had the curtains open on the window overlooking the municipal park and the statue of LaSalle with his foot up on a rock scratching his head over a map he had unrolled on his knee. The view was strictly for my benefit; Elda Chase had been blind since birth.

Not that you'd have known it from the way she got around that apartment, discreetly touching this chair and brushing that lamp as she bustled to catch the whistling teapot and find the cups and place the works on a platter and bring it over and set it down on the coffee table. When I leaned forward from the sofa to pour, I was just in time to accept the full cup she extended to me. She filled the other one then and took a seat in the chair opposite. She was a tall woman in her middle fifties who wore her graying hair pinned up and lightly tinted glasses with clear plastic rims. Her ruby blouse and long matching skirt went well with her high coloring and she had on pearl earrings and white low-heeled shoes. I wondered who picked it all out.

"The Braille edition of the Yellow Pages comes so late," she said, balancing her cup and saucer on one crossed knee. "I was half afraid your number had changed."

"Not in a dozen years. Or anything else about the office, except the wallpaper."

"Anyway, thank you for coming. You were the fourth investigator I tried. The first number was disconnected and the other two men referred me to the Humane Society. I'd called them right after it happened, of course. They wanted me to put up posters around the neighborhood. As if I could go out at all without my Max."

"Max is the dog?"

"A shepherd. I've had him three years. When Lucy died I was sure I'd never have another one as good, but Max is special. He's taken me places I'd never have dared go with Lucy."

I sipped some tea and was relieved to find out it was bitter. Watching her operate I'd begun to feel inadequate. "You're sure he didn't run away?"

"Trained seeing-eye dogs don't run away, Mr. Walker. But to lay your cynicism to rest, the padlock on the kennel door had been cut. You saw it in the yard?"

"A six-foot chain link fence to keep in a dog that wouldn't run away," I confirmed.

"The fence was to protect him. It didn't do a very good job. I knew dog stealing was a possibility, but I hate to keep a big animal cooped up indoors. The police were not encouraging."

"I'm not surprised, in this town."

"I like Iroquois Heights," she said.

"The park is nice."

She raised her face. With her sightless eyes downcast behind the colored lenses she looked like a lioness taking in the sun. "Can you find him?"

"There are markets for purebreds. I can ask some questions. I can't promise anything. My specialty's tracing two-legged mammals."

"I could have gone to someone who traces pets for a living. I don't like professional dog people. They're strident. They'd make me out the villain for not hiring a governess to look after the dog."

"Is there a picture?"

She groped for and opened a drawer in the end table next to her chair and handed me a color snapshot of herself in a wrap and gloves hanging on to a harness attached to a black-and-tan German shepherd.

"Marks?" I put it in my breast pocket.

"Now, how would I know that?"

"Sorry. I forgot."

"I'll take that as a compliment. He answers to his name with a sharp bark." She took a checkbook off the end table and started writing. "Seven-fifty is your retainer, I believe."

I took the check and put it in my wallet. I drank some more tea, peeled my upper lip back down, and stood, setting aside the cup and saucer. "I'll call you tomorrow. Earlier if I find out anything."

"Thank you." She hesitated. "It isn't just that I need him. If it were just that—"

"I had a dog once," I said. "I still think about him sometimes."

"You sound like someone who would."

Two

Mrs. Chase's landlady, a thin blonde named Silcox, lived on the ground floor. Mrs. Chase was her oldest tenant and Mrs. Silcox's son, a sophomore at the University of Michigan, had built the kennel at his mother's request. Neither was home when it was broken into.

From there I went to the office of the Iroquois Heights *Spectator*. The newspaper was the flagship of a fleet owned by a local politician, but the classified section was reliable. I asked for that editor and was directed to a paunchy grayhead standing at the water cooler.

"Rube Zendt," he said when I introduced myself, and shook my hand. "Born Reuben, but trust newspaper folk to latch on to the obvious."

His hair was thin and black on top with gray sidewalls and he had a chipmunk grin that was too small for his full cheeks. He wore black-rimmed glasses and a blue tie at half-mast on a white shirt. I apologized for interrupting his break.

"This distilled stuff rusts my pipes. I only come here to watch the bubbles. Got something to sell or buy, or did you lose something or find it?"

"Close. A local woman hired me to find her dog. I thought that holding down lost and found you'd be the one to talk to about the local market."

"Dog-napping, you mean. I just take the ads. Man you want to see is Stillwell on cophouse."

"He around?"

"This time of day you can catch him at the police station."

"What time of day can I catch him anywhere else?"

The chipmunk grin widened a hundredth of an inch. "I see you know our town. But things aren't so bad down there since Mark Proust made acting chief."

"Meaning what?"

"Meaning he spends all his time in his office. Tell Stillwell Rube sent you."

Three

The first three floors of a corner building on the main stem belonged to the city police. It was a hot day in August and the air conditioning was operating on the ground floor, but that had nothing to do with the drop in my temperature when I came in from the street. At the peak of the busing controversy in the early seventies a group of local citizens had protested the measure by overturning a bus full of schoolchildren; some of that group were in office now and they had built the city law-enforcement structure from the prosecutor right down to the last meter maid.

A steely-haired desk sergeant with an exotropic eye turned the good one on me from behind his high bench when I said I was looking for Stillwell of the *Spectator* and held it on me for another minute before saying, "Over there."

The wandering eye was pointing north and I went that way. He'd never have made the Detroit department with that eye, but with his temperament he was right at home.

Two big patrolmen in light summer uniforms were fondling their saps in the corner by the men's room, leering at and listening to a man with no hair above the spread collar of his shirt and a wrinkled cotton sportcoat over it.

" ... and the other guy says, 'Help me find my keys and we'll *drive* out of here!'"

The cops opened a pair of mouths like buckets and roared. I approached the bald man. "Mr. Stillwell?"

The laughter stopped like a bell grabbed in mid-clang. Two pairs of cop eyes measured me and the bald man's face went guarded with the jokester's leer still in place. "Who's asking?"

"Amos Walker. Rube Zendt said to talk to you."

"Step into my office." He pushed open the men's room door and held it. The cops moved off.

The place had two urinals, a stall and a sink. He leaned his shoulders against the stall, waiting. He was younger than the clean head indicated, around thirty. He had no eyebrows and clear blue eyes in a lineless face whose innocence could turn the oldest filthy joke into a laugh marathon. I gave him my spiel.

"Shepherd," he said. "There's not a lot of call for them without papers. No gold rushes going on in Alaska to goose the sled-dog trade."

"It's a Seeing Eye. That's an expensive market."

"They're handled by big organizations that train their own. They don't need to deal in stolen animals and you'd need papers and a good story to sell them one that's already schooled. Tell your client to place an ad with Rube offering a reward and stay home and wait to hear from whoever took the dog."

"Staying home is no problem."

"I guess not. Sorry I can't help."

"What about the fight game?"

"There's no fight game in this town."

"What town we talking about?"

"Yeah." He crossed his ankles then and I knew my leg had been pulled. "That racket's all pit bulls now. I can think of only one guy would even look at a shepherd."

I gave him twenty dollars.

"Henry Revere." He crumpled the bill into the side pocket of his sportcoat. "Caretaker over at the old high school. He's there days."

"School board know what he does nights?"

"Everyone knows everything that goes on in this town, except the people who pay taxes to live in it."

"Thanks." I gave him a card, which he crumpled into the same pocket without looking at it.

Coming out of the men's room I had the desk sergeant's errant eye. The other was on a woman in a yellow pantsuit who had come in to complain about a delivery van that was blocking her Coup de Ville in her driveway.

Four

It was a three-story brick box with big mullioned windows and a steel tube that slanted down from the roof for a fire escape. When the new school was built down the road, this one had been converted into administrative offices and a place to vote in district elections. I found its only inhabitant on that summer vacation day, an old black man wearing a green worksuit and tennis shoes, waxing the gym floor. He saw me coming in from the hall and turned off the machine. "Street shoes!"

I stopped. He left the machine and limped my way. I saw that the sole of one of his sneakers was built up twice as thick as its mate.

"Mister, you know how hard it is to get black heel marks off of hardwood?"

"Sorry." I showed him my ID. "I'm looking for a German shepherd, answers to Max. If you're Henry Revere, someone told me you deal in them."

"Someone lied. What use I got for dogs? I got a job."

"Also a lot of girlfriends. Unless those are dog hairs on your pants."

He caught himself looking, too late. His cracked face bunched like a fist. "You're trespassing."

I held up two ten-dollar bills. He didn't look at them.

"This here's a good job, mister. I got a wife with a bad cough and a boy at Wayne State. I ain't trading them for no twenty bucks. You better get out before I call the po-lice."

I put away the bills. "What are you afraid of?"

"Unemployment and welfare," he said. "Maybe you never been there."

Five

Back in my office in downtown Detroit I made some calls. First I rang Elda Chase, who said that no one had called her yet offering to return Max for a reward. I tried the Humane Society in three counties and got a female shepherd, a mix, and a lecture about the importance of spaying and neutering one's pets at sixty bucks a crack. After that it was time for dinner. When I got back from the place down the street the telephone was ringing. I said hello twice.

"Walker?"

"This is Walker."

Another long pause. "Ed Stillwell. The *Spectator*?"

I said I remembered him. He sounded drunk.

"Yeah. Listen, what I told you 'bout Henry Revere? Forget it. Bum steer."

"I don't think so. He denied too much when I spoke to him."

There was a muffled silence on his end, as if a hand clamped over the mouthpiece. Then: "Listen. Forget it, okay? I only gave you his name 'cause I needed the twenty. I got to make a monthly spousal support payment you wouldn't believe. What I know about dog fighting you could stick in a whistle."

"Okay."

"'Kay."

A receiver was fumbled into a cradle. I hung up and sat there smoking a couple of cigarettes before I went home.

Six

" ... believe the motive was robbery. Once again, Iroquois Heights journalist Edward Stillwell, in critical condition this morning at Detroit General Hospital after police found him beaten unconscious in an empty lot next to the *Spectator* building."

I had turned on the radio while fixing breakfast and got the end of the story. I tried all the other stations. Nothing. I turned off the stove and called the *Spectator*. I kept getting a busy signal. I settled for coffee and left home. As I swung out of the driveway, a navy-blue Chrysler with twin mounted spotlights and no chrome pulled away from the curb behind me.

It was still in my mirror when I found a slot in front of the *Spectator* office. I went inside, where everyone on the floor was hunched over his desk arguing with a telephone. Rube Zendt hung his up just as I took a seat in the chair in front of his desk. "The damn *Free Press*," he said, pointing at the instrument. "They want the rundown on Stillwell before we even print it. Those city sheets think they wrote the First Amendment."

"Which desk is Stillwell's?"

"Why?"

I counted on my fingers. "Stillwell gives me a man to see about a dog. A cross-eyed sergeant at the cophouse sees us talking. I see the man. Last night Stillwell calls me, sounding sloshed and telling me to forget the man. This morning the cops scrape Stillwell out of an alley."

"Empty lot."

"In Detroit we call them alleys. I'm not finished. This morning I've got a tail that might as well have UNMARKED POLICE CAR painted in big white letters on the side. Someone's scared. I want to know what makes Stillwell so scary. Maybe he kept notes. He's a newspaperman."

"I can't let you go through his desk. Only Stillwell can do that. Or Gerald Strong. He publishes the *Spectator.*"

"I know who Strong is. Where is he?"

"Lady, we don't *need* no warrant. We're in hot pursuit of a suspect in an assault and battery."

This was a new player. I turned in my chair and looked at a pair of hulks in strained jackets and wide ties standing just inside the front door dwarfing a skinny woman in a tailored suit. One, a crewcut blond with a neck like a leg, spotted me and pointed. "There he is."

I got up. "Back way."

Zendt jerked a thumb over his shoulder. "End of that hall. Good luck." He stuck out his hand. I took it hastily and brought mine away with a business card folded in it.

The detectives were bumping into desks and cursing behind me when I made the end of the hall and sprinted out the back door. I ran around the building to my car. One of the cops, graying with a thick moustache, had doubled back and was barreling out the front door when I got under the wheel. I scratched pavement with the car door flapping. In the mirror I saw him draw his revolver and sight down on the car. I went into a swerve, but his partner reached him then and knocked up his elbow. I was four blocks away before I heard their siren.

I backed the car into a deserted driveway and unfolded the card

Zendt had given me. It was engraved with Gerald Strong's name, telephone number, and address on Lake Shore Drive in Grosse Pointe Farms. I waited a little. When I was sure I couldn't hear the siren any more I pulled out. My head stayed sunk between my shoulder blades until I was past the city limits.

It was one of the deep walled estates facing the glass-flat surface of Lake St. Clair, with a driveway that wound through a lawn as big as a golf course, but greener, ending in front of a brownstone sprawl with windows the size of suburbs. I tucked the Chevy in behind a row of German cars and walked around the house toward the pulse of music. I should have packed a lunch.

Rich people aren't always throwing parties; it's just that that's the only time you catch them at home. This one was going on around a wallet-shaped pool with guests in bathing suits and designer original sundresses and ascots and silk blazers. There was a small band, not more than sixteen pieces, and the partiers outnumbered the serving staff by a good one and a half to one.

George Strong wasn't hard to spot. He had made his fortune from newspapers and cable television, and his employees had dutifully smeared his face all over the pages and airwaves during two unsuccessful campaigns for state office. His towhead and crinkled bronze face towered four inches over his tallest listener in a knot of people standing by the rosebushes. I inserted some polyester into the group and introduced myself.

"Do we know each other?" Strong looked older in person than in his ads. His chin sagged and his face was starting to bloat.

"It's about one of your reporters, Ed Stillwell."

"I heard. Terrible thing. The company will pay his bills, even though the incident had nothing to do with the newspaper. I understand he was drunk when they mugged him."

"Nobody mugged him. I think he was beaten by the police."

"Excuse us, gentlemen." He put a hand on my arm and steered me toward the house.

His study was all dark oak and red leather with rows of unread books on shelves and photographs of George Strong shaking hands with governors and presidents. When we were on opposite sides of an Empire desk I told him the story. Unconsciously he patted the loosening flesh under his chin.

"Ridiculous. The police in Iroquois Heights aren't thugs."

"Two of them tried to arrest me for Stillwell's beating in the *Spectator* office half an hour ago, without a warrant. They followed me there from my house where they have no jurisdiction. Your classifieds editor gave me your card. Call him."

He didn't. "I won't have my reporters manhandled. You say you want to go through Stillwell's desk?"

I said yes. He took a sheet of heavy stock out of a drawer and scribbled on it with a gold pen from an onyx stand. He folded it and handed it to me. "I'll pay double what the woman's paying you to forget the dog and find out who beat up Stillwell."

"Save it for your next campaign. If my hunch is right I'll find them both in the same spot." I put the note in my breast pocket and took myself out.

Seven

The navy-blue Chrysler was parked across the street from the newspaper office when I came around the corner from where I'd left my car. There was only one man in it, which meant his partner was watching the back door. I ducked inside a department store down the block to think.

There was a fire exit in Men's Wear with a warning sign in red. The clerk, slim and black in a gray three-piece, was helping a customer pick out a necktie by the dressing rooms. I pushed through the door.

The alarm was good and loud. Moustache had gotten out of the car and was hustling through the front door when I rounded the building and trotted across the street to the *Spectator.* The skinny woman in the tailored suit read Strong's note and pointed out Ed Stillwell's desk.

Reporters are packrats. While I was sifting through a ton of scrawled-over scrap, Rube Zendt came over and leaned on the desk. "Cops are watching the place," he said.

"Do tell."

"The older one with the moustache is Sergeant Gogol. The wrestler's Officer Joyce. They're meaner than two vice principals. When you're ready to go, hide in the toilet and I'll call in Joyce from the back—tell him Gogol's got you out front or something—and you can duck out the rear. It worked once."

"I guess you scribblers look out for each other."

"Stillwell? Can't stand the bald son of a bitch. But ink's thicker than blood." He strolled back to his desk.

Ten minutes later I found something that looked good, one half of a fifty-dollar bill with a scrap of paper clipped to it and "9 p.m. 8/8 OHS" penciled on the scrap in Stillwell's crooked hand. Today was the eighth. The torn-bill gag was corny as anything, but that was Iroquois Heights for you. I pocketed it, got Zendt's attention, and went to the bathroom.

Eight

I spent the rest of the day in a Detroit motel in case the cops went to my house or office. From there I called Elda Chase to tell her I was still working and to ask if she'd heard anything. She hadn't. I watched TV, ordered a pizza for dinner, and left three slices for the maid at 8:30.

The old high school was lit up like Homecoming when I presented myself at the open front door. A security guard in khaki asked me if I was there for the parents' meeting. I handed him the half-bill.

He looked at it, dug the other half out of a shirt pocket, and matched them. Then he put both halves in the pocket. "You're Stillwell?"

"Yeah."

"I heard you was in the hospital."

"I got out." I passed him ahead of any more questions.

A meeting was going on somewhere in the building; voices droned in the linoleum-and-tile halls. Acting on instinct I headed away from them, stepping around a folding gate beyond which the overhead lights had been turned off. A new noise reached me: louder, not as stylized, less human. It increased as I passed through twin doors and stopped before a steel one marked BOILER ROOM. I opened it and stepped into tropical heat.

I was on a catwalk overlooking the basement, where twenty men in undershirts or no shirts at all crouched around fifteen square feet of bare concrete floor, shouting and shaking their fists at a pair of pit bulls ripping at each other in the center. From the pitch of their snarls it was still early in the fight, but already the floor was patterned with blood.

The door opened behind me while I was leaning over the pipe railing trying to get a look at the men's faces. I stepped back behind the door, crowding into a dark corner smelling of cobwebs and crumbling cement. I wished I'd brought my gun with me. I'd thought it would slow me down.

Two men came in and stood with their backs to me, close enough to breathe down their collars. I recognized Henry Revere's white head and green workclothes. The other man's hair wasn't much darker. He was taller and white, wearing a gray summerweight suit cut to disguise an advanced middle-age spread. From the back he looked familiar.

"Which dog's that?" wheezed the man in the suit. I knew that broken windpipe.

"Lord Baltimore," said Revere. "Bart. He's new."

"He doesn't have the weight to start out that hard. He'll fold in five."

"That's a bull for you. Shepherds pace theirselves."

"Shepherds are pansies. I told you not to buy any more."

"I gots to buy something. We're running out of dogs."

"Sell what you got. I'm jumping this racket."

"Man, I don't like the other. That's heat with a big *H*."

"*I'm* the heat."

"What if one of them cons talks to the press?"

The man in the suit coughed. "Why'd he want to? What other chance he got to miss a stretch in Jackson? He should thank us."

"Not if he gets beat half to death like that reporter."

"Gogol and Joyce got carried away. They were supposed to just rough him around, maybe break something. Anyway he had his slice. He should've stood on his tongue."

"What I mean," Revere said. "If he talked, so could a con. And what about that detective?"

"I got men everyplace he goes. His wings are clipped."

"You say so, Chief. I feel better when he's grounded."

A shrill yelp sheared the air. Then silence.

"There, you see?" said the man in the suit. "No distance."

The door opened again. I squeezed tight to the wall. The pair turned, and I got a good view in profile of Acting Chief of Police Mark Proust's long slack face. His complexion matched the gray of his suit.

"Chief, that guy Stillwell's here. Thought I better tell you." The security man's voice was muffled a little on the other side of the open door.

"Impossible. What'd he look like?"

"About six feet, 185, brown hair."

"That's not—"

I hit the door with my shoulder, occupying the guard while I shoved Proust into the railing.

Revere moved my way, but his short leg slowed him down. I swept past him and threw a right at the guard, missing his jaw but glancing off the muscle on the side of his neck. He lost his balance. I vaulted over him.

"It's Walker!" Proust shouted. "Use your gun!"

Flying through the twin doors in the hall I sent a late dog rooter sprawling. Behind me a shot flattened the air. The bullet shattered the glass in one of the doors. I reached the folding gate, but the opening was gone; the guard or someone had closed and locked it. The guard was coming through the broken door, behind his gun. I ducked through a square arch in the wall, stumbled on stairs in the darkness, caught my equilibrium on the run, and started taking them two at a time heading up. A bullet skidded off brick next to my right ear.

I ran out of stairs on a dark landing. Feet pounded the steps behind me. I felt for and found a doorknob. It turned.

Cool fresh air slid over me down a shaft of moonlight. I was on the roof with the lights of Iroquois Heights spread at my feet. I let the heavy door slam shut of its own weight, got my bearings, and made for the fire chute. I had a foot over the edge when the security guard piled out the door and skidded to a halt, bringing his gun up in two hands. Gravity took me.

The inside of the tube smelled of stale metal. My ears roared as I slid a long way, as if falling in a dream. Then I leveled out and my feet hit ground and inertia carried me upright and forward. Officer Joyce, standing at the bottom, pivoted his bulk and brought his right arm down with a grunt. A fuse blew in my head and I went down another chute, this one bottomless.

Nine

I awoke with a flash of nausea. My scalp stung and an inflated balloon was rubbing against the inside of my skull. I got my eyelids open despite sand in the works, only to find that I was still in darkness. This darkness stank. As I lay waiting for my pupils to catch up I grew aware of an incessant loud yapping and that it was not in my head. Then I identified the smell. I was in a kennel.

Not quite in it, I thought, as objects around me assumed vague shape. I was lying on moist earth surrounded by wire cages with wet black muzzles pressed against the wire from inside and eyes shining farther back. These were the quiet ones. The others were setting up a racket and hurling themselves against the doors and trying to gnaw through the wire.

My arms had gone to sleep. I tried to move them, and that was when I found out my wrists were cuffed behind me. My ankles were bound too, with something thin and strong that chafed skin; twine or insulated wire. I rolled over onto my face and worked myself up onto my knees. The balloon inside my head creaked.

Something rattled, followed by a current of air that sucked in light. The walls were gray corrugated steel. A pair of shiny black Oxfords appeared in front of me and I looked up at Mark Proust. The battery-powered lantern he was carrying shadowed the pouches in his paper-pulp face.

"Cut his legs loose," he said. "He isn't going anywhere."

Feet scraped earth behind me. A blade sawed fiber and my ankles came apart. I got up awkwardly with my wrists still bound. Circulation needled back into my lower legs.

"When was the last time, snoop? The Broderick kill?"

I said nothing. Officer Joyce joined Proust, folding a jackknife. The crewcut gave his face a planed look, like a wooden carving with the features blocked in for finishing later.

"Shut up those dogs," Proust said.

I hadn't realized Henry Revere was present. The old black man came up from behind me and kicked the cage containing the loudest of the dogs. The dog, a sixty-pound pit bull, stopped barking and shrank back snarling. He kicked two more. The third dog hesitated, then lunged, fangs biting wire. Revere kicked again and it yelped and cowered. Its eyes glittered in the shadows at the rear of the cage. The rest of the animals fell into a whimpering silence. Two of the cages contained shepherds.

"Know where we are, snoop?" asked Proust.

"The Iroquois Heights Police Academy," I said. "Those are some of your new rookies."

"Funny guy. It's my little ten-acre retirement nest egg six miles out of the Heights. The old high school's nice, but it's too close to everything."

"Makes a good front, though," I said. "Like dog fighting, which is illegal but forgivable in case someone starts prying. Maybe he won't think to look further and find the real racket."

"What's that, snoop?"

I said nothing again.

"Smart." He smirked at Joyce and Revere. "A smart private nose is what we got here. Only he just thinks he's smart. Thinks if he acts dumb we'll let him go on breathing. Which makes him dumb for real."

I shrugged. "Okay. I heard enough to know you've graduated from fighting dogs to fighting inmates, probably from downtown holding. In return for their release or a word to the judge they agree to fight each other, probably in front of a crowd that's outgrown betting on dogs. Your piece of the gate must be sweet."

"It pays the bills. Especially when we put a black in the pit with a white. A lot of the residents here left Detroit to get away from the blacks. No offense, Henry."

"I'm surprised you didn't put one in with Stillwell."

"He wouldn't have lasted two minutes. Gogol and Joyce almost killed him without even trying." He paused, tasting his next words. "I figure you for a better show."

"I was wondering when we were coming to that."

"You might win, who knows?"

"What do I win, a bullet?"

"Warm up if you want. People are still coming. I'll send someone back for you." He went out, trailing Joyce and Revere. A padlock rattled.

It was a truss barn with a high roof and some moonlight seeping through cracks between the bolted-on sections. The cage doors were latched with simple sliding bolts. I backed up to them and worked them loose, hoping the agitated dogs inside wouldn't chew off my fingers. I left them engaged just enough to keep the doors closed. A good lunge would slip any of them. I came to the shepherds last.

In the gloom either of them could have been the dog in the picture Elda Chase had given me.

"Max."

One of them barked sharply. I called again. It barked again. The other looked at me and gave a rippling snarl. Just to be sure I left both cages locked. They were safer inside.

Some of the cages were empty and I sat on one. I wanted a cigarette but I didn't fidget. The last thing I wanted to do was startle a dog into breaking loose while I was still present.

After a long time of measured breathing and sweating beyond measure, I heard the lock rattle again and Gogol and Joyce came in. I stood. The detective with the moustache held his revolver on me while his partner led me out. Gogol followed with the gun.

We walked twenty yards through a jumble of cars parked on rutted earth to a steel barn bigger than the one we had just left. Henry Revere passed us coming out the door. He was going back to see to the dogs.

The interior was lit with electric bulbs strung along the tops of the walls. Crude bleachers had been erected on either side of a hole dug five feet deep and eight feet in diameter and lined with rough concrete. The bleachers were jammed with men and some women, all talking in loud voices that grew shrill when we entered. This building smelled as strong as the other, but the stink here was sharper, more foul, distinctly human. Proust sat in the middle of the front row.

We stopped at the edge of the pit and Joyce unlocked my handcuffs. Inside the pit stood a black man wearing only faded blue jeans. His hair was cropped short and his torso was slabbed with glistening muscle. He watched me with yellowish eyes under a ridge of bone.

I was rubbing circulation back into my wrists when Joyce shoved me into the pit. My opponent caught me and hurled me backward. I struck concrete, emptying my lungs. The crowd shrieked. He charged. I pivoted just in time to avoid being crushed between him and the wall. He caught himself with his hands, pushed off, and whirled. I hit him with everything, flush on the chin. He shook his head. I threw a left. He caught it in a hand the size of my office and hit me on the side of the head with his other fist. I heard a gong.

I backpedaled, buying time for my vision to clear. He followed me. I kicked him in the groin and punched him in the throat; he was no boxer and had left both unprotected. They didn't need protecting.

He wrapped a hand around my neck and reared back. "Sorry, man."

The fist was coming at me when a woman in the crowd screamed. The scream was higher and louder than any of the others and it made him hesitate just an instant.

I didn't. I doubled both fists and brought them up in an uppercut that tipped his head back and snapped his teeth together and broke his grip on my neck. Then I put my head down and butted him in the chest. He staggered back, spitting teeth.

The whole crowd was screaming now, and not at us. A torn and bleeding Henry Revere had stumbled into the building trailing a pack of enraged dogs that were bounding through the audience, bellowing and slashing at limbs and throats with the madness of fear and anger and pain. One, a red-eyed pit bull, leaped over the concrete rim and landed on my dazed opponent and I clubbed it with my forearm before it could rip out his throat. Stunned, the dog sank down on all fours and fouled the pit.

"You all right?" I asked.

He got his feet under him, a hand on his throat. It came away bloody, but the skin was barely torn.

"I guess."

"What'd they promise you, a clean ticket?"

"Probation."

"Give me a leg up and maybe you'll still get it."

After a moment he complied and I scrambled out of the pit, then stuck out a hand and helped him up. Most of the crowd had cleared out of the building. One of the dogs lay dead, shot through the head by one of the cops; the report had been drowned in the confusion. Another stood panting and glaze-eyed with its tongue hanging out of a scarlet muzzle. I didn't look for the others. My former opponent and I went out the door.

It was more dangerous outside now than in. Cars were swinging out of the makeshift parking lot, sideswiping one another and raking headlamps over scurrying pedestrians and dogs. I heard sirens getting nearer. I wondered who had called the cops. I wondered which cops they had called.

A maroon Cadillac swung into the light spilling out the barn door, illuminating Proust's pale face behind the wheel. I shouted at the black man and we ran after it. His legs were longer than mine; he reached the car first and tore open the door on the driver's side and pulled Proust out with one hand. The car kept going and stalled against the comer of the other building.

The black man took a gun from under Proust's coat and hit him with it. I let him, then twisted it out of his grip from behind. His other hand was clutching the acting police chief's collar. Proust was bleeding from a cut on his forehead.

"Police! Freeze! Drop the gun!"

I did both. A county sheriff's car had pulled up alongside us and a deputy was coming out with his gun in both hands. The door on the passenger's side opened and George Strong got out.

"It's all right," he said. "That's our inside man."

The deputy kept his stance. "What about the other?"

I said, "He's with me."

Strong looked from Proust's half-conscious face to mine. "I bribed the guard at the high school for this spot. I remembered I was a newspaperman and that maybe the biggest story in years was getting away from me. What about the ones who hurt Stillwell?"

"Sergeant Gogol and Officer Joyce," I said. "APB them."

His crinkled face got wry. "Did you find the woman's dog?"

I indicated the other barn. "In there. Take it easy on him," I told the deputy. "Take it easy on all of them."

"You a dog lover or something?"

"No, just one of the dogs." I walked away to breathe.

Safe House

One

Our host was a county deputy who wore a lumberman's checked jacket over his uniform blouse and non-issue wool pants. His name was Jerry and he had a long slab of blue chin and a .38 Chief's Special in a holster behind his right hipbone. I wanted to ask how the hunting was in that country but I'd been told not to speak to anyone except the two detectives who were guarding me. Jerry no longer looked at me, having filed me with the antlers over the door and the ulcerated leather sofa he said his father had died in with a .30-30 round in his chest during the 1966 deer season.

"Boys need anything?" he asked at the door. "How you fixed for eggs and shit?"

"Eggs we can use. Walker here gives us all the shit we need." Sergeant Coyne, seated as close to the oilcloth-covered table as his hard thick belly would let him, booted two cards out of his hand and accepted fresh recruits without looking up.

Jerry left. Outside, his Jeep Cherokee started up and clattered away. Officer Blevins, a long sinewy strip of busted University of Detroit basketball scholarship in an unbuttoned vest, as black as

Coyne was pale, bumped the pot up six bits and the sergeant threw in his hand with an oath.

"Two players sucks. Just pushing the same three sixty-seven back and forth. Sure you won't sit in?" Coyne looked at me.

"How long have you two partnered?" I asked.

He frowned at Blevins. "Six years?"

"Eight." The black detective raked in the pot and shuffled the deck.

I said, "I'll pass. I got cleaned out once playing checkers in Huron Metropark with this old wheeze who spent his retirement playing with his friend. Either one of them could tell you in three moves where the game was going from there."

"Hear that, Marcus?" Coyne said. "You and me are too good for the private flash." Blevins grunted and dealt.

Actually the sergeant was the worst poker player I'd seen in a long time. His face mirrored every card he drew and he fell like a piano for the most transparent bluffs; but I needed his good opinion.

They'd been shoving three bucks and change around the table for eight days, ever since I'd been tagged to testify before a grand jury investigating the death of a hood named Frank Acardo in front of my building. I'd missed the shoot, but I'd seen the Colombian hitters waiting for him earlier and so far I was the only witness who could place them at the scene. Rumor said the Colombians were laying out ten grand for me dead, which was a good deal more than I was worth alive. I hadn't had a client in weeks.

"Spicks got all the hotels staked out," Coyne had said when we'd arrived at the safe house, a hunting cabin in Oakland County arranged by a friend of the deputy's in the Detroit Police Department. "Sorry we got no mints to put on your pillow."

I didn't mind. There was nothing waiting for me at the office and the smell of knotty pine reminded me of hunting trips north, a long time ago. I ate Blevins' greasy cooking and read old paperback westerns and watched Coyne get himself bluffed out of everything but his shoulder rig.

He tossed in his cards again and leaned back, shoving his hands in his pockets. "Ten G's, that's a year's pay after taxes for me. How's come the Spicks got more to spend than the city?"

"Less overhead." Blevins reshuffled. "Spit-in-the-Ocean?"

"I ain't *got* spit. You cleaned me out." He rose to answer the telephone. "Coyne. Sure, he's still breathing. What time? 'Kay." He hung up. "Pack your panties, Sherlock. You go on at three."

I got up from the sofa. "I'll miss this place."

"You and Grizzly Adams," he said, shrugging into his sportcoat.

It was a 45-minute drive to Detroit and the City-County Building, where a soporific clerk directed us to a row of seats outside the jury room. The seats across from us were occupied by the man I was there to give evidence against and his entourage. This included his lawyer, young and black in a gray sharkskin suit and one of those bottle-top haircuts they go in for now and a pair of dark-skinned, long-haired bodyguards that would dress out to 500 pounds and look at home in Aztec ceremonial kit.

The man seated between the two hulks belonged to another species. Hector Matador was narrow enough in face and body to vanish when he turned your way, which may have been why he always presented a three-quarter profile, looking at you out of one eye. He had small hands and feet, big eyes, a hawk nose, and wore his black hair in bangs like Al Pacino in *Scarface*. Dressed like him, too, in fawn-colored suits with peaked lapels, pink silk neckties, and a camel's-hair overcoat flung across his shoulders cape fashion. He glanced at me with one mahogany-colored eye that had no bottom, then looked away.

He recognized me, all right. The last time I'd seen him he was seated beside the driver of the car that sped away from the scene of Frank Acardo's murder.

After a brief whispered consultation with the assistant city prosecutor, a big man named Fallon with red hair and the broken-knuckled hands of an Irish bricklayer, I went in to answer questions. Thirty minutes later I paused at the top of the outside steps to shake Fallon's hand.

"We'll get an indictment," he said. "I'll call you when we have a trial date. I wish you'd reconsider and remain in custody."

"Being a witness doesn't pay enough. I'll watch my back." I'd said good-bye to Coyne and Blevins outside the jury room.

"Watch your front, too. These Colombians don't care what direction they come at you from."

I took a cab to the office, circular-filed most of the mail I found waiting for me under the slot, paid some bills, and ran a duster over the desk. My answering service had no messages for me; just to make sure they asked me to repeat my name. The investigation business has more slumps than the Tigers. I was thinking of signing up for a course in word processing when the telephone rang.

"Walker's School of Dance. Fox-trots our specialty."

Pause. "Is this Amos Walker?" Female, middle register, 30 to 35. I took my foot off the file drawer and said it was. "My husband has been missing for a week."

"Do you want him back?"

"I wouldn't be calling you if I didn't. Do you know the Blue Heron?"

"It takes a month to get a reservation there," I said.

"I'll meet you there at six. Ask for Glasscock." She hung up.

Two

The restaurant was tucked back from four lanes of solid traffic in West Bloomfield, identified only by a blue long-legged bird taking off from a sign with no lettering. A rangy hostess in a white silk blouse and long black skirt came out from behind a trellis and towed me to a corner table looking out on the garden.

"I'm Natalie Glasscock. Thanks for coming."

I took a slim hand with a ruby the size of a typewriter attached and gave it back to the woman seated at the table. I'd guessed her age right over the telephone. She had a lot of black hair brushed back without ceremony and a little makeup on the kind of face that writers call handsome to keep from slobbering all over the keyboard. She wore a grayish-pink suit with no blouse that was plain enough to have cost plenty. The ring was her only jewelry. It would have been enough for Imelda Marcos.

I sat down. "Glasscock Bodies?"

"Now it's GlasCo, and we make everything from surgical lasers to those easy-exercise gadgets that get a ten-day workout and then wind up in the attic. Cars don't have bodies any more. Drink?"

She had a full martini glass in front of her. I got rye from the waitress who'd materialized when she made the offer. The help faded. "Your husband is a Glasscock?"

"My husband is an Emmett Firman. My great-grandfather founded the company. He's hypertensive."

"Your great-grandfather?"

"He died in 1930. Emmett's the hypertensive one. I thought it might help you locate him."

"You mean by making faces at strangers until one turns red and keels over?"

"I mean by canvassing drugstores. He needs medication. I brought his prescription." She took an empty plastic vial out of a purse with a clasp that looked like a Krugerrand and gave it to me.

I glanced at the typewritten label and pocketed it. "This is Detroit. People with high blood pressure outnumber the muggers. I could peddle Emmett's picture around drugstores every day for a month and not cover them all. That's a manpower job. Any reason you haven't called the police?"

"Just one. The same reason I haven't called the Six O'clock News. Except for the occasional wedding and death the name Glasscock has never wandered beyond the newspaper business page. As the last one to bear the name I'd rather keep it that way."

"When'd he leave?"

"Last Monday morning about eight o'clock. He has an office in the GlasCo Building on Grand. He never arrived."

"Did you have a fight?"

"Emmett and I never fought. He's entirely without passion. Frankly I was surprised when his doctors diagnosed hypertension. It was the first I knew he had any blood pressure at all."

"I guess that rules out a mistress."

Something stirred behind her face. She opened the purse again and handed me a matchbook. "I found that in the pocket of one of his jackets. He didn't take any of his clothes with him."

It had an advertising cover, THE DELPHI in blue on marble gray, with a telephone number and an address on Watson. I gave it back. "The Delphi's a gay bar," I said. "Is your husband a homosexual?"

"I can't believe he practices. He lacks passion as I said. But it wouldn't shock me to learn he leaned that way. We haven't had relations since our honeymoon, and *that* was a disaster."

Our waitress was back. Her flush said she'd heard more than she'd cared to. We read our menus and ordered appetizers. I waited until we were alone again. "Personal question."

"I married Emmett because my father's will stipulated I had to have a husband in order to collect my inheritance. A wedding was cheaper and less involved than an attempt to break the will. I don't think I have to tell you why he married me."

"Are you sure you want him back?"

"I'm used to him."

I asked her a few more questions and then the food came. "Another drink?" Natalie Glasscock asked.

"Not if I'm going to a bar later."

The waitress left. "Is that an acceptance?"

"Seven-fifty will do for a retainer."

Three

When you visit a gay hangout, and you're not trolling for truckers, it pays to bring reading material; it turns away all but the most rabid pick-up artists while you check the place out. I drank a beer at the bar and read a veiled piece in the *News* about my testimony in the Matador case. There was a sidebar listing Hector's various money-laundering operations under the umbrella of his dummy company, Corrida Ltd. I guess I was out of town the day the hoods moved from the police blotter to the financial pages.

Except for the lack of women, the Delphi didn't look all that different from a straight bar. These days they all have ferns and the Best of Broadway in the juke. The bartender was a cruelly handsome brute of twenty-two with short-cropped blonde hair and a curl on his lip. I ordered another beer and laid a twenty on the bar. When he picked it up I told him I didn't want change.

He gave me change. "There's a rule against dating customers," he said, "and if there weren't a rule against it I'd have one of my own, and if I didn't have one of my own I still wouldn't do it because I'm not gay."

"I like brunettes with big lungs myself. What I want is information." I dealt him a picture Natalie Glasscock had given me of her and Emmett Firman taken in a studio. He had one of those faces that made you think the photograph was fading in front of your eyes. "He been in lately?"

He handed it back, shaking his head.

"I'm not a cop, if that's what's bothering you."

"I knew that when you gave me the twenty. This guy could be sitting where you are and I'd forget what he looked like by the time I looked up from the picture."

"Got any regulars?"

"They're *all* regulars." He stroked the bills on the bar. I nodded. He folded them into the pocket of his green vest. "Try Rodney there in the booth. They built the place around him."

When I slid in I thought the man sitting opposite holding a stemmed glass was another youthful towhead, but as my eyes adjusted to the candlelight his face took on a burnished sheen and I saw the creases by his ears where the surgeon had folded back the skin. His hair was snow white under a blue rinse and curled over the collar of his tailored jacket. When he lifted his black, plucked eyebrows I held up another twenty. "Five minutes."

He smiled carefully, lest his face split. "I used to make twice that for five minutes."

I didn't withdraw the bill. "Everybody's into youth now."

He sighed and took it. I showed him the picture. "His wife wants him back."

"One wonders why."

"Do you know him?"

"Just to do business with." A wry look pushed at the taut skin.

"When?"

"The first time, about six months ago. It's been almost two weeks since the last time."

"Most people would have to think a little before being that specific," I said.

"Specificity's a tough habit to break. I was with the mayor's press corps for four years."

"What happened?"

He sipped wine. "Let's just say I prefer the people I'm working with now."

"Do you have a place near here?"

"Ernest did. That's where we always went."

"Ernest?"

"I never did believe it was his name."

"I take it he didn't confide."

"It was business as I said."

"Where was his place?"

"The Czarina, Room 201. Around the corner on John R."

"Thanks." I slid out of the booth. His eyes followed me up.

"Aren't you going to ask who did it to whom?"

"I'm a detective. Not Geraldo." I hung back. "I guess I wouldn't be the first to tell you to be careful."

He smiled a tragic smile and saluted me with his glass. "I'm an invert," he said. "Not an imbecile."

Gay, they're called.

· · ·

The Czarina had been an elegant hotel when Detroit was the stove-making capital of the world, before Henry Ford and the carburetor. Since then some aesthete had dropped a Styrofoam ceiling under the vault in the lobby, plastered over the marble, and laid linoleum on the parquet. You had to look twice to see where the dusty counter left off and the faded black clerk who was leaning on it began. "Two-oh-one," I told him.

Instead of ringing the room, he reached behind the counter without taking his other hand off it and gave me a key. I was still dizzy over the security of the place when the little coffin of an elevator deposited me on the second floor.

I knocked first, for delicacy, then used the key. Like the lobby, the room had been plastered and paneled into the twentieth century and truncated by a cheesy partition into something less spacious. The bed was unmade, the tub in the bathroom needed scrubbing, and there was a litter of change and pocket fallout on the glass-topped dresser. The drawers were empty, vacant hangers sagged in the closet. The scraps of paper on the dresser included a few odd cash-register receipts and a credit card statement in an open envelope. There was a charge from American Airlines for a one-way flight to Muskegon on the 10th. According to his wife, Emmett Firman had disappeared on the ninth.

I'd seen everything there was to see. There was no telephone in the room, so I added twenty cents to the expense account to call Natalie Glasscock from the lobby.

"Muskegon," she repeated, after we were through greeting each other. "Dear God, I forgot about the cottage."

"Now's a good time to start remembering." I didn't try to strangle the telephone cord. The desk clerk was watching.

"My father had a house in Muskegon. He called it his fishing cottage, but he never went there to fish. It was just a hideaway. I haven't seen it since he died. Do you think Emmett's there?"

I looked at my watch. "I'll know tomorrow. The airport will be closed by now. Have you got a key to the place?"

"I'll have it dug out by the time you get here."

I said tomorrow morning would be fine and told her good night. Hanging up, I waited for the rush that comes when the thing you've been hunting wanders into your sights.

It didn't come. This one hadn't wandered in at all; it had done a big fat brodie and landed on its face wearing a neon suit.

Four

That night I slept in my own bed for the first time in more than a week. I dreamed of hunting cabins and fishing cottages: Safe houses. When the alarm rang I called Fallon's office in the City-County Building. He was there early, shuffling papers in the Matador case. When I told him what I wanted he got one of his aides on the intercom and sent him after it. While we were waiting I asked Fallon how the hearing was going.

"We got an indictment last night."

"Congratulations."

"Save that for when we get a conviction. You still have to—just a second." The aide had returned. Fallon gave me what he'd brought. "That what you needed?"

"More or less."

"I won't ask why." He left a pause, which I didn't fill, and cleared his throat. "We need to go over your testimony before the trial. Where are you going to be?"

"Fishing."

Five

I swung through Grosse Pointe, where the maid who answered Natalie Glasscock's doorbell said her mistress was out and gave me the keys and the address of the house in Muskegon. I drove to city airport from there.

What the Glasscocks called a cottage would have housed Detroit's homeless with room left over for all the crooks on the mayor's staff. Sprawling over two acres of prime Lake Michigan shorefront, it was all glass and timber and stank architect. I parked my rental down the street and approached from the side.

I looked in on three empty rooms, then risked a peek through the big window from the deck overlooking the lake. If he hadn't worn a bright red sport shirt I might have missed him. Seated in a scoop chair reading a magazine, Emmett Firman looked even more faded than he did in his picture; and he wasn't alone. A burgundy loafer on a foot attached to a crossed leg in tan slacks showed in a corner of the window. Whoever was attached to the leg was sitting behind the wall.

I rang the bell on the street side. When Emmett opened the door I showed him my ID. "Natalie's worried," I said.

His face faded another tint. "Come inside."

I followed him through two of the rooms I had looked in on into the big sunny room on the lake. Out on the water a number of sailboats were flitting around like bright moths. Hector Matador, having risen from his chair to stand at the window, was watching them. He had on a fawn-double-breasted with the collar of his open shirt rolled over the lapels. His hands were in his pockets.

"Are you a sailing man, *Señor* Walker?" He didn't turn from the window.

"If God had meant us to sail he wouldn't have given us gasoline."

"Is too bad." His head slid my way. "By now I guess you have figured out that *Señor* Firman was never missing."

I said, "Thanks. Up until you said that I wasn't sure his wife was in on it."

"He came here to lead you away from your official friends in Detroit. We could not stop you from talking to the grand jury, but there is no reason you should be made to repeat yourself at the trial."

"You must have driven all night to get here ahead of me. How'd you make bail so fast?"

"I have official friends as well."

"Where's the Aztec backfield?"

"If you mean Luis and Francisco, they are making my house look lived-in for the police who think they are watching me." He shrugged. "I am among friends, no? So who needs bodyguards?"

Emmett said, "May I go now?"

"What I can't figure is why you ran me through the Delphi," I said. "Natalie Glasscock could have told me about the cottage."

"Then you would have asked why she didn't check on it herself. It was more convincing to say she forgot. We knew you'd find the room at the Czarina and the airfare bill to Muskegon sooner or later. Almost *too* soon, as it turned out." He grinned.

I took the Smith & Wesson out of my coat pocket. "Get your hands out where I can see them."

Still grinning, he turned from the window and drew them out of his pockets, empty. "*Señora* Matador's eldest son is too smart to drive two hundred miles carrying a firearm while he is out on bail," he said.

But Sergeant Coyne wasn't. He came out of a side door behind his department-issue automatic, pale and thick-bellied as ever in the same rumpled suit he'd worn for eight days at the safe house in Oakland County. "Ditch the piece, private flash."

I hung on to it. "When'd you go over?"

"Always was. Couldn't cap you while you was in custody, now, could I? Not with Straight-Ass Marcus Blevins giving me the fish-eye the whole time. Ditch it, I said."

Emmett said, "I'm going."

Matador said, "You stay."

"I don't want to be part of this."

"You already are. You stay through or you go sailing tonight with *Señor* Walker. Either way you don't talk, *comprende?*"

Emmett opened his mouth, closed it, fumbled in a pocket, and took a pill from a vial like the one his wife had given me.

"I won't tell you again." Coyne gestured toward my Smith & Wesson with the automatic.

I said, "You still made it too easy, Matador. That's why I called Fallon this morning and had him give me a rundown of all the companies your Corrida, Limited uses to launder money. When GlasCo came up I knew Natalie Glasscock had called you last night to tell you I was coming today. She and Emmett owe you too much to refuse when you tell them to set somebody up. Did you think that after all that I'd come here without the cops to back me? There are fifteen of them surrounding this place right now."

Nobody said anything.

I don't know how I was doing with Matador. I was watching Coyne. Uncertainty flickered on the sergeant's face and I shot him in the stomach before he could activate his gun hand. By the time he thought of it he was firing at the floor.

He was still falling when Matador lunged for the automatic. I took two quick steps, kicked the Colombian's legs out from under him, and booted the automatic out of Coyne's weak grip. I needn't have bothered; Emmett Firman was busy chewing his own hand in a corner.

I used the telephone in the room to call the law and an ambulance. I would have hollered cop earlier, but GlasCo hadn't been on Fallon's list and I thought I'd guessed wrong. But Coyne didn't know that. As I said, he was easy to bluff.

Kill the Cat

Rivertown

It was right at dark, one of those evenings when you saw it as a black diagonal against the light, like the title sequence of the old soap opera *The Edge of Night.* The river smelled like iron, and the People Mover—Coleman Young's electric train set—chugged along several stories above the street, empty as usual, shuttling around and around in its endless circle as in one of those post-apocalyptic science-fiction stories about a depopulated world, still going about its automated business decades after doomsday, jungle vines crawling up the sides of vacant glass buildings. Detroit had a start on the last, in weedy empty lots where pheasants roosted among the rats and cartridge casings. I was thirty seconds from downtown and might have been driving through Aztec ruins.

The address I'd scribbled in my notebook belonged to a barely renovated pile in the shrinking warehouse district, one of the last places where the city still shows its muscle: miles of railroad track and a handful of gaunt brick buildings where steering gears and coils of steel once paused for breath on their way to becoming automobiles. In a year or two it'll be gone. City Hall and the Chamber of

Commerce are busy gentrifying it into riverfront condominiums. This address was poised square in the middle, the edge of the edge of night.

I was working on a teenage runaway. Mark Childs had slid through a crack in the *über*-upper class of Grosse Pointe, getting the boot from the University of Michigan three weeks into his first semester and then falling in with low company, in this case three boys studying at Wayne State University. I'd gotten the last from a kid who hung doors at Chrysler in order to attend classes in library science at WSU. Childs had taken his place when he'd opted out of sharing rent so he could sleep in his parents' house and save money for cigarettes and tuition.

Where the new roomie found cash to keep up his end, I didn't know and never did, although the family suspected an indulgent aunt. Childs was seventeen, a young high school graduate coming into a trust fund when he turned eighteen in two months. The family didn't like that, thought if they got him back under the parental roof they could teach him some responsibility in sixty days so he · wouldn't blow it all on Internet poker or the Democrats. I hadn't said anything to that. When work comes your way you don't get into a debate situation with the client.

A simple job: Confirm the kid's location and notify the parents so they could call the cops and tell them to take a mixed-up boy off the streets and deliver him to their door.

I parked on gravel off Riopelle and walked down to the river to finish a cigarette, stepping carefully over chunks of brick and Jell-O pudding tops. The lights of Windsor, Ontario made waffle-patterned reflections on the surface where the Detroit River squeezes between· countries. The spot where I stood hadn't changed since Prohibition, when rum boats docked there and men who weren't dressed for the work offloaded the cargo into seven-passenger touring cars with a man standing sentry holding a tommy gun. It was late August and already the air felt like October. We were in for one of those winters that shut up the global-warming people for a while.

The place I wanted stood fifty yards away, with all the character sandblasted off the brick and yellow solar panels replacing the multiple-paned windows. The concrete loading dock was intact, but above it someone had substituted a faux-wrought iron carriage lamp for the original bare bulb. It was an amateur facelift, done on the cheap by a landlord who'd seen too many local renaissances fizzle out to put any faith in the current one.

The big bay doors were chained and padlocked, but decks had been built around the corner with steps zigzagging up four stories and doors cut into each level for the tenants, with small windows added to let in light and accommodate the occasional window-unit air conditioner. The only lights burned on the ground floor. The kid at Chrysler had said none of the other apartments was ready for occupancy.

When no one answered I tried the knob. It turned freely. There might have been nothing in that; college housing is always getting burgled because the students are careless about locking up. The boxy window unit that stuck out of the nearest window was pumping full out. I didn't like that. The damp air off the river was too cool to bother running up the utility bill. I went back to my car and transferred the Chief's Special from its special compartment to my pocket.

Still no answer. I opened the door as quietly as I could, just wide enough to step inside around the edge with my hand on the revolver. It was like walking into a refrigerator truck.

The first one lay on a blown-out sofa near the wheezing air conditioner. He was in his underwear, lying on his side facing the back of the sofa, as if he'd been caught sleeping. I found the next one on his back in an open doorway connecting to a hallway and had to step over him to inspect the rest of the apartment. I had the gun out now.

Number three was twisted like a rag on the floor halfway down the short hallway. I eased open the door to a small bathroom, dirty but unoccupied, found an untidy bedroom with no one in it, checked out a narrow closet with sports equipment piled on the floor, and finished the inventory in another bedroom at the back. This one, more cautious than the others, sprawled on the bed with his legs hanging over the footboard, arms splayed. When I stepped in for a closer look, my toe bumped into something that rolled: an aluminum baseball bat. He'd dropped it when he fell backward. He was naked, the others nearly so. No one wears pajamas anymore.

I put away my weapon. There was nobody left to shoot.

I noticed the smell then, faint but bitter, mixed with the slaughterhouse stink. They'd all been blasted at point-blank range by a heavy-caliber shotgun.

Checking for pulses would have been redundant. I went back to the first corpse. The back of his head was a mass of pulp; stray pellets had torn fresh holes in the upholstery, but he'd taken most of the charge. The others had been struck in the chest or abdomen. Mr. Sofa was the only white victim. Mark Childs was white.

I wished it was that easy, but I had a report to make. Setting my jaws tight, I grasped his bare shoulder to pull his face into view. The skin was cold and the body turned all as one piece, stiff as a plaster cast. Death alters features, but he looked enough like his picture to give him a name. The birthmark on his upper lip settled the question.

The front room was as big as the rest of the apartment. The sofa was part of a rummage-sale set facing a home theater from a box, with a kitchen at the other end. Disposable food cartons littered a folding card table with four mismatched folding chairs around it, but plastic forks and smeared paper napkins suggested more nomadic dining habits. My breath made gray jets. I thought about turning down the air conditioner but didn't. Whoever had touched the controls last wasn't present.

The place didn't seem to be wired for a telephone. I found a cell on the sticky kitchen counter and called police headquarters. I bypassed 911 and asked for Lieutenant Mary Ann Thaler.

"Why felony homicide?" she asked. "Why not plain homicide?"

"It looked like a drug thing," I said.

"It still looks like it."

"So I called you to avoid a handoff."

"I appreciate it. I've been on duty thirteen hours now."

She sat across from me at the folding table, dangling a tea bag on a string in a big cardboard cup with a Powerpuff Girl printed on it. Now that she no longer wore glasses the tiredness showed, but she was still the best-looking thing I'd seen all day, and mine had started as early as hers. Her skin was fair, she had her light brown hair tied in a ponytail with a yellow silk scarf, and a fitted jacket and pleated slacks didn't distract the admiring male gaze from the rest. Her SIG Sauer would be on the left side of her belt, the gold shield on the right. Her brown eyes were as big as wheel covers.

The place buzzed with assorted professionals. A happy Asian medical examiner hummed show tunes and probed at wounds with the nightmare tackle from his tin box. Young people of both sexes measured spatter patterns and bumped into a big black radio-car cop who kept grunting and moving out of their way and into someone else's. Every light was on and a couple of arcs had been brought in for a better look.

Finally the air conditioner stopped. A fingerprint tech had lifted latents off the controls with a gizmo that took pictures like a camera phone.

"That should wrap this," Thaler said. "The heat wave broke night before last; the tenants had no reason to crank up the cold. Whoever did wanted to keep them from getting ripe long enough to split and set up an alibi. I figure these boys have been dead since early this morning or they wouldn't have been undressed for bed."

She sipped tea and twisted in her chair to gesture with the cup. "Your boy Charles died in his sleep. The next two came running when they heard the noise and Shotgun popped them, one, two, like birds. Number Four stuck it out in his room in batter's position, but rock breaks scissors. That how you see it?"

"Clear as gin. Can I smoke?"

She nodded, watched me light up while she rotated the cup between her palms. She kept her nails short and polished clear. "What else you see?"

"Not a thing. I called you right after I ID'd my runaway." I drew in a lungful and staggered it out through my nostrils.

"You didn't snoop around for dope? Funny money? Stolen rubies?"

"I'm not as curious as I used to be."

"Who else you call?"

"The client. It's all in your notebook."

"Before or after you called me?"

"After."

She was still deliberating my case when a sergeant or something in a sharp suit and cowboy boots came over carrying two Ziploc bags. The one he dropped on the table contained four spent shotgun shells. "Twelve-gauge double-O buck, L.T.," he said. "Nothing surer, richer or poorer."

"Rick McCoy, Amos Walker. Walker called it in."

He took my hand in a hickory grip. He wore his hair to his collar and a soul patch in the hollow of his chin. I figured he was working undercover with a Wild West show.

"What else?" Thaler said.

McCoy flipped the other bag onto the table. We didn't have to open to smell what was inside. "In the fridge."

"Nothing harder?" Thaler asked.

"The gunner left with it if so. But if my honker is working this isn't nickel-bag stuff. There's right around six or seven grand in there." He had an accent, Arkansas or farther.

"How'd he miss it?"

"Maybe he found another stash and stopped looking."

"Okay. Tag both bags and get them to the Poindexters downtown."

"Who's McCoy?' I asked when he left with the evidence.

"Narcotics. He caught the squeal and hitched along. He thought the same thing you and I did when it came down."

"I did then."

"You saw the pot. Either a buy went wrong or word got out the stuff was here. You've seen it before."

"Not over pot. Not even the premium kind. Someone who knows his way around a shotgun might stick them up, but he wouldn't cut loose for anything less than heroin, or high-grade coke on the outside. He was methodical, if not professional. And any idiot who's ever seen *Cops* knows enough to look in the refrigerator."

"McCoy's people will run a check on the stiffs as we make them. One of 'em will cash back."

"That sounds like racial profiling."

"Not if it turns out it's Childs."

"His family never said anything about drugs."

"That's reliable." She raised and plunged the tea bag a couple more times; the contents of her cup were nearly black. "You're out at first base, Walker. If you think Homicide rides its fence you don't know anything about those cowboys in Narco."

I dragged in everything but the filter and put it out in a carton of moo shu pork. "I told you I'm not as curious as I used to be."

"You were more convincing the first time."

• • •

Mark Childs was the product of a broken home; the home in his case being a nine hundred square foot house in old Delray. At age three he'd traded it for a Cape Cod on Lake St. Clair, with grass and clay courts and a skiff tied up at the dock out back with *Childs' Plaything* scripted on its transom. Orson Childs, Swedish on one side, English on the other, with equal shares in Volvo and British Petroleum, had adopted Mark after his mother's divorce and her marriage to Orson. If I understood right, Orson's own mother had commemorated the occasion by endowing the boy with a trust fund that after nearly fifteen years of compound interest looked like the annual budget for the state of Rhode Island.

The houseman, a fine-featured Micronesian in a white coat, left me standing in the entrance hall while he found out if anyone was home at 11 o'clock on a weeknight. It was a room meant for standing, despite the presence of a row of straight shieldback chairs and an antique oak hall tree with a bench. I got the nod finally and followed him into a carpeted living room with a sunken conversation pit and Mrs. Childs drinking from an umbrella stand in a white leather armchair. She was a horsey-looking woman of fifty, not horsefaced but the type you pictured riding to hounds in a red habit and black helmet, and to hell with the animal rightists, in a gray silk blouse, black stirrup pants, tasseled loafers on her bare feet; fencerail-lean with high cheekbones and straight auburn hair swept behind her ears. She'd been crying. She offered me a drink. I said no thanks and she threw out the houseman with her bony chin.

I remained standing. "I'm sorry."

"Why should you be? You didn't kill him. Did you?" She had a flat Midwestern accent. In those surroundings, with her features, it should have been New England, but then she'd been married to a construction worker before Orson came along.

"Have the police been here?"

"They just left. They were polite; sincere, even. They asked if Mark was into drugs. I said no. They didn't believe me, but they were polite about it, so I didn't throw anything at them. I suppose we owe you money."

"We're square. You gave me a three-day retainer but I only used two days. Actually, it's your husband I wanted to talk to. Is he around?"

She said he was in his workshop and gave me directions. Then she swirled the ice in her glass and drank from it and I stopped existing.

It was a metalworking shop in a small building behind the house, a shed that was supposed to be an old carriage house that had been converted into a shed but had always been a shed. It was one of the newer estates in Grosse Pointe, less than sixty years old; no vintage auto money there of the Dodge and Ford and Durant type. I knocked, but it was noisy inside, so I let myself into a room filled with blue smoke and the sharp stench of scorched metal and sparks from Childs's cutting torch. He was a hobbyist who made sculpture from rescued driveshafts, leaf springs, and gold dental retainers scrounged from salvage yards and dumpsters behind schools. At the moment he was cutting up a length of steel pipe clamped in a vise bigger than my head.

I waited, hands in pockets, not wanting to startle him while he was handling dangerous equipment. When he saw me he jumped a little anyway, then tipped up his visor and screwed shut the valve on the acetylene tank. I said I was sorry about Mark.

"Yes." He spoke in clipped tones: stiff-upper-lip Brit by way of Vancouver, where the American branch of his family emigrated after the colonies declared independence from England. "I consider our transactions at an end, barring outstanding expenses. If you'll submit a statement, we can put an end to this sad business." He produced a checkbook from a hip pocket. He had it on him with a leather apron.

"We're fine," I said. "I just wanted to clear up some details before I type my report."

"Clarissa's the detail person. Why don't you come back when she's in a condition to answer your questions?"

"Stepfathers tend to be more objective considering their wives' children. Was there anything about Mark's behavior that suggested he might have been into the drug scene?"

He tugged off his gauntlets. He was a good-looking man creeping up on sixty, with a receding hairline and a long upper lip fighting the old battle between pickled youth and premature old age. "I liked Mark," he said. "I couldn't really love him, because he came to me fully assembled, but I think we might have been friends if I hadn't married his mother. It never occurred to me he had anything to do with drugs, but then I didn't pay as much attention to that sort of thing as I suppose I should have. It would explain some things, wouldn't it?"

"Things such as what?"

"Well, his poor academic performance and his running off. He wasn't a rebellious boy. He was a sickly child, always on some kind of medication. Maybe that's where it started."

"His real father might know something."

"Hank? I doubt it. They haven't seen each other in years."

"That's what he said when I called to ask if Mark had moved in with him. Then he hung up."

"That's Hank Worden. I suppose I should be grateful he's such a miserable son of a bitch. He's made me look like the ideal husband by contrast."

I thanked him and thought of some more words of sympathy, but he had his gloves back on and the visor down and was firing up the torch for another go at his project. People grieve all sorts of ways.

The houseman was standing in the path between the house and the workshop when I let myself out. His hands hung at his sides and his white coat glowed blue under a mercury light mounted on top of a tall pole.

"We talk," he said.

He asked me to call him Truk. That was the name of the archipelago where he'd grown up; he said his real one was even harder to pronounce than it was to spell. His room in the walkout basement contained popular fiction on the shelves and stacks of *People.* I guessed he read them to improve his English. He sat cross-legged on a neatly made twin bed, showing bare ankles and the smooth brown line of his throat when he tipped his head back to draw on the cigarette he'd bummed.

I smoked and waited in a wicker armchair and wondered how old he was, thirty or sixty. His bowl-cut hair was glossy black, but Micronesians are a long time going gray.

"Police?" he asked.

"Private," I said.

His face crumpled into a wrinkled mask. Sixty, definitely. "I don' know what this is, *private.*"

"It means I can't shoot if you run away from me. Apart from that the work's the same."

He smiled, showing gold teeth and smoothing out his face. Thirty, maybe. "I thought Mark is dead before this."

"Bad habits?"

He puffed and said nothing. He didn't inhale, just filled his mouth and let it out like cigar smoke. His grin set like plaster of Paris. Forty, probably. I got out a twenty, folded it lengthwise, and held it up between two fingers. He drew his lip down over his teeth and shook his head.

I started to put it away.

"Kidneys," he said.

I stopped; "What about them?"

"Like he didn't have none. None that worked."

"He didn't die because his kidneys failed. His kidneys failed because he died."

"I mean before. Three year, four. He got a new one."

"His mother and stepfather didn't mention that."

"He didn't get it from them."

"Who donated it?"

He dropped the filter into a jar lid on the nightstand and asked for another cigarette. I tucked the twenty into the pack and flipped it onto the bed. I'd guessed the answer, but I might have to come back for more later.

He pocketed the pack with the bill inside. He didn't take out a cigarette. "His father, the real one."

"The mother's type didn't match?"

He shrugged.

I said, "I heard Mark and his father weren't that close."

He smiled again and patted his pocket.

I misunderstood. "That's all you get. I'm dipping into capital."

"Money's what I meant. They pay."

"Hank Worden sold one of his kidneys? For how much?"

He lifted and dropped his shoulders again. I asked him how he knew about the deal.

"I didn', then. Later, Worden comes back, drunk, loud. Mr. Childs he say, 'I call police.' Then he leave."

"What was he mad about?"

"I think maybe he wants more and Mr. Childs says no. I guess. My English is not so good as now."

"Was Mrs. Childs here at the time?'

"She is out. It is after the operation, she goes to see Mark in the hospital."

I got up and put out my cigarette in the jar lid. "Anything else?"

"Nothing else. I hear you talk to Mrs. Childs, I think maybe you want to know." I was at the door when he spoke again. "You no police?"

"When's the last time a cop gave you money?"

He lifted his bangs to show me a thin white scar on his scalp. "Sixteen stitch, ten year ago. All I ever got. So why you want to know about Mark?"

"I'm more curious than I thought I was."

The radio news had more details on the victims in the apartment. Du'an Reeves, twenty, was a sophomore at Wayne State. Gordon Samuels and LeRon Porter, both twenty-one, were juniors.

Porter had done short time in County for nonpayment of child support to a seventeen-year-old former girlfriend in Redford Township. None of the others had a record, including Mark Childs. The police were still investigating drug connections. I switched off.

Hank Worden, Mark Childs's father and Clarissa Childs's ex, lived in a bungalow that needed a new roof on West Vernor, the old Delray section, now mostly Mexican. The disrepair wasn't uncommon in houses where construction workers lived; the work is all outgo and no income. His lights were on at midnight, so I knocked on his door. I had my gun with me on a hunch, but I didn't need it to get in. I accomplished that by sticking my foot in the door and pushing a twenty through the gap.

He sat in a quagmire sofa drinking Diet Pepsi from a can, a man in his middle fifties but fit, tan from rugged outdoor work, in jeans and run-down tennis shoes and a plaid flannel shirt with the sleeves rolled up past his elbows. He had all his hair, splintered with silver, and from the look of him it was easy to see why his kidney passed muster. But you don't have to socialize with a vital organ.

"So you got the boy killed." That's what he opened with.

I remained standing. All the seats in the place looked like sinkholes and I didn't want to have to wallow my way out of one to clock him. "According to the cops he was dead almost before I started looking for him. Do you want to fight? I sure don't. It's been a day."

He shook the last drops onto his tongue and tossed the can toward a raveled straw laundry basket heaped over with empties. "I don't want to fight. I been in fights and I never got a thing out of them, not even the sense to stop picking 'em. Last time I saw Mark he was in Pampers. I know I ought to feel something, but I don't. Bastard, ain't I?"

"Who told you, the cops?"

"They make the family rounds when something like this happens. Greasers next door get a visit every time one of their uncles gets squiffed. They got more uncles than a rabbit. Ought to loan 'em out to colored boys that got no daddies."

"You thought enough of Mark to give him a kidney."

"First thing I thought when they told me. 'Well, there's a piece of me wasted.' You know about that, huh?"

"I told you, I'm a detective. So what about it?"

"That was strictly a business deal. Ten thousand bucks and all expenses paid. See, Mark and me was a perfect match. Is that a hoot? Clary took him when she left and she had less in common with him than me."

"Ten grand doesn't go as far as it used to. That was true even three or four years ago. So you went back for more, and Childs threw you out."

His face darkened under the tan. "That what he said?"

"It's what I heard."

"I ought to go back up there and bash in his skull with one of them nutty statues he makes out of scrap."

I didn't like the way he said it. He was too calm. "If the cops heard you say that, they'd be down here tossing the place for a shotgun."

"Go ahead, it's in that closet. I used to bring it along when I had a job in the country, in case I saw a deer. Now I just keep it around to punch holes in the sky on New Year's Eve."

It was a Remington twelve-gauge in good condition. The barrel smelled oily and there was a little dust in it when I turned it toward the light. It hadn't been fired recently. I put it back. "Of course, it could be one of a set."

He made a kazoo with his lips. "I can barely afford to buy pop in six-packs. Get me one, will you? Take one for yourself. I ain't had a real drink in twelve years; that's why my kidney was so rosy pink." He took one of the two I got from the refrigerator in the kitchenette and watched me snap the top on mine. "If Childs told you I got greedy, then he's a liar on top of a deadbeat. I only went to that barn of his to get what was promised me. That check he wrote me ought to be tied to a paddle with a string."

"It bounced?"

"Man, I had to duck when I tried to cash it." He popped open his can. "I guess his insurance took care of the hospital bill, but I don't go in to get carved on just for the rush."

"You didn't take it to court?"

"No contract. He said it was dicey legalwise. What you think of that, man lives like that, hanging paper like some goldbrick?" He poured half the can down his throat.

"Maybe he lives better than he is off." I sipped. No matter what they put in place of sugar it always tastes like barbed wire left to steep. "I don't guess you told any of this to the police."

"I would've, if they asked. Why should I cover up for a squirt like Orson Childs?" He spoke the name with an effete accent.

"No reason, except they might look at it as motive for murder. You made a deal to save Mark's life, Childs reneged, so you decided to repossess."

He paused in mid-guzzle, swallowed. "Jesus, that's cold."

"It should be. I just took it out of your refrigerator."

"I mean what you said. So why'd I wait four years?"

"Murder plots have been known to stew a lot longer than that."

He drank off the second half and flipped the can toward the basket. It wobbled but didn't fall off, as some of the others had. "Do I *look* like somebody who'd wait that long?"

• • •

I drove away from there, yawning bitterly and hoping Barry Stackpole's lights would be out so I could go home and go to bed. But Barry lived without sleep, a journalistic vampire who that season had sublet lodgings downtown, five minutes from each of the city's three legal casinos. He had a theory that the owners were building a Mafia outside the Mafia with no ties to what the gaming commission interpreted as organized crime, but with all the benefits attendant. He might have had something, at that; the owners were exclusively male, and the mob is not an equal opportunity employer. Traditional gangsters had taken one of his legs, some fingers, and put a steel plate in his skull, so he was less than reasonable on the subject of thugs incorporated. In that vein of mind he'd hacked into every hundred-thousand-dollar bank account between Puget Sound and Puerto Rico. Thirty minutes after I dropped in on him and his computer arsenal, I found out Orson Childs had been selling off his family's stock for five years, trying to bolster investment losses and personal indulgences, from *Childs' Plaything* to a racehorse named Lightyear that couldn't hold its own beside a California redwood. I promised Barry a case of scotch and left him to his obsession of the season.

The rest was as glamorous as it gets. I caught a few hours' sleep in my hut on the west side of Hamtramck, got up at the butt-crack of dawn with black sludge in a thermos, and camped out across the street from the Childs house in Grosse Pointe. That morning happened to be trash collection. I was out of the car the second Truk wheeled the household refuse bin to the curb and started back up the drive, puffing smoke from one of the cigarettes I'd given him.

I worked fast, because the trash truck was snorting its way up Lake Shore Drive, the collectors evaluating the inventory for personal aggrandizement before feeding it to the crusher. I found what I wanted among the empty single-malt bottles and plain garbage, put it in my trunk, and went home to hose off and change. Rich people are never available before 9:00 anyway; not even rich people who aren't really rich, mathematically speaking. In America, even the broke are divided into classes.

Truk let me in with no expression on his face to indicate he knew me from anyone else who came to the door. He didn't even glance at the red and blue gym bag I was carrying. After a little absence he came back and led me through a room I hadn't been in and outside to a flagged courtyard where Orson and Clarissa Childs sat in fluffy white robes drinking coffee; Mrs. Childs's out-of-focus gaze said there was as much Kentucky as Colombian in her cup.

The houseman faded and I set down my bag, which clanked when it touched the flagstones. Childs, looking up from the *Free Press*, glanced back at it, then at me. Portrait shots of the shooting victims bordered a grainy picture of the murder scene on the front page.

"Anything new?" he asked. "There was nothing on the radio that wasn't there last night."

"There wouldn't be. The press doesn't know yet about the kidney."

The woman started, spilling coffee on the table. Childs folded the paper and laid it on the vacant chair. "It didn't have anything to do with what happened. I assume you've been talking with Worden."

"What happens to Mark's trust fund now that he isn't around to collect it?"

"It goes to his heirs and assigns. Before you go any further, you might want to consider the penalty for slander."

"What lawyer would press the case after your retainer check came back from his bank?"

The couple locked gazes. He blinked first. She set down her cup with a double click.

Childs said, "You should be having this conversation with Worden. He's an angry man and simple. His thought processes are easy to predict when he thinks he's been cheated. Not that there is anything to whatever he told you. Buying organs is shaky from a legal standpoint."

"So's murder. His shotgun tests clean. How about yours?"

"I don't own a shotgun."

"Not anymore. You decided to get rid of it after you used it on Mark and then his roommates to make it look like he wasn't the only target."

He lengthened his upper lip. "Evidence?"

"Me, for starters. I'm a witness." I leaned down, unzipped the bag, and took out one of the pieces I'd retrieved that morning. The barrel had been cut into eight-inch lengths, then split down the middle. When I laid it on the table, Mrs. Childs squeaked, got up, and half ran inside, holding a hand over her mouth. I let her. "If I'd known this was what you were slicing up last night, it would've saved me a dive in your Dumpster. No wonder you jumped when I walked in on you."

Childs turned his head slowly from side to side, as if he were trying to get out of my shadow. "Assuming that's where you found it, what's it prove? You can't trace scrap."

"You know a lot less about shotguns than you do about metalwork. Cutting up the barrel's a waste of time; it's smooth, leaves no striations on the pellets. In order to connect the weapon to the murder, all the cops have to do is match the firing pin to the marks on the shells found on the scene." I was holding the bag now. I took out the heavy Browning receiver and laid it on the table. The incriminating evidence was intact.

He stared at it while I let the bag drop with the rest of the pieces inside.

"Planting that high-grade pot was smart," I said. "It should have been coke or heroin, but maybe a man in your circumstances doesn't know how to go about finding them. Smart, and stupid: It diverted the investigation, but it put it in the hands of a narc named McCoy, who'll have all the upper-end dealers in the area in his data bank. The one you bought it from will turn you if it means ducking four charges of homicide."

"It's true," he said. "I don't know much about dope or shotguns."

"Don't say anything, Orson. All you did was buy marijuana."

I turned around. Clarissa Childs was standing in front of the door to the house with the twin of the chopped-up Browning raised to her shoulder. The barrel looked as big as a culvert.

"He wasn't lying to you, Mr. Walker," she said. "Orson has never fired a shotgun in his life. My first husband taught me how to hunt. I've been putting game on the table for years."

I thought about the revolver in my belt. She read my mind. The shotgun twitched. I held my hands out from my body.

"Clarissa—" Childs began.

"I said don't say anything!" She kept her eyes on me. "Nothing that ever came from Hank was any good. His son was defective; even his kidney didn't fix what was really wrong with Mark. After everything Orson and I did for him, he turned his back on his education and ran away. Why should he fall into money when we've got three mortgages on this house?"

"Clarissa?" This time his throat throbbed with warning.

"Drop it!"

We turned our heads together. Childs sat motionless, staring at Lieutenant Mary Ann Thaler, Rick McCoy, and three uniforms standing with sidearms pointed at the woman with the shotgun. I'd called them early enough to avoid a standoff, but they must have taken the long way around the house.

"Drop it!" Thaler shouted again.

Clarissa Childs hesitated, then lowered the shotgun. The officers were advancing when she swiveled the butt down to the ground, jammed the muzzle up under her chin, and tripped the trigger with the toe of her slipper.

. . .

"We got a partial off that air conditioner knob that puts the mother on the scene," Thaler said while my statement was being typed up. "For what it's worth."

"It closes the case. That must be worth something to someone."

She was drinking tea again, from one of those mugs they sell downstairs with the police seal on it. Headquarters is running a boutique to catch up on repairs. Today she had on a grayish-pink suit; ashes of rose, I think they call it. She looked less tired. "All we've got on Orson Childs is attempting to destroy evidence. I don't think we can make accomplice after the fact stick. Some mother, huh? I used to think there was something to maternal instinct. I thought I was missing something."

"Not wanting kids and killing the one you have don't walk under the same sun."

"Plus three other mothers' sons just for garnish. Sometimes I hate this town. Other times I just dislike it a little."

"It started in Grosse Pointe."

"It's all Detroit." She worked the tea bag. "I'd sure like to know how you confirmed the Childses had money troubles. If I thought you knew your way around a computer I might ask the boys in white-collar crime to keep an eye on you."

"You don't have to log in to run a bluff."

"On," she said. "You log on to the Internet, not in. But you knew that. You're overdoing it."

"The less people think you know, the better for you."

"If that's true you'll live forever."

I said nothing.

She said, "I know about you and Barry Stackpole. You two are the evil twins of amateur law enforcement." She took out the tea bag and dumped it into her wastebasket. "Any questions?"

"None I can think of."

"Well, you know what they say about curiosity." She sipped.

Slipstream

The blue flashers made me slow down. The red flashers made me pull over and stop to see if I could help scrape someone off the pavement. When the state troopers and the county sheriffs both come out, it means there's been more than just a merger of fenders.

The light bar on the EMS van was stuttering in a desultory kind of way, splashing colors off the dewy asphalt and into the faces of the usual human detritus that gets pulled into the slipstream of accidents, fires, and drive-by shootings: guys in quilted vests and base-ball caps, cigarette-puffing women in head scarves and denim, teenage boys reeking of Stroh's, and big cops in leather jackets writing birthdates and license numbers into spiral notebooks with doodles on the covers. The air smelled of scorched metal, gasoline, and carbon tetrachloride. A plume of dank smoke hung over a charred blob of something that might have been a Ford Escort or a Cadillac Seville or the tail section of the *Hindenburg,* kneeling on bare wheels with its front end accordioned against the trailer of a flatbed truck parked across Square Lake Road, somewhere in No Man's Land between Southfield and Iroquois Heights, seven miles north of Detroit.

"See anything you like, mister? Oh, Christ."

This cheery greeting, altered when I turned to face him, came from a man mountain in a Chesterfield with velvet collar and a tweed cap, who answered to Killinger. He wore amber shades astraddle his Irish pug and an impressive set of handlebars that must have set him back an hour each morning in the bathroom. He topped off at six and a half feet, high normal among the Michigan State Police, and dressed out at around two hundred fifty.

"Evening, Lee," I said. "This is a piece out of your pen, isn't it? I heard you were commanding the Northville post."

"Your hearing's just fine. I'm meeting friends for dinner at the Machus Red Fox. Or I was." He checked his watch, a steel aviator type. "They probably think I've pulled a Jimmy Hoffa by now. Anyway I caught the squeal and that makes me the ranking officer on the scene. What about you?"

"Just rank. I thought I had a client up in the Heights. If she'd said over the telephone her missing Ambrose was a pit bull I'd have saved a trip. Is that a K?" Two EMS attendants in navy were busy zipping up a vinyl bag on a stretcher on the gravel apron.

Killinger nodded. "Charbroiled in the can. The M.E., who's been and gone, thinks male, between twenty and twenty-five, but he says he's been wrong before. Sheriff's men put out the fire. No skid marks. Poor son of a bitch came over the hill and met God."

"What was the truck doing blocking the road?"

"We'll know that when we find the driver. He might've jackknifed and been trying to straighten out when the car came. Probably he was drunk. Ninety-nine times out of a hundred that's the case when somebody rabbits."

"No witnesses?"

"Just rubberneckers. Video arcades must be closed."

"What'd you get on the plate?"

He might have smiled under the moustaches. In any case, it wouldn't have meant anything. "Rita Donato."

"Seriously?"

"No, I always joke around whenever I help pull a Crispy Critter out from under a steering wheel in my supper suit."

"Then that'd make this—?" I nodded at the bag being slid into the back of the van.

"At a guess, Albert. The son. Heir to the department store chain, currently in receivership while the widow of its late humanitarian founder stamps books in the library in Milan on a three-to-seven for income tax evasion." Then he did smile. "Didn't I call him a poor son of a bitch?"

Walter Donato, dead five years, had been named for his adoptive parents and reared in Dearborn, where he inherited his foster father's five-and-dime at age thirty and within sixteen years ran it into the largest chain of cut-rate department stores in the Middle West. After spending several millions of his personal fortune probing fruitlessly into the mystery of his birth, he had diverted his energies toward the establishment of a foster-care foundation that became a model of its type and put his face simultaneously on the covers of *Time* and *Newsweek*. When bronchial pneumonia took him at sixty-two, the President of the United States authorized an annual grant in his name to be awarded to deserving projects in the area of child placement. The local archbishop had been overheard to remark—and was censured by Rome for so doing—that he'd consider nominating Donato for canonization if he were anything but a Baptist.

The take on his widow was different. A former professional dancer, Rita had met Donato shortly after the death of his first wife, married him within six months, and buried him before their second anniversary. The terms of his will placed her in sole charge of the store chain until the majority of his son Albert, a role she took far more seriously than those of helpmate and stepmother. She remodeled the stores from top to bottom, threw out all the no-brand merchandise, and replaced it with clothing lines named for TV miniseries actresses whom she hired to do commercial endorsements. In no time at all she had stores on both coasts and became a sought-after speaker at gatherings of women who wore shoulder pads and hyphenated their surnames. When the Democrats finally got into the White House there was even talk of a cabinet post.

Just about then someone in the IRS found out she hadn't paid taxes in three years, each of which showed more profit than the chain had seen during Walter's lifetime. After the usual protracted trial, appeal, and counter-appeals, reparations forced the Donato organization into Chapter 11 and Rita into the federal penitentiary at Milan, Michigan, pronounced *Meye*-lin, where at the time of the accident that took the life of her stepson Albert she had served eighteen months. In the meantime some things had come out about her general comportment that removed her name from *Cosmopolitan's* list of the twenty most admired women.

Albert Donato's death and its circumstances led all the local news reports and received heavy national play for the better part of a week. The Oakland County Sheriff's Department traced the truck driver, one Owen Subject, to his house in the suburbs and arrested him for leaving the scene of the accident with a charge of manslaughter to follow, too much time had elapsed for a blood-alcohol test to be considered conclusive, and so no drunk-driving accusation was made. An independent trucker, Subject told the cops he'd been on his way home from delivering a diesel tractor to a farm implements dealership in Iroquois Heights when he swerved to miss a deer and wound up stalled across Square Lake Road. Albert Donato's Chrysler LeBaron had slammed into him and burst into flames, panicking him into running. Subject's basset-hound features and freestanding black hair became a staple on the front pages of both Detroit papers for days. Then another one of the mayor's relatives got caught dealing dope and the story went inside.

That was when a party named Sporthaven with caps on his teeth and a brown leather portfolio under one arm looked me up in my little toy office on West Grand River and asked me to drop in on Mrs. Donato in Milan.

*   *   *

"*Hell* no, I never said it. They made that one up at Channel 2 and all the networks took it and ran with it. That's what convicted me. Otherwise I could have bought my way out."

We were sitting in the visitor's room—a not really uncomfortable place with orange scoop chairs and laminated tables that looked more like the cafeteria in an auto plant than a room in the House of Doors—Rita Donato, Lawyer Sporthaven, and the detective in the story. She had on a cotton blouse open at the neck, twill slacks, and loafers, no stripes or work denims. Things are a little more relaxed in the federal lockup, and if you can afford them you'd be surprised how much you'd be willing to pay for the simple comforts. They didn't include hair dye, and hers had gone back to its natural gray, but it was done in a style becoming to her lean angular face, parted to the left of center and curling in at the base of her neck. She was fifty and looked it, but a patrician fifty, and the large round lenses of her glasses masked the bags under her eyes.

The question, asked by me and answered by her, was whether she had really been overheard to say that only losers pay taxes.

"Pity," I said. "Nobody ever says what everybody says they say." I lit a Winston and waited for the conversation to come to a point, any point. So far all she'd done was sit across the table from me with her legs crossed, bouncing one foot and holding up one end of an interview for "Prime Time Live." I had the impression she was starved for company.

"A man named Killinger gave me your name," she said then, without transition. "I gathered he's something with the state police."

"Commander. He issued me my license the first time."

"He was decent enough to come here in person and tell me about Albert before I heard it on the news. He mentioned your name and what you do. He didn't say why. Maybe he knew the local authorities were going to sweep Albert's death under the rug."

"Are they?"

"Sporthaven tells me they're about to drop all charges against Owen Subject."

I looked at the lawyer's young-old face: nipped, tucked, stitched, peeled, creamed, and smoothed by many hands until it had all the character of a rounded stone in a riverbed.

"I got it from a legal secretary at County," he said. "Albert should have had his car under control. The trucker took adequate steps to avoid hitting an obstruction in the road."

"What about his leaving the scene?"

"There was nothing anyone could do. The car was instantly engulfed. Even had he stayed and risked his life to pull Albert out of the car, a corpse would have been all he saved."

"That part's true enough," I said. "I saw the car."

"They're blowing it off." Mrs. Donato had both feet on the floor now. "If Albert were anyone but my stepson they wouldn't have dared. Read the polls. I'm the most hated woman in America."

"What do you want me to do?"

"Investigate Subject. Killinger said he thought there was alcohol involved. If he's got a record I want it brought out into the open. If it leads to something else I want that to come out too. I'm no wicked stepmother, Walker. I was very fond of Albert. I won't have his life wiped off the books just because the woman his father married made a mistake in arithmetic."

Sporthaven reached inside his portfolio. "Under the conditions of her personal bankruptcy, Mrs. Donato cannot own anything for five years. However, my firm has authorized me to issue you a letter of credit for up to five thousand dollars." He handed me a crisp sheet of expensive bond containing three paragraphs printed in boldface with justified margins. "Should you be successful, whatever is left is yours. Your standard fee is guaranteed, of course."

"Of course." I folded it as carefully as if it were the Declaration of Independence and interred it in my inside pocket. "What if nothing turns up?"

"Come now." The woman sat back and recrossed her legs. "In your profession and mine, where would we be if we went around looking for the good in everyone?"

* * *

I spent an hour in the periodicals section of the Detroit Public Library downtown reading up on the accident. I knew most of the details, but I needed one in particular. When I had it I went back to the office and rummaged through my desk looking for business cards. I still have every card that was ever handed me. Twenty minutes of that and I had a match. I propped it against the base of the desk lamp, looked up Owen Subject in the metropolitan directory, and dialed the number. His wife answered, a break. She said Owen wasn't home; another break. I read the name and title off the business card and arranged an interview at the house for seven that evening. She said Owen would be in by then.

The house was in Redford, one of a tract of brick ranch styles that had been poured in an ice cube tray and dumped out in the pattern in which they were formed. A small woman with red hair and gray roots snatched the door open under my knuckles.

"Owen? Oh." She clutched her quilted housecoat together at her throat.

"Anson Wold, Mrs. Subject. We spoke earlier. I'm with Midwest Casualty. It *is* Mrs. Subject?" I handed her the card.

"Yes. I'm afraid Owen isn't home yet. I expected him before this." She stood aside.

The living room was full of glazed furniture and factory art. Stacks of supermarket tabloids occupied most of the chairs. The same alien seemed to have cropped up on the front pages of most of them. I found space on the couch.

"I just need a couple of details before I can finish processing Mr. Subject's claim. I understand the truck is his property."

"Yes. Um, I didn't know he'd filed a claim. He's been so busy with this court thing. They arrested him, you know." She perched on the edge of a straight-back chair.

"Released on his own recognizance, I believe."

"Right. Even at the arraignment the judge knew they had no case."

"I imagine your finances are pretty tight with his truck in impoundment."

"Well, there's not much coming in. But the mortgage is paid off and so is the truck, and we have enough in savings to take care of incidentals."

I made some scratches in my prop notebook. "He must be a hustler. Making a go of a small business in this economy is a twenty-six-hour-a-day job."

"That's what I said when he left the trucking company and made a down payment on the rig. I told him if he lost the house I'd leave him. It was tough at first, but then he got a loan and right after that work started coming in. We're better off now than when he was punching the clock, and his time's his own." That made her think to look at her watch. "I can't imagine what's keeping him. He was just going to see the lawyer."

"Where did he get the loan?"

"Loan? Oh. Do you need to know that?"

"It's for Records."

The magic phrase brought her to her feet. "I forget the name of the company. I think there's a card." She went to a desk holding up a telephone shaped like a duck and pawed through drawers. "He got the name from a friend in the union. He almost gave up. He'd tried all the places that advertised in the yellow pages and on television. Here it is! Ever hear of them?"

I looked at the card she brought over. "Oh yeah," I said. "I've heard of Gryphon Collateral."

• • •

I spotted the blue Chevy two turns after I left Redford. It was a closed tail and he was good, but traffic was light at that hour and the routes I take around the city are my own and make no sense to anybody but me.

I had three good chances to shake him. I didn't use them. Thanks to Mrs. Subject I had a fair idea who was sending his kid through medical school, and it was handy to have someone close by I could ask questions of in case I hit a wall.

When I turned into the driveway in Highland Park the guy kept driving, reading the numbers on both sides of the street as if he were looking for one in particular. I heard him cut his motor down the block while I was waiting for someone to answer the front door.

"Chevies. What's the world coming to?" Barry Stackpole trained a pair of graphite binoculars through the window of his home office. "Something important went out with bulletproof Cadillacs."

"Ten'll get you twenty when you run the plate it'll kick out Gryphon Collateral," I said.

The room, converted from a small bedroom on the second floor, was full of books and videotapes that had boiled out of the shelves onto the desk ad chairs and all but a narrow twisted walkway on the carpet. Some of the books bore his byline. All of the tapes belonged to the program he had hosted on local cable until someone decided that reruns of "Three's Company" would skew better in his time slot. The program, titled "Know Your Neighbor," had highlighted a different Detroit area crime figure each week. Barry had been a Mob watcher only a little longer than he'd been getting around with an artificial leg, two missing fingers, and a steel plate in his skull, souvenirs of the first time someone had suggested canceling him.

He put down the nocs and limped over to the desk to pour scotch into two glasses from a bottle of Glen-Something. "I want to thank you for bringing him here, Amos. I still have three limbs I don't know what to do with." He handed me a glass. "Cold steel."

"Hot lead." I lifted mine and tossed it back. "I brought him here on purpose. When he reports the address and they look it up, maybe they'll panic and do something dumb."

"Here's hoping they do it to you." He drank and leaned a hip against the desk. "Gryphon, you said?"

"I hear they got two floors of a high-rise in Southfield, no more dealing loans over a card table behind Tino's Billiards on Livernois."

"Michigan," he corrected. "Livernois was Jake the Shake. Gryphon's lost a lot of color. They figured out they don't make anything when they have to break bones. That's when they added Collateral to the company name. Small business is their specialty. If you can't pay they grab a piece or take it out in trade."

"That explains why Owen Subject isn't hurting for money."

"Milton Thorpe."

"Is that a name or another toast?"

"Milton likes to block roads," he said. "He used to use cars, but someone got around him once by going up the bank. A truck is better. He used a truck the day he capped Guillermo Zuma."

"Zuma I heard of. Someone named Milton Thorpe doesn't sound like he attends the same cockfights."

"Zuma always had a WASP front for him. This one had ambition. Loan sharks generally have plenty of indy truckers in inventory. And Milton Thorpe juices most of the sharks in town."

"I don't remember Zuma getting killed in a crash. I heard it was bullets."

"You can't count on a crash. He got it from the car following behind. He couldn't go forward on account of the truck blocking the road and he couldn't back up because the car was on his bumper. They squoze him in between, put it in Park, got out, and shot him and his driver in the barrel. Cops down in Ecorse snagged the trucker out of the river three days later."

"Owen didn't show tonight," I said. "His wife was worried."

"He'll turn up in three days. That's how long it takes the gas to bring them to the surface."

"Lucky for Albert Donato he was driving so fast. It saved him from getting shot."

"It would explain why Subject powdered and left the truck behind. Nobody told him there might be flames. The car with the guns would have done the same once Albert was toast." Absently he scratched the wrong leg. "That store receivership wouldn't have lasted long. What was a kid with his bucks doing playing around with someone like Milton Thorpe?"

"Maybe he wasn't. Maybe it was a message for his stepmother."

"Are you suggesting your client might not have come across with the whole story?"

"I'm shocked too." I drained my glass and set it on Barry's face on the back of one of his books. "Thanks for the whiskey and information. I'll be taking my tail and leaving."

"Don't forget you owe me a bottle."

"I can't afford your brand."

"Hell, neither can I. That's why I give out information."

He stopped smiling. "Stay alive, buddy. Don't leave me alone with the politically correct."

"Don't worry. I'm fire-retardant."

I left the driver of the Chevy looking for a space near my building and went up to place some calls. First I tried Rita Donato at Milan, but after a long wait some prison brass came on and said she'd used up her allotment of calls for that period and would I care to leave a message? I hung up and got Lee Killinger at the Northville state police post.

"I'm out the door, Walker. Unless you're calling for an address to send money you borrowed from me, which no keyholer will do ever, I got no time for you."

"Sorry to hear it, Lee. So will a lady dispatcher I know at the Brighton post. Wasn't her kid born just about the time you transferred over on your last promotion?"

"You can only draw that one so many times before it misfires," he said after a pause. "What is it this time?"

"I'm wondering if Rita Donato ever had any dealings with a drug lord by the name of Milton Thorpe."

"That's federal."

"I hear the computer in Lansing has coffee all the time with the one in Washington."

"Anyway, all that would have come out during her trial. When they really want you they dig deep."

It was a point, one sharp enough to deflate. I asked him to feed it through anyway. He said he'd get back to me in twenty-four hours and banged off. I was getting to be as unpopular as my client.

Next I called Owen Subject's wife to ask if her husband had showed up. I knew what the answer would be when she speared the telephone halfway through the first ring. It was three minutes after ten. He'd been missing eight hours. I said something comforting. It made me unpopular with myself.

•   •   •

The next morning I was shaving with the bathroom door open when the TV morning-show hostess, a blonde on Percodans, reported that the body of a middle-aged male had been found snagged in brush on the American side of the Detroit River south of Flatrock. I wiped off the lather and made a call.

"Wayne County Morgue. Fitzgerald."

"Walker, Fitz. How was Bingo Saturday night?"

"I'm still answering the phone here, ain't I? What's the rumpus so bright and early?"

"I may have an ID on that floater they gaffed down-river."

"Too late. His wife identified him an hour ago."

"How'd she take it?"

"Better than the son. He was leaning on the old lady when they left."

"Son?"

"Clean-cut kid. You wouldn't think he came from such rotten loins."

"Fitz, I have an idea we're not both talking about Owen Subject."

"Never heard of the gentleman. Customer's name is LoPolo."

I groped for the pack in my shirt pocket and realized I was wearing my robe. "LoPolo comma Francisco in parentheses Pancho Polo?"

"Yeah, all of those. Plenty of places he could've landed between Bogotá and here, but he, chose the Renaissance City. Two in the melon. Nine millimeter."

"Didn't he used to work for Guillermo Zuma?

"Uh-huh. Some folks thought he'd step into the old man's pointy patent leathers. He didn't and I hear it made him surly."

I found a half-smoked Winston in the ashtray ant set fire to it. The smoke cleared the bees out of the skull. "Have you got an address for LoPolo?"

"His wife left it. Second." He came back on after twenty. "Nice little cottage on Square Lake. Probably thirty-two rooms. Number's—"

"Not necessary. Thanks." I broke the connection and tried Killinger in Northville. The turn-out sergeant I spoke to said he wouldn't be in until eight. I finished grooming, dressed, and drove to the office. The blue Chevy followed.

"I said twenty-four hours," Killinger growled when I got him. "It's been ten."

"Forget it. I'm betting five thousand dollars Rita Donato didn't know Milton Thorpe from Robert Young." I told him about Francisco LoPolo and where he'd lived.

He blew air. "Snaps right in there, doesn't it?" What about the trucker?"

"He'll pop up in a couple of days. By then he'll be the forgotten man. How'd you like a plush office in Lansing?"

"Depends on the deposit."

I told him.

When the manager came on, shortly before noon, I tipped him, opened the manila envelope, studied what was inside, and transferred it to a No. 10 I'd already addressed and stamped. I slipped it into my inside breast pocket. Before I went out I checked the load in the Smith & Wesson .38 I'd had longer than my wife and clipped it to my belt.

The man behind the wheel of the blue Chevy shielded his eyes with his left hand when I came out of the building and lost himself in a map of what looked like Nebraska. He jumped when I tapped on his window with the muzzle of the revolver. I made a twirling motion with my free hand. He cranked down the glass.

I got out the envelope and held it in front of his face. It was addressed to the Detroit office of the Drug Enforcement Administration. His lips moved as he read. His hair was moussed forward rather than slicked back and he had on turquoise-colored contacts, but the rest of him had plainly come from someplace where the written language included tildes and accent marks.

"Yeah?" he said. "So?"

"Oh, the repartee." I pocketed the item. "You probably saw the messenger deliver it in a different envelope. It was sent by Owen Subject's wife. She found it among his papers. You know, 'To be opened in the event of my etcetera.' It's going to a safe deposit box I keep up in Iroquois Heights." I pointed at the blue cellular telephone standing to attention at his elbow. "Tell Milton he knows where to reach me when he's ready to deal."

"Milton who? I don't know you, mister."

Grinning, I holstered the .38 and walked. Only the faces change. The patter stays the same.

My car was parked in the deserted service station across the street. Once behind the wheel I shook the silver-dollar-size object out of the envelope and clipped it to the sun visor. The messenger had come from Lee Killinger, not Mrs. Subject.

I don't keep a safe deposit box In Iroquois Heights. Mostly what I keep there is away. But the road that leads there is one of the few empty stretches in the metropolitan area and crosses Square Lake Road, where Albert Donato got cooked to death and near where Francisco LoPolo had lived in dope-financed splendor until somebody shot him in the head and tipped him into the river. I made a face at the doohickey on the visor. For a man who didn't own a computer or even a digital watch I was counting an awful lot on modern technology not letting me down.

I picked up the truck at Thirteen Mile Road. A big yellow tanker labeled CAUTION TOXIC CHEMICALS, wheeled into my lane from the right without stopping for the light, forcing me to use the brake to slow down. The Chevy, which had been hanging back a block and a half since I left downtown, closed in then. This would require timing.

Although it was cool September, my window was open to allow maximum oxygen into the car and my brain. Now I poked my cigarette butt into the slipstream and rolled up the window. I wanted as little resistance as possible when the time came to maneuver.

It came sooner than expected. The traffic had thinned out to just us three, but we were a mile south of the Square Lake crossing and the straight stretch that afforded an unobstructed view in both directions. The tanker accelerated with a black jet of diesel smoke from its stack and went into a hard turn. Its rear tires skated sideways, laying down molten rubber. The truck filled my windshield.

My instincts screamed brake. I didn't listen. I wrenched the wheel left and leaned with the inertia. My tires yelped. Thanking God and Goodyear for steel-belted radials, I stood on the brake then, and while my insides were still straining toward the firewall I straightened the wheel and banged the lever into Reverse. The tires spoke again. My rear wheels struck the curb with a vibration I felt in my teeth. I spun the wheel and hit the accelerator. The blue Chevy slid into view square in the middle of the windshield. I saw the driver's narrow dark face, his eyes and mouth forming a triangular rack of O's, one hand diving inside his coat.

I hit him hard.

The Mercury was fifteen years older than his little outsourced GM and outweighed it by fifteen hundred pounds. His front end crumpled like foil, throwing belts, bursting hoses, and spraying steam. After killing the ignition I unbuckled myself and piled out behind the .38.

I didn't need it. He hadn't worn a seat belt and was sprawled over the console, out cold and bleeding from the piece of scalp that was caught in the jagged star on his windshield. I found his pulse, unburdened him of the 9-millimeter Beretta he carried in a shoulder rig under his coat, and used it to cover the driver of the tanker. That was unnecessary too. He was sitting hunched over the wheel of his stalled truck with that poled-ox look that says the round is over.

That's how things looked when the state police radio car arrived carrying Commander Killinger, its roof-mounted halo homing in on the little electronic gizmo attached to my visor.

● ● ●

The matron held the door for my client more in the manner of a maidservant than a turnkey, which meant all her bills were being paid. Prisonwear today was a pink cashmere sweater and pleated skirt split as if for riding. Mrs. Donato nodded to Sporthaven and sat down opposite me with the table in between.

"You've been busy," she said, when I'd delivered my report. "Do you think this Hidalgo will testify against Milton Thorpe?"

Feliz Hidalgo was the name on the green card the state police found on the driver of the blue Chevy. I moved a shoulder. "If the cops match that Beretta I took off him to the slugs they dug out of LoPolo's brain, he might trade his boss for a sentence less than life. If he's the pro I think he is, they won't. The tanker driver is another story. I hear he's talking already. That ties Thorpe to the attempt on me."

"I don't want that. I want him to answer for Albert."

"That's up to Hidalgo. Or Subject, if he surfaces. The judge put out a warrant on him when he didn't show at his preliminary this morning. No body yet, so it's possible he just ran."

"So Albert wasn't the target after all. The wanted LoPolo that night."

"It makes sense," I said. "LoPolo lived on Square Lake and always took the same route home from his headquarters in Detroit. He drove a gray Cadillac, Albert drove a gray Chrysler. They look alike to the owner of a Chevy. Your stepson just got sucked up in the slipstream. Later, when they found out their mistake, they took LoPolo out more quietly."

"Poor Albert. I really was fond of him."

"You'll get over it. In time," I added sympathetically. She was as easy to feel sorry for as a battlewagon.

Sporthaven shifted his briefcase. "You've earned the five thousand, Walker. Send us the bill when you buy a new car to replace the one you wrecked."

"Thanks, I'll get it fixed. I've seen what the new ones are worth." I rose. Rita Donato's eyes followed me up.

"I won't forget you when I'm paroled. That may not sound like much now, but I won't be your average ex-convict any more than I was your average rich widow."

"Just don't put your first hundred million into electronics," I said.

Lady On Ice

Outside, it was eighty-nine degrees at ten P.M., with percentage of
humidity to match, and I was experiencing the early stages of frostbite.

I was sitting on a bench otherwise occupied by semi-professional
hockey players, each of whose pads, jerseys, and weapons-grade
adrenaline were more effective insulation against the proximity of
the ice than my street clothes. The arena had been conjured up out
of an old Michigan Company stove warehouse on the Detroit River,
with the Renaissance Center undergoing a public-friendly renova-
tion on the one side and twenty toxic acres being parceled out to
gullible buyers wanting riverfront condos on the other. Veteran Detroiters were aware that asbestos and car batteries had been leaking
poisons into the earth there since Henry Ford, and so the athletes
on the ice outnumbered the fans in the bleachers.

I wasn't playing, and I was only half paying attention to the
game. When I want to see apes brawl, I can always tune in to the Discovery Channel. I was providing security for a Detroit Lifters guard
named Grigori Ivanov who, at the moment I realized I could no
longer feel my face, was busy pummeling a French-Canadian center
skating for the Philadelphia North Churches. Ivanov didn't seem to
need my help with that.

The team owner, a Fordson High School dropout who'd made a couple of hundred million selling pet grooming products over the Internet, had gambled most of his capital on the notion that a summer hockey league would go over as big as Sergeant Spaniel's Tickbuster Spray. Now he was finishing out the team's second season under a court order forcing him to play his team or pay off the remaining time on the players' contracts.

In the midst of all this, Ivanov had started receiving letters from an anonymous party threatening to throw acid in his face if he didn't remand his salary over to a fund to save the Michigan massassauga rattlesnake from extinction. Since most people, particularly those with small children, aged relatives, and beloved pets, would just as soon see the region's only venomous viper go the way of the passenger pigeon, and since hockey stars in general looked as if someone had already thrown acid in their faces, no one was taking the threats seriously.

No one, that is, except the owner's attorneys, who warned him of the legal consequences on the off chance Mr. Anonymous wasn't just blowing smoke. But Ivanov was a reclusive type, with relatives in the Ukraine awaiting money from him to make the journey to America and no wish for any undesirable publicity that might move the State Department to deny them entry visas. That ruled out the police. I'd come recommended on the basis of an old personal-security assignment that had wound up with no one dead or injured (three cracked ribs didn't count, since they were mine), and since I was on my sixth week without a cent and considering trading a kidney for the office rent here I was on the night of the hottest day of summer rubbing circulation into my face while visions of hot toddies danced in my head.

The score was lopsided in Philadelphia's favor. By the final buzzer, the only audience left was either too drunk on watered-down beer to move or sweeping up Bazooka Joe wrappers in the aisles. I pried my stiff muscles off the bench and moved in close to Ivanov as the Lifters started down the tunnel toward the showers.

The kid had on a bright green T-shirt, or I might not have spotted him bobbing upriver through the red-and-yellow jerseys. The concrete walls were less than ten feet apart, and the players averaged six feet wide. It was a tight crowd, and I had to wedge myself in sideways to keep from being squeezed to the back, which is no place for a bodyguard. As it was, I couldn't get to my gun and had to bodycheck Ivanov out of the way when the kid's arm swept up and yellow liquid sprayed out of the open vial in his hand.

I hadn't time to see where the liquid went. I hurled myself between two padded shoulders, grabbed a fistful of green cotton, and pulled hard. A seam tore, but the kid's forward momentum started him toward the floor, and I came down on top of him and grasped the wrist of his throwing arm and twisted it up behind his back. The empty vial rolled out of his hand and broke into bits on the concrete floor.

I placed a knee in the small of his back and ran a hand over him for weapons. He hadn't any. By this time, the players had backed off to give us room. I got to my feet, pulling the kid up with me by his twisted arm, and slammed him into the wall, pinning him there while I looked at Ivanov.

"He get you?" I asked.

He'd put a hand against the wall to catch himself when I'd shoved him aside. He pushed himself away from it and touched his face, a reflexive gesture; the lawyers weren't the only ones who'd suspected something was behind the letters besides a crank. "No. I am OK."

The kid was shouting something. I took hold of his hair and pulled his face away from the wall to hear it.

"I didn't want to hurt anybody!" he was saying. "I just wanted to scare him. It was just colored water."

I looked at the wall farther up the tunnel. It had been painted green until a moment before. Now there was a large runny patch with smoke tearing away from its bubbling surface. A patch about the size of a man's face.

"Your name's Amos Walker?"

I'd seen the speaker once or twice at police headquarters, but we'd never exchanged a word except maybe to ask for a button to be pushed on the elevator. He was a big Mexican in his forties who bought his sport coats a size too large to leave room for his underarm rig and wore matching shirt-and-tie sets to save himself time dressing. His graying hair was thick enough to be a rug but wasn't, and he had a red, raw face that looked as if he exfoliated with emory paper. The name on the ID clipped to his lapel was Testaverde. He was a detective sergeant with Special Investigations.

I said my name was Amos Walker. He was holding my ID folder, so there didn't seem any point in denying it. We were standing in a hall at headquarters by the two-way glass looking into the interview room where the kid with the stretched-out T-shirt was answering a detective's questions in front of a camcorder. The air conditioner wasn't working any better than it did in any other government building, which was all right with me. My nose was still running from the chill in the arena.

Testaverde returned the folder. "That was quick thinking. Baby-sitting your specialty?"

"I almost never do it. Hours of sitting around on your hip pockets, seasoned by ten seconds of pure terror. But a job's a job."

"One might say *our* job. Why do people pay taxes if they're going to hire the competition?"

"If they refused, you'd arrest them. Anyway, this one had a muffler on it. It's the only edge I've got. You've got all the people and whirlygigs."

"Well, the rabbit's out of the hutch now. Let's have a listen." He flipped the switch on an intercom panel next to the window. The kid's shallow voice wobbled out of the speaker.

"... vegetable dye, I don't remember what kind. All I know is there wasn't any kind of acid."

The detective, a well-dressed black man named Clary, read from his notebook. "'High concentration of sulphuric and hydrochloric acid.' That's what Forensics scraped off the wall. It scarred the concrete, Michael. Think what it would have done to Ivanov's face."

"I filled the tube from the tap and put in the coloring. I wouldn't even know where to lay hands on that other stuff. "

"Hydrochloric you can get in any hardware store. People soak their faucet filters in it to remove rust. Sulphuric you can drain out of an ordinary car battery. I want to believe your story, Michael, but you're not helping much. Who could have switched the tubes?

"I don't know." His mouth clamped shut on the end.

Clary scratched his chin with a corner of the notebook. "Let's go back to those letters you wrote. You said you were jealous of Ivanov's success."

Testaverde switched off the speaker. "Robin Williams is funnier. But he has to make sense. This punk's got serious problems if he's jealous of a third-rate stickman on a crummy semi-pro hockey team."

"Red Wings players are harder to get close to."

I was barely listening to myself. Michael Nash was seventeen but could pass for two years younger: an undernourished towhead in an old T-shirt without lettering, faded carpenter's jeans, appropriately baggy, and pretend combat boots. He was only an exotic dye job and a couple of piercings away from the common run of self-esteem-challenged youths you saw taking up space at the mall. Nothing about his story made sense, unless you fitted in the one piece he was leaving out. After that, it came together like a Greek farce. I didn't bother suggesting this to Sergeant Testaverde; he'd already have thought of it. Cops aren't stupid, just overworked.

Grigori Ivanov got away from the Criminal Intelligence Division after recording his statement and autographing a hockey puck for an officer whose kid followed the Lifters. I waited and rode down with Ivanov in the elevator. I asked him who wrote the letters.

He gave me that eyebrowless look you saw a lot of on Eastern European faces before the Iron Curtain rusted through; the one they showed KGB agents and officials of the U.S. State Department. "The boy," he said. "Michael Nash?"

"You wouldn't show me the letters before. Can I see them now?"

"What is point? It is over. Send bill."

"You said they weren't typewritten. I'd like to see the handwriting."

He smiled. It would take a good dentist to decide which teeth hadn't grown in his mouth. "You wish to determine personality?"

"No, and I don't read head bumps either. But I can usually tell a man's writing from a woman's."

"What woman?"

"The kid's protecting someone. When you're a seventeen-year-old boy, the someone is usually female. But then, you'd understand that. You're protecting the same person."

The elevator touched down on the ground floor. He gathered himself to leave. I mashed my thumb against the Door Close button. He grew eyebrows then. I'd seen that same look when he was trying to pry off the Philadelphia center's head with his stick.

"It's a theory, anyway," I said. "The cops will buy it; they don't care as long as the case closes. If there's another reason and I have to go out and find it, I might take the long way back, past Immigration."

The fight went out of him then. In a sport coat and silk shirt, he looked smaller than he did in pads, and now he was almost human scale. "We go somewhere?"

The cop shop is just off Greektown, which is always open, thanks to the casino. The street was speckled with zombified strollers whose air-conditioning had broken down at home. There was a scorched-metal smell in the air, peculiar to that city of wall-to-wall automobiles on a heated summer night. We ordered coffee in a corner booth in a place that reeked of hot grease and burnt cheese. Ivanov hunkered over his cup, looking like a nervous goalie.

"She is—was—underage."

"What's her name, and how far did it go?"

His story started in the old country. Trinka Svetlana, a Ukrainian figure skater with Olympic hopes, had met Ivanov when he was skating for a team in Kiev. He was twenty-three; she was sixteen. When Detroit bought his contract and started unwinding red tape to import him, the pair had been living together secretly for six months. He promised to send for her the moment he had the cash. That was three years ago. In the meantime, she'd made her way over with an aunt's help and was living with her in Rochester Hills. Trinka surprised Ivanov one night, waiting for him outside the arena. She'd expected a joyful reunion, but the look on his face when he recognized her ended that. He'd been married to the daughter of the owner of the Lifters for a year.

She fled when he broke the news. Two weeks later, the first of the letters came, threatening to throw acid In Ivanov's face if he didn't agree to leave his wife and return to her.

"What about the Massassauga Relief Fund?" I asked.

"I read about some such thing in the newspaper. Everyone in America supports a cause, no? I thought it would, how you say, throw off the suspicion." His eyebrows disappeared again. "This thing, it is like that movie. *Fatal Extraction?*"

I didn't correct him. His dumb hunkie act had worn through. "She hasn't assimilated," I said. "The thing to do in America is to bring charges against you for statutory rape and contributing to the delinquency of a minor, not to mention encouraging the hopes of innocent rattlesnakes under false pretenses. That means deportation. No wonder you wanted private protection instead of going to the cops."

"Well, she is scared off now. What is your interest?"

"There's a kid in Holding because he thought he was throwing a pie in your face, and it turned out to have a rock in it. I'm curious to meet the person who put it there."

"What pie? What rock?"

I got up and put down money for the coffee. He seized my wrist in an athlete's grip.

"You won't tell Immigration?"

I broke the grip with a maneuver I hadn't used since Cambodia. "Too busy. I need to get an estimate on putting the Berlin Wall back up." I went out into the scorched-metal air.

There was a V Svetlana listed in Rochester Hills. I tried the number from a booth, and a husky female voice confirmed the number and told me to leave a message. I disobeyed.

I opened the window in the car, mostly to let out the stale air. My congestion was clearing, and I had just begun to feel the heat. Coming up on one A.M., and the stoops of apartment buildings and single-family houses were occupied by men in damp undershirts and women in shorts and tank tops, smoking and drinking from cans beaded with moisture. Some of them looked as if they'd been hit over the head with something, but most were smiling and laughing. Winter had been long and cold and not so far back.

It was one of the homes in the older section of Rochester Hills, which means it didn't look as if it came with a heliport. The roof was in good shape, it had been painted recently, and the lawn would pass inspection, free of miniature windmills and lighthouses.

"Mrs. Svetlana?" I asked the creature who answered the doorbell.

She looked at me with slightly sloping Tartar eyes in a face that had given up its first wrinkle—a vertical crease above the bridge of the nose—and probably got something well worth having in the trade. Her hair was an unassisted auburn, cut short at the neck but teased into bangs to lighten the severity. The nose was slightly aquiline, the cheekbones high. Stradivari had made a pass at her lips and taken the rest of the week off. She had on a blue satin dressing gown and flat-heeled sandals and looked me square in the eye at six feet and change.

"Miss," she corrected. "It's late for visitors."

"Not many women would open the door this late." I showed her my ID. "Are you Trinka Svetlana's aunt?"

"You woke me up to ask me that?"

I liked her accent: Garbo out of *Ninotchka* by way of Nadia Komanich. "Trinka's boyfriend is in jail. I want to ask her a couple of questions about how he got there." ·

A light glimmered n the Oriental eyes. "Grigori?"

"Michael."

Her face shut down. It had never been fully open. "She's a beautiful girl. I can't keep track of her young men." She started to push the door shut. I leaned against it.

"I'm betting she can. Girls are organized about that kind of thing."

"She isn't here." She pushed harder. She had plenty of push, but I had thirty pounds on her, and it was too hot to move. She gave up then. "She's at the rink downtown, practicing her routine." She rolled the *r*.

"Routine?"

"Her figure skating act. Everything today is a show. To skate expertly is no longer enough. She wants to go to the Olympics."

"She wanted that in the Ukraine. She wanted Grigori, too. Does she still want Grigori?"

"Grigori is a pig." Spittle flecked my cheek.

"No argument from the U.S. Which rink?"

"There is only one."

I straightened, and she pushed the door shut. By that time it was redundant. With women like V. Svetlana around, it was a wonder there weren't still missiles in Cuba.

The Iceland Skating Rink's quarter-page ad in the Yellow Pages said it closed at midnight. There was a light on in the city block of yellow brick building when I parked in a lot containing only a two-year-old Geo and a Dodge Ram pickup with a toolbox built onto the bed. When no one came to the front door, I walked around to the side and kicked at a steel fire door until it opened wide enough to show me a large, black, angry-looking face and a police .38.

"What part of CLOSED you need me to explain to you?"

It was a deep, well-shaped voice. Motown had a lot to answer for when it moved to L.A.

"You left a light on. I'm with Detroit Edison."

He looked at my ID. "That ain't what it says."

"One of us is lying. I need a minute with Trinka."

"Don't know no Trinka."

"Yeah. I'm just the scrub team. The first string won't like that answer any more than I do. It's a long drive from Thirteen Hundred and a hot night. They'll be sore."

Thirteen Hundred is the address of Detroit Police Headquarters. He opened the door the rest of the way and put away the .38. His uniform was soaked through. The air-conditioning budget at Iceland went into keeping the rink from turning into a swimming pool.

I followed him down an unfinished corridor to a glass door. "See if you can get her to go home," he said. "I like her, but I need this job." He left me.

Inside, a trim figure in a royal blue leotard glided around on the ice. It was just her and me and Sarah Vaughan singing "Dancing in the Dark" on a portable CD player propped up on the railing that surrounded the rink. I leaned next to it and violated another rule by lighting a Winston.

Trinka Svetlana was as tall as her aunt and could have been her daughter. Her hair was longer and a lighter shade of red, but disregard fifteen years and the laws of physics, and I might have been looking at the same woman. She had an athletic build and muscular legs, more shapely than the broken Popsicle sticks they use to sell hose on television.

Her white skates cut wide, nearly silent loops on the ice. I found the volume on the CD player and turned it down. I didn't want to startle her by switching it off. She noticed the change and slowed down, looking at me. She didn't stop.

"Nice form," I said. "I give it a ten, but my favorite's the luge."

"Who are you?" Her accent was heavier than her aunt's, but she didn't sound any more rattled.

"Not important. Michael's in jail."

Even that didn't stop her. She drew a wide circle around the edge of the rink. "Michael?"

"Nash. *N* as in *nice-to-a-fault*. *A* as in *adolescent*, *S* as in *stupid*. *H* as in *hell*. Or *holding*. Same definition. He threw a bottle of acid at Grigori. Grigori Ivanov? *I* as in *infidelity*—"

"I know who he is." It was the first emotion she'd shown. "Michael's a nice boy. Why would he want to do that?"

"He believed your letters. Don't say, 'Letters?' No more spelling bees." My face was stiffening all over again, That night in summer was the coldest winter I'd ever spent.

"He thought it was colored water in the vial. Any thoughts on where he got that idea?"

She skated in silence. Sarah had stopped singing. I switched off the player.

"He said he filled it himself from the tap," I said, "but I figure he lied about that, too. Whoever filled it used hydrochloric and sulphuric acid in concentrate. Very hard on the complexion."

She stumbled and almost fell. She caught her balance and skated up to the rail. Her eyes were larger than her aunt's, but they hadn't been so large a moment before

"Who sent you?"

I told her.

"Aunt Vadya?" She was breathing heavy, and her face glowed with moisture. It had collected in beads along the top of her collarbone. On TV you never saw how much they were sweating.

"She didn't rat you out. In the Ukraine she grew up in she learned how much truth to tell when. What I want to know is, why didn't you do the job yourself? Your aim probably would've been more accurate."

"It *was* water. I filled it and put in the coloring. Are you the police? Why did you arrest Michael? He's just a boy."

This sounded like truth. It didn't have the ring of conviction that went with a lie. But then she was a performer. I put cop in my voice. "We arrest them whether it's nitro or Kool-Aid. If it's Kool-

Aid, we don't hold them. When it's something else, we try them as adults."

She believed me then. I wouldn't have bet money on it a minute earlier. "Grigori. Did—"

"Did his face melt? Six inches this way or that, and it would've. It sure made a mess out of a painted concrete wall. Not that he'd have had to look at himself in a mirror. He'd have had to skate for a team for the blind."

"That's impossible! I never—it—"

She stopped, not because I'd interrupted her. Something had clicked for both of us.

"Was that vial ever out of your sight after you filled it?" I asked.

She started shivering.

• • •

I told her she could pick up her car later. I drove her to 1300, got Sergeant Testaverde out of his office, and introduced him to her. He locked himself up with her for twenty minutes. At the end of it, he sent a car to Rochester Hills.

The four of us waited in the office. Michael Nash and Trinka sat on the vinyl-upholstered sofa—close, but not touching, and without speaking. She'd put on a sweatsuit over her leotard and changed from her skates into a pair of pink running shoes. Dressed like that and with her hair twisted into a ponytail, she looked younger than nineteen, closer to Michael's age. She stared at the linoleum, he looked at a CPR chart on the wall and chewed his lower lip. The sergeant, seated behind his desk, mopped at his face and neck with a hand towel and glowered at me sipping hot coffee from a Styrofoam cup in the scoop chair.

"Do you have to guzzle that in front of me?" he snarled. "It just makes me hotter."

"That's your problem. I think I'm coming down with a cold."

"You can stay home and nurse it after Lansing jerks your license. Impersonating an officer."

"I did an impression of one. There's a difference."

"I'd sure as hell like to know what it is."

"It wouldn't do you any good. You have to shut off half your brain, and half's all you got."

"That a Mexican joke?"

"I don't know any Mexican jokes. They haven't been up here long enough. It's a cop joke. Force of habit. You'd have got around to Trinka after you finished sweating Beaver Cleaver."

"Thanks for the vote of confidence." He reached back and twisted the knob on the window fan, looking for a speed faster than High. Maintenance turned off the air conditioner at midnight.

A uniform poked his head in and said the suspect was in Interview Room 3. Testaverde stood and pulled his shirt away from his back. "Keep these two company." He stabbed a finger at me. "Let's find out what half your brain turned up."

Detective Clary was still at his post, but he wasn't asking many questions. Vadya Svetlana, having changed into a simple but by no means unfashionable green dress, but otherwise looking much as she had standing on her own doorstep, sat at the table Michael Nash had occupied, speaking directly to the video camera.

"You Americans talk of family until it means nothing," she said. "You couple it with other words—family *values*, family *workplace*, *extended* family—as if it needed the help. I will tell you about family. When the Nazis shelled Leningrad, my grandmother was visiting friends outside the city. She tried to sneak back in, carrying her baby—my uncle—and holding her firstborn's hand—my mother's hand—and almost stumbled into an SS patrol. She took cover in a doorway. When the baby began to cry, she smothered it with her hand so the soldiers wouldn't hear and slaughter them all. She killed her son to save her family."

After a moment, Clary cleared his throat. "Let's move closer to the present. Why did you replace the colored water in the vial with acid?"

"Because my niece is a fool."

The camera whirred, wanting more.

"Most kids are," prompted the detective. "Most guardians don't turn it into a reason for mayhem."

"Most guardians don't have Cossack blood. When someone dishonors you, the name of your family, you don't just scare him. You say, 'Boo!', what is that? No, you say it with a knife in the belly."

"If you feel that way, why didn't you do it yourself?"

"The boy wanted to do it. He said it was too dangerous for a girl. When a boy wishes to play at soldiers, it is not a woman's place to interfere."

"Except in the business of the vial."

"You frighten a pig, it runs away squealing. The fright goes away, the pig comes back. What you expect, he will stop being a pig? If you want a pig to stop being a pig, for the honor of your family, you must kill him."

"But you didn't try to kill him."

She shrugged. It was an entirely Slavic gesture, not to be imitated. "It is America. You make the adjustment."

Officer Clary was silent. We were silent. She lifted her eyebrows and looked directly at us. The glass was a blank mirror on her side.

"What did I say?" she asked. "It is my English?"

Testaverde switched off the intercom. I thought he shuddered a little. It could have been the cold.

Snow Angels

One

They were the unlikeliest visitors I'd had in my office since the time a priest came in looking for the antiquarian bookshop on the next floor.

She was a comfortably overstuffed sixty in a plain wool dress and a cloth coat with a monkey collar, gray hair pinned up under a hat with artificial flowers planted around the crown. He was a long skinny length of fence wire two or three years older with a horse face and sixteen hairs stretched across his scalp like violin strings, wearing a forty-dollar suit over a white shirt buttoned to the neck, no tie, and holding his hat. They sat facing my desk in the chairs I'd brought out for them as if posing for a picture back when a photograph was serious business. Their name was Cuttle.

I grinned. "Ma and Pa?"

"Jeremy and Judy," the woman said seriously. "Ed Snilly gave us your name. The lawyer?"

I excused myself and got up to consult the file cabinet. Snilly had hired me over the telephone three years ago to check the credit rating on a client, a half-hour job. He'd paid promptly.

"Good man," I said, resuming my seat. "What's he recommending me for?"

Judy said, "He's a neighbor. He sat in when we closed on the old Stage Stop. He said you might be able to help us."

"Stage Stop?"

"It's a tavern out on Old US-23, a roadhouse. Jeremy and me used to go there Saturday night when all our friends were alive. It's been closed a long time. When the developers gave us a hundred thousand for our farm—we bought it for ten back in '53—I said to Jeremy, 'We're always talking about buying the old Stage Stop and fixing it up and running it the way they used to, here's our chance.' And we did; buy it, that is, only—"

"Dream turned into a nightmare, right?"

"Good Lord, yes! You must know something about it. Building codes, sanitation, insurance, the liquor commission—I swear, if farming wasn't the most heartbreaking life a couple could choose, we'd never have had the sand for this. When the inspector told us we'd be better off tearing down and rebuilding—"

"Tell him about Simon," Jeremy snapped. I'd begun to wonder if he had vocal cords.

"Solomon," she corrected. "The Children of Solomon. Have you heard of it, Mr. Walker?"

"Some kind of Bible camp. I thought the state closed them down. Something about the discipline getting out of hand."

"A boy died in their camp up north, a runaway. But they claimed he came to them in that condition and nobody could prove different, so the charges were dropped. But they lost their lease on the land. They were negotiating a contract on the Stage Stop property when we paid cash for it. Solomon sued the previous owner, but nothing was signed between them and the judge threw it out. They tried to buy us off at a profit, but we said no."

"Took a shot at me," Jeremy said.

I sat up. "Who did?"

"Well someone," Judy said. "We don't know it was them."

"Put a hole in my hat." Jeremy thrust it across the desk.

I took it and looked it over. It was stiff brown felt with a silk band. Something that might have been a bullet had torn a gash near the dimple on the right side of the crown. I gave it back. "Where'd it happen?"

"Jeremy was in front of the building yesterday morning, doing some measuring. I wasn't with him. He said his hat came off just like somebody grabbed it. Then he heard the shot. He ducked in through the doorway. He waited an hour before going back out, but there weren't any more shots and he couldn't tell where that one had come from."

"Maybe it was a careless hunter."

"Wasn't no hunter."

Judy said, "We called Ollie Springer at the sheriff's substation and he came out and pried a bullet out of the doorframe. He said it came from a rifle, a .30-30. Nobody hunts with a high-powered rifle in this part of the state, Mr. Walker. It's illegal."

"Did this Springer talk to the Solomon people?"

She nodded. "They denied knowing anything about it and there it sits. Ollie said he didn't have enough to get a warrant and search for the rifle."

I said he was probably right.

"Oh, we know he was," she said. "Jeremy and me know Ollie since he was three. Where we come from folks don't move far from home. You'll see why when you get there."

I hadn't said I was going yet, but I let it sail. "Can you think of anyone else who might want to take a shot at you?"

She answered for Jeremy. "Good Lord, no! It's a friendly place. Nobody's killed anybody around there since 1867, and that was between outsiders passing through. Besides, I don't think anybody wants to hurt either one of us. They're just trying to scare us into selling. Well, we're not scared. That's what we want you to tell those Solomon people."

"Why not tell them yourself?"

"Ed Snilly said it would mean more coming from a detective." She folded her hands on her purse in her lap, ending that discussion.

"Want me to scare *them?*"

"Yes." Something nudged the comfortable look out of her face. "Yes, we'd like that a whole lot."

I scratched my ear with the pencil I used to take notes. "I usually get a three-day retainer, but this doesn't sound like it'll take more than half a day. Make it two-fifty."

Jeremy pulled an old black wallet from his hip pocket and counted three one hundred-dollar bills onto the desk from a compartment stuffed full of them. "Gimme fifty back," he said. "And I want a receipt."

I gave him two twenties and a ten from my own wallet, replaced them with the bills he'd given me, and wrote out the transaction, handing him a copy. "Do you always come to town with that much cash on you?" I asked.

"First time we been to Detroit since '59."

"Oh, that's not true," Judy said. "We were here in '61 to see the new Studebakers."

I got some more information from them, said I'd attend to their case that afternoon, and stood to see them out.

"Don't you wear a coat?" I asked Jeremy. Outside the window the snow was falling in sheets.

"When it gets cold."

I accompanied them through the outer office into the hallway, where I shook Jeremy Cuttle's corded old hand and we said good-bye. I resisted the urge to follow them out to their car. If they drove away in anything but a 1961 Studebaker I might not have been able to handle the disappointment.

Two

I killed an hour in the microfilm reading room at the library catching up on the Children of Solomon.

It was a fundamentalist religious group founded in the 1970s by a party named Bertram Comfort on the grounds that the New Testament and Christian thought were upstarts and that the way to salvation led through a belief in a vengeful God, tempered with the wisdom of King Solomon. Although a number of complaints had been filed against the sect's youth camp in the north woods, mostly for breach of the peace, the outstate press remained unaware of the order's existence until a fourteen-year-old boy died in one of the cabins, his body bearing the unmistakable signs of a severe beating.

The camp was closed by injunction and an investigation was launched, but no evidence surfaced to disprove Comfort's testimony that the boy died in their care after receiving rough treatment Solomon only knew where. The Children themselves were unpaid volunteers working in the light of their faith and the people who sent their children to the camp were members and patrons of the church, which was not recognized as such by the state.

There was nothing to indicate that Comfort and his disciples would shoot at an old man in order to acquire real estate in South-eastern Michigan, but before heading out the Cuttles' way I went back to the office and strapped on the Smith & Wesson. Any place that hadn't had a murder in more than 120 years was past due.

Three

An hour west of Detroit the snow stopped falling and the sun came out, glaring hard off a field of white that blended pavement with countryside; even the overpasses looked like the ruins of Atlantis rearing out of a salt sea. The farther I got from town the more the scenery resembled a Perry Como Christmas special, rolling away to the horizon with frosted trees and here and there a homeowner in Es-kimo dress shoveling his driveway. The mall builders and fast food chains had left droppings there just like everywhere else, but on days like that you remembered that kids still sledded down hills too steep for them and set out to build the world's tallest snowman and lay on their backs in the snow fanning their arms and legs to make angels.

Judy had told me she and Jeremy were living in a trailer behind the old Stage Stop, which stood on a hill overlooking Old US-23 near the exit from the younger expressway. At the end of the ramp, an aging barn she had also told me about provided more directions in the form of a painted advertisement flaking off the end wall. I turned that way, straddling a hump of snow left in the middle of the road by a county plow. Over a hill and then the gray frame saltbox she had described thrust itself between me and a bright sky.

As it turned out, I wouldn't have needed either the sign or the di-rections. The rotating beacon of a county sheriff's car bounced red and blue light off the front of the building.

I parked among a collection of civilian cars and pickup trucks and followed footsteps in the snow past the county unit, left unattended with its flashers on and the two-way radio hawking and spitting at top volume, toward a fourteen-foot house-trailer parked behind the empty tavern. A crowd was breaking up there, helped along by a gangling young deputy in uniform who was shooing them like chickens. He moved in front of me as I stepped toward the trailer.

"We got business here, mister. Please help us by minding yours."

I showed him the license, which might have been in cuneiform for all the reaction it got. "I'm working for the Cuttles. Who's in charge?"

"Sergeant Springer. Until the detectives show up from the county seat, anyway. You're not one of them."

I held out a card. "Please tell him the Cuttles hired me this morning."

He looked past me, saw the first of the civilian vehicles pulling out, and took the card. "Wait." He circled behind the trailer. After a few minutes he came back and beckoned me from the end.

The sergeant was a hard-looking stump about my age with silver splinters in the black hair at his temples and flat tired eyes under a fur cap. The muscles in his jaw were bunched like grapeshot. He was standing ankle-deep in snow fifty feet from the trailer with his back to it on the edge of a five-acre field that ended in a line of firs on the other side. A few yards beyond him, a man and woman lay spread-eagled side by side on their faces in the snow. The backs of the man's suitcoat and the woman's overcoat were smeared red. More red stained the snow around them in a bright fan. They were dressed exactly as I had last seen Judy and Jeremy Cuttle.

"Figure the son of a bitch gave them a running start," the sergeant said as I joined him. "Maybe he told them if they made it to the trees they were home free."

"Who found them?" I asked.

"Paper boy came to collect. When they didn't answer his knock he went looking."

"Anybody hear the shots?"

"It's rabbit season. Day goes by without a couple of shotgun blasts…" He let it dangle. "Your name's Walker? Ollie Springer. I command the substation here." I could feel the wire strength in his grip through the leather glove. "What'd they hire you for?"

"To hooraw the Children of Solomon. Jeremy thought they were the ones who took a shot at him yesterday. Who identified them?"

"It's them all right. I started running errands for the Cuttles when I was six and my parents knew them before that. If Comfort's bunch did this I'll nail every damn one of them to a cross." His jaw muscles worked.

"Any sign of a struggle?"

"Trailer's neat as a button. Judy was the last of the great home-makers. Bastard must've got the drop on them. Jeremy didn't talk much, but he was a fighter. You don't want to mess with these old farmers. But you can't fight a jinx."

"What kind of jinx?"

"The Stage Stop. Everybody who ever had anything to do with the place came to no good. Last guy who ran it went bankrupt. One before that tried to torch the place for the insurance and died in prison. I took a run at it myself once—nest egg for my retirement—and then my wife walked out on me. I guess I should've tried to talk them out of it. Not that they'd have listened."

"Mind if I take a look inside the trailer?"

"Why, didn't they pay you?"

"Excuse me, Sergeant," I said, "but go to hell."

He went over me with his cop's eyes, grunted. "Go in with him, Gordy. Make sure he doesn't touch anything."

There was a door on that side of the trailer, but the deputy and I went around to the side facing the Stage Stop. Gordy should have set up his post closer to the road; the path to the door had been trampled all over by curious citizens, obliterating the killer's footprints and those of any herd of Clydesdales that might have happened by. Inside, Judy Cuttle had done what she could to turn a mobile home into an Edwardian farmhouse, complete with antimacassars and rusty photos in bamboo frames of geezers in waistcoats and glum women in cameos. A .20-gauge Remington pump shotgun, still a fixture in Michigan country houses, leaned in a corner of the tiny parlor. Without touching it I bent over to sniff the muzzle. It hadn't been fired recently.

"Jeremy's, Ollie says," the deputy reported. "He used to shoot pheasants till he slowed down."

The door we had entered through had a window with a clear view to the tavern and the road beyond. The purse Judy had carried into my office lay on a lamp table near the door. The quality of the housekeeping said she hadn't intended it to stay there for long. I wondered if they'd even had a chance to take off their hats before receiving their last visitor.

An unmarked Dodge was parked next to the patrol car when we came out. On the other side we found a plainclothesman in conversation with Sergeant Springer while his partner examined the bodies. Their business with me didn't take any longer than Springer's. I thanked the sergeant for talking to me and left.

So far the whole thing stank; and in snow, yet.

Four

Judy Cuttle's directions were still working. A houseboy or something in a turtleneck and whipcord trousers answered the door of a gray stone house on the edge of the nearby town and showed me into a room paneled in fruitwood with potted plants on the built-in shelves. I was alone for only a few seconds when Bertram Comfort joined me.

He was a well-upholstered fifty in a brown suit off the rack, with fading red hair brushed gently back from a bulging forehead and no visible neck. His hands were pink and plump and hairless, and grasping one was like shaking hands with a baby. He waved me into a padded chair and sat down himself behind a desk anchored by a chrome doodad on one end and a King James Bible the size of a hand-truck on the other.

"Is it Reverend Comfort?" I asked.

"Mister will do." His voice had the enveloping quality of a maiden aunt's sofa. "I'm merely a lay reader. Are you with the prosecutor's office up north? I thought that tragic business was settled."

"I'm working for Judy and Jeremy Cuttle. I'm a private investigator."

He looked as if he were going to cry. "I told the officer none of the Children were near the property yesterday. I wish these people could lay aside the suspicions of the secular world long enough to understand it is not we but Solomon who sits in judgment."

"I notice you refer to it as *the* property, not *their* property. Do you still hope to obtain it for your camp?"

"Not *my* camp. Solomon's. All the legal avenues have not yet been traveled."

"It's the illegal ones I'm interested in. Maybe you've got a rebel in the fold. It happens in the best of families, even the God-fearing ones."

"The Children love God; we don't fear Him. And everyone is accounted for at the time of yesterday's unfortunate incident."

"Yesterday's yesterday. I'm here about today."

"Today?"

"Somebody shotgunned the Cuttles behind their trailer about an hour ago. Give or take."

"Great Glory!" He glanced at the Bible. "Are they—"

"Gone to God. Knocking on the pearly. Purgatory bound. Dead as a mackerel."

"I find your mockery abhorrent under the circumstances. Do the police think the Children are involved?"

"The police think what the police think. I'm not the police. Yesterday somebody potted at Jeremy Cuttle, or maybe just at his hat as a warning. Today he and his wife engaged me to investigate. Now they're not in a position to engage anything but six feet of God's good earth. I'm a detective. I see a connection." I looked at my watch. "It's three o'clock. Do you know where the Children are?"

Again his eyes strayed to the Bible. Then he placed his pudgy hands on the desk, jacked himself to his feet, and hiked up his belt, the way fat men do. "I have Solomon's work to attend to. 'Go thou from the presence of a foolish man when thou perceivest not in him the lips of knowledge.'"

"'Sticks and stones may break my bones,'" I said, rising, "but any parakeet can memorize sentences." I went me from his presence.

Five

Ed Snilly, the lawyer who had recommended me to the Cuttles, lived in an Edwardian farmhouse on eighty acres with a five-year-old Fleetwood parked in the driveway sporting a bumper sticker reading HAVE YOU HUGGED YOUR HOGS TODAY? His wife, fifty-odd years of pork and potatoes stuffed into stretch jeans, directed me to the large yellow barn behind the house, where I found him tossing ears of dried corn from a bucket into a row of stalls occupied by chugging, snuffling pigs.

"One of my neighbors called me with the news," he said after he'd set down the bucket and shaken my hand. He was a wiry old scarecrow in his seventies with a spotty bald head and false teeth in a jaw too narrow for them. "Terrible thing. I've known Judy and Jeremy since the Depression. I'd gladly help out the prosecution on this one gratis. Do you suspect Comfort?"

"I'd like to. Did you represent the Cuttles when they bought the Stage Stop?"

"Yes. It was an estate sale, very complicated. Old Man Herndon's heirs wanted to liquidate quickly and wouldn't carry any paper. Jeremy negotiated to the last penny. I also stood up with them at the hearing with the State Liquor Control Commission. A license transfer can be pretty thorny without chicanery. I'm not sure we'd have swung it if Ollie Springer hadn't appeared to vouch for them."

"I'm surprised he spoke up. He told me the place was jinxed."

"I can see why he'd feel that way. Old Man Herndon was Ollie's father-in-law. The Stage Stop was going to be a belated wedding present, but that ended when Herndon's daughter ran out on Ollie. The rumor was she ditched him for some third rate rock singer who came through here a couple of years back. I think that's what killed the old man."

"So far this place is getting to be almost as interesting as Detroit."

"Scandals happen everywhere, but in the main we country folk look out for one another. That's why Ollie helped Judy and Jeremy in spite of his personal tragedy. To be honest, I thought they were getting in over their heads too, especially later when they talked about digging a wine cellar and adding a room for pool. They were looking far beyond your usual mom-and-pop operation."

"Is gaming that big hereabouts?"

"Son, people around here will go to a christening and bet on when the baby's first tooth will come in. Phil Costa's made a fortune off the pool tables in the basement of his bowling alley out on M-52. Lord knows I've represented enough of his clientele at their arraignments every time Ollie's raided the place."

"Little Phil? Last I heard he was doing something like seven to twelve in Jackson for fixing the races at Hazel Park."

"He's out two years now, and smarter than when he went in. These rural county commissioners stay fixed longer than the city kind. Phil never seems to be around when the deputies bust in."

"So if the Cuttles went ahead and put in their poolroom, Little Phil might have lost business."

"It's a thought." Snilly picked up his bucket and resumed scattering ears of corn in the stalls. "A thought is what it is."

• • •

The Paul Bunyan Bowl-A-Rama, an aluminum hangar with a two-story neon lumberjack bowling on its roof, looked abashed at midafternoon, like a nude dancer caught under a conventional electric bulb. A young thick-shouldered bouncer who hadn't bothered to change out of his overalls on his way in from the back forty conferred with the office and came back to escort me past the lanes.

Little Phil Costa crowded four-foot ten in his two-inch elevators, a sour-faced baldy in his middle years with pointed features like a Chihuahua's. Small men are usually neat, but his tie was loose, his sleeves rolled up unevenly, and an archaeologist could have reconstructed his last five meals from the stains on his unbuttoned vest. He didn't look up from the adding-machine tapes he was sorting through on a folding card table when I entered. "Tell Lorraine the support check's in the mail. I ain't about to bust my parole over the brat."

"I'm not from your ex. I'm working for the Cuttles."

"What the hell's a Cuttle?"

I told him. He scowled, but it was at a wrong sum on one of the tapes. He corrected it with a pencil stub. "I heard about it. I hope you got your bread up front."

"Talk is Judy and Jeremy were going to add a pool room to the Stage Stop."

"How about that. What's six times twelve?"

"Think of it in terms of years in stir." I laid a hand on top of the tape. "A few years back, two guys who were operating their handbook in one of your neighborhoods were shotgunned behind the New Hellas Cafe in Hamtramck. The cops never did pin it to you, but nobody's tried to cut in on you since. Until the Cuttles."

The farm boy-bouncer took a step forward, but Costa stopped him with a hand. "Get the bottle."

It was a pinch bottle filled with amber liquid. Costa took it without looking away from me and broke the seal. "You a drinking man, Walker?"

"In the right company. This isn't it."

"I wasn't offering. This stuff's twenty-four years old, flown in special for me from Aberdeen. Seventy-five bucks a fifth." He upended it over his metal wastebasket. When it gurgled empty he tossed in the bottle. "On their best night, that's what the Cuttles' room might cost me. Still think I iced them?"

"I'm way past that," I said. "Now I'm wondering who takes out your trash."

"You trade in information, I'll treat you. Check out a guy named Chuckie Noyes. He's a Child of Solomon, squats in the cemetery behind the Stage Stop property, the old caretaker's hut. I knew him in Jackson before he got religion. He did eleven years for killing a druggie in Detroit. Used a shotgun."

"Why so generous?"

He tipped a hand toward the adding-machine tapes. "I got a good thing here, closest I ever been to legit in my life. Last thing I need's some sticky snoop coming back and back, drawing attention. Time was I'd just have Horace here adjust your spine, but if there's one thing I learned on the block it's diplomacy. Dangle, now. I open at dusk."

"Seventy-two," I said.

"What?"

"Six times twelve."

"Hey, thanks." He wrote it down. "Come back some night when you're not working and bowl a couple of lines. On the house."

• • •

For the second time that day, police strobes had beaten me to my destination. They lanced the shadows gathering among the leaning headstones in what might have been a churchyard before the central building had burned down sometime around Appomattox. Near its charred foundation stood a galvanized steel shed with a slanted roof and a door cut in one side. As I was getting out of the car, two uniformed attendants wheeled a body bag on a stretcher out through the door and into the back of an ambulance that was almost as big as the shed. Sergeant Springer came out behind them, deep in conversation with a man six inches taller in a snap brim hat and a coat with a fur collar. The two were enveloped in the vapor of their own spent breath.

"I'll want it on my desk in the morning," said the big man, pausing to shake Springer's hand before pulling on his gloves.

"Will do, Lieutenant."

The lieutenant touched his shoulder. "Bad day all around, Ollie. Get some rest before you talk to the shooting team." He boarded an unmarked Dodge with a magnetic flasher on the roof. The motor turned over sluggishly and caught.

"Chuckie Noyes?" I asked Springer.

He looked up at me, then down at his fur cap. "Yeah." He put it on.

"Who shot him, you?"

"Uh-huh."

"He do the Cuttles?"

"Looks like."

"You're not the only one having a bad day, Sergeant."

"Guess you're right." He fastened the snaps on his jacket. "I came here to ask Noyes some questions, thought he might have seen or heard something living so close. He had an antique pin on this chest of drawers by his bed. Judy wore that pin to church every Sunday. Don't know how I missed not seeing it in the trailer. Noyes saw it same time I did. He tried for my gun."

"Were you alone?"

"What?" He lamped me hard.

"Nothing. You folks in the country do things differently."

"I don't expect to lose sleep over squashing a germ like that, but it doesn't mean I wanted to. Now we'll never know if he was work-

ing for Comfort or if he slipped the rest of the way over the edge
and acted solo. He had a record for violence."

"So Little Phil said."

"That germ. Guess you'll talk to just about anybody."

"It's a job."

"A stinking job."

"Everything about this one stinks," I agreed. "Sleep tight, Sergeant."

Six

I'd always heard God-fearing people went to bed with the chickens.
Another myth gone.

At 11:45 P.M. I was still parked down the road from Bertram
Comfort's gray stone house, where I'd been for over an hour, warm-
ing my calcifying marrow with judicious transfusions of hot coffee
from a Thermos and waiting for the lights to go out downstairs. A
couple of minutes later they did. I was tempted to go in then but sat
tight. Just after midnight the single lighted window on the second
story went black. Then I moved.

I'd brought my pocket burglar kit, but just for the hell of it I
tried the knob on the front door. Comfort had the old churchman's
prejudice against locks. I let myself in.

I also had my pencil flash, but I didn't use that either. There was
a moon and the glow reflecting off the snow shone bright as my best
hopes through the windows. I found my way to the study without
tripping over anything.

I didn't waste time going through the desk or looking behind
the religious paintings for a wall safe. During my interview with

Comfort his eyes had strayed to the big Bible on the desk one too many times for even the devoutest of reasons.

The book was genuine enough. There were no hollowed-out pages and an elaborate red-and-gold bookplate pasted to the flyleaf read TO MR. BERTRAM EZEKIEL COMFORT, FATHER OF THE FAITH, FROM THE CHILDREN OF SOLOMON, flanked by Adam and Eve in fig leaves. A dozen strips of microfilm spilled out of a pocket in the spine when I tilted the book.

I carried the strips over to the window and held them up to the moonlight. They were photographed documents bearing the identification of the records departments of various police organizations. The farthest came from Los Angeles. The closest belonged to Detroit. I read that one. Then I put it in my inside breast pocket, returned the others to the Bible and the Bible to its place on the desk, and left, my sabbatical completed on the bones of another Commandment.

Seven

The next day was clear and twenty degrees. The sky had no ceiling and the sun on the snow was a sea of cold white fire. Breathing was like inhaling needles.

The air was colder inside the empty Stage Stop building with the raw damp of enclosed winter. The old floorboards rang like iron when I stepped on them and my breath steamed around the gaunt timbers that held up the roof. Owls nested in the rafters. The new yellow two-by-fours stacked along the walls were bright with the anticipation of a dead couple's exploded vision.

"Jesus, it's cold in here," said Ollie Springer, pushing aside the front door, which hung on a single scabbed hinge, "Is the cold locker closed at Pete's Meats?"

"It's a hall. The Cuttles might have appreciated the choice. Thanks for coming, Sergeant."

"You made it sound important over the phone. It better be. The lieutenant's waiting for my report on Chuckie Noyes."

"I've got something you might want to add." I handed him the microfilm slip I'd taken from Comfort's Bible.

"What is it?"

"Noyes's arrest report on a homicide squeal he went down for in Detroit a dozen years ago. Since you mentioned his record yesterday I thought you'd like to see the name of the arresting officer."

He was holding it up to a shaft of sunlight coming in through an empty window, but he wasn't reading.

"The city cops are jealous of their reputations," I said. "When they take a killer into custody they sometimes forget to release the name of the rural cop who actually busted him during his flight to freedom; but a report's a report. Just a deputy then, weren't you?"

"This doesn't mean anything." He crumpled the strip into a ball and threw it behind the stack of lumber.

"Detroit has the original. Bertram Comfort maintains the loyalty of the more recalcitrant members of his flock by keeping tabs on their past indiscretions; that's where I got the copy. I figure when you found out Noyes was back in circulation and hanging around your jurisdiction, you either hired him to kill Judy and Jeremy or more likely threatened to bust him on some parole beef if he didn't cooperate. Then you offed him to keep him from talking and planted Judy's pin in the caretaker's hut where he was living. The simple plans are always the best. As a Child of Solomon he'd be blamed for try-ing to help secure the Stage Stop property for Comfort's new camp.

"I guess I'm responsible for accelerating their deaths," I went on. "Someone—you, probably—made a last ditch attempt to scare them off the other day by taking a potshot at Jeremy. When he and Judy hired me instead to investigate, you switched to Plan B before I could get a foothold. You're one impulsive cop, Sergeant."

"Why would I want to kill the Cuttles? They're like my second parents." He rested his hand on his sidearm, a nickel-plated .38 with a black knurled grip.

"It bothered me too, especially when I found out you spoke up for them at the hearing before the State Liquor Control Commission. But that didn't jibe with what you told me about thinking this place had a hoodoo. I should have guessed the truth when Ed Snilly said they decided later to expand the Stage Stop. At first I thought it was their plans for a pool room and the competition it would create for Phil Costa, but that was chump change to him, not worth killing over. It was the wine cellar."

"What wine cellar?"

"There isn't one now, but there was going to be. You were right in there cheering them on, in spite of your own bad luck with the place and the wife you said left you, until you found out they were going to dig a hole." I paced as I spoke, circling a soft spot in the floor where the old boards had rotted and sunk into a depression eight feet across. He was watching me, trying to keep from staring at my feet. His fingers curled around the grip of the revolver. I said, "I made some calls this morning from my motel room in town, got the name of that rock singer everyone says your wife ran off with. I called eight booking agents before I found one who used to work with him. He didn't skip with anyone's wife. He died of a drug overdose in Cincinnati a couple of months after he played here. Nobody was with him or had been for some time."

"If you stayed at the motel you know she spent a night with him there," Springer said. "It was all over the county next day. They were both gone by then."

"Your wife didn't go as far as he did. No more than six feet from where we're standing, and all of it straight down. Those rotten boards lift right out. I checked before you got here."

"Plenty of room under there for two." He drew his gun.

"Drop it, Ollie!"

He pivoted, snapping off a shot. The bullet knocked a splinter off the big timber the sheriff's lieutenant had been hiding behind. The big man returned fire. Springer shouted, fell down, and grasped his thigh.

"Drop it, I said."

The sergeant looked down at the gun he was still holding as if he'd forgotten about it. He opened his hand and let it fall.

"Thanks, Lieutenant." I took the Smith & Wesson out of my coat pocket and lowered the hammer gently. "Sorry about the cold wait."

He holstered his own gun under his fur-lined coat. "Ollie was right about this place." He shook loose a pair of handcuffs.

I left while he was reading Springer his Miranda and went out into the cold sunshine of the country.

Major Crimes

One

Deborah Stonesmith was a tall black woman with auburn-tinted hair sprayed into hard waves and heavy hips tastefully disguised under a tailored gray herringbone suit. The steel desk in her office just came to her knees when she rose like a man to grasp my hand. The gesture didn't seem out of place at all; but for a spray of daisies in a cut-glass vase on the desk, the room might have belonged to any of the male detectives in the squad. When we were seated, she put on a pair of gold-rimmed glasses hanging from a chain around her neck to read my ID, then took them off and returned the folder and leaned back in her yellow leather swivel, steepling a pair of surprisingly slender hands without a ring or long nails.

"What brings you down to Major Crimes, Mr. Walker?"

Her voice fell around the middle register, a little hoarse at the edges like a saloon singer's. I said:

"I'm working for Midwest Life, Automobile & Casualty this month. Stan Draper there hired me to look into this Gendron kill that went down Tuesday. Gendron's wife stands to collect a quarter million on the double indemnity clause and its Midwest's policy, excuse the expression, to investigate all claims above fifty thousand. I understand it's your case."

She smiled tightly. "How *is* Stan?"

"Three sheets to the wind, same as always. You know him?"

"We pulled stakeout together once when I was in uniform. That was before they broke him for keeping a pint of Ten High in the glove compartment." She turned the chair to the left and back again. "We made a collar in the Gendron case this morning. This kid tried to buy a tape deck at a Radio Shack downtown with bills on the hot serial number list. He's rolling over on his partners right now."

"I heard. When can I talk to him?"

"Not until after he's arraigned, and maybe not even then. The P.D. on this one's a real nutcracker and I'm not going to stray from the book and take a chance on blowing it all over some technicality. We got a textbook arrest on a drugstore heist and the murder of an innocent bystander and that's how it's going to stay."

I tapped a Winston out of my pack and spiked it between my lips. "I'd like to see the autopsy report on Gendron."

"So would I. We're still waiting on it. All I've got so far is the bullet that killed him, a .38. The kid didn't have a gun on him when we picked him up and his apartment is clean, if you call a drawerful of controlled substances and a stack of naughty pictures clean. He says it was one of the others pulled the trigger. I would too."

"Yeah. Did you ever find out what a PR consultant was doing in a drugstore in the middle of the morning on a weekday?"

"Getting cigarettes, his secretary said. Look, you think his wife sent him there to get squiffed? One of the scroats popped him in front of four witnesses on their way out the door."

"The questions have to get asked." I lit up and flipped the match into the glass ashtray on the desk. "This kid got a sheet?"

She fingered her eyeglasses, smiling the tight smile. "Three disorderlies and a shoplifting. Copped a pair of nylon panties from the downtown Hudson's, when there was a downtown Hudson's. His size. Did I say those pictures we found in his apartment were all of men?"

"Not exactly Machine Gun Kelly."

"These days you don't have to be. All it takes is an expensive hobby, like doing pills and cruising the fag bars on Woodward."

"Any provocation for the shoot?"

"Witnesses say no. Just another good-bye kill. We get them."

"Was Gendron killed instantly?"

"Twelve paces, straight through the heart."

"They're getting better."

"I've got a ballistics expert wants his autograph."

I burned some more tobacco. Then I squashed out my butt half-smoked and rose. "Thanks, Inspector. I hope you get the others."

"We will. We don't see many mysteries in Major Crimes. You see Stan, tell him Deb said hi."

She put on her glasses and I let myself out. She looked as much like a Deb as I look like an Irving.

Two

The Gendron house stood in St. Clair Shores a block off the lake, really just a broad spot in the Detroit River where rich people from Grosse Pointe with nothing better to do sail catamarans and worry about their putting. It was a brick colonial with a midget windmill on the front lawn and a yellow Citroen parked behind a black Camaro in the circular driveway. I parked behind the Citroen and got out and when I rang the doorbell a tall party with receding gray hair answered. He had on a camel-hair sportcoat over a white turtleneck and black wool peg-topped pants. His face was tanned.

"I'm Amos Walker," I said, before he could say, "Yes-s?", and handed him a card. "I'm an investigator with the late Mr. Gendron's insurance underwriters. I wonder if I might ask Mrs. Gendron a few questions."

"I doubt it." His gaze fell somewhere behind me. It was a powder-blue gaze. What color it was behind the contacts was anybody's guess.

I said, "It has to do with whether or not Midwest pays off her claim."

"Mrs. Gendron is under sedation. I'm Dr. Redding, the family—her physician." He made the change with a slight twitch of his very black eyebrows. They looked lacquered on. "Perhaps later, when the shock has worn off—"

"Did you know Mr. Gendron well?"

"Very. He was my friend before he was my patient."

"Maybe I could talk to you."

He moved his eyebrows, then stood aside to let me in. The living room was done in beige, with blonde furniture and a twist of bleached driftwood resting on the mantel of a pale stone fireplace. A bloodless room, professionally decorated. He offered me the ivory-colored sofa and helped himself to a thin cigar from his inside breast pocket.

"Shocking habit, especially for a doctor." He lit it with a Zippo and got a Winston burning for me. I noticed he chewed his nails. "We're as weak as everyone else."

"Didn't I see your name in Gendron's file?"

"I conducted his physical when he applied for the policy last year."

"Was that the last time you examined him?"

"No. I gave him his annual just six weeks ago. He was in excellent condition for a man of forty, though he could've stood to lose ten pounds."

"Every doctor says that. You knew him socially?"

"Dick and I became friends when he was a freshman at Michigan and I was interning in the hospital there. I introduced him to his wife." He flipped some ash into the tray on the blonde coffee table.

"How was he emotionally?"

"In good spirits. Maybe a little harried. Public Relations is a cannibal profession. I've referred a number of Dick's colleagues to stress counseling. Not him, though. He coped."

I added some ash of my own to the pile. The tray contained two of his cigar stubs and a number of shredded cigarette butts with pink lipstick stains on the tips. "Would you know if he had money troubles?"

He stroked the brown underside of his chin. "Is there something suspicious about Dick's death? I thought it was established he was killed at random by some strung-out bandit."

"That's how it looks. I'm just stitching up the loose corners. People who live in nice houses like this have a tendency to go into the hole."

"I wouldn't know about that."

It sounded stiff. "Just asking," I said. "Friends usually know about those things. How were relations between him and his wife?"

"They were devoted to each other. Really, I'm curious. Does someone imagine he threw himself in front of that bullet just to cheat the insurance company?"

"It's happened."

"Not with Dick. He had too much to live for." He killed his cigar. "I think that if Lynn were standing where I am she'd be asking you to leave about now."

"He's just doing his job, Tim."

I'm some detective. I hadn't heard her entering the room through the doorway behind me. I stood and turned to look at a small brunette in her mid-thirties, wearing a pageboy haircut and a blue satin dressing gown trimmed in ruffles. Her feet were bare in flat-heeled sandals and she was without make-up but for a touch of pink on her lips. She wouldn't need much else. Her eyes were a little puffed.

"I heard you talking," she said. "I'm Lynn Gendron, Dick's— widow."

"Then you can answer the questions I was asking Dr. Redding."

"Lynn, you should be resting."

"What does it matter? Dick's the first thing I think of when I wake up. My husband was a happy man, Mr.—?"

"Walker."

She smiled her thanks sadly. "He worked hard and it took its toll on his nerves, but he liked the work and he loved me. We had the usual debts, nothing we couldn't stay on top of. The house is mortgaged and we—I owe three more payments on the car. If that's something to panic over, this whole neighborhood should be half berserk."

"That's the Camaro you owe on?" I asked.

"Yes," offered Redding. "The Citroen is mine. *All* mine."

The cigarette was burning my fingers. I got rid of it. "It's good you still make house calls."

"Only in special cases. Lynn is a dear friend. Now, I really must insist you go. Despite what Lynn says, time alone is the best cure for grief."

"Alone with you, you mean."

He did the trick with the eyebrows. "I think I resent that."

"When will you know?"

"Good-bye, Mr. Walker," cut in Mrs. Gendron. She sounded more tired than angry. I thanked her for her help and left while Redding was still making the effort to be civilized.

Three

Hegelman Associates, advertising and public relations, occupied the twenty-second floor of the Penobscot Building, a grand old pile of granite and red marble in downtown Detroit that looked as if it was willing to tolerate all that space-age plastic going up along the river-front for a while longer anyway. I followed a short carpeted corridor from the elevator to a desk behind which a China doll in a stiff blouse and Max Factor directed me to Richard Gendron's office. The woman I found there wasn't quite as pretty, but she didn't work as hard at it. I liked her slight overbite and the wisp of soft brown hair that strayed out over her forehead. She read my card and her face got drawn.

"Mr. Hegelman said someone from the insurance company would be coming by," she said quietly. "He said we should all cooperate."

Her voice broke a little. I said, "Gendron was a good boss, huh."

"He was a good *man*. When I threw out my back bending over to open a file drawer, the company tried to deny me compensation. Dick—Mr. Gendron stormed into Mr. Hegelman's office in the middle of a conference and threatened to quit if my claim wasn't honored. I got my first check two days later. He took care of his people."

"All his people, or just you?"

Her chin came up. "I'm happily married and so was he. Ask anyone on the staff; they've all got stories just like mine. He did right by all of us, even if it meant breaking the rules."

"Sorry. I'm starting from scratch, that's all. Can I look in his office?"

She said the door was unlocked and I went inside. It was a corner room, looking down on Griswold to the west and out on the Renaissance Center to the south, a giant poker-chip caddy with the handle gone. An original architect's drawing of the Penobscot Building hung on the east wall and a framed studio shot of Gendron's wife Lynn shared the desk with a telephone pad and a complicated intercom. The drawers yielded pens, stationery, a paperback book, and a carton of Pall Malls.

The telephone pad was blank. I picked it up and riffled through it. A business card slid out onto the desk. I read it.

I studied the buttons on the intercom for a minute, then gave up and went back into the outer office. Gendron's secretary looked up from her typing.

"Your boss said he was going to the store for cigarettes?"

"Yes. We had an agreement: I wouldn't try to talk him into quitting, and he wouldn't send me out to maintain his habit. We—"

"What brand did he smoke?"

"What brand? Pall Malls."

"Any thoughts on why he'd go out for cigarettes—when he had a ten-day supply in his desk?"

She shook her head.

I laid the business card on top of the typewriter. The legend was embossed in tasteful blue on pebbled beige stock:

Reliance Investigations
"Courtesy, Efficiency, Confidentiality"

"What business would he have had for a private investigator?" I asked.

"It must have fallen out of the Turner file," she said, and stopped. Something fluttered across her face; a confidence betrayed.

"Who's Turner?"

"I'm sorry, I can't answer that."

"Not even if it means finding out why Gendron died?"

She looked up at me with dry eyes. "Discretion was very important to Dick. He practiced it in everything he did. He'd want me to do the same no matter what."

"Okay." I left the card where I had put it. "Did he confide in you personally?"

"Such as what?"

"Such as his health." I brought out the paperback book I had found in Gendron's desk. A pastoral cover, doves circling a meadow in blossom, the title in gentle script: COPING WITH TERMINAL ILLNESS.

She stared at it a long time. "Maybe it was someone he knew. His mother or father. Or his wife."

"Maybe. Have the police been here?"

"Just to talk. None of them went into the office."

"No need, for a simple robbery killing. Can I use your telephone? It's a local call."

She said go ahead and I dialed police headquarters and asked for Deborah Stonesmith in Major Crimes. After a minute her saloon-singer voice came on the line.

"Walker, Inspector," I said. "Did that autopsy sheet come through?"

"On my desk. What do you need, if it's quick?"

"Gendron's physical condition at time of death. Was he suffering from cancer, heart disease, anything that would snuff him if the bullet didn't?"

"Nope. I should be so healthy."

"Okay, thanks. How's the investigation?"

"Hot as hell. We found the kid's partners right where he said we would. They're being processed now."

"Names?"

"After the arraignment tomorrow morning."

I thanked her again and we were through talking. The secretary's eyes were on me. "Gendron was sound as a rock," I said.

"Surprised?"

"Only a little."

Four

Back in my office I removed the *Free Press* movie section from the telephone and called Hal Needham at Reliance Investigations. When I wasn't working for Midwest or following someone's husband through the after-hours places downtown or looking for someone's daughter in the Cass Corridor, I sometimes farmed myself out to Reliance, and Hal and I had worked in tandem enough times to owe each other some favors. I recognized his Kansas twang as soon as he answered.

"Walker? Call you back."

The telephone rang a minute later. When I picked it up he said, "Sorry. Krell's got a tap on all the incoming lines. This one's clean."

"How can you work for him?"

"I got a gifted daughter and I'm starting a bail fund for my son. What's the favor?"

"Guy named Richard Gendron at Hegelman Associates did some business with Reliance a while back, something to do with someone or something named Turner. I need the details."

He whistled. "It gets back to Krell he'll play the 'Rogue's March' over the office P.A. and break my men's room key over his knee."

"He won't get it from me."

"This one's worth a dinner. At least."

"You pick the place."

"Whose sheet are you on?"

"Midwest is picking up the expenses on this one."

"In that case, make it the London Chop House. Give me a half hour."

I said okay and broke the connection. Next I tried Lee Horst downtown. Lee's an information broker, and if you're on his accepted list he'll hand you the inside track on anyone or anything in the Detroit area, provided you meet his price. He picked up the receiver himself; no secretaries or assistants to undersell Lee.

"Timothy Redding," he repeated in his high soft voice, after I had told him what I needed. "M.D.?"

"I'll get back to you."

The counter down the street from my building served me a three-course dinner—tuna fish sandwich, coffee, and a bill—and I unlocked the door to my office again just as the telephone started ringing. It was Hal Needham.

"Turner Chemicals," he said. "They went to Hegelman looking for a better public image and Gendron got the assignment. He observed their operation for a month and made recommendations that included a dress code for office personnel and a pink slip for the dispatcher in their Warren plant."

"How come the canning?"

"Gendron didn't think it was good business practice to keep an armed robber on the payroll. Guy's name was Phil Hardy and he had priors going back to the riots. Also he was driving a new red Pontiac Firebird that he didn't buy on a dispatcher's salary."

"I like that part," I said. "I like it a lot. Tomorrow night okay for the chop house?"

"I'm not eating a bite until then." He laughed shortly and hung up.

Lee Horst didn't call back that day. I dialed my service and asked them to reroute all calls to my home telephone, then closed the office. At home I watched a little TV, dealt myself a couple of losing games of Solitaire, and turned in early. All that dialing can really take it out of you.

Five

In the morning I showered, dressed, and turned on the radio for the news while the coffee was brewing. When the announcer had finished with Washington and the Middle East he noted that three men had been arraigned ten minutes before in Recorder's Court in connection with Tuesday's drugstore robbery and the murder of Richard Gendron. He gave two names I didn't recognize and we pronounced the third one together. Philip Hardy.

"Yeah. I want his finances, but if you find anything else juicy I'll take that too."

Stonesmith was a few minutes getting rid of the reporters and coming to the telephone. I congratulated her on the arrests. She said, "Save it for the convictions. Jay Albert Matthews represented them at the arraignment."

Matthews had defended a millionaire's daughter or two and written a best-selling book, *Mistakes of Darrow* or something on that order. "Who's paying him?" I asked.

"Privileged information, *he* said. It sure isn't any of those three."

"I think I know."

"Well, spill it."

"Privileged information, Inspector."

I hung up on whatever name she was calling me and lifted the receiver again and got Lee Horst just as he was entering his office. He apologized for not calling.

"Computer was down, and isn't that the most popular new lie this season?" Keys clattered on his end. "Okay, I got a readout on Dr. Redding. You want it over the phone or on paper?"

I said over the telephone was fine, and smoked two cigarettes while he was feeding it to me.

When he was through I asked him how much.

"For you, a hundred."

"You're a fraud, Lee."

"My informants like to eat, what can I say?"

I promised to get a check off to him that week. Then I went out without finishing my coffee.

Six

The yellow Citroen was parked in the same spot behind Lynn Gendron's Camaro when I climbed out of my own crate. It might not have moved since yesterday, but Redding was too discreet for that. A discreet fellow was Dr. Redding.

"What now?"

He had shed the camel-hair for a sober blue serge suit and knitted black necktie. This time he stood across the doorway with his feet spread, a graying sentinel with a Palm Beach tan. I said, "We can go inside or we can talk out here. My voice carries."

After a beat he let me pass. Gendron's widow was sitting on the sofa in a snug-fitting black dress that caught her just below the knees. A pair of gray cotton gloves lay on the coffee table in front of her, next to a barrel glass half-full of amber liquid.

"Dick's funeral is this morning." Redding closed the door. "Can't this wait until after?"

"What'd you tell him, cancer?" I said.

His lacquered eyebrows squirmed. "What?"

"Cancer, probably. It's a buzzword, bound to have the extreme effect you were after. How deep are you in debt really, Redding? My information says six figures."

"Are you drunk? You're babbling."

"This is a computer society. Everything's on record. Your house in Grosse Pointe has a third mortgage and you dumped a ton of preferred stock at a loss to keep the loan sharks happy downtown. You're into the IRS for sixty grand, you owe every bookie between here and Miami. You told me the truth about your car, though; you own that, at least until the government or some guy named Big Tony the Hippo seizes it."

"Keep talking," he said. "You're constructing an ironclad case for slander and invasion of privacy."

"You need that quarter-million insurance money, Redding. It means surviving or staying out of jail, depending on which of your creditors gets to you first. Murder was a little out of your reach, and since your old friend Gendron wasn't going to accommodate you by committing suicide, you decided to supply him with a good reason. So when you gave him his last physical you told him he had terminal cancer."

"Now I know you've been drinking. He was in excellent health."

"You knew that, but he didn't. The symptoms of stress can be made to seem like the early stages of something much more serious, and he trusted you enough not to get a second opinion from another doctor. I found a well-thumbed self-help book in his office about living with death. It didn't take, though. With your help he chose a sudden end over letting his insides rot away slowly."

Redding smiled grimly. "Very inventive, but you forgot one

thing. Suicide would have voided the policy."

"Only if it looked like suicide. Being an old friend, you planted a simple idea in Gendron's head: Set up your own murder. He pulled the file on a man named Phil Hardy, a man he'd persuaded a client of his to fire in the interest of a better public image, a known armed robber who would organize the hit for an inducement—something up front, say, plus whatever he got away with from the robbery and a good attorney if he got caught.

"Jay Albert Matthews is the direct link. Gendron could supply the advance payment, but you had to hire Matthews to represent Hardy and his partners, because Gendron wouldn't be around to do it once he kept his appointment in that drugstore, and if you reneged on the deal they'd spill the details. The law says Matthews doesn't have to divulge his client's name, but once it gets out you set the whole thing up, he'll turn you to save his own reputation. Lawyers are like that. That's where you went sour, Redding. You didn't have the guts to arrange the kill yourself, so you let Gendron do it. Only in the end you had to get your hands dirty too."

"I wasn't Dick's beneficiary, Walker. Lynn was."

I looked at her on the sofa. "He's trying to lay it off on you."

The skin of her face drew tight. "The hell he will."

"Shut up, Lynn."

"I guess she's in love with you, or thinks she is," I said. "Otherwise she wouldn't have gone along with it. A divorce would only have given her part interest in a car with three payments to go on it and half a house with a mortgage, but her husband's death by misadventure was good for a quarter million. It would make a nice dowry when you two got married after a suitable interval. Don't move, Redding. Let's keep my gun in my belt holster and this conversation civilized."

"Don't be melodramatic. I was just reaching for a cigar."

"That's another thing. You really should have emptied the ashtray in your Citroen. I took the liberty of inspecting it on my way up to the door just now. The pink lipstick on the cigarette butts I found there isn't your shade. Bet there are more in your house."

"You're a man."

I looked again at Mrs. Gendron. Her glass was empty now but she was still holding it, her knuckles white. "You don't know what it's like being married to a dull man in a dull job who never took a chance in his life. Dick was horridly, stultifyingly *dependable*. Try living with that."

"Don't say anything more," Redding warned her. "Matthews won't talk and Hardy and the others don't know either of us from Adam."

"You should be grateful he was so dependable." I lifted the receiver off the telephone stand near the door and used that same hand to dial police headquarters, keeping my gun hand free and my eyes on Redding. "Gendron took his responsibilities seriously, and hang the rules. That's why he tried to see that you got his insurance money. He took chances, all right, but not like yours. All of his were for other people."

The police switchboard put me through to the Major Crimes unit.

Seven

"Matthews won't turn," Deborah Stonesmith said. "Why should he? He's not guilty of anything but being a lawyer. Even if he did talk it wouldn't prove anything."

We were seated in her office, waiting for the stenographer who had taken my statement to finish typing it up so I could sign it. The inspector had on a light blue suit today, over a white ruffled blouse that on her looked like a lace doily on an armored car. She was playing with the glasses on the chain around her neck.

I said, "Keep working on the Gendron woman. She might crack."

"More likely it'll be Redding. A funny thing happens in these inequal partnerships when they go into Interrogation; they reverse roles. The strong one spills his guts and the weak one clams up tight. If it happens at all."

"In any case, Midwest saves having to payoff. If your hunch is right and Hardy folds on Gendron, it's suicide any way you slice it."

"So why aren't you happy?" she asked.

"Why aren't you?"

She smiled. There was no joy in it. The light of a gray Detroit sort of day came through the window at her back and painted a red nimbus around her head of hard hair. "So it was just an ordinary domestic murder after all. Not a major crime."

"They're all major," I said, admiring her halo through the smoke of my Winston. "Every last one of them."

Square One

The bar in the new Hilton Garden Inn in Harmonie Park is a pleasant place to sit and listen to the bartenders clinking their instruments and watch baseball on the liquid-crystal screen in the corner—two or three more games and it will be a year-round sport. I don't go there often. I spend less on a bottle of red wine than the place charges for a glass of decent scotch.

That day I went. Ed Warburton had done me a favor as commander of the eleventh precinct when he could just as well have jailed me as a material witness, and had a round bought in his honor at the local cop hangout that evening. I'm unpopular there as a rule. The break had given me a chance to close out an my investigation I'd been working three weeks, and Warburton to clear up a police case that had hung fire for more than a year. When he called me at the office and asked me to meet him in the Hilton bar, I took out a loan and drove down.

I didn't ask why he'd chosen a spot so far from his home park. When a cop stumbles and falls on his sword, his colleagues give him a door-busting going-away party in a private room above a saloon and then the dustoff. It isn't that they're ashamed, or disapprove of what he did. Cops are superstitious and convinced that bad luck is contagious. No one is safe if a Detroit police commander can get caught with his thumb in the till.

Not that he had. Six officers from his precinct had gone up on charges of substituting confectioners' sugar for twenty kilos of cocaine in the evidence room, and brass is expected to know about such things. Even then he might have come off with a reprimand and possibly demotion to inspector, but when the jury voted to acquit the officers, the department had had to let blood somewhere. He'd resigned after being relieved of his duties.

It was the middle of the afternoon. A man and woman in business dress had the bartender to themselves at the bar. No one was watching the game. Warburton lifted a hand, and when I went over to his booth raised himself six inches to shake hands. He was fifty and looked it with less hair than I remembered, and the stoop was new, but if I'd had twenty years on him I wouldn't have chosen him. He stood six two with no body fat and his grip would bend a coconut.

"Thanks for coming, Amos. What are you drinking?"

I knew then the occasion wasn't social. Cops only call me by my first name when they want something. "What are you?"

He held up his glass, a narrow tumbler half filled with sparkling water, with a lemon wedge straddling the top. "French fizzie. I haven't had a nibble in a week."

"Program?"

"Experiment. I like the stuff. I want to see if I need it. No pink eels yet." He drank and made the sort of face a seasoned drinker makes over carbonated water. He had a long, humorous face, like the put-upon father in a 1950s sitcom. His suit was pressed but his tie was at half-mast. That and the teetotaling were his only visible concessions to his situation. I lured the help away from the couple at the bar and ordered a scotch.

"What's your fee?" Warburton asked when I had it and we were alone again.

I drank. It tasted sweet, not like the paintstrip I kept at home. "Depends on the work. I can run a credit check in an hour, that's forty. Otherwise, five hundred a day, with three days up front for seed. If you want me to scratch up dirt on the chief, I'll need a little more. No hospitalization," I explained.

"You wouldn't have to dig too deep. She's the mayor's creature, and we know what he is. You never see those two apart. I wouldn't take them on in a sack race."

"She slam-dunked you pretty hard."

"I don't hold it against her. Not much. She's got the feds sitting in her lap. A whole line of chiefs crooked the joint before she came along. I want you to put in a word," he said. "It shouldn't take three days."

"I don't know the chief. It would take that long to get past the reception room, and then I might as well hit her up for a personal loan while I'm there. I'll get the same answer."

"Not with the chief. With Inspector Alderdyce. You two go back."

"Our fathers ran a gas station together. We entered training the same day. I washed out a week short, he stayed on. That's our history. We swap favors now and then, but right now I'm in the red. Even if I weren't, there's no way an endorsement from either of us will put you back in charge of the eleventh."

"I don't want that. I'm asking you to ask him to ask the chief to green-light my application to rejoin the department at entry level."

I drank again. "You want to get back into the blue bag?"

"I'll take cadet if I have to. I'd rather not. They're making those scaling walls higher than they did thirty years ago. I can file, hold down the front desk, get coffee for the C.I.D. Free up a younger man for the streets. I know I can't be Supercop. See? No delusions. Next week maybe I'll go back to drinking beer." He drained off his glass and set it down with a thump.

"What's the gag?"

"It's legit. I bit the moose hard; lost my pension, almost lost my wife. My daughter won't speak to me. The twerp she married wants to be drain commissioner, but that won't happen thanks to good old dad. I could write a book, or take security work, but I don't want that. I want to go back to square one and this time roll the dice with the other hand."

"The chief won't go for it," I said. "It's like cutting the end off a blanket and stitching it back on the other end. They'll fry her in the media."

"Everybody deserves a second chance. That's the spin. I'm physically fit, no misdemeanors or felonies, and it wouldn't be the first time a middle-aged man was accepted for duty."

"It's her head if you screw up again. She won't go for it."

"She's forgotten what it was like in the ranks. She put me down as incompetent because I couldn't offer evidence against those six officers. It never occurred to her I wouldn't because you don't rat on a brother cop."

"You knew?"

He frowned. "This conversation is like attorney-client privilege, right? To you, I mean; it doesn't swing a flea's weight in court, but I know you've gone into the cage over it in the past. Your file makes good reading at the dentist's."

"If I entertain you, I've done my job. I'm not writing my memoirs anytime soon, if that's what you're worried about."

"Not worried. Just wanted to know how wide I can open up. I wouldn't have to explain this brothers-in-blue business to Alderdyce. He may run Homicide, but his heart's still in uniform."

"So ask him to put the word in with the chief. What do you need me for?"

"You might have noticed I'm not shaking friends from the department off my lapels just now. Being seen with a disgraced character like me might not make a grease spot in his jacket downtown, but it wouldn't win him points next time he comes up for promotion. A man like John wouldn't refuse to see me, but I can't do that to him."

"I'm not exactly a photo op myself," I said.

"Don't flatter yourself. You're a bug on the radar at best."

"Since you put it that way, go to hell." I drank off my scotch and slid to the end of the booth.

Warburton had the reflexes of a rookie. His hand clamped my wrist.

"Let's not fight," he said. "When you've been called six kinds of an imbecile where your wife and your kids and all their friends can see it, you let fly at whatever's in range."

I settled back against the seat. I still felt the pressure of his fingers on my wrist after he let go. "I have to work in this town," I said, "which means getting along with chiefs and inspectors, inspectors especially. Forget about convincing the chief for now. First you have to convince me you're not just dicking around."

"My God, man, I'm degrading myself in front of the world. Why would I make it up?"

"It's got Spike TV all over it. All you'd have to do is stick it out long enough to interest some hack, sell the idea to New York and L.A., and bug out before your appointment comes up for the department physical. That makes everyone else look like an imbecile, and guess who takes the heat? I don't like security work any more than you do, but that's all I'll have left this side of a refrigerator box on Gratiot. That's if they let me."

"I'm not grandstanding. I took an oath to serve and protect, that's the job. I got so busy trying to keep the job, I forgot to do it. This is the one shot I've to make up for it."

If he'd popped a tear, or put a throb in his throat, or hauled out the speech about a man's word being all he has left in the finish, I'd have paid for my drink and left there and then. But his face was as calm and clear as a reflecting pool. I believed him.

"I'll talk to him," I said. "That's as far as the promising goes. Working on keeping jobs is the slogan they ought to paint on the squad cars."

He reached inside his coat and slid out a checkbook bound in marbled blue leather. I stopped him before he clicked his pen.

"Pay the bartender. Stand up for me at my next arraignment."

I caught up with Inspector John Alderdyce in the Detroit Athletic Club, swimming laps around the pool where Johnny Weissmuller had trained for the Olympics. The gymnasium was more brightly lit than it had been for thirty years, when a brick wall had blocked the view of the encompassing city. Now it looked out on the larger-than-life statues of dead ballplayers in Comerica Park.

Anthropologists say that black men haven't the buoyancy to break records in the water, but they hadn't seen Alderdyce, dark and gleaming, arms and legs slicing the surface like a water rocket. There was no one present to enforce the rules, so I lit a cigarette and waited while he circled twice and climbed out. The water came off him in sheets, like rain from a locomotive. He'd put on weight around the middle, but he was all slabbed muscle through the chest and shoulders, with a head hewn roughly like a chainsaw sculpture from a living tree.

"Put that out," he said. "I'm on probation here six more weeks."

I squashed out the butt on the tiles while he toweled off and put on a terrycloth robe with the DAC monogram above the pocket. We sat down in a pair of folding chairs with woven plastic seats and I got right to it.

"Why didn't Ed come see me in person?" he asked when I'd finished.

"He says he's a pariah."

"You're not?"

"I made the same argument. He said I wasn't in his league."

"He doesn't know you like I do."

"What do I tell him?"

"I'll think about it."

"That means no."

"No means no. 'I'll think about it' means I've got a stack of homicides on my desk that won't investigate themselves. What's your end?"

"Not a cent. I owed him a solid."

"I don't."

"He knows that."

"What's my end if I deliver?" he asked. "I mean from you."

"There isn't one from me. Personally, I don't care if Ed Warburton's name shows up in the morning roll or not. He got a raw deal if he's telling the truth, but this mayor and this chief hardly ever deal any other way. I don't have the time or the capital to square up the deck every week."

"Think he's on the level?"

"He made all the right faces when he was talking, but you cops all got more personalities than Mel Blanc. For what it's worth, I think he wants to clean the slate."

"Tell Ed I'll call him."

Warburton called me at home a week later. I don't know where he got the number. It was late and he was drunk.

I said, "I guess you didn't see any pink eels."

"I'm celebrating," he said. "You're talking to Officer Edward Thomas Warburton. That's unofficial until they give me the oath, but I'm taking it out for a test drive."

"Congratulations."

"Thanks, Walker. John gave me the news an hour ago. The chief waived training. All I have to do is pass the physical and qualify on the range."

"Bet she's hoping you'll fail one or the other."

"I won't, though. I've never missed a doctor's appointment or a target. I've got fifteen years till mandatory. I might make lieutenant. Then I'll be in a position to even things up with you."

"If I'm still doing what I'm doing fifteen years from now, that might mean asking you to put a round in my head."

"I'd like to buy you another drink."

"No, you don't. A fresh fish like you can't afford to be seen in public with a disgraced character like me."

We continued in that vein for five seconds more and then we were through talking. We were back to last names and that was just fine. I never heard from him again. But I heard about him plenty.

A writer who'd ghosted three presidential memoirs spilt a publishing contract with Warburton and brought out his story under the title *Second Chance*. Before it appeared, a Hollywood studio bought the rights to adapt it, but the circumstances themselves were public domain, and at one point a movie company, a broadcast TV network, and a satellite station had all announced plans to dramatize the story: Kevin Costner, Kiefer Sutherland, and Denzel Washington entered into negotiations to play the lead. No cameras turned on any of the productions and the book went into remaindering after one printing.

Ten months after Officer Warburton raised his right hand and promised to serve and protect his community on CBS, NBC, ABC, and CNN, officers with the General Service Bureau arrested him for embezzling forty thousand dollars from the stash the department kept for buying drugs in sting operations. Subsequent investigation revealed he's lost that much at least in the three casinos in town.

He was dismissed by order of the chief of police, found guilty of grand theft, and sentenced to serve eight to twelve years at hard labor in the state penitentiary in Jackson, where he was placed in isolation to protect him from the convicts he'd helped send there. His wife divorced him, his daughter's husband lost his bid for public office, and his son changed his name. Meanwhile, the FBI informed the chief it was expanding its probe of the department, and Inspector John Alderdyce was suspended for three weeks with pay while General Service investigated his connections with Warburton. His membership in the Detroit Athletic Club was canceled.

My name didn't come up in any of the press conferences that accompanied the story, but I got my car into a garage to bring all the safety equipment up to date. These days I can't afford to be stopped for even a broken taillight in the city of Detroit.

The Man Who Loved *Noir*

One

The address I'd written down belonged to a house in Lathrup Village three miles north of Detroit, the only one in a cul-de-sac that ended in a berry thicket and a cyclone fence. It was a cool, sprawling ranch-style of brick and frame with four great oaks in the yard arranged in such a way that the house would always be in shade. I felt the sweat drying on my body during the short walk from my car to the front door.

A woman in a gray dress and white apron with her hair caught up by combs led me into a sunken living room and went away. They're no longer called maids, but they still can't speak English.

"Thank you for coming on such short notice, Mr. Walker. I'm Gay Cully."

She'd come in through an open sliding glass door from a patio in back when I was looking in another direction, a small compact red-haired woman with the sun behind her. Assuming she'd planned her entrance, that put her over forty. She had large eyes mascaraed all around, a pixie mouth, and a fly waist in a pale yellow dress tailored to show it off.

"I like your home." I borrowed a warm, slightly moist hand with light calluses and returned it. "They don't design them this way since air conditioning."

"Neil has an eye for that kind of thing. He's a building contractor."

"Neil's your husband?"

"Yes. Can I get you something? I'm afraid Netta has narrow ideas about her housekeeping duties."

"Just water. Anything stronger's wasted on a day like this."

She agreed that it was hot and came back after a few minutes with two glasses and a bowl of crushed ice on a tray. When we were seated on either side of a glass occasional table she said, "Neil's officially missing. Twenty-six hours. I trust the police but they're outnumbered by their cases. That's why I called you."

"This puts me even up. I take it he isn't in the vanishing habit."

"No. He's never been gone without an explanation except for the time he was in the hospital."

"Accident?"

She drank and set down her glass. "He checked himself into a sanitarium. That was eighteen months ago, when the construction business was in a slump. Our lawyer advised him to declare bankruptcy, but Neil insisted on paying back every creditor in full. It was too much for him, the worrying, the long hours. One day he left for work and never showed up. The police traced him to the hospital after three days."

"I guess you checked there this time."

"I called every hospital in the area, public and private. No one answering his description has been seen in any of them."

"How's he been lately?"

"A little keyed up. We're just now getting back on our feet. I didn't think it was anything serious until his partner called yesterday to ask where he was."

I had some water. I wasn't thirsty any more, I just never liked asking the question. "Any reason to suspect he's involved with another woman?"

"Yes, but I called her and she swears she hasn't seen him in months."

"You know her?" I stroked my Adam's apple. A piece of ice had stalled in my throat during her answer.

"Vesta is her name. Vesta Mainwaring. She was the bookkeeper at the office until I made Neil fire her." She leaned over and touched my wrist. The light found hairline creases in her face.

"I should explain something before we go any further. My husband is an obsessive personality, Mr. Walker. He's subject to binges."

"Alcohol?"

"No, but just as intoxicating. Come with me to the basement." She rose.

We went through a stainless steel kitchen and down a flight of clean sawdust-smelling steps into a cellar that had been turned into a den, mahogany paneling and tweed wall to wall. It contained a wet bar, Naugahyde chairs and a sofa, and a television set whose forty-eight-inch screen dwarfed the videocassette recorder perched on top. A set of built-in shelves that looked at first to hold books was packed with videotapes instead.

"My husband's favorite room," said Mrs. Cully. "He spends most of his time here when he's not working."

I read the labels on the tapes. They were all movies: "The Dark Corner," "Night and the City," "Criss Cross," "Double Indemnity"—not a Technicolor title in the bunch, and none of them made after about 1955. "He likes murder mysteries, I see."

"Not just murder mysteries. Dark films with warped gangsters and troubled heroes and fallen women. There's a name for them; my French isn't very good—"

"Cinema noir," I said. "Black films. I like old movies myself. So far it hasn't landed me in psychiatric."

"You just like them. Neil sucks on them. In the beginning I watched with him. They were interesting, but not as a steady diet. I don't think he even noticed when I stopped watching. Lately he's been spending every spare minute in front of this set, exposing himself to I don't know how many murders, deceits, and depressing situations. It's not healthy."

An empty cassette sleeve lay on an end table. "Pitfall," starring Dick Powell, Raymond Burr, and Lizabeth Scott. I went to the VCR and punched Eject. A tape licked out. "Pitfall." It hadn't been rewound.

"He was watching this one when?"

"Night before last. He disappeared the next day."

"When was the last time he got on this kick?"

"Just before he entered the hospital. About the time I found out he was having an affair with Vesta Mainwaring."

"How'd you find out?"

"The police told me. The little slut caved in pretty quickly when they started asking questions about his disappearance."

I slid the tape into its sleeve. "Where can I find Miss Mainwaring?"

"She's listed. But as I told you, she doesn't know where he is."

"I'd like to hear her say it. What's the name of your husband's firm?"

She'd anticipated that and gave me a business card from the pocket of her dress. CULLY AND WEBB, it read. "Webb is the partner?"

"His first name's Leo. They've been together longer than Neil and I."

"Can I take this with me?" I held up the videotape.

"Of course. You'll need a picture of Neil too."

Upstairs she took a five-by-seven out of its frame and handed it to me. Cully was a craggy-looking party in his late forties with sad eyes and dark hair thinning in front. "Any ideas on what he might be up to?" I asked his wife.

She hesitated. "It might sound crazy."

"Try me."

"You have to understand that he might be unbalanced," she said. "I didn't put it together the first time, but I've seen enough of these things now to recognize the plot. I think Neil wants to be one of these *noir* heroes, Mr. Walker. I think he thinks he's in a film."

Two

Cully and Webb had a small suite on the seventeenth floor of the Michigan Consolidated Gas Company Building on Woodward, a furnace-shaped skyscraper with a lobby out of Cecil B. DeMille, complete with sparkling blue lights mounted under the thirty-foot ceiling and a bronze ballerina pirouetting among exterior pools. The offices themselves were just offices. A gray-haired woman with reading glasses suspended from a chain around her neck spoke my name into a telephone and Leo Webb came out to shake my hand.

He was a short wiry sixty with white hair slicked back, a power nose, and eyes like glass shards. His suit was tailored snugly and there was something about the knot of his silk tie that said he'd given it a jerk and a lift just before his entrance.

When I told him my business he steered me into his office, a square room full of antiques and statuary, trembling on the rim of bad taste. I admired the view of downtown Detroit through his window and managed to sit without upsetting a plaster cupid notching an arrow into its bow on a pedestal next to the chair.

"Gay's overreacting," Webb said, settling himself behind a

French Empire desk crusted all over with gold inlay. "Cully's just off on a toot. He's that age. He'll be back when he's had enough."

"Vesta Mainwaring told her she hasn't seen him in months."

"This town's full of squirming women. I know. That's why I never bothered to get married."

"How's he been acting lately?"

"Same as anyone in this goddamn business, jumpy. Every time it rains on Wall Street mortgage rates go up and people stop building houses. If you're looking for security, keep going."

"You wouldn't know that to see this office."

He smiled and ran a finger down the side of a Dresden Marie Antoinette on the desk. "I'm a sucker for nice things. We're into developing in a small way. You get a sixth sense for dying old widows looking to unload their property in order to have something to leave their grandchildren. The bargains would surprise you."

Bet they wouldn't. "Do you know where Miss Mainwaring is working? I can't get an answer from her home phone."

"Her new employer called us for a reference." He slid the pointer down the side of one of those nifty message caddies and punched up the cover. "Ziggy's Chop House on Livernois." He gave me a telephone number.

I wrote it down in my old-fashioned notebook. "Do you always hang on to the new numbers of former employees?"

"Everybody has their own records system and they take it with them when they go. Calling them saves a lot of decoding time."

"Can I see Cully's office?"

"I'll have Frances show you." He picked up his telephone.

"Partners sometimes take out insurance policies on each other," I said when he was through. "Anything like that here?"

"The premiums are too dear for the shoestring we operate on most of the time. His half of the business goes to his wife. Are you suggesting I did something nasty?" A pair of shard-like eyes glittered.

"Just sweeping out all the corners." Someone knocked and the woman I'd spoken to outside stuck her gray head into the office. I stood. "Thanks, Mr. Webb. I'll let you know if he turns up."

He remained seated. "Just tell him to wash off the powder and perfume before he reports to work."

Neil Cully's office was a poor working cousin of his partner's, containing a plain desk and file cabinet and an easel holding a pastel sketch of an embryonic building. The only personal items were a picture of Gay Cully on the desk and a framed movie poster on one wall for "This Gun for Hire," with Alan Ladd looking sinister in four colors under a fedora. Frances stood in the doorway while I went through the file cabinet and desk. I found files and desk stuff. The message pad by the telephone was blank, but there were indentations in the top page.

"The police called this morning," Frances said. "They said not to disturb anything in the office."

I looked at my watch. "Okay if I call my answering service?"

When she said yes I lifted the receiver and dialed the number for Cully and Webb. The telephone rang in the reception area. Frances excused herself and withdrew. I laid the receiver on the blotter and tried the trick with the edge of a pencil on the message pad. It made the indentations clearer but not legible. I smoothed out some unedifying crumples in Cully's wastebasket, found a sheet that had been torn off the pad, and got it into my pocket just as Frances returned. I cradled the receiver.

"Odd, there was no one on the other end," she said.

"Kids." I thanked her and left before she could work it out.

In the elevator I looked at the sheet. An unidentified telephone number. I tried it in a booth on the street.

"Musuraca Investigations," wheezed a voice in my ear.

I hung up without saying anything. I knew Phil Musuraca; not personally or even by sight, but the way a hardworking gardener knows a destructive species of beetle. Where he had gone, no honest investigator could follow without risking having a safe drop on him with Musuraca's name on it. What his number was doing in Neil Cully's wastebasket was one for Ellery Queen.

Three

"Hello?"

A low voice for a woman, with fine grit in it, like a cat's lick. Conversations collided in the background with the snarling and cracking of a busy griddle. I could almost smell the carcinogens frying at Ziggy's Chop House. "Vesta Mainwaring?"

"Speaking. Listen, I'm busy, so if this is another obscene call, get to the dirty part quick."

I introduced myself and stated my business. I was looking across my little office at Miss August, kneeling in yellow shorts, high heels, and nothing else behind some convenient shrubbery on the calendar. I wondered if Miss Mainwaring ever trimmed hedges.

"Like I told Mrs. Cully and like I told the police, I haven't seen Neil since last fall," she said. "I got work to do."

"Not seeing him doesn't cover telephone calls and letters."

"You forgot telegrams, which I didn't get either. I lost one good job over that crumb, you want me to lose a lousy one too?"

There was no reason to play the card, just the fact I hadn't any other leads. "What about Fat Phil, heard from him?"

The little silence that followed was like tumblers dropping into place. When she spoke again the background noise was muffled, as if she had inserted her body between it and the telephone.

"What do you know about him?"

"Meet me and we'll swap stories."

"Not here," she said quickly. "Do you know the Castinet Lounge on Grand River? I get off at ten."

"I'll find it." I hung up and checked my watch. Quitting time. Five hours to kill. I had dinner at a steak place on Chene and stopped at a video store on the way home to rent a VCR from a kid I wouldn't have let follow me into an arcade after sunset.

At the ranch I fixed a drink, hooked up the recorder to my TV set with the help of the instructions and a number of venerable Anglo-Saxon words, and fed the tape of "Pitfall" I had borrowed from Gay Cully into the slot. It was a tight, black-and-white crimer the way they made them in 1948, starring Dick Powell as an insurance agent who has an extramarital affair with sultry Lizabeth Scott, only to run afoul of her embezzler boyfriend and a sex-driven insurance investigator played by Raymond Burr at his pre-Perry Mason heaviest. Powell kills the boyfriend and Scott kills Burr, but not before Powell's marriage to Jane Wyatt is threatened, leaving their lives considerably darker than they were when first encountered. There were plenty of tricky camera angles and contrasty lighting and one clever scene involving Powell and Burr with guns in a room full of shadows and reflections.

It was a good movie. It wasn't worth going off the deep end over, but then neither are most of the reasons men and women choose to walk away from a perfectly good relationship. When it was over I caught a rerun of "Green Acres," which made more sense.

Four

The Castinet Lounge was the latest in a series of attempts to perform shock therapy on Detroit's catatonic nightlife. A foyer paved with blue-and-white Mexican tiles opened into a big room covered in fake adobe with a bar and tables, a dance floor, and a mariachi band in sombreros and pink ruffled shirts. At a comer table I ordered scotch and soda from a waitress dressed like Carmen Miranda who wouldn't remember Sonny and Cher.

Ten o'clock came and went, followed by ten-thirty. A few couples danced, the band finished its set, rested, and started another. They were playing requests, but everything sounded like the little Spanish flea. I nursed the first drink. What I did with the second and third was more like CPR. I was sure I'd been stood up.

Just before eleven she came in. I knew it was her, although I'd never seen a picture or been given a description, and my opinion of Neil Cully went up a notch. Coming in from the floodlit parking lot she was just a silhouette, square shoulders and a narrow waist and long legs in a blue dress and a bonnet-like hat tied under her chin with a ribbon, but as she stopped under the inside lights to look around I saw eyes slanted just shy of Oriental, soft, untanned cheeks flushed a little from the last of the day's heat, red lips, a strong round chin. If you were going to kick over the traces you could wait years for a better reason. When her gaze got to me I rose. She came over.

Seated, she took off her hat, shook loose a fall of glistening blue-black hair, and traded the hat to Carmen Miranda for a whiskey sour. When we were alone she said, "You don't look like someone who'd be working with Phil Musuraca."

"Never met him."

"Did Neil tell you he was following me?"

"Who hired him?"

She seemed to realize she'd tipped something. She took a cigarette from her purse and fumbled for a light. I struck a match and leaned over. I didn't smell onions. Whatever she had on made me think of blossoms under a full moon. She blew a plume at the ceiling. "You haven't talked to Neil."

"Me and the rest of the human race," I said. "That part I've been spending time with, anyway. Tell me about Fat Phil."

"First tell me why you're asking."

"I found his number in Cully's wastebasket. Did Cully hire him?"

"I suppose you could find out anyway. Musuraca's working for my ex-husband. His name's Ted Silvera."

"Where did I hear that name?"

"He pushed over a bunch of video stores downriver two years ago. They called him the shotgun bandit."

"I remember the trial," I said. "The prosecution offered him a deal if he agreed to tell them where he'd stashed the money."

"Eighty thousand dollars, can you believe it? I keep telling Ziggy he should sell the griddle and rent out tapes. Anyway Ted spit in their face and he's doing eight to twelve in Jackson. The police followed me around for a while, but when they got the idea I didn't know what Ted did with the money they laid off."

"But not Musuraca."

"Ted's jealous," she said. "He got wind about Neil somehow and had his lawyer retain Musuraca to tail me. Then Neil's wife found out and I got fired. Musuraca gave up after that. But a week ago I turned from the counter at Ziggy's and there he was looking at me through the front window. He tried to duck, but he wasn't fast enough. I'd know that fat slob in the dark."

"Sure he's working for Silvera?"

"I went to Ted's lawyer and he said no. But you can't trust lawyers. Who else would care what I do and who I see?"

"Dicks like Fat Phil are simple organisms. They don't give up as easily as the police. Maybe he thinks you'll lead him to that eighty grand."

"If I knew where it was, would I be flipping burgers?"

I lit a cigarette for myself. "It's only been two years. Inflation isn't so bad you couldn't wait a little longer for the coast to clear."

"Thanks for the drink, mister." She stood.

"Sit," I said. "I don't care if you've got the money sewed inside your brassiere. I'm looking for Neil Cully."

"I don't know where he is."

"What was he doing with Musuraca's number?"

She sat. Carmen drifted over and I ordered another round. Our glasses were less than half-empty but it was that kind of night. Vesta said, "I don't know why he'd still have it. I told Neil about Ted and Musuraca—well, before. After that I couldn't get rid of him. He thought he was protecting me."

"Did you know he had mental problems?"

"What makes him special? My father died when I was little and if I didn't marry Ted when I was sixteen to get out of the house my stepfather would've hung me on his belt with every tramp in Detroit. When Ted got sent up I saved everything I made waiting tables to pay for my bookkeeping classes. Cully and Webb was my ticket out of places like Ziggy's. Some protection job. Neil cracks up and goes to a cushy sanitarium and I'm back behind a counter."

"He's got a movie complex, his wife says. Your situation comes right off a Hollywood B lot. If he's gone bugs again he might look up you or Musuraca to write himself in as the hero."

"I haven't seen him. I haven't heard from him. I don't know how to say it so you'll believe it."

"I believe it. Were you followed here tonight?"

"I wouldn't be surprised. Musuraca doesn't make a lot of mistakes."

"Okay, go home."

"What are you going to do?"

"Get a look at Fat Phil."

"You'll be the first who ever wanted it." She got up. "You know, I usually get taken home from this place."

I held up a fifty-dollar bill. "That ought to cover gas."

She didn't take it. "I'm not a whore."

"You're a bookkeeper who waits tables. Put this in your ledger."

She smiled briefly, took the bill, and left, carrying her hat. I crushed out my cigarette, put down money for the drinks, and went out after her. Out front the parking lot attendant held the door of a four-year-old green Fiat for her and she gave him a dollar and drove away. A moment later a pair of head lamps came on and a black Olds 98 covered with dings pulled out of the first row in the lot and burbled after her. By that time I was sliding under the wheel of my Mercury eight spaces over. I waited until the Olds turned left on Grand River, then swung out into the aisle behind it. Fat Phil and I had one thing in common: We never used valet parking.

Five

Vesta Mainwaring lived in a house that had been converted to apartments in Harper Woods. She parked in a little lot behind the house and let herself in the back door. After a minute a light went on upstairs. The big Olds coasted to a stop.

I parked around the corner and walked back. The car was still there with its lights off. I got in the passenger's side.

Fat men are often fast. He sprang the gun from its underarm clip with an economy that would have impressed Hickok. But I showed him my Smith & Wesson while he was still drawing and he let his hand fall to his lap with the gun in it.

"You should lock your doors this time of night," I said.

"Who the hell are you?" It was a light voice for so much man. In the glow from the corner he had on a dark suit that could have been used for a drop cloth and a porkpie hat whose small brim made his face seem bloated. Actually it was in proportion with the rest of him. He would run three hundred stripped, a picture I got out of my mind as quickly as it came in. He had one eyebrow straight across and a blue jaw. I smelled peppermint in the car.

"Trade you my name for the cannon." When I had it—one of those Sig-Sauer automatics the cops are so hot on—I put it on the dash out of his reach and lowered the Smittie. "So much gun for such a little girl. The name's Walker. You wouldn't know it."

"Don't count on it. The town ain't that big and the racket's smaller. What's the play?"

"Who's paying you to tail the Mainwaring woman?"

"Never heard of her. I was getting set to take a leak when you busted in."

"They arrest you for that here. How about Neil Cully, ever hear of him?"

"Uh-uh."

"He had your number written down in his office."

"So what? I ain't so busy I'm unlisted. Listen, I got a sour gut. There's a bag of peppermints in the glove compartment."

I opened it. The second my eyes flicked away his hand went up to his sun visor. I swung the Smith, cracking the barrel against his elbow. He yelped and brought down the arm. With my free hand I reached up and slid a two-shot .22 off the top of the visor. "For a guy that knows nothing from nothing you've got plenty of ordnance," I said. "What's Vesta Mainwaring to you?"

"Eighty grand." He rubbed his elbow. "She's got that dough stashed somewhere. She can't stay away from it forever."

"You gave up on that once. What makes you think she knows where it is now?"

"Just a hunch I got."

"Save it, Phil. There's too much divorce work in this town for you to give up any of it on a hunch. What's your source?"

"I got a note in my inside coat pocket." He didn't move.

"Fish it out. If it's more iron I'll shoot you in the head. It's not much of a head but it'd be a shame to spoil that hat."

He took the note out slowly. I pocketed the .22 and took it, a square of coarse Big Chief notepaper with two words printed on it in block ballpoint capitals: VESTA KNOWS. "Who sent it?"

He shook his head. "Came in the mail yesterday. No return address and a USPS postmark. Same printing on the envelope."

"You'd drop everything and take off after her on an anonymous note?"

"I'd do it on less than that for eighty thousand."

I put the note in my pocket and showed him Neil Cully's picture. His eyebrow rippled. "Sure, he was sniffing around the Mainwaring broad last year. I ran his license plate through the Secretary of State's office but he wasn't nobody. I guess Cully could of been the name. I ain't seen him lately."

"Maybe you did and forgot. Like you forgot his name."

"Hey, I hear a lot of names."

I opened the door. "If I find out there's more to it I'll be back and you and I will go a round."

"What about my guns?"

"Go straight home from here and I'll mail them to your office. Tell anybody you feel like shooting to take a number till then." I left him.

Six

I caught six hours' sleep and was standing in front of the Detroit Public Library when they unlocked the doors. The film section had several picture books on *cinema noir* and one scholarly tract, *Dark Dreams: Psychosexual Manifestations of Hollywood Crime Movies Circa 1945-1955*, by Ellis Portman, Ph.D. It had been published that year by Wayne State University Press. I lugged the thick volume over to a reading table and waded through a grand's worth of four-dollar words, then turned to the author's biography at the back. Ellis Portman, it said, taught psychology and film courses at Wayne State.

I also found a withdrawal card at the back bearing signatures of those who had checked the book out recently. I took it.

A public telephone on the main floor put me in touch with Dr. Portman and an acquaintance in the Detroit bureau of the FBI who owed me a favor. I made an appointment with Portman and stopped at the Federal Building on the way to give my acquaintance the note Phil Musuraca had given me.

The room number I'd gotten from Portman belonged to a small auditorium lit by only the black-and-silver images fluttering on a square screen at the far end. I found a seat in time to watch Robert Mitchum and Jane Greer careening down a country road in a big car with bug-eye headlamps toward a roadblock. Spotting the armed men in uniform, Jane Greer said, "Dirty double-crossing—" and shot Mitchum, who sent the car into a spin while the woman traded fire with the officers. After she was killed and the car came to a stop, a cop opened the driver's door and Mitchum flopped out, dead.

The lights came up and a small man with a big head, half the age I associated with a college professor, dismissed the students with a reminder that their papers were due Monday. As they filed out, discussing the movie, I introduced myself and shook Portman's hand. Up close he was older than he looked from the back of the room. I sketched out the case on the way to the projector.

"Just another manifestation of the Don Quixote complex," he said when I'd finished. "How can I help?"

"Most books on *noir* are for buffs. Yours takes on its psychology. I thought you might translate the Latin."

He switched off the projector and removed the take-up reel. "We've always identified with gods and heroes. The appeal of the *noir* protagonist is he's more approachable than Beowulf or Sherlock Holmes. He's an ordinary guy with tall troubles, but he usually comes out on top, even if it does kill him sometimes."

"Kind of a complex world to want to be part of."

"Actually it's simplistic. You've got your good guy, your heavy, your good girl, and your tramp. Upon examination the *noir* landscape makes more sense than our world. I don't wonder that an obsessive like your client's husband would prefer it to his own tangled affairs. His wife, whom he perceives as the good girl, represents the crushing responsibilities that landed him in therapy the first time. The girlfriend, whose situation might have come out of any crime movie of the forties, promises adventure and uninhibited sex and a respite from his oppressive routine. The whole thing might have been made to order for a man with his fixation."

I watched him place the reel in a flat can labeled OUT OF THE PAST and seal the lid. "What would shake him out of it?"

"Nothing, if he's too far gone. If not, the shock of reality might do it. Our world has more twists than any screenplay. Villains turn out to be just guys trying to get along. Bad girls are just good girls in trouble. Angels become whores in front of your eyes. If that doesn't bring him back, electrodes won't."

Seven

Later, in my office transcribing the notes I'd taken in Dr. Portman's classroom to my typewritten report, I took a call from my FBI acquaintance. We spoke for five minutes, after which I hung up and placed two calls. The first was to Gay Cully, who agreed to see me at her place that night.

It was just past dark when Netta, the Cullys' maid, answered the bell and told me her mistress would be with me in a few minutes. I asked her to send Mrs. Cully to the basement when she was ready and went down there.

I slid the videotape I'd brought into Neil Cully's VCR and turned on the giant-screen TV set. As the black-and-white credits for "Pitfall" came on I turned down the sound and switched off the lights in the room. Now the only illumination came from the screen. Shadows crawled in the silver glow on the tapes perched on their shelves.

"Mr. Walker, is that you?"

I hadn't heard her coming down the stairs. She was standing on the second step from the bottom, a small trim figure in a fresh-looking pale tailored dress like the one she'd had on when we met. One hand rested at her throat.

"It's not Neil," I said. "Is that what you thought, Mrs. Cully?"

"I—well, yes, for a moment. He used to sit down here with no lights on and a movie on the—"

"Couldn't be him, though. You know that better than anyone."

"I don't—do you have news? Where is he?"

I was standing in shadow beside the TV set. The full light of the screen fell on her, as I'd planned. I said, "You were okay for a novice. You only made two mistakes. One was natural: Who'd expect Phil Musuraca to show me the note or that it would find its way to the FBI? The second was just plain stupid.

"Printing VESTA KNOWS was good," I went on. "No handwriting expert could pin that small a sample on you. But that coarse paper holds prints like soft wax. When I had a fed friend check them against yours on file from an old job, it didn't take long."

"What are you implying?"

"Nuts. You've seen enough of these films to recognize the obligatory explanation scene. The note was smart, all right. It got Musuraca back on Vesta Mainwaring's case and made him a prime suspect: Poor crazy Neil got himself involved all over again in Vesta's troubles and stubbed his toe, permanently. Just in case the cops missed it you hired me, knowing I'd turn Musuraca eventually. The law couldn't convict him without a body, but his interest in eighty thousand dollars stolen by Vesta's ex would divert suspicion from you. You even read up on *cinema noir* to make sure your story about Neil's obsession would hold water. But that was where you made your second mistake, the bonehead one." I took the card out of my pocket and held it up to the light.

"What's that?"

"A withdrawal card from the Detroit Public Library with your name on it, dated a week before you reported your husband missing. You shouldn't have checked out Dr. Portman's book. That was like signing your own name to a murder contract." I put it away. "How much is Neil's half of the contracting firm worth?"

Shadows and light played over her face. "Fifty thousand. More if I liquidate the real property. But that's not evidence. A note, a card with my signature. They won't convict."

"No, but they're enough to obtain a warrant to dig up that berry patch at the end of this street. Before I rang the bell tonight I poked around with a flashlight. I found a lot of turned earth. With Neil's corpse, the note and the card will convict."

"You don't know what it's like."

I said nothing.

"Listening to him babble about those stupid films," she said. "Even when he had his affair it wasn't with a woman, just a character in a movie. I'd have killed him for that alone; the half-partnership will just be compensation for the past two years I spent living with a zombie."

"How'd you kill him?"

"Guess." She raised a gun in the hand she'd had resting on the banister. I hadn't seen it in the shadows. "I sent Netta out just now," she said. "Call it a feeling I had."

"Drop it, sister."

I almost laughed. It was the one cliché the scene needed and you could count on Phil Musuraca to deliver it. His bulk filled the upper stairwell. The Sig-Sauer automatic I'd sent to him by messenger after calling him was in his hand. I took advantage of Gay Cully's confusion to remove the Smith & Wesson from my pocket.

"Make that three mistakes," I said. "You're as much a sucker for that *noir* schtik as Neil. Just because a P.I. is greasy enough to hound a woman for eighty grand doesn't mean I can't call on him for help. You've seen the pictures, Mrs. Cully. A staircase is no place to make a successful play."

Her gun dropped, bounced down two steps, and landed on the carpet. Just then Dick Powell shot Byron Barr onscreen.

Fat Phil said, "I didn't care for that *greasy* crack."

Eight

I got away from the Lathrup Village cops around midnight. On the way home I stopped at the video store, rented some tapes, and watched Doris Day movies until I fell asleep.

Sunday

They were having one of those runs for a disease on West Grand River. Most of the streets leading into it were blocked off with sawhorses and large Detroit Police officers in uniform, and some peace-loving soul had installed a loudspeaker on every third lightpole to blast a running commentary on the participants. I didn't catch the name of the disease but it was a cinch it wasn't a hearing disorder.

Normally on Sunday morning I'd have been sleeping through it all in my little cottage by Hamtramck, but my taxes were due the next day. So far I had located most of my canceled checks under the desk blotter in the office and was putting off pulling the file cabinet away from the wall to look for some missing receipts when the door to my reception room opened.

The buzzer was switched off, but the connecting door to the private office was ajar and I had a clear view of my visitor. I couldn't have seen any more of her if the door had been open all the way, because she was as naked as an onion.

She was a tall brunette with her hair swept up from a long neck that hadn't gotten much sun.

Her breasts were small but self-sustaining and she had athletic hips and legs with a little more meat on them than the current fashion allowed, which was okay with me because I hadn't caught up with it either. Her feet were pretty in a time that emphasizes hands and faces, the nails neatly pruned and unpainted. It was a pale body like you don't see any more—it shone in the sunlight canting through the window at my back—and she hadn't had any bikini waxes recently. She was in her late twenties.

For a beat after she closed the hall door she leaned against it, breathing in shallow gusts and looking around jerkily like a doe that had jumped the wrong fence. Then she saw me, standing half-turned toward the file cabinet, and seemed to realize her naked condition suddenly, because she blushed clear down to her bosom. It was like spilling red ink over a marble statue.

The loudspeaker under my window crackled and spewed some irrelevancy that gave me the best line I could dredge up under the circumstances. "The race is downstairs."

She started, as if the additional discovery that I was capable of speech was too much for her to take in. "Next door," she said; and fell on her face.

I couldn't have caught her on a moped. Still, I sprinted through the connecting doorway, knelt and felt her carotid for the strong pulse I found there, and lifted her up onto the upholstered bench where the potential clients were expected to sit, thumbing through copies of *U.S. News & World Report* from the Carter administration. She'd skinned her nose when she fell, but the rest of the inventory checked out. She'd only fainted. I took my raincoat off the halltree and spread it over her. Then I went out, locking the dead bolt behind me.

The office next door belonged that month to a graphic artist, a bitter-faced old mutterer still waiting for his one-man show at the Detroit Institute of Arts—or failing that, next month's rent—who hadn't said a word to me all the times we'd passed each other on the stairs. I nodded to the workman painting someone's name on a glass door down the hall, knocked at the artist's door, and tried the knob. It wasn't locked. Nothing about the workman's resigned expression told me he'd seen any good-looking naked women that day.

The office consisted of one room, slightly larger than my private tank. It had been converted into a studio, with unframed canvases covered with riotous slashes of paint hung on the walls and a sheet tacked over the south window to simulate north light. A foot-high wooden platform occupied one corner; across from it stood an easel holding up a canvas with the outlines of a nude human female form brushed on and a low zinc-topped table smeared all over with paint from half a dozen squashed tubes. A bouquet of brushes stood in a chipped coffee mug on one corner.

The air smelled of turpentine and something else even stronger, that didn't belong in a studio or an office or anywhere else except the firing range at Detroit Police Headquarters. I went over and wrenched up the window to let some of it out. The run was still going on below, with accompanying commentary from the loudspeakers. Every corner wore a cop in uniform.

The room where an artist works is never tidy. There are always things lying around, props and half-empty containers and yards of canvas tarpaulin and piles of paint-stained clothing. The pile of clothing at the foot of the easel contained a man.

He lay on his side with his legs drawn up and one arm flung across his face. When I moved the arm to get to the artery on the side of his neck, the collar of his old streaked shirt shifted, exposing a blue-black hole the size of my finger in the back of his head, just below the occipital bulge. There was no reason to expect any activity in the artery, but I looked for some anyway. No surprises there.

The face was the one I knew from the stairs. It looked a little less bitter. Death will do that, even the violent kind.

His right fist was wrapped around a long-handled brush. I made a mitten of my handkerchief and grasped the brush and pulled. It slid easily out of his grasp. I slid it back in. I straightened, touched the paint on the canvas with a corner of the handkerchief, and looked at the cloth. No stain. There was a sink, paint-splotched like everything else in the room, with a square plank table covered with charcoal sketches on rough paper, and a wobbly kitchen chair, where presumably the next Van Gogh sat with his back to the door, drinking coffee and brooding over his dark visions. A split, empty Styrofoam cup stood on the table. It smelled of grounds and was still warm.

One corner of the room was obscured by a sheet hanging down like a drape from tacks in the ceiling. Behind it was another rickety chair, with a woman's dress folded on the seat. A pair of low-heeled pumps lay underneath and a bra and panties hung from the back. I touched the dress lightly with a palm.

I found the telephone on the floor under an open Little Caesar's box with a bit of crust stuck to it and a couple of flies stuck to that. I made a call.

The painter in the hallway was gathering up his equipment. According to the fresh legend on the door, I was about to be blessed with another lawyer for a neighbor. My building ate them like peppermints.

"See anyone today?" I asked.

The painter shook his head. "I hate working Sundays. Dull as a washtub."

My visitor was standing in the middle of my waiting room, wearing my raincoat with her hands in the pockets. It nearly wrapped around her twice. A little of the frightened-doe look had gone from her eyes.

"You locked me in." She sounded accusing.

"I didn't want to lose the raincoat. Put these on instead."

I held out her dress and shoes and undies.

"You went in there?"

"Uh-huh. You want to talk about it?"

"Turn around."

I admired the view of the inner office while the raincoat rustled to the floor behind me and hooks hooked and elastic bands snapped.

"I'm a model," she said. "I work nude."

"I know. I'm a detective."

"I didn't see it. I was posing with my back to him. I heard the door open and close, but I didn't turn around. In my work you learn to stand still no matter what. I heard a sharp crack. Just a crack, like a brush dropping to the floor. I thought guns made more noise than that."

"Depends on the gun. Also whether it's wearing a suppressor."

"Suppressor?"

"Silencer to you. It was probably a twenty-two automatic, which is one of the few guns you can suppress successfully. It's a pro's weapon. What happened then?"

"He made a little noise and fell. I turned around then, just in time to see someone going out the door. It was a man—I think. That's all I can tell you. All I saw was his back."

"What was his name?"

"I told you, I didn't see his face. I wouldn't—"

"Not the shooter's, the artist's. I like it when the dead men I find have names. It helps me sort them out."

"Oh. Tontine. Victor Tontine." She hesitated. "He's really dead?"

"Didn't you check?"

"No. I just ran out. I didn't even bother to dress. I was afraid he'd come back and kill me. Don't they do that to witnesses? I panicked. I knew I couldn't go outside all undressed. Yours was the first door I came to. Thank God it wasn't locked."

"If what you say is true, you aren't much of a witness. Do you know why Tontine was killed?"

"I know nothing about him. He hired me through the agency where I'm listed. Thirty minutes, that's how long we knew each other. That's how long I'd been posing." A zipper shrilled. "Can you take me to the bus stop? There's a crowd on the sidewalk and my legs are too wobbly to fight my way through. I need to go home."

"We need some law first. You can sit down till they're through with you. It shouldn't take long, since you didn't see anything." I started toward the inner office and the telephone.

"Turn around."

I did. She looked just as good with as without, a rarity. The dress was a simple blue frock with double-reinforced pockets sewn in. Some women just didn't like to carry purses. This one preferred to hold a gun. It looked familiar.

"You should have locked the door to your office, Mr. Walker," she said. "You never know who might walk in and plunder the arsenal."

"Poor judgment. You didn't have any pockets when I left." I raised my hands.

"It was going to stay in my pocket until we got away from the crowd; but I never make plans that won't stand alteration. You're going to take me to my car, arm in arm, just like we're going steady. This gun's going to be in your ribs just in case you can't stand commitment."

"You should've wet down the paint."

She frowned. "What?"

"The paint on the canvas Tontine was working on. It was dry. He wasn't painting when he was shot. He was sitting at the table drinking coffee. After you shot him you pried the cup out of his fist, splitting the Styrofoam, dumped it out in the sink, dragged him to his easel to make it look like he was working, and stuck a brush in his fist. It was looser than it should have been if his muscles had contracted the way they usually do at the moment of death, but that wasn't evidence. The dry paint was. Also your clothes. They were still warm from your body. They wouldn't have been if you'd been posing for a half hour, like you said."

"Well, well. You *are* a detective."

"You were working under a deadline, or you wouldn't have hit him with a charity run going on down in the street and cops hanging from the lightpoles. You like your anonymity, or you wouldn't worry about being seen by one of them, a woman alone leaving a building where a murder was committed. And then there was the painter in the hall. He didn't see you slipping in; painters take breaks, just like everyone else. But you couldn't go back downstairs without passing him. You could have killed him, too, but that's one too many bodies on the same premises for a true professional. What's a girl to do?"

"What, indeed?" She seemed to be enjoying herself. She had the weapon.

"Easy. You shucked your clothes, ditched the gun somewhere in the clutter—the cops will find it, but it won't have prints or a serial number or a past history to spoil a job well done—waited till the painter wasn't looking, and slipped down the hall and through my door. Chances are you saw me through the window from the street on your way here and took a chance that I'd be working on a Sunday with my door unlocked. If you were wrong, you could always go back for your gun and kill him. He wouldn't be likely to run from a good-looking naked woman."

She laughed. She really was having a good time. "Thanks for the compliment. I work out. You have to stay in shape in my line, but

I'm a woman too. I like to look good. Good enough anyway to ask a handsome gentleman to see me to my car and keep his mouth shut."

"Permanently, of course. If the painter was worth killing, so is a detective. There can't be so many lady mechanics in this town the cops won't put two and two together."

"Here's where I say I prefer to be called a 'hitperson.'" She wasn't laughing now. Nothing like amusement had ever crossed that face. "On second thought, you may not be worth the commitment. Never let it be said I ever needed a man for any purpose, let alone slipping away in a crowd." She slid back the hammer on my revolver.

"Lose the piece *now!*"

She hadn't heard the hall door opening behind her. Now it swung around the rest of the way and Mary Ann Thaler charged in, accompanied by a pair of Detroit Police officers in uniform. They spread out inside the door, crouching, their service pieces clamped in both hands. The Felony Homicide lieutenant had on stone-washed jeans, black high-top Reeboks, a satin jogging jacket, and a baseball cap with a brown suede visor and her hair tucked up inside.

The game of cops and robbers was starting to require all new equipment: compacts and curlers and an extra pair of pantyhose for those pesky runs during high-speed chases. I was beginning to feel even more like an endangered species than usual.

The piece was lost. The officers flung Ms. Raskolnikov against the wall and put on the cuffs.

I lowered my hands and looked at my watch. "Twenty minutes for a murder. That's some kind of record."

"You try finding a place to park with barricades all over the neighborhood." Lieutenant Thaler returned her nine-millimeter to the shoulder rig under her jacket. "Where's the cold cuts?"

"Next door."

In the studio, she squatted on her heels to look at the dead man's face. "That's Tontine, all right. He's wanted for questioning by the FBI for an art forgery scam with connections to the Benevolent Brotherhood of Sicilians. We got a flyer. I guess someone was afraid he could talk as well as he could paint." She looked up at the embryonic painting on the easel. "That's where she got the idea to impersonate a nude model, huh? She got a nice body?"

"If you like one with a murderer inside," I said. "You'll find my prints on the telephone when you dust the place. I called you from here."

She stood up. "What are you doing at work on a Sunday, anyway?"

"What are you? I thought you had weekends off this month."

"The IRS doesn't recognize weekends."

"You shouldn't put things off till the last minute," I said. "You can get in all kinds of trouble."

Necessary Evil

Rosecranz, the building super, met me in the foyer. He was the oldest thing in the place after the plumbing, and whether he existed outside it was a mystery no one had yet paid me to solve. At midnight and change he had on the same greasy overalls and tragic expression he wore at noon. At the moment it was directed at the ruins of the front doorframe, shot to splinters by a solid professional kick to the deadbolt lock that had torn the screws from the pre-Columbian wood.

"You didn't hear anything?" I said by way of greeting.

"I had on *M.A.S.H.* It must have been during the shelling."

"Uh-huh." I didn't elaborate. Whatever the corporation that owned the building was paying him, it didn't cover acts of valor. "How many offices got hit?"

"Just yours."

"Uh-huh."

I got the rest during the climb to my floor. After the sitcom rerun had finished, he had stepped outside his office/apartment to check the front door before bed and had found it in its present condition. He'd snatched up the monkey wrench he kept around for pipes and crackheads, tried the doors to all the offices, and learned that mine alone had been forced. By then the intruders had left. He'd called me instead of the police on the theory that they hadn't changed since they put him in the hospital for attending a rally for Sacco and Vanzetti in 1922. I couldn't see any holes in the theory.

The lock to my outer office—the one with A. WALKER INVESTIGATIONS on the door—had been slipped with a credit card or a strip of celluloid. The furniture and magazines inside were undisturbed. I'd secured the door to my private brain trust with a dead bolt, but they're only as sound as the woodwork; the white gash where the frame had shattered was so worm-tracked it looked like Sanskrit.

"You went inside?" I asked. Rosecranz nodded.

I believed him, but I unlimbered the Chief's Special and poked the muzzle into all the holes and corners. A good break-in artist can hide behind a dust bunny.

Mounds of papers leaned at Dali-esque angles atop the old desk, crumples lay around the kicked-over wastebasket, the blinds hung crooked over the window. Everything just the way I'd left it when I locked up the evening before.

Everything except the two green file cabinets. Even there they'd made a tidy job, springing the two simple bar latches that secured all the drawers, the same way every file case had locked since Eve hired Cain to get the goods on Adam. All the missing files had been scooped from the top drawer of the second cabinet, between Beeker and Day.

"Something?" The super's sad eyes had followed every movement like a dog's.

"Something." I slammed the drawer shut with a boom they heard in Alberta.

"Police?"

"Why? I've already been robbed."

He called Detroit headquarters downtown anyway, for the insurance company. I skinned him a twenty to forget all about my office when he filed his statement, and got to work.

I couldn't get to who without going through why, and why wasn't worth banging my head against until I figured out what. That meant identifying which files were gone.

With the back of the customer chair tilted under the doorknob for privacy, I sat on the floor surrounded by spiral pads and transposed my notes onto a legal tablet, focusing on the names of clients that fit the hole. As experiences go, it was about as nostalgic as cramming for a tax audit.

When I finished the room was full of daylight and cigarette smoke. My throat burned and my eyes felt pickled. I wrenched open the window, sucked in my morning's helping of auto exhaust, and sat down at the desk to place the first of many telephone calls.

It was wild goose season. Two of the older numbers were invalid. Owen Caster's machine answered, and I left a message asking him to call me back. April Berryman hung up—divorce case.

I wound up with six no-answers, four new-parties-at-old-numbers, and three appointments for interviews. That was swell, provided I could think of some questions.

• • •

"Amos Walker. I hoped I'd never hear that name again."

Evelyn Dankworth met me at the Caucus Club. Her deep auburn hair and mahogany-colored eyes went with the stained glass and paneling, her tall highball with her two-fisted legacy. Her great-grandfather helped found General Motors and drank himself to death in 1930. Her parents had gone in an alcoholic murder-suicide, and after a long custody battle she had been raised by an uncle who later stood trial for drunk driving and manslaughter. These days she divided her time between Betty Ford and a clinic in Toledo where cosmetic surgeons removed the fresh-burst blood vessels from her cheeks.

"I get that a lot," I said. "I'm only bothering you to prevent someone else from bothering you worse." I told her about the burglary.

"I hired you to rescue my daughter from a cult. You didn't deliver. That's hardly a scenario for blackmail."

"You hired me to find her. When I did, you tried to pay me to kidnap her and deliver her to some professional deprogrammers you'd hired to scare the cult out of her. I turned you down because she was eighteen and an adult. I'd have stood trial for abduction."

"In any case I haven't heard from her in two years. She might be dead."

"Someone who knew about the situation might want to shake you down. That case file would help."

"You know my family history. Do you honestly think I could be hurt if any of this was made public?"

I sipped my scotch, a single malt that tasted like the smoke from an iodine factory. "I wasn't talking about blackmail. Someone might make contact with you and offer to deliver her for a consideration. A phony who got all his inside information from the stolen file."

"Very well. You've told me and I'm forewarned. May I now consider our association to be at an end?"

I said that was fine with me, but reminded her I was in the book in case she heard from someone. She climbed back into her sable wrap and left. She wasn't in such a hurry she forgot to finish her drink.

. . .

I found Chester Bliss sitting on a broken foundation on Woodward, eating his lunch in what was left of the third largest department store in the world. He was one of the workers hired by the city to clear away the debris after a demolition crew blew up J. L. Hudson's to make room for a mall or a casino or maybe just another empty lot. The big black face under the yellow hard hat was a mass of bone and scar tissue. He'd sparred with Joe Louis and Floyd Patterson and quit the ring in 1962 after a kid named Clay laid him on his back forty seconds into the third round. When he spotted me wading toward him through the dust and broken bricks, he put down his sandwich and took my hand in a grip I can still feel.

"They're selling those bricks for five bucks a pop down the block," I said when I got it back. "You could slip one in each pocket and wait for the market to rise."

"Suckers. Bricks ain't history. My foreman said you called. Don't tell me you found it after all this time."

I hated to shake my head. Fourteen months earlier I'd spent a week on his retainer trying to track down some items that had been stolen from his apartment. The only one he really cared about getting back was the Golden Glove he'd won in 1954. "Someone pushed in my office last night and made off with some files, yours among them. I wanted to let you know in case someone called and offered to sell you back your glove."

He grinned. He had all his teeth—a testament to how good a fighter he had truly been—but there was no sunshine in the expression. "They wouldn't eat out on what they got. All I own's my pride, and they can't have that."

"The B-and-E community's pretty tight. If I turn up this clown, he might know who hit your place."

"You think?"

I shook my head again. "Not really. It's just something I'm supposed to say."

He picked up his sandwich then and resumed eating. He managed dignity without stained glass and paneling.

• • •

My third appointment showed up at the Scott Fountain on Belle Isle just as I was getting ready to leave. The gunmetal-colored stretch limo crunched to a stop alongside the two-lane blacktop that circled the island and stood there with no one stirring inside while I finished my cigarette. That was apparently as long as it took to determine there were no snipers in the trees or FBI men within eavesdropping range. The driver, six-three and two-fifty in a camel-hair coat and dark glasses on an overcast day, got out then and opened the rear passenger door.

Boy Falco gestured to the driver to stay with the car and trotted up the steps to the fountain, swinging his club foot out in a half circle with each step. He'd dropped the *d* from the end of his first name about the time of his first face-lift. Scuttlebutt said he hoped to win the sympathy of the grand jury with the illusion of innocent youth. They'd voted to indict anyway. He was out on bond pending a new trial; a witness had recanted.

"Entertain me." He stuck his hands in his alpaca pockets and leaned back against the railing.

"Aren't you supposed to shoot at my feet?"

"I forgot you're a comic. Somebody cut out my sense of humor in the shower at Jackson. This about that stolen credit card?"

"You used the name on the card, Cruickshank, to fly to Miami and pick up a shipment from Bogota. The client died while I was working the case, bum ticker. I proved he wasn't on that plane so the

Widow Cruickshank wouldn't have to pay the bill. There was no reason to ID you as the card user."

"There was one damn good reason not to. You shaking me down after all this time."

"What would it buy me, a better coffin? No one would see it. The file walked out of my office last night. I don't want your boys coming to me in case someone calls you looking for Christmas money."

"That could be a fancy P.I. way of putting the sting on me without fingering yourself as the stinger."

I moved a shoulder. "Don't pay."

"I never do. In money." He pushed himself away from the railing. "If the credit card turns up in court, you won't."

"I thought you'd say something like that. I'd hoped it would be more original."

"The old ways are the best. That's why they're the old ways." He went back down the steps and swung his club foot into the car.

• • •

The telephone was ringing when I got back to the office. It was Owen Caster, replying to the message I'd left on his machine that morning. He was an investment broker with a juvenile theft conviction that had been sealed for thirty years. On his behalf I'd broken a couple of things in the living room of the former court stenographer who'd tried to sell him a duplicate transcript, and the threat had gone away.

"Someone else called after you," Caster growled. "He offered to sell me my file for a thousand."

I sat up. "What did he sound like?"

"I'm not even sure it was a he. It was a whisper. Twice I had to ask him to repeat himself. It might have been a woman."

"Disguise. Anything unusual?"

"Foreign accent, maybe. Probably another disguise. Tell me, do I have to hire you again to clean up your own mess?"

"This one's on me."

"I'm starting to think I should have paid the stenographer and kept you out of it."

"You'd still be paying him."

"Him, Mister or Miss Whisper, what's the difference? What the *P* stand for in P.I., Pandora?"

"Paradox. Clients hire me to take away their grief. Most of the time I manage to do that. Sometimes I just exchange it for a different kind of grief. I'm a necessary evil at best."

"Maybe not so necessary. Call me when you sort this out."

"When I do, can I get a tip on the market?" I was talking to a dead line.

The receiver rang right out from under my hand. A jovial Chester Bliss told me he got a call after his shift asking how badly he wanted his Golden Glove. The old fighter hand danced around with the caller for a minute, but the party got suspicious and hung up.

"Man or woman?"

"Woman, I think," he said. "She was whispering."

"Did you notice any kind of accent?"

"Couldn't say. I don't hear so good over the phone. Patterson busted my eardrums good."

"Thanks, Chester."

He hesitated. "You don't suppose she really has my glove?"

"I wish she did."

"Mr. Walker."

"Did you get a call, Mrs. Dankworth?" I'd just had time to get a cigarette going. I flipped the match at the ashtray.

"Ten minutes ago. When I asked for a description of my daughter, they quoted from the one I gave you. I hung up."

"Was it a woman?"

"Certainly not. I can tell a man's whisper from a woman's, even if he was European."

"What kind of accent was it?"

"Oh, I don't know. One of these eastern countries we're always sending food to. What are you going to do?"

"Make a call."

• • •

Boy Falco was a while coming to the telephone. He didn't have one in his office above the meat-packing plant he owned on Michigan and took all his messages through the realtor next door. So far the federal judges don't okay wiretaps on instruments belonging to gangsters' neighbors. "This better be something," he said.

I asked him if he got a call.

"You mean besides this one?"

"That answers my question. There's a good chance you will. Whoever copped those files has been running up his bill all day. When he calls you, I want you to arrange a drop."

"Be glad to." He sounded too pleased.

"I'm not setting up target practice for your boys. Once he agrees to the details, I want you to forget all about them."

"What if I don't?"

"Then I'll send my notes to the Federal Building."

"What do you want done with the ashes?" he snarled.

"You'll be too busy sweeping out your cell in the Milan pen to make the arrangements."

"Where do you want the drop, meat?"

"Four thirty-one Howard."

There was a long silence. "That's the DEA!"

"He'll feel safe there."

"I sure as hell won't."

"That's the idea, Boy. If your word were your bond, the judge wouldn't have had you put up half a million to stay out."

He had me repeat the details several times; writing things down wasn't his long suit. "I want those notes," he said then. "The file too, when you get it back."

"Too rich."

"I ain't asking."

"You've got enough on your plate without hanging me up on one of your hooks," I said. "You know a lot of people. A client of mine had his Golden Glove stolen a little over a year ago. He wants it back."

"Baseball?"

"No, the other one. Boxing."

"Trophies are tough to unload. I might know a fence with a soft heart. I ain't promising nothing."

"Me neither. I may not get that file back."

"I'll make some calls."

"Don't tie up the line," I reminded him.

I killed the time browsing through the yellow pages for a locksmith whose name I liked to replace the dead bolt on my office door. The telephone rang while I was deciding between Sherlock's Home Security and Lock You.

"The puke called," said Falco by way of greeting. "It's set for seven thirty tonight."

I wrote down six o'clock. I trusted Boy like pro wrestling. "How much?"

He snorted. "Thousand bucks in small bills, brown envelope. I got no respect for leeches in general, but I got less than no respect for a cheap one."

"Was the leech male or female?"

"Male. I guess I know a chick when I don't hear one. That whispering dodge has got hair growing out of its ears." He paused. "I think I found your glove thing. There's a name engraved on the plate. Sailor Jack Moran."

"Wrong name." I winched my heart back up where it belonged. "Wait. Does your fence do engraving?"

"Not for free."

"I'm good for it. Tell him to match the plate." I spelled Chester Bliss's name.

• • •

I left the office in plenty of time to buy a current *TV Guide* at a Rite-Aid, check a listing, and call Channel 2 from a public telephone to confirm something. Then I drove to Howard Street.

There was a wire city trash basket on the corner near the plain building with the flag flying out font. I slid the brown envelope under a Little Caesar's pizza box and walked around the corner out of the pool of light from a lamp. I came back on the shadowed side of the street and pegged out a spot in a doorway across from the basket. An empty crack phial crunched under my foot, ten yards from the Detroit office of the Drug Enforcement Agency.

It might have been the trouble he was in, but for once Boy Falco kept his word. In an hour and a half a handful of people walked past the trash basket, and not one of them was packing a tommy gun. I had a palpitation when an old woman in a knitted cap and a torn and filthy overcoat stopped to root through the trash, but she stopped when she found a piece of petrified pizza in the little Caesar's box, claimed it, and moved on.

Seven-thirty came and went. The temperature had dropped since sundown, and I had begun to lose all feeling in my toes when he showed up.

He had on a shapeless fedora and a faded mackinaw over his old overalls. His breath frosted in the air while he poked among the newspapers and Styrofoam cups in the basket, then lifted the pizza box, plucked up the thick envelope, tested its heft, glanced around, and stuck it in a side pocket. He turned and started back the way he'd come, his heels scraping the sidewalk.

I crossed the street and fell in step behind him. I followed him a full block before he turned his head.

He didn't try to run when he recognized me. Instead he leaned against the lamppost, collapsing a little like a sack of old fruit. I circled around to stand in front of him and held out my hand. I had my other hand in my coat pocket with the Chief's Special, but it didn't come out. He slid the envelope out of his mackinaw and laid it in my palm.

"What is inside it?" Rosecranz asked. "Not money."

"*TV Guide.*" I put it away. "You shouldn't have trusted it. *M.A.S.H.* was listed last night, but it didn't air. A programmer at Channel Two told me the president's speech threw off the schedule. The last half hour of *Steel Magnolias* ran in that time slot. That soundtrack wouldn't have drowned out a mouse's burp, let a lone a burglar kicking in two doors."

The building super moved a shoulder. "The same thing runs every night at the same time for two years. Who knew?"

"What did you need the money for?"

"I didn't. I don't." He leaned his cheek against the lamppost, sliding his hat off center. "I am eighty-six Friday. I never did nothing. Nothing since I came to this country."

"What about Sacco and Vanzetti? You were arrested at a rally."

"That was my cousin. I tell that story. I never did nothing. Nothing in eighty-six years."

"You're hell on locks."

"I smash the dead bolts with a monkey wrench. Forty years I have spent opening file cabinets when tenants lose keys."

"You shook down a fighter, an heiress, and a racketeer. That's not nothing. What did you do with the files you took?"

"I will show you."

I drove him back to the building, where he unlocked his single room on the ground floor, complete with steel desk, Murphy bed, and a teenage soap playing out in black-and-white on his ancient TV set. His tools lay in a pile on a folding table designed for lonely dinners in front of the tube.

He moved a stack of *Popular Mechanics*, and there were the manila folders in a dilapidated egg crate. I went through the files quickly. Nothing was missing.

"Comfy setup. Ralph Kramden ever drop by?"

I turned around. With Boy Falco and his family-size driver standing inside it, the room was barely big enough for oxygen. Rosecranz was watching them without hope.

"See what happens when you leave the front door open?" I said.

"You're a laugh hemorrhage." Falco's smile was dead on arrival. He was looking at the stack of folders in my hands. "Mine in there?"

When I hesitated, the driver unbuttoned his overcoat. The fisted handle of his Magnum stuck up out of a holster two inched left of his navel. I shuffled the stack and gave Falco the folder tabbed CRUIK-SHANK. He riffled through the pages, paused to examine the signature he'd forged on the airline receipt—all the feeds needed to tie him to the Miami drug scene—then put it back and stuck the file under his arm.

"What's it doing in here?" His tone was almost pleasant.

"I asked Rosecranz to hide the files in his place until I got a better set of cabinets."

"Thief give you any trouble?"

"Trouble's my name. I changed it to Amos when the other kids laughed."

He wasn't listening. He was looking at the super.

"Whisper something," he said.

Rosecranz looked sad. "What should I whisper?"

"That's the accent." He jerked his chin at the driver. The Magnum came out.

"You got what you came for," I said. "What's the point?"

"The point is I don't get crapped on by private creeps and janitors. Make it neat. I'll be in the car." He turned toward the door.

As he passed in front of the big man, I snatched the monkey wrench off the folding table, the same wrench Rosecranz had used to demolish the front door lock and one to my office. It was fourteen inches long and as heavy as a handtruck; it swung practically without help. The case-steel head struck the knobby bone on the driver's wrist with a crack and the gun went flying.

That was it for the muscle. He doubled over, gripping his shattered wrist between his knees, and I stepped around him and laid the wrench alongside Falco's head, a little more gently. I didn't want to crush his skull, God knew why. He folded like a paper fan.

When I turned around, Rosecranz was covering the driver with the Magnum.

The big man wasn't paying much attention. He was still bent into a jackknife and his face was gray. Rosecranz looked as tragic as ever. The hand holding the gun was shaking. I took it from him, put it in my pocket and drew out my on .38. I have a thing against playing with someone else's clubs. I told the old man to search Falco for weapons while I kept an eye on the driver.

Rosecranz knelt beside Falco and rose a minute later hefting a paper sack. "He had this under his coat."

I went that way, still holding the gun, and peered inside the sack. I reached in with one hand drew out the heavy object. The engraved brass plate was riveted to the base.

"Whaddaya know," I said. "He spelled Chester's name right."

The super looked around. "Just like *NYPD Blue*."

"You do need to get out more." I reached over and turned off the TV.

"Police?" he asked.

I nodded. "Police."

"Me?"

"No."

He didn't look any happier. "Why?"

"You're a necessary evil." I put the Golden Glove back in the sack, pocketed the .38, and picked up the Cruikshank file from the floor while Rosecranz worked the rotary dial on his old telephone.

Trust Me

"Every cockfight looks pretty much like all the rest, until you get to know it for the sport it is," Jackie Brill said.

"Football's a sport," I said, "and you don't have to watch a guy mop up blood and feathers at halftime."

"No, football's a game. Sport is life and death and taking risks."

"The roosters take the risks. I like my chickens flame broiled."

"Trust me on this. I've traveled enough in it to write a book on the subject, like that Irish guy that invented bullfighting. Hennessey."

I lost a beat, and two or three sentences of Jackie's high-octane pitch, before I realized he'd meant Hemingway. He was a drawn strip of forty-year-old jerky with shoulder-length dirty blond hair, a wind-sock moustache, and blue eyes pickled in scotch—the pizza delivery man in 1970s stag films—whose daily uniform only varied by which color of plaid flannel he wore over his jeans and black Surfaris T-shirt. He belonged to the fifth generation of a family whose fortune had built the Detroit Opera House, the public library on Woodward, and Joe Louis Arena.

His approaching me at Ford Field didn't increase my chances of making the Social Register that season; his relatives paid him to travel in circles other than theirs. I was only giving him time because I was stuck there until the parking lot cleared, and he'd come over to wait with me in the vacant seat next to mine.

When I'd heard enough about beaks dipped in poison and feed laced with antifreeze—the tricks of the cockfighting trade—I asked what he wanted. With the elaborate care of a proud father, he un-shipped a crocodile wallet, stripped off the rubber band that kept it from falling apart, and handed me a Polaroid of the biggest, ugliest rooster this side of Lyle Lovett.

The bird stood straight as a reinforcing rod, glaring through chicken wire at the camera, with its head tilted like a boxer's and a blood-red comb that flopped to one side like Hitler's lock. It had a gorilla chest and railroad spikes for spurs. I gave back the picture. "That's not a chicken. It's the love child of my ex-wife and a California condor. Just out of curiosity, who was on your lunchbox as a kid, Strangler Lewis?"

"I went to Grosse Pointe schools. My lunch was catered." He admired the snapshot, then tucked it away carefully and returned it to his hip. "He's Prince Cortez, out of Montezuma III by Queen Isabella, whose father took top money at the world tournament in Tijuana three years ago. He's just a year old and undefeated in three matches. Think Mike Tyson at eighteen."

"How much you got down on him?"

"Betting's for rubes. I'm buying him outright: two thousand cash."

"He must be a hundred percent white meat."

"I told you, you don't understand the sport. One more win and the price goes to five."

"If he's that good, why's he for sale?"

"His owner's got INS on his neck; something about lying on his visa app about his connections with those Zapatistas a dozen or fifteen years back. He needs juice wherever he can squeeze it. He's overextended."

"So buy the bird. You make that much a week just by staying away from Symphony Hall."

"See, that's why I'm glad I bumped into you. He wouldn't sell Prince Cortez to me for ten grand. I need somebody to carry the pony down to Mexicantown and pick up the goods by proxy."

"What'd you do, sleep with his wife?"

"His daughter." He broke eye contact. "Carmelita's a ripe little peach. I wasn't the first to pick her, but I was the one she expected to stick. When that didn't happen she went to the old man. So now Zorboron's prejudiced against my case."

"*Tiger* Zorboron?"

"*El Tigre del Norte*, they call him down in DelRay. His right name's Emiliano. That's like Mac in Mexican."

Jackie's local roots were showing. The old Hungarian section of town, once called DelRay, had been Mexicantown for years, attracting immigrants from south of the border to lay brick and pour mortar so their children could practice medicine and law. There was a gang element among them, of course, promising Old Country justice to new Americans and extracting tribute for the service. Emiliano Zorboron kept the tally.

I stood. The stands were still a quarter full, and the exits from the lot would be jammed tighter than Calcutta, but just then my car seemed a safer place to be. "Forget the prince, Jackie. You can mail order baby chicks by the crate for a lot less than two thousand. Try raising your own champ."

He slouched in his seat, thin as the slats but loose as the peanut sacks blowing about the field. "I heard you had *cojones*."

"If I didn't, I wouldn't worry so much about machetes."

"I'll pay two thousand to deliver two thousand. You went worse places for less for my uncle's law firm. I was brought up soft, but I've been down there a hundred times."

"It's the hundred and first I'm worried about." I left.

• • •

He was found in an alley behind a restaurant off West Vernor, the Mexicantown main drag. The cheap trash bag fell apart when a sanitation worker lifted it and Jackie Brill's head rolled out.

They'd cut him in six pieces, tucked them together as neatly as Legos, and if they'd used a Hefty Steelsack Jackie might have been buried in a landfill and forgotten, which is the fate of heirs who fall out of favor and vanish.

As it was he fell back in when his remains were identified. The Grosse Pointe Brills turned the screws on the mayor, the mayor put the squeeze on the chief of police, and the chief cracked the whip on the precinct commanders, who set loose the dogs. The restaurant belonged to a cousin of Emiliano Zorboron's, and even though the cousin lost his English under interrogation, and forgot his Spanish when a Hispanic detective clocked in, street informants were helpful; the story of the Tiger's strained relations with Jackie was known from one end of Vernor to the other. Within twenty-four hours of the discovery of the corpse, Zorboron was under arrest for murder.

Run-of-the-mill homicides don't make the local columns or see airtime. This space-saving policy pays off whenever a Jackie Brill dies under grisly circumstances. He was still on page one and ahead of the first commercial days later, when Mexicantown paid a call to my office.

I leave the door to the reception room unlocked during the day. You never know when loose money might blow in from the street while you're at lunch. The doorknob turned while I was reaching for it and an Aztec idol invited me inside. He was three hundred fifty pounds stretched out six and a half feet in a Hawaiian print shirt, cargo pants, and what looked like blue fur on his arms but which on closer inspection turned out to be tribal tattoos. His feet were disproportionately small—about size fourteen—in shining loafers, but his head was the size of a temple bell and looked larger still with a bushy mane of black hair combed up and over and down to his collar.

"Aloha," I said.

"*Buenos dias.*" His bass rumbled like someone rolling a piano through an empty warehouse. "We've been waiting."

He was big enough to be plural, but when I stepped inside from the hall, a human being who could have sat on his shoulder rose from the upholstered bench. She was about nineteen, olive-tinted, with full lips, eyes as big as the giant's in a head half as large, and black hair hanging loose and glistening to her waist. She wore a white blouse tucked into black slacks cinched by a belt with a heavy silver buckle, cork sandals on her bare feet. She'd have looked appropriate in a mantilla and lace, or a cape made of turquoise, sitting on a sandstone throne.

The season was past for Hawaiian shirts and sandals, but those traditions don't exist in Mexico or its northernmost branch.

"Mr. Walker?" said the woman. "I'm Carmelita Zorboron."

"I was afraid you'd say that. I was hoping you were Dolores, the patron saint of private detectives."

"You're not surprised. My picture has been in the papers and on TV. I'm sure that upsets my father. Before this, the only time his picture was ever published he was wearing a black bandanna across his face and holding a rifle."

"That was him? I thought that Zapatista story was a gag."

"Not to him. He is a proud man. He denied it just once, when he wanted to bring his family to the United States."

I thought she was more Anglicized than she acted. Her accent was too pronounced, her English too careful. But seeing her made me feel better about the hunk of pre-Columbian architecture in my little waiting room. I had an idea she could control him.

"Let's go inside." I rattled my keys. "This half of the building's been unstable since they blew up Hudson's Department Store. Senor Colossus exceeds the load capacity."

"Felipe," rumbled the big man.

"Okay if I call you Flip?" I opened the private door and held it. He said nothing, hanging back for Carmelita to enter first.

Inside the brain trust he pulled out the customer's chair and hung on until she was perched on the edge. He remained standing while I took my seat behind the desk. There were no other chairs, but he looked as if he'd feel at home sitting Indian fashion on the floor.

"You spoke with Jackie two days before he was killed," the woman said.

"Did I?" I didn't hesitate while taking a cigarette out of the pack.

"You don't have to deny it. I'm not accusing you of anything. One of my father's people saw him at the football game. He saw you talking, and when you left he followed you and got your license plate number. He told me this after my father was arrested. He did not tell the police."

"It wouldn't have looked good for your father if he had. They'd have wanted to know why he was so interested, and who for. Did he happen to overhear this conversation?"

She shook her head. "That is one of the reasons why I am here, to ask you what it was about."

"What does anybody talk about at Ford Field? Someone should sue the team on behalf of real lions for character assassination."

Felipe shifted his weight from one foot to the other, punishing a floorboard.

"Please," Carmelita said.

I blew smoke at the dark spot on the ceiling. "It won't help your father's case."

"Please."

"Por favor," said Felipe, without tone.

"I didn't take the job," I said, "so it wasn't privileged communication. He wanted to hire me to buy a fighting cock from Zorboron. Your father wouldn't deal with him."

"Prince Cortez." Carmelita nodded. "Jackie was right. Papa was not pleased with our relationship."

"If he were any less pleased, Jackie'd be cut in twelve pieces instead of six."

"My father did not do that."

"There's not a lot of difference between swinging the machete and giving the order."

"He did not do that either," she said. "If he had, do you not think he would have arranged to be seen engaged in some innocent activity at the time the police think Jackie was murdered?"

I smoked my cigarette in silence. It was a point.

Carmelita lifted her chin. "My father is not an angel. Nor is he a fool. He has no illusions about his daughter's virtue. Even if he had, he would do nothing during his time of trouble with Immigration. He would wait. He has the patience of a hunting cat. That is why they call him *El Tigre.*"

"Okay; so you've established reasonable doubt. You'd better get going if you want to convince the rest of the jury pool."

"I want to hire you to find the real killer."

"I don't hunt killers. My specialty's missing persons. The first rule is not to become one."

"You can at least demonstrate that my father was not the only one in Mexicantown who had a reason to kill Jackie."

"Why should I? My books are in good shape right now. One Emiliano Zorboron more or less won't affect the local tax base."

"My father is the one man my people can go to for justice when they are preyed upon by their own. The police file reports and do nothing. If he is convicted and deported there will be no one to defend them." She paused, a fist on her thigh until her breath stopped coming in short, shallow gusts. "I should not need to add that deportation would be a death sentence. The Mexican government tried him in absentia after the Zapatistas failed. His enemies will see to it he does not survive his first six weeks in prison."

I took one last bitter drag—a mistake I make twenty times a day—and mashed out the stub. "Where would I start? Your people don't pour out their secrets for Anglos."

Talk to my father. He is like a priest, and Mexicantown is his flock. There is no affair so private he does not know it in detail. He will not see me, and I suspect he distrusts Felipe's ability to act upon any information he might give him."

"The justice system has laws against outside competition. If he can open up to me without incriminating himself in another area he knows the language better than I do. A turnkey would be listening, and he'd wind up with a dozen more charges against him. I'd have to be working for his lawyer in order to arrange a private interview."

Felipe trundled forward and handed me a business card:

Felipe Quintas De La Merida
Attorney at Law

I ran my thumb over an embossed coat of arms. "You represent Zorboron?"

"*Sí.* Yes. Since before Carmelita was born."

"Okay, Mr. Merida. I need fifteen hundred to start."

"Felipe?"

The big man nodded and went out. He made very little noise crossing through the reception room. They say elephants walk quietly too. "Where's his briefcase?" I asked Carmelita.

"In his head."

"He could fit the entire Michigan Penal Code in there."

When he returned, Merida was carrying what might have been a medium-size safe by a handle on top. The handle stuck up through a hole in a heavy black cloth that covered the boxlike shape on all sides. When I realized he was about to set it on my desk, I cleared room for it. He hoisted it onto the corner without much effort. It seemed to be a lot lighter than a safe.

"What's in it?"

"Your retainer." He twitched off the cloth, startling the thing inside, which made a shrill squawk of a battle cry and hurled itself against the wooden staves that caged it. I shoved away from it as if a snake had struck at me. Merida, who seemed to know his way around a few things other than torts, made cooing noises until the dervish in the cage stopped whirling and flapping. It stood erect on its newspaper carpet, glaring at me from under its floppy comb with feathers floating down all around.

"His highness, the prince." Carmelita crossed her legs. "You know his worth. Jackie was many things, but he was not a liar."

"I meant cash, not livestock."

"Immigration has frozen all my father's accounts. I wait tables for minimum wage in my cousin's restaurant, the one where Jackie was found." Her throat worked. "Cortez is all I can offer in the way of security."

"Where would I put him? This place only looks like a barnyard until the cleaning service shows up."

Merida said, "He needs sunlight and air and cracked corn. Water. A goldfish is more trouble."

"Keep him. I'm appointing you his conservator."

He dropped the cloth back over the cage, choking off the rooster in the middle of some avian blasphemy.

"You will find him at this address," said the lawyer, writing on the back of another card. "Raul is in charge. Show him this card to collect."

I took it. "I'll need a letter for the cops, confirming I'm acting as your agent. On stationery without the Kentucky Colonel's picture on it."

He produced an envelope from a pocket of his cargo pants. His name and an address on West Vernor were engraved on it in gold and on the computer-printed letter it contained, both good linen stock. His signature might have been written by Prince Cortez. That made him genuine.

Carmelita Zorboron rose and grasped my hand in a fine slim one strung with hidden cable. "Thank you, Mr. Walker. Please report to Flip." Her smile burst like an incandescent bulb and was gone. In a minute she and Merida were as well.

I stared at the door for a while. Then I stared at the window and the wall. I'd bartered my services for jewelry and friendship and debts outstanding. It was bound to come to chickens sooner or later.

• • •

"Trust me," I said. "I'm the only one you've talked to in forty-eight hours who doesn't have an axe to grind."

"Felipe told me Carmelita wanted to hire you. I said no. Jail has robbed me of the respect of my servant and my child."

"Yeah, well, what are you gonna do? Up here they don't let you stick them in cages and feed them cracked corn." ·

I had no idea how that sat with him. Emiliano Zorboron looked as much like a gang leader as Felipe Quintas de la Merida looked like an attorney; small for a tiger, with the cuffs of his orange Wayne County jumpsuit turned back to let his hands poke out, and fine featured to the point of transparency. But when it came to showing what he was thinking, he was as transparent as a drill press. He might have been thirty-five or fifty. His accent was less obvious than his daughter's, which confirmed my suspicion she leaned on hers a little for effect.

We were seated facing each other at a plain maple table in a room reserved for lawyer-client conferences at the jail. I didn't think it was bugged, but just in case, I'd brought along a transistor radio and tuned it in to a gassy talk show to confuse eavesdroppers. RICO and the Patriot Act had danced a flamenco all over the First and Fifth Amendments.

"I had no part in Jackie Brill's death," Zorboron said.

"I'm being paid to believe you, so okay. Who did?"

"Someone with good sense."

"I didn't care for him either, but you've got the best motive so far."

"What does it matter whether they send me home for murder or committing perjury when I applied for my visa? I am sure you know something of my trouble there."

"The immigration beef you can beat, if Merida's half as good as his stationery. Murder's ten times tougher. We got all the killers we need domestic. We can export one now and then."

"Felipe is the best. I paid for his education. We worked side by side in a meatpacking plant in León when we were boys. I trust him with my life."

"Trust me. So far the prosecution has a case, and all he's got is a chicken."

"He had no right to offer you Prince Cortez. I am in here because I refused to let Brill dirty his feathers."

I played with a cold cigarette. You can't smoke in jail now, which is what they call kind and usual punishment. "You're in here because someone dirtied his hands good on Brill. And no one owns a fighting cock, except apparently me. It's illegal."

"That is America. Execute men, but do not abuse fowl." He scratched his chin. He had an eagle tattooed between two fingers so that it opened its wings when he spread his hand. "Speak to my cousin, Nolo Suiz. He may know something."

"The one who owns the restaurant where the body was found?"

"*Sí.* I do not know if he had dealings with Brill. But I think he thinks I should be frying tortillas and he should be running Mexicantown."

•   •   •

The restaurant was a single story of cinder block, with every square inch of concrete painted gaily and crudely with dancers and bullfighters and vaqueros on horseback, and evidently no name. The same stylized Aztec eagle that Zorboron wore between his fingers spread its wings above the door. In Detroit, you learn to read gang signs like cattle brands, without taking them too seriously. The most notorious band, Young Boys, Incorporated, was mainly a fiction of the late mayor's to derail an investigation into his personal finances.

A middleweight Hispanic in uniform stood in front of the yellow police tape across the entrance. I showed him the letter from

Merida, who seemed to be a familiar figure on that detail because he let me duck under and go in without any more foreplay. I passed through a room full of tables and upended chairs and paused inside the swinging kitchen doors to watch a dissection.

A Mexican built along Zorboron's delicate lines, but with coarser features and forearms as big around as melons, quartered a pig on a great butcher-block table in less time than it takes to say it, ambidextrously using a big cleaver to chop bone and a curve-bladed knife to slice sinew. He operated with a surgeon's lack of extraneous motion and made as much noise as a tyrannosaur eating a tenor.

"Nolo Suiz?"

He looked up, startled, with a sharp instrument in each hand and an expression that made me glad I always go armed on a homicide case. The medical examiner had said that whoever had cut up Jackie Brill had known a thing or two about bones and joints.

"*¿Quien es?*"

"Amos Walker. I'm representing your cousin Emiliano's attorney."

I showed him my ID, with the honorary deputy's badge pinned to the bottom of the folder.

"*El Tigre* don' go to cops. Get out."

I put away the folder and went for another pocket. He raised the cleaver high enough to throw. The Baby Ice Age never moved slower than my hand drawing out Merida's letter. I stepped his way, holding it out. He put down the cleaver to take it but hung on to the knife in his other hand. He read for a long time.

"I don' like Felipe." He gave back the letter.

"If there was a law against hating lawyers, the jails would burst."

I put up the letter, letting my coat slide open to show the revolver on my belt. He put down the knife then and mopped his hands on his apron. It looked like a bloody test pattern.

"Who takes out the trash here?" I asked.

"Me, sometimes. Sometimes staff. My cousin, Carmelita. You think she carved up her *hombre*?" He leered.

"It's a thought. She's healthy enough, and if she spent much time in this kitchen she'd know where to make the cuts. Same goes for the rest of the help."

"Me too. Back home I work in a *carniceria* since before I was big enough to lift a side of beef. You think it was me?"

"Not on that evidence. Zorboron told me he worked in a meat-packing plant. Butchering's practically a spectator sport in Mexico. Half the neighborhood's wise to the moves. But the Tiger has a motive, and Jackie Brill turned up in a sack behind your establishment."

"It wasn't even one of my bags. Health Department wouldn't let me use nothing cheap like that."

"If you were dumb enough to use one of your own, you're too dumb to operate your own cash register."

"Dumb enough to dump 'em behind my own place, though."

"You did a good job playing dumb with the cops and ducked an accessory charge. Zorboron and Brill had a bad history. Being related to the owner of the restaurant would make this a comfortable place to make the drop. Nothing dumb about that on your side."

"I don' even know Brill."

"You knew Emiliano didn't like him. Word's out you think you're better qualified to run things than your cousin. Maybe you found a way to vote him off the island."

I'd bet the odds and blew it. He'd seemed more comfortable with the cleaver, so I'd focused my attention on his right hand hovering near it. When the knife flashed into his left fist I made a late backhand swipe and got a nasty cut on the base of my palm. The blade tinkled in a corner, and I drew my weapon.

"Cops wasn't outside, I'd take away that piece and grind you up for a burrito." His big forearms bent at an angle in a wrestler's stance.

"Let's have them in." I held my free hand out to the side dripping blood. "What's *your* immigration status?"

His face paled beneath the natural pigment. His features were sharper than Zorboron's, rodentlike. "Why shouldn' I run things? I came here six years before Emiliano. I sent him money to come and bring Carmelita. I loaned him money to rent a garage and buy his first rooster. He paid me back with money only. Didn' offer me a partnership in his loan and protection business. Instead he trusts that big donkey Felipe. I am his blood!"

"Speaking of which, you got a Band-Aid?"

He found a kit in a steel drawer. I put away the gun and watched him as I poured on antiseptic and bound my hand in gauze, but he'd spent his wad. INS means TNT in ethnic circles. "So far you've convinced me you wouldn't help your cousin out of a ditch now: much less help him dump a corpse. If he did it alone, he wouldn't choose here and put ammo against him in your hands. Good work, Nolo. Before this, he was clean on just a working basis. You make a better defense lawyer than Felipe."

"I didn' kill this Brill," he said. "I didn' even know what he looked like till I saw his picture on TV."

"I believe you. You'd have deposited the evidence in Zorboron's back yard just to make sure it stuck. Who else hated Brill, or hated Zorboron enough to hang a frame on him?"

"Sister Delia."

That rattled me. So far the case had fathers and daughters and cousins and all of Jackie Brill's relatives. Brothers and pets seemed to be all that was left. "*¿Quien es?*" I said.

"She used to be a nun, but she quit when the old pope died. She runs her own mission now, across from Most Holy Redeemer, and she ain' so Christian about what she thinks of *El Tigre.*"

.   .   .

I don't know what I expected; a squat old dragon, probably, with a ruler in her fist and a prominent moustache. Sister Delia turned out to be a tall, handsome, horsy-looking woman with bobbed red hair and a grip best suited to a polo mallet. I shook circulation back into my fingers and sat in a shabby but clean armchair in a storefront whose plate-glass windows looked out on the Gothic pile of the church. Her coffee would float the Ark. I bit off a chunk and put cup and saucer on a folding card table.

"I haven't met Señor Merida," she said cheerfully. "If he represents Zorboron, I'm not sure Christ Himself could keep him from the flames."

"That doesn't say much on my behalf. I'm trying to get the Tiger out of the pit."

"You're just misled. The residents of Mexicantown are honest and hardworking—that whole cliché—and they're raising a generation whose accomplishments will establish whole new stereotypes, like the ones Asians enjoy now, as thinkers and innovators. The only thing that can stop them is prejudice. A gangbanger like Zorboron feeds that with every breath he takes."

"You don't think he can be saved?"

"I don't. That's where I parted with the Vatican. I stayed on from loyalty, but when the guard changed I got out. Cock fights; can you think of any symbol more demeaning to a people?"

"He isn't in for that."

That didn't pierce her armor. She sat in a cracked plastic scoop chair with her long legs crossed in pleated slacks. The mission seemed to be a place where the poor and homeless came in from the weather to thaw their veins with hot soup and that nerve-shredding coffee and listen to Scripture in Spanish. It was a nice day, and we had it all to ourselves.

"His daughter thinks he was set up," I said. "I think so too. Did you know Jackie Brill?"

"He tried to rent this building for his filthy exhibition." she said. "When I said no, he offered me a cut of the take. He spouted some nonsense about having to get to know it for the sport it is. He left when I threatened to call the police."

"He made me the same pitch."

"You see what I'm talking about? Zorboron's plague has spread to the white suburbs. He's the worst thing to happen to the Chicano image since Pancho Villa."

"You're not Chicano, are you?"

Her smile chilled the steam off my coffee. "I'm one of those white liberal meddlers you hear so much about; the people the KKK hate more than themselves. What about you?"

"Just a meddler. When did Brill approach you?"

"Last week. If you think I killed him and cut him up and dumped him at Zorboron's door, thank you for the compliment. I'm not that devious, but if I were I'd have done it just for the way Brill treated Carmelita. She's a sweet girl."

"You know her?"

"Everyone knows everyone here. Most of them came from the same three villages. Sooner or later they all showed up at Most Holy Redeemer."

"Did she go there to confess?"

"Technically, I can't say. I never saw her use a booth."

"Technically, bees can't fly," I said. "Let's put that word aside."

"A doctor knows medicine, but a nurse knows patients. It's the same with priests and nuns. People would trust me with things they'd never tell the father. I won't violate that just because I no longer wear the habit."

"You'd make a good lawyer."

The smile evaporated. "These days anyone can be a lawyer; anyone at all. Being a nun takes *cojones.*"

• • •

I had everything now but a motive, and I could guess at that. It was some kind of record for me in an investigative quagmire like murder. But it's a small community, where events take place in closer order than they do out in the world. I called Felipe Quintas de la Merida and agreed to meet him and Carmelita in his office.

It was above a garage around the corner from Nolo Suiz's restaurant, close enough to smell the hot grease and cilantro. Merida's diploma hung in a frame on imitation wood paneling behind an easy-assembly desk. I figured the second door led to his living quarters. Today he wore a lightweight gray suit off the big-and-tall rack and a dark blue shirt-and-tie set that made him look like a bouncer in one of the better strip clubs north of the county line. Carmelita, in a yellow dress and open-toed pumps, sat facing me on the customer's side with her hair up. She looked drawn, and pretty as end of day.

"Nice setup," I said. "What goes on downstairs?"

Merida didn't stir behind his desk. "They fix cars. We don't stage cockfights in Mexicantown anymore. It's become a suburban sport."

"Outsourcing. Very American. I don't guess Jackie Brill made himself any more popular than always when he tried to reintroduce it to the neighborhood."

Carmelita perked up. "He did? Do you think that's why he was killed?"

"No, it was over you. The police are right about that."

She drooped.

"Who told you Brill wanted to do that?" asked the lawyer.

"Sister Delia."

I'd picked a spot where I could watch both their reactions. Merida's face was an adobe wall. Carmelita's fell apart in little pieces. I decided to start with her.

"He tried to cut a deal to use her mission," I said. "She was a hard sell. She's not exactly an aficionado, but she was even less inclined because of you. You were a lot more forthcoming with her than you were with me. All I knew was you and Brill had a history."

She gripped the arms of her chair. "She swore she wouldn't—"

Merida broke in. "You covered a lot of ground in a day."

"It isn't Acapulco. You can do the place in an hour." I was still looking at the young woman.

"It was a scare," she said before the lawyer could speak again. "I was—late. He offered to make all the arrangements. He insisted. He said he'd pay for everything. I reminded him I'm a Catholic. He threatened me. He was terrified, I could see that. He knew Papa would kill him if he found out."

"Carmelita—" Merida began.

"Did he hit you?"

"No. He was afraid to go that far." The pieces came back together. She was the Tiger's child. "But you know that, if you spoke with Sister Delia."

"She kept your confidence. I've been working this job since before you were born. I get the most I can out of what little I get."

"*¡Bruto!*" Merida's face showed color for the first time. "She's your client, not a defendant on trial."

"They're all on trial until I separate them from their lies and omissions. She held back the pregnancy because she knew it was the best motive on earth for a father to kill an unwanted suitor. She said it herself; that's why Brill was desperate to terminate it on the q.t. What happened?"

"It was a false alarm," she said. "I was just—late. But the episode determined me to end the relationship." Her accent was softer now. She'd given up on playing the heiress apparent.

"That explains how he found the grit to go ahead and try to buy Prince Cortez through me. It also leaves only one person with reason enough to kill Jackie and the skill to process him like prime rib." I looked at Merida. "Sister Delia said anyone can be a lawyer. She wasn't speaking generally, was she?"

"*Cuidado, amigo.*" The big man's tone was at low idle. "You're coming close to grounds for action."

"I've been sued before," I said, "if that's the action you mean. You've got the doublespeak down, but you'll never be a successful criminal attorney if you think the cops are dumb enough to arrest Zorboron's cousin just because you ditched the body behind his restaurant. You were loyal enough to the Tiger to try to implicate his most outspoken rival; but that would just be a collateral benefit, wouldn't it? How long have you been in love with Carmelita?"

He laughed. The noise lacked resonance of his speech and had a nasty little rattle in it.

"Felipe?" Carmelita was staring at him.

"Remain calm. He swings his machete in the dark." It had the sound of an Old Country saying.

"No good, Flip. She knows. I knew, too, but I was too busy being sure Zorboron was guilty to read anything into the little things like the way you hold doors and chairs for her. Sister Delia knew because Carmelita told her. There's no other explanation for why she'd drag out that remark about lawyers when the subject came up."

"Felipe." She wasn't questioning him now. The syllables came out in a slow snarl of accusation.

I said, "You and Emiliano worked in the same meatpacking plant when you were kids. You never forget your first job or how to do it."

The desk erupted, coming up and over and almost clipping me before I could jump out of my chair. I knew he'd have strength, but I'd misjudged his speed. But Carmelita was slower to react. The near edge of the desk landed in her lap and the momentum threw her chair over onto its back with her still in it. She screamed, a clear, bell-like, south-of-the-border cry like you only hear now in old movies about lusty banditos and dancing senoritas, drowned out before it hit its peak by a horrified roar as Merida saw what he'd done and lunged across the desk to catch it before it pinned her to the floor.

He made it with an inch to spare and time for me to draw down on him where he stood clutching the heavy piece of furniture with his great arms strained to the limits of their tendons.

$$\bullet \quad \bullet \quad \bullet$$

We sat on the stoop in front of the door to his office, which belonged to the garage above which Felipe Merida had practiced law until yesterday. Zorboron conducted business inside only when rain or cold prevented him from making high-interest loans and promises from that concrete pedestal sprayed all over with graffiti in Spanish. I was in my shirtsleeves, the Tiger in a black T-shirt that showed raw muscle stretched over bone with no flesh to spare. The day was warm, not precisely Indian summer because we hadn't had a frost yet, but nice enough for two acquaintances to drink Dos Equis from the bottle on the street, knowing there wouldn't be many like it for a long time.

"He was the friend of my youth," he said. "He should have told me of his intentions toward my daughter."

I said, "He hadn't any, apart from mooning around in her orbit until she found someone closer to her age and type. You'd have taken even that away if he'd opened his mouth."

"Yes, but he should have showed me the respect. Carmelita is different. She tells me nothing and I know less."

"Congratulations. That makes you an American dad. She knew how he felt without his having to tell her. Women are born with that talent, both sides of the Rio Grande."

"Poor Felipe. I would help him if it were not for my problems with Immigration."

"He's confessed. He'll get off with less than a life sentence if Brill's rich relatives stay out of it. I think they've made all the noise they're going to. He's off their hands, and they don't have to pay him any more to keep him off."

He swigged beer. "I cannot even reimburse you."

"We're square. I've got Prince Cortez, don't forget. I don't think you're stupid enough to fight him with Uncle Sam watching, and he'll be past his prime by the time you jump through the hoop in Washington."

"Will you fight him?" He looked at me. It was the first time I'd seen his eyebrows move more than a bubble off level.

I scratched my hand. The cut was starting to heal. "I spend most of my day in a sweaty little room. I don't want to spend my nights in one. My building super has family out in farm country. His Highness can perch on a fence and annoy the neighbors at sunrise."

"You are an animal lover?"

"Only the ones with fur and cold noses. I thought about eating him, but he's too stringy."

"I do not see the profit to you."

"I told your daughter at the start my books are in good shape. I got some sun and found good takeout across the street. I don't think I want to eat in your cousin's place. He told me he grinds the meat for his burritos. Authentic Mexican cooks shred theirs."

"He is Bolivian on his father's side." Zorboron chipped at the label on his bottle with a manicured thumb. "I, too, am disenchanted with the spectacle of birds mauling one another for the entertainment of imbeciles. It does not suit a man of standing in his community. I will be disappointed if after all you have said you take advantage of my withdrawal to mount an enterprise of your own."

"You'll have to trust me on that."

"This thing I will do." He offered me the hand with the tattoo. We shook.

The Woodward Plan

Emory Freemantle had been with the Detroit Public Library almost as long as the 1950 Wayne County Manual and had spent even less time outside its doors. His job was to wear a uniform and wake up the odd bum when he started drooling on Shakespeare's sonnets. I'd been bribing him for ten years to unlock the back door for me midnights and Sundays when I needed to check a fact in one of the newspapers on microfilm.

I parked next to the white marble Main Branch on Woodward and rapped on the fire door. He'd been waiting for me; a key rattled immediately in the lock on the other side and he swung the door open just wide enough for me to slide in around the edge.

"Thanks for coming, Mr. Walker. I know I haven't any hold on you. Our account's square." He gripped my hand gently; he was as big as a city bus and didn't need to prove anything by crushing bone. He had skin the color of oiled walnut, faded a little with age, and pale eyes like Christ on the cross.

"You never know when I might want to take out a reference book," I said.

"The librarians hate that. Meanwhile they let a hundred thousand in rare books crawl out through the ductwork. I pulled a guy out of a ventilator just last month." He spoke carefully as he led me through a mile of metal stacks to the little room where he took his breaks. He read a lot when he wasn't rousting drug dealers and book thieves and liked to make himself crazy diagramming the sentences of politicians.

The break room had a Mr. Coffee, a microwave, a camp-sized refrigerator, and a round table covered with magazines, as if there weren't enough to read on three floors. It smelled of strong Colombian and uncensored literature; Emory's little borrowed stack on the counter included *Ulysses* and Harry Potter.

He poured me a cup from the carafe, tossed a handful of coins into a Town Club box on the counter, and sat down at the table opposite me, folding his big hands on the top. "My nephew's in Receiving Hospital, hooked up to a pinball machine. He may come out, or not. He hurt his head."

"Hurt his head on who?"

His grin lacked heat. "I oughtn't forget you're a detective. He wrapped a Porsche around a lightpole four blocks up on Woodward. You might've heard about it."

I nodded. "It had to be a Porsche. A Chevy wouldn't have made Section A."

"Cops called it a carjack. Lester stuck a gun in a guy's face in the parking lot at the Whitney, they said, and took off for Eight Mile Road. City cruiser got in behind him up past Kirby; he had it up to a hundred when he spun out. They don't know if he'll walk again."

"Should've picked a Chevy."

He worked his hands together. Powerful hands, with balloons of scar tissue on the knuckles; they must have given him hell in damp weather. He never got to the Golden Gloves, but he'd sparred with many who had, and one winner.

"My sister did as good a job raising him as she could, but she done it alone. There's some juvie stuff on his record, but that was years ago, and he never raised so much as his fists on no one. Jacking that car wasn't his idea."

"Cops didn't pull anyone else out of that wreck. How long since you talked to Lester?"

"They ain't let me in to see him. I seen him a week before the thing. He had him a job installing car stereos, was saving to buy speakers for his Jeep. You can't put speakers the size he wanted in no Porsche."

"A Porsche buys a lot of speakers. I'm not trying to be tough, Emory. Nobody knows anybody."

"You want to see the gun?"

"Cops said he threw it out of the car. They didn't find it, so it went down the sewer."

"Them sewers swallow up a lot of ordnance. You wonder how the shit gets out to the river." He leaned back to snake a hand inside his pants pocket and clattered something onto the table.

I caught it before it bounced over the edge. It was black plastic, about the size of a cigarette case, with a red muzzle. A spring snapped inside when I pulled the trigger. It was made for shooting plastic darts with rubber suction cups on the ends. I chuckled and slid it back his way. He made no move to pick it up.

"You get points for originality, but that's all," I said. "It won't buy you thirty seconds downtown."

"I gave him that toy gun in a box with a set of darts and a target board for his tenth birthday. I never seen it again till Old Willie brought it to me yesterday. You seen Old Willie. Begs his dinner off folks coming out of the Whitney with doggie bags and eats it in Periodicals."

"He the one with the football helmet?"

"No, that's Cap'n Kirk—he gets messages from Jupiter. Old Willie wears a sock cap with a deer on it. He picked up the gun in the parking lot where Lester threw it when he took off in the Porsche."

I retrieved the toy and turned it over. "It wouldn't make a difference to the charge. It's still armed robbery. They put teeth in the law after too many toy-gun users walked on the weapons beef."

"That's 'cause some toys look real to the victims. You think anybody would be fooled by this one? They don't put red tips on real guns."

"It could happen," I said. "If it was dark enough, and the victim was Mr. Magoo."

"They light the lot at the Whitney brighter'n the MGM Grand. But let's go out on a limb and say somebody might mistake this hunk of plastic for the real thing. You think anybody'd mistake Buzz Bernadotte for Mr. Magoo?"

Bernadotte was the owner of the Porsche. A Chevy might have made Section A at that, if it had been carjacked from him; only if it had been a Chevy, it wouldn't have been Buzz Bernadotte.

"Richie Rich, maybe," I said. "Not Magoo. You think the carjacking was phony?"

"You're the detective."

I twirled the gun Tom Mix fashion on my finger. "Old Willie sell you the gun or what?"

"It was a gift. I let him curl up in the stacks sometimes when I'm supposed to be sweeping him out the door. He don't cause trouble, and he's afraid of shelters. He got his teeth kicked in once for grinding 'em in his sleep."

"He see anything?"

"I asked, but he went dummy. Half these boys talk to theirselves all the time. The other half wouldn't open their mouths to tell you you're parked on their foot. Guess which half is Willie's."

"You say he hangs out in the Periodicals section?"

"All day every day, except dinnertime, when he's at the Whitney. And today," he added. "Today he didn't show up."

"He ever miss before?"

Freemantle shook his close-shorn head. "Not since I know him. That says something, don't it? I mean if he saw something."

"Not to the law." I put down the toy gun. "It wouldn't be the first time a policyholder mistook his insurance company for an ATM. If that's the case, Lester might do a jolt for fraud, but not armed robbery. He'll take his physical therapy in minimum security, be out in ten months. The gun's cheesy enough to make the cops ask Buzz some hard questions, but it's no good if they can't place it at the scene."

"That's why I didn't go to the cops." The guard got a worn wallet out of his hip pocket and laid five one-hundred dollar bills side by side on the table between us, dealing solitaire. "That's all I got. I know you get three days up front. I'll write you a check for the rest, if you don't mind hanging on to it till Friday. That's when I get paid."

I picked up one of the bills. "Case dough. I'll be back for the rest when I have something to sell. Give me a description of Old Willie. Maybe he's found a new hat."

• • •

Buzz Bernadotte's line stretched back to Detroit's French Colonial period. The family had built its fortune on the trade in beaver pelts, invested it in railroads, then automobiles, and more recently in fast food and sports franchises. Since the1967 race riot, the Bernadottes had been living in Grosse Pointe Farms, where they grow nothing but billionaires, but Buzz's father Alec had been pouring money into a number of restoration projects along Woodward Avenue, Detroit's main street: Theaters, restaurants, and art galleries had begun to appear on sites formerly occupied by crack houses and ladies named Chenille. Alec, Jr.—Buzz to the people who trailed him picking up fifty-dollar bills—made most of his investments in low-slung cars, high-breasted women, and dinners at restaurants like the Whitney, where his tips alone would keep a Democrat in dates for a year. It was one of the few places on Woodward not owned by his father.

I went to the Whitney, but not to see Buzz. It was dinner-time, and rumor had it the best of the local color could be found at that hour in the parking lot.

How this many-spired monument to the bad taste of a lumber baron managed to survive the years of civil unrest, soaring homicides, and mayoral plundering is one for Ellery Queen. It was serving sliced salmon hips smothered in champagne sauce while the rest of the city's nightlife was roasting rats in the vacant lot down the street.

The parking attendant was a good-looking black kid in a burgundy blazer. When he opened my door, I folded a twenty into a slim rectangle and held it between two fingers. If I'd started with a ten, then changed my mind when I caught a whiff of clarified butter from inside. "I'm looking for Willie."

He measured out a centimeter of careful smile. One look at my suit and the car it came out of had told him I wasn't dining there. "That's the first time I've heard anyone call it that."

"This one's homeless. Short, black, about sixty, wears a knitted cap like a hunter's with a deer embroidered on it. Begs doggie bags off customers."

"Him, yeah. I shoo him off every night."

"What about tonight?"

"Not yet. He usually shows up about ten."

"Was he here the night of the carjacking?"

"Probably. I had my hands full with the police that night. I'm the one who called them. I saw the whole thing."

"What'd you see?"

His face showed animation for the first time. "After I brought up Buzz's car, he took it to the end of the drive and waited to turn. This guy stepped from behind a pillar waving a piece. Buzz got out with his hands up, and the guy got in and took off."

"You saw the gun?"

"He had something in his fist. I didn't think it was a pocket calculator and neither did Buzz."

"Did you see him ditch it?"

He shook his head. "Cops said he must have thrown it out during the chase."

"The cops know everything," I said. "That's why there's no crime in the city. Willie show up last night?"

"I wasn't in last night."

"Who was?"

"I don't know. I wasn't here, remember?"

"I forgot. People forget things and think they never knew them." I gave him the twenty.

"I'll get my supervisor. He's here every night."

His supervisor had sixty pounds on him and gray hair.

He'd witnessed the carjacking too, but he hadn't seen anything the kid hadn't. He thought Old Willie had been hanging around about that time. It cost me another twenty to find out he hadn't seen him since.

I hung around the lot until ten-thirty, smoking cigarettes and watching foreign cars and the odd Cadillac come and go, taking on and unloading well-fed men in Frank Lloyd Wright ties and glittering women. They left carrying filets of Tibetan yak wrapped in swan-shaped foil, and no one came forward to relieve them of the burden. That nailed it for me. Men who hadn't eaten all day didn't miss such opportunities. I cranked my battered old American make out of the corner where the employees parked and paid a call on the Wayne County Morgue.

• • •

My contact there was a neat little guy with bright eyes behind windowglass spectacles he thought made him look older. He looked like Mr. Peabody's boy Sherman. He said, "You're going to have to be more specific. This place is a clearinghouse for the homeless, and the *living* population's eighty percent black."

I told him about the knitted cap. "It might not be natural causes. No wood-alcohol poisoning or OD or passing out on the Penn Central tracks?"

His eyes brightened further. "We got a g.s. early this morning. That's gunshot."

"N.s.," I said. "That's no shit. Show me the body."

"Anywhere else, that'd be a euphemism." He put down his carton of chocolate milk and led the way to a drawer. The naked body was bluish gray, the face shrunken to the skull. He might have spent the last ten thousand years in a crevasse, except for the blue hole just above his left nipple. Bright Eyes scooped the rolled-up paper sack from the foot of the drawer and pulled out a knitted stocking cap, blaze orange the way they wear them in the woods, grimy from constant wear and no laundering. The deer wasn't talking.

"Him, I guess," I said. "Where'd they find him?"

He returned everything to the drawer, shut it, and went back to his desk to consult his clipboard. "State fairgrounds. Ditch along

Woodward. M.E. says he was moved. He dug out a twenty-two long. Pro job, or a good amateur who wanted it to look that way."

"Straight shot. No pun intended. They were waiting for him on his way to the Whitney, or more likely on his way back to the library, after ten p.m. when it was quiet. Probably offered him a handout; that's how they got him in front. Then they rode him up to the first deserted stretch and dumped him."

"Doesn't say that here. Who's your snitch?"

"Andy Jackson." I poked a twenty into the pocket of his white coat.

Alec Bernadotte was easier to find than his son; it's often that way with philanthropists. They like to be seen and have their pictures taken, shaking hands with crippled children and giving out big dummy checks loaded with zeroes. It was a morning reception in the baroque lobby of the Fox Theater on Woodward; not his project, which was why he didn't hesitate to rest the plastic glass containing his mimosa on the head of one of the plaster lions flanking the staircase.

I got in line to shake his hand. He was a small-boned man in his fifties with black, Gallic eyes and a tanned bald head, a hundred and fifty pounds of nervous energy in a pinstripe suit measured and cut under the direct supervision of God. When he stuck out his hand I showed him my ID.

"Amos Walker, Mr. Bernadotte. I need to ask a couple of questions about the incident at the Whitney."

The practiced twinkle in the black eyes became a stony glint. Two large men in blue suits stepped forward to flank him. They looked just like the lions. He said, "If you're working for the insurance company, you'll have to talk to Buzz. He and I don't communicate these days."

"Not at all?"

The thrum of voices was loud in the cavernous room, but he lowered his a notch. "I'm a venture capitalist, Mr. Walker. Once an investment has revealed itself to be a losing proposition, I stop putting money into it. My son is a junk bond. He's been on his own for months."

"Where can I find him?"

"You might try the DAC. He likes to keep fit. It's the one thing he does that makes sense. He needs to stay in front of his creditors."

I thanked him and started to leave. Turning back, I pulled the toy gun out of my side pocket.

Bernadotte shrank back. The bodyguards went for their shoulder rigs. They were trained for speed and would probably have gotten off a couple of shots after I'd pumped half a clip into the man they were paid to protect. I think one of the lions gasped. Then the bodyguards saw what I was holding and relaxed. Bernadotte's nervous laugh joined theirs, a beat behind. Echoes of it rippled through the crowd in the room.

"Is life that boring?" Bernadotte asked.

"Calculated risk," I said. "I knew you could afford the best and that their reflexes would work just as well both ways. You knew it was a gag, huh?"

"I'm not an idiot. It might as well have a flag sticking out with 'bang' printed on it in big letters."

"Is your son an idiot?"

"Only when it comes to money. He thinks I have my own printing press. Or thought it, until I cut him off. But he knows a toy gun from the real thing."

I thanked him again and put away the toy. It was worth almost getting shot.

Woodward Avenue was named for Augustus B. Woodward, who in 1807 proposed his "Woodward Plan" for rebuilding Detroit after the great fire burned it to the ground two years earlier. The plan called for a series of great circles after the fashion of Washington, D.C., beginning downtown and radiating out to where Outer Drive now encloses the central city. The building I walked into, on Madison a quarter turn along the great circle off Woodward, stands just about where the Plan petered out and the gridded blocks begin. That's where we lose most of our visitors; they circle the octagonal lots for hours, fingers clamped to the steering wheel and only the ghosts of hope on their faces.

I hadn't visited the Detroit Athletic Club since the old mayor died. The stately Italianate box had gone up in 1915 to give the old auto pioneers a place to hide from their fan base, but it had taken the optimism of a new administration to rescue it from demolition. Now, gentry like the Bernadottes were re-upping in herds, and restorers were uncovering the ornate painted ceilings and scraping the gum off the Pewabic tiles on the floors. I rode a brass elevator up to the gallery overlooking the Olympic-size swimming pool and gazed down on the spot where a pre-Tarzan Johnny Weismuller had trained for the 1924 games.

Buzz wasn't hard to spot. He was the one dripping in a Speedo at the far end, selecting a towel from among the half dozen offered him by a group of young men his age, all of whom dressed as he did in photographs, in loose unbleached cotton and khakis hand-stitched in Manila or someplace equally difficult and expensive to import from. and went to his hairdresser to tame their cowlicks. He was a slender, muscular twenty-two, with his father's Gallic eyes and a five o'clock shadow that was hard to maintain unless you wanted to eliminate it, as I did. It cost him plenty to look as disheveled as Old Willie had for free. I wondered where the money came from.

By the time I descended the stairs to the pool area, Buzz had put on a terrycloth robe and flip-flops and was on his way to the locker room. I showed him the bottom half of my ID folder, containing the honorary sheriff's star. "It's about the Whitney. It'll just take a minute."

"Minutes are what I'm fresh out of," he said. "The Detroit police have my statement. Don't you boys talk to each other?" He started to push past.

I took my other hand out of my pocket and stuck the palm under his nose with the toy gun lying on it. "Minutes aren't the only thing you're fresh out of, Buzz. Who's paying your dues?"

He recognized the item. His eyes seemed to get blacker. That was just the effect of the color leaving his face.

"Buzz, you want me to get security?'? This from one of the youths clustered about him. He still had his baby fat.

"No. Meet me in the bar later. Set yourselves up on me." That cleared the room. Buzz and I stepped through a door into a locker room that was like no other, with a carpet and a little, leather-upholstered sitting area around a big-screen TV and, if you wanted them. a shower and a couple of rows of lockers. We sat down facing each other. He held out a hand. "I'll take a closer look at that popgun."

I smiled and patted my pocket. "It's evidence of nothing if I can't put it in Lester's hand, but I'll hang on to it just the same. Who are you in to and how deep?"

He shook his head. "What's County's interest? My car was stolen in Detroit."

"The badge is a toy, like the gun. I'm private. They hung the wrong rap on Lester, and I'm out to correct it."

"His family." He showed me his orthodontia; his feet had found the shallow end of the pool. "How much for the gun and to forget you ever saw it?"

"Thanks, Buzz. That saved me some, time. There was a bare chance you thought the gun was real, silly as that sounds, and didn't set up the carjacking. What's the insurance tag on the Porsche, couple of hundred thousand?"

"Half a million. It's a commemorative model. But you've got nothing. Even if you can enter the toy in evidence, my lawyers will hang up the case for years."

"What lawyers? You can't pay them. You can't even pay for your friends' drinks. Your old man sent you packing. That's why you decided to run a number on your insurance company, to keep up your lifestyle."

He sat back and crossed his arms behind his head. "You're just like the old man, as you call him. You think he's the only source of income in the world."

That puzzled me for a minute. Then it didn't. My contact at the morgue had said Old Willie was a pro job, or made to look like one. I'd hung up on the second choice and hadn't stopped to consider the first.

"Your father said you weren't an idiot, except when it came to money," I said. "He'll be relieved to know you've learned something. Who's Daddy now, and does he speak with an accent or is he one of the new breed?"

The black eyes shifted slightly. "I don't follow."

"Sure you do. You just didn't expect me to. Alec Bernadotte doesn't care anymore if his kid gets in Dutch, but someone else does. Someone who wouldn't hesitate to put a hole in the only witness who saw the carjacking close enough to know it was fake, then run him up to the fairgrounds and dump him."

"What? I don't—"

"The boys in the Combination like long-term investments. They know if they help you out now with cash, it will come back a hundred thousand times over when Bernadotte dies and his only son takes over the family finances. Except all that goes south the minute you draw a conviction for insurance fraud. Any good conservator would freeze you out forever."

His hands came out from behind his head. "I don't know anything about murder. Who?"

"You wouldn't know him. I doubt you ever stopped long enough to throw him a pheasant leg on your way out of the Whitney. He only became important when he could place a silly toy gun in the hand of a kid who wanted some money to buy stereo speakers. That's why he agreed to fake a carjack and stow the Porsche someplace until the policy paid off.

"I thought at first you killed Old Willie yourself," I went on. "Telling your mob friends about him, knowing what they'd do to correct the situation, amounts to the same thing. That's how the judge will see it."

He gripped his knees through terrycloth. Very slowly his hands relaxed. He shook his head. "There's a flaw. If I had this wonderful source of money, why did I decide to hold up the insurance company?"

"You were looking for a buyout. Maybe you didn't like the way they eat with their mouths open. Too bad you couldn't ask your father for advice. He'd have told you an investment is not a loan. A one-time payoff wouldn't satisfy them."

He smiled with some of his old cockiness. "It's all smoke without—what did you call him? Without Old Willie. You could have bought that gun at Wal-Mart."

"You forgot Lester. He's staring at hard time, and in a wheelchair. Your Woodward plan totaled itself against a lightpole."

"He's in a coma."

"If he wakes up with this same story, without prompting, everything else falls into place: the gun, the dead bum, your bottomless bankroll. If I were the prosecutor, I'd spin the wheel. But you can always hope he doesn't wake up. It'll help pass the time." I got up and left him there. The place was beginning to smell like a genuine locker room.

I filled a glass from my private stock in the file drawer where I never filed anything but my portfolio on whiskey futures and drank it down at my desk. I was working up stimulation to dial Emory Freemantle's line at the library. The case against Buzz wouldn't hold water in a hurricane; without it, Lester would be wheeling up to a drill press at the state penitentiary in Jackson until they ran commuter flights to the moon. By then everyone would have his own robot private investigator and I'd be living on other people's leftovers like poor Old Willie.

Deciding that bad news went down a little less bad in person, I got up and reached for the doorknob just as someone came in. He was quiet; I hadn't heard him in the outer office. He was built slighter than expected, and fair, with long lashes most women would sell their bodies for, although if they had them they'd get a better price. Well, there are blond Sicilians. He didn't even have to be Sicilian at all, or Italian, for that matter. All he had to have was a gun, in this case a .22 target shooter with a silencer.

"Don't waste your time denying you're Walker," he said. "I pulled your picture from a file at the *Free Press.*"

I raised my hands without waiting for orders. He liked that. He was young, and not the type to be patient with aging boomers. He patted the usual places, shook the flaps of my suitcoat for telltale weight. The toy gun in my side pocket weighed almost nothing and was too slim to make a bulge.

"I'm disappointed. I thought all you old-time P.I.'s went around loaded for rhino." He gestured with the .22. I backed up and he cocked a leg over a corner of the desk. "I'm waiting for a call," he said. "Then we'll finish."

"I'll guess. Receiving Hospital."

"Maybe a pay phone outside. He might be in a hurry. Maybe not, though, if he rings for the nurse just before he sticks the ice pick in Lester's chest. That'd give him another forty-five minutes." He laughed. It was a boy's laugh, light and completely unclouded.

"Buzz didn't waste any time getting in touch."

"I like Buzz. We got a special interest in Buzz." He liked saying Buzz. "He shouldn't try to think like us, though. Lester installed the sound system in Buzz's Porsche—that's how they met. If the cops felt like digging, they could link them up."

"I'd wondered about that. "That the same piece you used on Willie?"

"Willie? Oh, the homeless guy. No, that's in the river. Guns are cheap."

"Almost as cheap as shooters."

He laughed. "I like you. I'm going to regret this, I can see. It may not even be necessary. But why take the chance?"

The telephone rang and I started toward it, as if from habit. He raised the pistol an inch, stopping me, and lifted the receiver. But he didn't make me go back.

"Hello." He listened, watching me through his long, pale lashes. "No Alderdyce here. Wrong number. You're very welcome." He hung up. "You'd think with all this technology—"

He stopped when the muzzle touched his temple. I didn't raise my voice. We were only separated by the length of my right arm. "Your frisking needs work."

His finger whitened on the trigger of the target pistol. I pressed harder. "Twenty-two's big on accuracy," I said. "Lousy stopper. You can hit something vital and I'll still have time to blow your brains out the other side."

"That's not a real gun. That's that toy Lester used." His eyes were mostly white, straining to see it.

"Probably. Then again, guns are cheap."

We were like that for a while. We might have been like that all day, but the telephone rang. It startled him; he jerked the trigger. But I was already slashing down with the arm holding the toy gun. I hit his hand and the bullet went into a baseboard. It's still there. I crossed with my left fist and caught him on the temple, where his brains would have gone out if I'd been loaded for rhino. I reached down and twisted the .22 free as he tipped off the desk.

The air smelled like a struck match and there was some smoke, but the silenced pistol had made no more noise than a drawer slamming shut. The telephone was still ringing. I picked up. "Me, John," I said. "You took a chance. This character might have known there was an Alderdyce with Homicide."

"He caught me off guard," the lieutenant said. "I didn't expect anyone but you to answer your phone. You all right?"

"Peachy. What about Lester?"

"Still asleep. They say he might come out of it. He missed the excitement. Someone ought to tell these bozos a phony doctor's smock is no place to carry an ice pick."

"I didn't think they'd move this fast. Good thing you beefed up the guard."

"We'd have got him anyway." John never gave an inch. "We picked up Buzz an hour ago. A car's on its way to your office. Should I radio them what to expect?"

"Tell them to bring a real gun. This one's ready for the toy box." I laid it on the desk and sat down with the .22 to wait for my visitor to wake up.

Rumble Strip

I ran off the road in the Lake Superior State Forest, straight at an old-growth pine. It was a rumble strip that woke me. The rubberized chevrons in the asphalt made my tires buzz and my hands tingle on the steering wheel and I stomped on the brake.

I'd driven eleven hours one way, following a bad-check artist clear from Detroit to Manistique, giving him time to lay down a paper trail long enough to hang himself. Now that he was in the capable hands of the state police and off my client's, I was on my way back and hoping to make Mackinaw City before I turned in. A judge in Detroit expected me in the Frank Murphy Hall of Justice at two P.M., dewy eyed and with my head chock full of salient facts in an unrelated case.

The trunk of the tree I'd almost smashed into was so wide my lights didn't show around it. The woods were as black as Lake Michigan on the other side. There wouldn't be any motels for a while.

I hate the woods at night; doesn't everyone? They're okay by day, with Disney creatures scampering about, but after dark, give me any gloomy alley and keep those black holes for yourself. When I'm in a deep funk I'm convinced I'll end up in some shallow depression covered with dead leaves instead of a cozy luggage compartment in Long-Term Parking. The Upper Peninsula is a great place to visit, but I don't want to die there.

I took the last tepid swallow of Mountain Dew from the two-liter jug I kept in the car for surprise marathons—my hand had begun to shake from the delayed reaction—backed around, and got back onto Highway 2 to look for a place that poured coffee. A modern one, I hoped, with cheery fluorescents and expired hot dogs revolving on a carousel.

No such luck. Happy's Diner looked like a New Deal roadhouse, built low and square from local pine and covered with cheap stain that still showed in shiny patches like peanut brittle. More recently it had been a bowling alley, but from the condition of the six-foot wooden pin by the entrance, no strikes or spares had been rolled there this century. The windows and glass door looked new and ground spots illuminated the name on a square sign in the little parking lot. All the lights were burning. I pulled in next to a new Escalade with heavily tinted windows and got out. Crickets serenaded me with their sprightly little ode to Restless Legs Syndrome.

The SUV was backed into its space, concealing the license plate from the road, but my instincts were on low battery. I got a whiff of coffee and pushed through the door like a herd smelling water. A gong sounded when it opened.

The air was dense with roasted beans, pine, and layer upon layer of fried grease. Machine-embroidered tapestries of deer in the wild hung from gilded ropes like Rotarian banners, and Windsor chairs surrounded eight or ten round wooden tables, deserted at present and probably usually. There was a counter with stools upholstered in green leather, separated by a sliding frosted-glass panel over a pass-through. I sat on a stool and asked for coffee.

"We're closed." The woman behind the counter, a creature of pumpkin-colored hair, sharp bone, and skin like Saran Wrap, stood in a pink uniform and white utility apron with her hands hugging her upper arms. She wasn't looking at me. I didn't know just where she was looking at first.

"The sign says you're open all night."

"Cook's got the flu."

"All I want's coffee."

"Last batch boiled away. You don't want coffee the way I make it."

"I thought everyone was born knowing how to make coffee. If you think it's too strong it's just right."

"Closed, sorry." Her voice went up half an octave.

I followed her eyes then. The pass-through panel was open a crack. That woke me up. An airhorn next to the ear would have been too subtle.

"Well, tell him get well soon." I got up and headed toward the door, moving as casually as a marching band.

Which wasn't casual enough. The gong rang again and I lunged for the bar across the glass door, to pull it shut on the hand coming around the edge with a gun in it, but the panel behind me opened with a whoosh and a bang and a shell slid into a chamber with an oily metallic slam that can't be duplicated any other way. That was to get my attention; the shell that was already there made a brassy tinkle when it landed on the floor.

"I'd stop," someone said.

I was already stopped. The door was open now, and the man standing there held a deep-bellied Magnum braced against his hip. He was big and broad, soft looking, in a gray hoodie and old black jeans, which with his dark, mixed-blood face had blended with the shadows inside the tinted windows of the Escalade out front. "I should flag you for trying to bust my wrist." His tone was a bottomless guttural. A hundred fifty years ago he'd have worn buckskin leggings and plaited his hair. It was as black as the woods at night.

"Plenty of time for that. Feel him up."

This was one of those hand-me-down Swedish singsongs you still hear sometimes in the North Country. I turned around and held out my arms while the Indian went over me with one hand top to bottom. The man leaning inside the square opening to the kitchen—the owner of the singsong voice—might have been his photographic negative, drawn thin: colorless hair cut close to the skull, narrow pale face, and a tubular torso in a plaid flannel shirt over a black Zevon T-shirt. The hand resting on his stainless-steel nine-millimeter had a swastika tattooed on the back. Maybe there's hope for peace when skinheads and redskins start hanging out together.

The Indian pried my wallet out of my hip pocket. "Amos Walker. Private investigator, from Detroit."

"I knew he was a cop when he made for the door. Where's your piece, Amos?"

"I left it home. It's not big enough for bear."

He watched me. He didn't appear to have developed eyelids. He raised the semiautomatic.

"Don't!"

He looked at the woman behind the counter. She had her hand to her mouth. "He some kind of friend of yours?" he asked.

"I never saw him before. Just don't kill him—please."

"Suppose I decide to kill you. Think he'll beg for you?" He turned the pistol on her. He held it sideways, the way you see in movies. I hoped he was that green.

I made a decision and started toward the counter. The muzzle swung back my way and squirted white flame. The slug smashed through a glass display case containing a slice of coconut cream pie on a stand and buried itself in drywall. The woman screamed hoarsely. The echo of the shot rang like raining hubcaps.

"Man said no shooting," the Indian said.

"That's 'cause he's a city feller. Somebody's always popping off in the woods." Skinhead looked at me. "First jokes, now this. You're starting to tick me off. I was saving that pie for later."

"No more shots. State cops patrol these roads."

"You sure spook easy for an injun." But he put down the pistol.

That was all the encouragement I needed. I took another long step. I just wanted to get closer to the kitchen. The floorboards shifted behind me. I turned away from the blow and lifted a shoulder, hoping to absorb most of it with tendons and muscle and not skull.

I was only partially successful. The barrel of the Magnum caught a piece of posterior lobe on the follow-through. Sparks flew and I sprawled out full-length on the floor. I didn't try to catch myself; that's how wrists get broken, and I needed all my limbs now more than ever. The Indian kicked me hard in the ribs and told me to get up. I groaned—it came easily—pushed with both hands, and when I was standing I had the ejected cartridge from Skinhead's pistol between two fingers.

"Get him in here out of sight before anybody else comes in. You, lock the door and turn off the outside lights."

The Indian said, "They might miss the place in the dark."

"The man picked it out, not us." He looked at the woman. "Lock. Lights. Now!"

She hurried around the end of the counter while the Indian shoved me toward the swinging door to the kitchen, using his empty hand. He'd handled hostages before; enough anyway to know better than to use the one holding the big revolver. His was the stable half of the partnership. I wasn't sure which one to take out first.

In a little while we were all crowded in a narrow room with the usual equipment, including a six-burner electric range: the woman, the gunmen, me, and a black man as big as the Indian but older and harder-looking, sitting on the floor in a corner with duct tape around his ankles and across his mouth and his hands behind him. One eye was swollen shut with a gash over it that had bled down the side of his face onto his white T-shirt. He raised his head high enough to take me in with his working eye, then put his chin back on his chest. That's the kind of confidence I usually inspire.

I said, "He doesn't look happy."

"Shut up." The Indian made a motion with the gun as if measuring its heft.

"Let 'em jabber." Skinhead had my wallet now and was going through it. "Passes time. What kind of diner don't have no TV or radio?"

The woman found her voice. "Luke says it distracts him."

"Who the hell's Luke?"

"That's his name. We called the place Happy's to get people's attention."

He'd lost interest. He took out my cash and threw the wallet on the floor. "No credit cards. No pictures neither. Looks like nobody's going to miss you, Amos."

"You and Luke are partners?" I asked the woman.

"Fifty-fifty . We're married."

"Hear that, Roger? That's what this country's coming to, mixing the races like chocolate chip cookies. I'm glad now I didn't eat that pie."

The Indian grunted. He didn't look like a Roger. "I'm French-Irish on my mother's side."

"I wouldn't eat pie in your place neither." Skinhead grinned at me. His teeth seemed to have come in any old way. "Luke gave us grief. Them people don't understand the basic principles of occupation."

"Military man," I said. "Power Rangers or Hitler Youth?"

The grin went. He played with the pistol, then shook his head. "You're tired of living, but I'm tireder of being the only white man in the room. It ain't natural. But we brung plenty of duct tape."

"We need to save some," Roger said.

"We're good."

His voice dropped. "We talked about how this was going to go down."

"You talked. I thought all you people said was 'ugh.'"

I smiled at the woman. The name Pearl was embroidered above her breast pocket in white script. "Bake your pies here?"

"No. We order them from a place in Marquette." She stroked her upper arms as if she were cold. Actually it was close in the room even with the stove turned off.

"Jo's Bakery," Skinhead said. "Our Christmas pies came from there."

Roger said, "Now who's talking too much?"

I said, "All this pie talk makes me hungry. Okay if I ask Pearl to fry me a couple of eggs?"

"Mister, you don't want me to cook. I burn salads."

"Anybody can fry an egg," I said.

"You heard her," Skinhead said. "Be hungry."

"I need to keep up my blood sugar. I could faint."

"So faint. We could use some quiet around here."

"I'll do the cooking." I took a step toward the stove.

Roger shifted his weight to his gun side. I stopped. But I was in reach of the controls.

Luke started coughing, a strangling sound behind the tape across his mouth. Everyone looked at him, bent forward and looking a little green, his chest heaving; everyone but me. I made a try for the knob under the nearest burner.

Pearl spoiled it. She pushed me out of reach and started toward the man convulsing on the floor.

"Whoa." Skinhead jerked up his pistol. His lidless eyes had all the humanity of dripped paint.

She put on the brakes. Her face was white. "He has trouble breathing through his nose. He broke it playing football."

"Why ain't I surprised?"

"Please! He'll suffocate."

"I guessed that already."

Roger stuck his revolver in his hoodie pocket and crossed the room in two strides. Luke's eyes were rolling over white when the Indian bent down and tore away the tape. Luke sucked in air like a swimmer breaking the surface and fell back against the wall, rattling all the pots and pans hanging from it. His chest emptied and filled and emptied again and his natural color returned.

"Buzzkill." Skinhead lowered his weapon.

Pearl sagged. I caught her. She hadn't fainted; the wire that had been holding her up all this time had worn through.

"Shoot 'em both if he opens his mouth for anything but oxygen."

Skinhead looked around, eyes bright. "Well, what do we do for fun now?"

"The man said no killing," the Indian said.

"He should've told his boy that years ago. It was the same way with my old man: Too little, too late."

Something glimmered then; this was no ordinary hostage situation. I gave Pearl's thin shoulders a reassuring squeeze and she straightened and stepped away from me. "What about those eggs?" I said. "I can't be the only one who can use a bite."

"It's always eggs with you," Skinhead said. "What are you, part weasel?"

Roger said, "I could eat."

"No time."

"We don't know how much time we got. These things never come off on schedule, the man said."

"Mitchell don't know squat about how things work up there."

The Indian looked around at the rest of us, then went over to his partner and whispered something.

"You worry too much. Big Chief Worry Wart, that's you."

Roger retreated, falling silent. He was troubled by something other than results.

His partner stuck the nine-millimeter under his belt. "I'm going to the can. Keep 'em covered, and see he makes mine runny. I like to lick the plate."

The Indian grimaced. "Jesus, Benny."

He looked like a Benny. I wasn't sure why.

I wasn't crazy about the timing. Electric burners take time heating up, and Benny didn't seem like the type who stopped to wash his hands. I didn't know if I could take both men at once. I didn't know if I could take even one, but from the way the skinhead slung information around, there was only one way this thing was going to end if I didn't start cooking. I knew who Mitchell was. For once in my life I wished my hunch had been wrong. I turned to the range and twisted the knob all the way to High. "Eggs, please."

Pearl stared at me a moment, but the Luke incident seemed to have sapped her of the will to protest. She opened a Sub-Zero refrigerator and took out a carton.

"Skillet."

Roger was standing by the pots and pans. When he turned his head to take one down, I took the pistol cartridge out of my pocket and tucked it back between my fingers.

"No butter." He passed me the skillet by way of the woman. "I'm fat enough."

I put it on the burner. "I hear they pile on the starch in Marquette. Makes it hard to squeeze your gut through a tunnel."

"You and Benny both talk too much," he said.

"Give me some credit. Prison's the only circle the two of you would ever travel in together."

"He's got his good points. Up there you need a friend in the White Power gang if you want to live till parole."

"The joint's a great leveler. Where else would a couple of bums hook up with a rich kid like Emmet Mitchell Junior?"

"He drops names, Benny does. I told him it wasn't cool."

"I didn't need the hint. I keep current. Emmett Senior spent millions trying to acquit his boy. Looks like he had a few left over. Junior's a serial killer. Benny's got an excuse; he's a psychopath. What's yours?"

"Mister, you don't get no more unemployable than an Indian ex-con. Even the casinos won't touch me. What's it to me how many night-call nurses got themselves raped and killed so long as the old man pays cash?"

"Emmett Mitchell," Pearl said. "I heard that name."

I said, "They moved him to maximum security in Marquette State Prison after he tried to escape from Jackson. That was before DNA linked him to Victim Number Six. Not even the press knows when they're taking him downstate for the hearing. But Roger and Benny know. It's tonight. You need a bankroll like Emmett Senior's to buy that kind of information."

The eggs were starting to sizzle, but just then Benny came back in. I could tell by his face he'd overheard plenty, but he wasn't upset. He looked like a man who had won a bet with himself. He leveled the pistol at me.

"Private cop walking in just when he did," he said. "He was laughing at us the whole time, us talking all around what he knew already."

"You're wrong, Benny. Why would he have his ID in his wallet if he was undercover?"

"Cops are dumb, that's why. They keep talking about the world's dumbest criminals, but they're the ones make all the mistakes. Our boy Amos made two: The day he was born and the day he died."

I concentrated on the eggs. It was an argument I couldn't win. The trick was to keep him close without pushing him over the edge.

"You're smarter than you look," I said. "If Old Man Mitchell is paying the officers transporting Emmett Junior to stop here, and he's paying you to tie them up and maybe knock them out to make it play like an old-fashioned escape set up by a couple of Junior's former inmates, you can be sure he's paid someone else to make sure you don't turn state's evidence against him when you get caught." I chose that moment to let the cartridge drop into the middle of a yolk to avoid making noise.

"So we don't *get* caught." The skinhead placed the muzzle against the bone behind my right ear.

That was too close. Any sudden disturbance would startle him into jerking the trigger.

"Pearl, they're fixing to kill all of us."

This was a new voice, hoarse from lack of use. Luke had recovered from his choking fit. He sat in his corner perfectly alert, his good eye glistening. Benny didn't move. "Roger, I told you what to do the minute he opened his mouth."

"I don't flag people. They only got me because I wouldn't shoot."

"Luke's right," I told him, watching the skillet. The brass shell was almost submerged in yellow goo. "Mitchell Senior can't afford to leave anyone behind, Benny knows that. Not even the cops he bought. That's the way the two of them worked it out. You won't need any more duct tape."

"Benny?" Roger's tone was less guttural, almost shallow.

"Don't be a dumb digger injun. If you wasn't so skittish we'd've done this at the start and saved all this jabber."

I knew then I couldn't wait for a diversion. If I moved fast enough…but no one was that fast.

No one except Luke. He shoved himself away from the wall, rolling, and caught Roger behind the knees with a bulky shoulder. The Indian folded like a cardboard cutout, the gun flying from his hand when his elbow struck the floor, but for a man running to fat he wasn't clumsy. He dove to retrieve it.

Benny pivoted that way, taking the pistol away from my head. I swung the skillet with all I had, catching him square on the corner of the jaw with the edge, spraying hot egg over both of us, grabbed his gun arm in both hands, and broke it over my knee. He shrieked and his fingers lost their grip. I caught the pistol as it fell, but by then I didn't need it.

Pearl was faster than all of us put together. She'd beaten Roger to the Magnum and stood in a feral crouch, covering him with the weapon in both hands. He remained motionless on all fours.

A loud report made us all jump. The pistol cartridge from the skillet had continued to heat up for a second after it hit the floor, and went off like a kernel of popcorn. The slug dug a hole in a baseboard. I'd worried about what direction it would take.

"You work for Mitchell?" Pearl seemed ready to include me in her firing trajectory. Her pumpkin-colored hair hung in her face.

"Don't make me lose respect for you. I'm only here because of a rumble strip."

"What?"

"You know. Those things they put on the edge of the highway to warn you you're drifting off the road."

"We can use those other places," she said.

I found the roll of duct tape and trussed up Benny, clucking over his screams when I jerked his shattered arm behind his back. I remembered to take my money out of his pocket. Then I saw to Roger. There was enough tape to go around after all. Finally I helped Pearl cut Luke loose.

"Good tackle," I said.

He grinned lopsidedly; his bruised eye was a kaleidoscope of color. "You should've seen me on the field."

"NFL?"

"St. Helens High. They overlooked me in the draft."

"Too bad I'm not a scout."

"Now what?" Pearl repaired her hair, a pin in her teeth. "They cut the phone wire."

"Now we stop a prison van and reunite father and son." I went out to the car to get my cell.

Sometimes a Hyena

Why I told the joke at all I can't say. It wasn't that good, but then neither was the bar I told it in nor the bartender I told it to. I was drenched through with the sweat of a long day, with nothing else to show for it but the thought of an unpleasant telephone conversation with the client the next morning. Sometimes you stick with the subject like his own bad taste in aftershave, sometimes he drops you like a weak signal; but the guy paying your freight is never a philosopher.

I'd driven past the place a hundred times without noticing. I hadn't been thirsty the first hundred times. A long way back it had been someone's idea of home, a square frame eight-hundred-square-foot house with a shingle roof and tile siding that reminded you you'd missed three appointments to have your teeth cleaned. It didn't identify itself: The owner had just bought an orange LED sign that said OPEN and stuck it in the front window. But in that neighborhood a bar was all it could be. I still think of it, when I think of it at all, as the Open.

Inside was permanent dusk, two piles of protoplasm dumped on stools at the end of the bar, and a tabletop shuffleboard game whose pine boards had been slapped with a varnish that went tacky in high humidity so that one of the shuttles had stopped halfway down its length one day and decided that was where it would stay. A paint can opener would be needed to pry it loose.

I don't remember what the bartender looked like. He would be a middle-aged guy running to flab who had seen Cocktail once, pictured himself in some swanky joint juggling shakers and stem glasses, and like the shuttle had come to everlasting rest in that spot. Normally I wouldn't have spoken to him beyond ordering a double scotch, but while he was siphoning it out my gaze lit upon a sepia picture in a frame on the wall above the beer taps. Someone had cut a photo of zebras grazing in the veldt from National Geographic and put it behind glass to make the place seem exotic.

"Guy walks into a bar," I said.

"Guys do, pleased to say." He slapped a paper napkin in front of me and set my drink on it. "This is a joke?"

"That's the punchline from another 'Guy walks into a bar' joke; but you tell me. There's a kangaroo mixing the drinks. Kangaroo looks at the guy and says, 'I see you're surprised to find a kangaroo behind the bar.' Guy says, 'I'll say. Did the zebra sell the place?'"

He grunted, which told me all I needed to know about how he'd wound up in a dump like the Open. A really first-class barman laughs when the joke isn't funny and shakes his head when the story isn't that sad. Now that I think of it, his face belonged on the other side of the bar, tie-dyed with red gin blossoms and yellowed lost opportunities. But then that might just have been my face in the peel-and-stick mirrors in back of the bottles with recycled premium labels. An unexpected glimpse of one's reflection on that sort of day is no treat.

I'd thought of leaving him change from my ten, but I put it away. His kid could scrub pots and pans for his tuition, just like all the other self-made millionaires. I was in what the poets call a dark humor. I looked around for someone to kick sand in my face.

"Fucking cops," the bartender said.

He'd flicked on the TV on the corner shelf under the ceiling, in case my opening routine might lead to a set.

I wasn't the least bit curious. That state of mind is the first off-duty casualty in the life of a detective. I couldn't care less about what the cops were up to that put him out of his sunny mood. So of course I looked up at the screen.

A female reporter stood on a street cross-hatched with yellow caution tape, pretending to read from a notepad while red and blue strobes pulsed in the background. An Early Response Team—downtown Detroit jargon for SWAT—had charged a house on the northwest side where an armed man was said to be barricaded with his wife. The husband was in custody, but the wife was dead with a slug in her heart. An unidentified source swore that no firearms were found in the house. An investigation was under way to determine whether a stray police round had killed the woman.

The bartender backhanded his remote at the TV and the screen went black. "They'll sweep that one under the rug toot-sweet. State should make them buy a hunting license."

"I guess you've never been in on a bust."

"I been on the receiving end. Cops think they own the town."

"Anything can happen when the adrenaline kicks in and the guns come out. A little girl got killed the same way last spring. That time they were looking for an armed robber."

"I remember it. Seems to me a cop got an unpaid vacation. He's back on the job and the girl's still dead. You a cop?"

"If I said I was, would you spit in my drink?"

He grinned sourly. "For starters."

• • •

The story metastasized over the next few days. A DPD spokesman confirmed the report that no gun was recovered from the house and the bullet, which had shattered when it penetrated the woman's sternum, was a soft-nose .38, a common police weapon. The lab rats in Ballistics were working to reassemble the fragments in order to match them to the gun. So far none of the officers on the scene had admitted to discharging a sidearm. The spokesman refused to say whether their guns were being examined, but that would be SOP.

Another press conference was called by Philip Justice, who announced he'd been retained by the husband to sue the police department for excessive use of deadly force and false arrest. Justice—it was his real name, and maybe the inspiration for his choice of occupations—was a pit viper who specialized in representing ordinary citizens against authority. His strategy never changed. He went in fast and hard, shrill with outrage, blindsiding the opposition before it could get a toehold and wresting pricey settlements with his teeth.

I admired his performance over my morning coffee. He removed his hand from his recently released client's shoulder only to stab a finger at the camera and paraphrase the First Book of Samuel; he'd know the passages on David and Goliath by heart, but he needed the sympathy of atheists too.

It was live coverage. I'd just turned off the set when my telephone rang. It was Justice.

I'd worked for him a couple of times, so I wasn't shocked that'd he tag me to investigate, but the timing was a surprise. I thought he'd be on the line with a judge or the New York Times, or anyway someone higher up on the food chain so quickly after going public. I said I wasn't working hard and agreed to meet him in his office in twenty minutes.

• • •

He operated high up in the American Building in Southfield, a glass-and-steel arrangement that towered over the horizontal suburb like a birthday candle on a cupcake. The suite was medium gray and pale yellow, and his desk was a glass wafer on composition legs. He got up from behind it, and as usual his six feet six was a shock to the system; sitting down he looked built to ordinary scale. His hair grew straight back and close to the scalp like an otter's and he blinked a lot—I guess from all those TV lights and flash attachments he lived among. He took my hand in a swift, firm grip and gave it back. "Amos Walker, Claud Vale."

I remembered his client spelled his first name without an E. He rose from a yellow leather chair, shrinking in on himself unlike Justice as he did so, and lowered and raised his chin in greeting while letting his hands hang at his sides. He was fifty but looked older, with once-red hair like rusted iron and muddy eyes wallowing in bags behind bifocals. A blue blazer hung from thin shoulders, showing four white stitches on one cuff where the manufacturer's label had been removed, a nice lawyerly touch that said the man was unaccustomed to dressing up but had made the purchase to appear presentable in court. The black silk armband was unobtrusive but impossible not to notice.

When we were all seated, me in gray leather, Justice in the ergonomic item behind the desk, he said, "Mr. Vale neither said nor hinted that he was armed. When he refused to open the door to police answer a domestic disturbance complaint by neighbors, the officers assumed the worst and the situation escalated from there."

"Ernestine was divorcing me," Vale said, in a voice like a cassette tape dragging over tired spools. "When GM laid me off and I couldn't find nothing, she said she'd be better off getting a job and looking after herself and nobody else. That's what we fought about. I never laid a hand on her, not in seventeen years. I sure didn't want her dead." He dug out a handkerchief, blew his nose, and lifted his glasses to wipe his eyes.

"We know a shot was fired," said Justice. "We know from which gun. An ERT sergeant admitted it after Ballistics examined his weapon. He claims it went off when Mr. Vale grabbed his arm."

"That's a lie!"

"Of course it is, Claud. Try to calm down. The bullet recovered from Mrs. Vale's body was too fragmented to match conclusively to a weapon, but with only one shot fired and one slug found, we don't need it to build our case."

I crossed my legs. "All I know is what I saw on TV. The cops who answered the domestic complaint swore he shouted through the door he'd shoot if they tried to come inside."

"I never did."

"Claud, please. You're among friends. Even if that were so, it would only have given the department probable cause to enter the house. I'm not debating that, although I believe they mistook what they heard. The fact that no gun was found in the house or within throwing range of any of the doors or windows emphatically demonstrates that the authorities failed to exercise due diligence. We're asking for ten million."

"This is all starting to sound familiar," I said.

"The circumstances are almost identical to those involving the death of a little girl six months ago on the East Side: An Early Response Team officer investigating a felony-harboring situation said the grandmother on the scene struggled with him and his gun went off, killing the child. I wasn't the attorney of record in the suit that followed, but the officer was dismissed and the judge awarded the family five million. I believe double that amount is justified by the fact that the department failed to learn from its earlier mistake."

"You've got it all figured out. So what's my end?"

"I want to swat that mosquito about whether Mr. Vale threatened to shoot the first responders. If one of them doesn't recant I can still make the case, but if there's no truth in it, the city will settle and this never goes to court."

I got out a cigarette, to play with, not to smoke; state law says you can buy them but don't light up. "In other words I ask a couple of cops if they're liars."

"You've got the best lawyer in town, if that's what you're worried about."

"It's not. My insurance carrier might consider stupidity a pre-existing condition." But I proved the point and took the job.

• • •

I met Officer Bender in a booth in the Thermopolis, a cop bar in Greektown, in the shadow of 1300, the ornate crumbling headquarters of the Detroit Police Department. It was early, and the staff was clearing away the debris of the morning rush and laying tables for the noon crowd. We had the place to ourselves apart from them and a couple of tired-looking plainclothesmen from Major Crimes drinking coffee at the bar over baklava and waiting out the end of their shift.

Bender was the junior half of the two-man team that had responded to the domestic disturbance complaint at Claud Vale's house. He was built like a college basketball player, tall and sinewy in his autumn uniform, and during the brief small talk. I learned he'd been offered a full-ride scholarship at the University of Michigan, but had gotten tired of the hoops and dropped out to join the twelve-week police training course in Detroit. He was a good-looking light-skinned black who liked plenty of cream and sugar in his strong Greek coffee.

He finished looking at my credentials and handed them back. "'I'll shoot the first man through the door,' that's what I heard. Book says that implies probability of a weapon. What's it say in yours?"

"It says step off and call for backup," I said. "Only I don't have backup, so I'd just step off. How do you and Wallace get along?" Sergeant Wallace was his partner, a fifteen-year-man with the Uniform Division; three letters of commendation in his jacket and two months' unpaid suspension over a home-invasion suspect who'd died of asphyxiation in the course of a bust.

"He's my partner. I trust him with my life."

"That's what the book says. I'm not taking notes."

"I don't think he'd give me his sister's hand if I asked, but we got plenty of that in the department. He's a good cop. That thing two years ago could've happened to anyone. Guy had a glass throat."

I let that one eddy with the current. "This thing goes the way it went on the East Side last spring, a lot of good cops'll wind up in private security. That goes from the bottom up and never reaches the brass."

He added still more sugar to his cup and stirred it; a weaker man would've had to use two hands. "Call me a liar again, I'll cuff you for whatever I can dream up between here and down the street. Just as soon as I finish my coffee."

That was it for the interview. I thought of paying his tab along with mine, but the bribery charge might be too much temptation.

Cops, even young ones, are rarely so thin-skinned. I'd taken a wild shot and drawn blood.

. . .

Sergeant Wallace was temporarily unavailable. He'd taken a personal day and the woman who answered at his home—I assumed it was his wife—said he'd gone bow hunting in Washtenaw County. She didn't expect him back before nightfall.

I couldn't get within a mile of the ERT sergeant who'd fired the round that had reportedly killed Ernestine Vale. He was on paid administrative leave pending the outcome of the internal investigation and not even Philip Justice could get a contact number for him outside of 1300. But I couldn't think of anything to ask him that the shoot team wouldn't, so I didn't waste time pumping my unofficial sources, who are all more or less legitimately employed and keep jacking up their rates according to the risk of selling confidential information: Homeland Security had become involved, and Justice's pockets aren't that deep. No one's are.

Just to kill time while waiting to corner young Officer Bender's partner I got a pass through Justice to walk through the scene of the shooting. The cop at the door looked at the pass, confirmed it on the Star Trek radio clipped to his shoulder strap, and stood aside to let me open the door and duck under the yellow tape.

It was a building of historical interest, which locally is as good as an order of condemnation; ninety years ago Henry Ford built dozens and dozens of narrow frame houses with steeply pitched roofs to shelter laborers who had streamed in from the Deep South and eastern Europe to earn five dollars a day assembling Model Ts in Dearborn. This was one of the few left, and despite intermittent remodeling preserved the shape and character of the original better than most of the rest.

I climbed the nearly vertical staircase and looked at the bedroom purely out of cultural curiosity. All the action had taken place on the

ground floor, where according to her husband Mrs. Vale was down
with the flu on the living room sofa when the bullet entered her heart
at an oblique angle, the coroner said, which corresponded with Vale's
version of the event. She'd moved to the sofa anyway preliminary to
cutting herself loose from her husband permanently. The sheets had
been removed for evidence, but the cushions were stained dark where
she'd bled.

On the way out I nodded to the gatekeeper and tried the house
next door, a shotgun-style ranch built on the site of what would have
been another Ford construction; he created whole neighborhoods
from barren fields and reclaimed swamp. The woman who cracked
the door two inches at my knock had thick fingers, a suspicious blue
eye, and a Ukrainian accent. The eye studied my credentials from
top to bottom, but the door didn't budge. "I tell the police everything," she said.

"I won't walk you all the way back through it. What did you hear?"

"I hear bang when the police are there. I think it must be a shot."

"Any sound of struggling?"

"No, just bang. Without police I would think it is a door slamming. Doors are slamming there all the time, yelling, like that day.
The people, they don't get along so good."

"Are you the one who complained to the police about the domestic disturbance?"

"I don't want to get into no trouble."

"You won't."

She said it again. I moved on. I was sure now it was her, not that
it mattered who'd called. "What about when just the two policemen
were there? Did you hear Mr. Vale shouting?"

"I hear shouting. I don't know who or what. Then the two go
away. Later more come. One comes to this door and says don't go

out, stay away from the windows. I tell him, today is no different from all the rest. I might have stayed in Kiev."

I thanked her. She pressed the door in my face and was still snapping locks when I stepped off the porch.

·   ·   ·

"I had a sweet shot, a heart shot," Sergeant Wallace said. "This little-bitty birch you couldn't even see deflected the arrow and the best rack I've seen in years went sailing off over a barbed-wire fence."

Veteran cops are masters at dividing their work and home lives. I was there to ask about his part in an affair that had left a woman dead with a slug in her heart and he was telling me about the deer heart he'd missed that afternoon in rural Michigan; no irony in his voice or expression.

We were sitting in his small kitchen in Redford Township, with a group of mismatched appliances that had been replaced as needed and no two at the same time. The pattern was worn almost completely off the linoleum and the table we sat at was sheet metal over pine. He had a squat brown beer bottle in his squat right fist and I could have connected the broken blood vessels in his broad fleshy face like dots. Mrs. Wallace, a small, wrenlike creature who gave the impression of a nervous type until you noticed the steel wire underneath, was in the laundry washing spray-on doe hormones from her husband's camo suit. He wore loose-fitting old suitpants and his back hair curled like tropical undergrowth over the shoulder straps of his BVD undershirt.

I said, "I won't take up much time. What did Claud Vale say when you showed up at his house?"

"'Go away or I'll shoot right through this door.'"

"Those words exactly?"

"They're in my report."

I looked at my notebook. "Your partner said it was, 'I'll shoot the first man through the door.'"

"What's the difference?"

"The second version threatened your lives. The first threatened his door."

He swigged beer and thunked down the bottle. "You work for a lawyer, all right. You know same as me he meant only one thing either way."

"The lawyer I work for would go to town on the difference in phrasing. He'd make it sound like one of you lied and the other backed him up, as partners do, only he got the words wrong. He'd say it was your idea, being the senior man; but anyway he'll play it so both your testimonies wind up in the ashcan."

His face got so dark I couldn't pick out the burst vessels.

I said, "I'm just the messenger. If that's how it went down, fine: Tell it on the stand and let Justice do what he can with it. Just don't lose it there the way you're losing it here in your own kitchen. I wouldn't be talking this way if Bender didn't lash out like a snake when I told him his career might depend on what he said in court. He's got a guilty conscience."

"Finished?" He pointed at the beer he'd given me. I hadn't touched it, but I put away my notebook and got up. At the front door I heard the hollow snap and whoosh of a fresh bottle being opened.

• • •

Philip Justice subsided into the cushions of his desk chair, closing his eyes and folding his hands across his spare middle as if he'd just finished a feast. "Damn fine work. I had Wallace figured as the weak link, based on that blot on his record. But Bender's our pigeon. I may not even have to call his partner to the stand."

"Thing is," I said, "I think Wallace is telling the truth. I believe Vale made a threat of some kind. Bender didn't hear it—making out emotional words through a thick door comes with experience. Bender decided to back him up after they compared notes. You need a good reason for calling for reinforcements when you write your report, especially after what went down."

"Made a threat with what? He didn't have a gun."

"Not when a search was made. The next-door neighbor heard doors slamming earlier. A handgun report heard through two walls can be mistaken for a door slamming."

He opened his eyes and came forward. The feast had turned into indigestion. "She heard yelling too."

"I can go back and find out if any of that yelling sounded like Ernestine Vale's voice."

"I didn't hire you to make a case for the police. God, you make him sound like a criminal mastermind. You're saying he shot his wife, then staged a fight to bring the cops to his door and set up the Detroit Police Department for her murder."

"It wouldn't be the first time someone tried to get tricky. If he shot her long enough before the complaint went through, he'd have plenty of opportunity to sneak out of the house, dump the gun in a storm drain a dozen blocks away, and sneak back in and fake a fight."

"There'd be a record of a firearm purchase. He's clean. Don't you think I had that checked out? You're not the only P.I. in town."

"You're right. Where would anyone go in Detroit to get a gun without leaving a paper trail?"

"He's an unemployed auto worker, not a penny-ante hit man. He wouldn't know where to look."

I played with a cigarette. "All I'm saying is I'd like to run it out. You don't want this blowing up in your face in public."

"What do you want from me?" Now he sounded like a successful man being put upon by a poor relation.

"Two things. First: When did his wife file for divorce?"

He fired up the computer on his desk. "April eleventh."

"This is part of the first thing. When did the cops screw up and kill that little girl on the East Side?"

"You can't think those two things are connected. The circumstances—"

"—are almost identical. Your words. When?"

Keys got tickled. He frowned at the screen, showing the kind of reaction he never showed in court. "April fourteenth."

I wrote both dates in my notebook, not that I'd forget. "Second thing: Which plant did Vale work for before he was laid off?"

• • •

I found Dix Sommerfield working the employee parking lot at the GM assembly plant in Warren. He was a third-generation member of a Kentucky family that had come North in a body to build tanks for the automobile factories-turned-defense plants during World War II. He could usually be found, a pot-bellied presence in a reverse ball cap, selling unlicensed bottles of whiskey and cartons of cigarettes and certain other contraband from the trunk of his wired-together Chevy Nova during shift changes. Tuesdays and Thursdays found him at Chrysler, Mondays at River Rouge, where he spent a lot of time looking over his shoulder for Ford's private police force. The other days of the week you could depend on his being in Warren, his sentimental favorite; his father and grandfather had been loyal to General Motors ahead of Uncle Sam and the Southern Baptist Church.

"I'm looking for a thirty-eight revolver," I said, after we'd exchanged greetings. I'd bought information from him in the past, cash on the barrelhead, and no backlash from the authorities.

Not that he wasn't cagy; the balance had shifted after 9/11, and you never knew when interference from the amateurs in Washington might louse up a smooth system. "I don't deal in that stuff no more," he said, moving the toothpick that lived in his mouth from one corner to the other. "You want a piece, go to Dick's Sporting Goods."

"I want to know about one you sold. Dix, do I have to pull that spare tire out from under all those boxes of Marlboros and look into the well? It was a soft-nose slug, so it couldn't have come from an automatic."

"Wearing a wire?"

I unbuttoned my shirt and spread it.

"That ain't nothing. Drop your pants."

I kicked him in the shin, and when he bent to cradle it gave him a chop with the side of my hand on his elbow. Forget the groin: If you really want to make a painful point, go for the little knobs of bone that stick out from the joints. When the tears stopped flowing I took out a Free Press clipping with Claud Vale's picture and stuck it under his nose.

He wiped his eyes with his sleeve and squinted. "Jeez. I been praying for days that one wouldn't come back and bite me in the ass."

"God answered. He said stick to cigarettes and booze. You can't go wrong with the basics."

• • •

One week after the story broke, Philip Justice announced he was dropping his suit and that he'd resigned as Claud Vale's attorney. The cops, knowing what that meant, re-arrested his former client and went to work on him; no physical abuse, no coercion other than the reliable aggressive questioning in Supreme Court-mandated increments with periods of rest in between, tying the suspect up in his own lies until telling the truth was the only path to sanity. He confessed to murdering his wife, threatening the first responders so that back-up was required from 1300, and grabbing the arm of the first cop through the door, forcing his gun to go off, as guns will in that situation. A more thorough search of the crime scene turned up the ERT sergeant's slug in a place where two baseboards met unevenly in a corner. That had been a break for Vale, who hadn't considered what would happen if it were recovered anywhere but in Ernestine Vale's heart. He'd had the foresight to score an X in the nose of the slug he'd used before firing it, making it burst apart on entry so that it couldn't be traced to the gun he'd used; the rest was beginner's luck.

The gun itself was never found, but it was no longer required for evidence. I didn't have to go to jail for keeping Dix Sommerfield's name out of the record.

Philip Justice bought me a drink at the Caucus Club downtown. He was still bothered by the loss of what looked like a big settlement and more crusading glory to his name, but he was grateful not to have been made a clown on the evening news. He sipped at his twelve-year-old cognac. "So you got all this on what a couple of cops told you?"

"Some of it." I stirred the ice in my scotch and tossed the swizzle. "The timing cinched it. Vale was brooding about the divorce, losing half of what little he had in the outcome, when that little girl died. He saw a way to get clear and be rich besides."

"That was an armed-robbery investigation, not murder."

"It was enough the same as what he had in mind. When I first heard of Vale I was in a bar."

"Imagine that."

"I'll ignore the implication. I'd told the bartender a joke. I got the idea from a picture of zebras he had on the wall." I told it.

He didn't laugh. "I heard that one. Seems to me a different animal was involved."

"Sometimes it's a hyena sold the place. It's always a kangaroo behind the bar, for some reason. Who knows what makes these things work?"